Pestilence in the Darkness

Pestilence in the Darkness

Havoc in Wyoming, Part 6

Millie Copper

Written by Millie Copper

Edited by Ameryn Tucker

Proofread by Light Hand Proofreading

Cover design by Dauntless Cover Design

Original cover design by Kesandra Adams

Also by Millie Copper

The Havoc in Wyoming Series

When a series of coordinated attacks devastate the United States, the people of Bakerville, Wyoming, must come together to survive. Unfortunately, not everyone has the town's best interest at heart. Some are striving for personal gain during the apocalypse.

The Montana Mayhem Series

A group from Bakerville, Wyoming strikes out on their own while searching for the desires of their heart. Unfortunately, the road will not be easy, and sometimes the heart is hardened and deceitful. When things don't work out as they hoped, will they become stranded in the wilderness? Or will each be able to find their way home?

The Dakota Destruction Series

After a series of coordinated attacks devastate the United States, Katie and Leo sacrifice everything to help their country. But some things aren't as they seem. Is it time to go home and start fresh, or can something good come out of this terrible situation?

In The October Fall World

In the blink of an eye, an EMP changed everything for Lauren and her family. Now they are in a fight for survival, trying to keep their loved ones alive as society collapses around them. Their once peaceful town of Cody, Wyoming has turned into a powder keg. And with law enforcement a thing of the past, evil lurks around every corner.

In The As The Light Dies World

Lisa Bentley thought having her daughter attacked and left for dead was the worst thing that could happen. She was wrong. She and her family lived an ideal life operating a bed and breakfast in the perfect Wyoming town. That world came crashing down when her daughter was attacked.

Nonfiction Books

Millie has penned seven nonfiction, traditional food focused books, sharing how, with a little creativity, anyone can transition to a real foods diet without overwhelming their food budget. Many of her books also include preparedness and food storage tips.

Find these titles at MillieCopper.com

Join My Reader's Club!

Receive a complimentary copy of *Wyoming Refuge: A Havoc in Wyoming Prequel*. As part of my reader's club, you'll be the first to know about new releases and specials. I also share info on books I'm reading, preparedness tips, and more. Please sign up on my website:

MillieCopper.com

Who's Who

Jake and Mollie Caldwell: A bachelor until age thirty-seven, Jake married Mollie and suddenly became a dad to four girls. A couple of years later, they added a son. Malcolm is *almost* eleven and is Jake's right-hand man. They've sacrificed for years to build a safe retreat for their children, sons-in-law, grandson, extended family, and close friends. Many times, they thought they were crazy. Now, in a new world full of danger and heartache, they realize their plans weren't enough.

Sarah Garrett: Sarah is Mollie's oldest daughter. She and her husband Tate are expecting their first child and have recently adopted Marc, Sissy, and Andy after their mom died. Tate's parents, Keith and Lois, and his sister, Karen, were visiting from out of state when the attacks started. Tate and his dad were on a community hunt when they went missing. They haven't been found.

Angela and Tim Carpenter: Angela is Mollie's second oldest. She and Tim are parents to Gavin, age two. Tim's dad, Art, reluctantly joined Tim and Angela at the Caldwell homestead. To everyone's surprise, farm life seems to agree with Art.

Calley and Mike Curtis: Calley is Mollie's third born. She married Mike, the boy next door, two years ago. Mike's parents, Roy and Deanne, along with Mike's recently single sister, Sheila Stapleton, escaped Casper for the Caldwell homestead with Calley and Mike.

Katie and Leo Burnett: Katie is Mollie's youngest daughter. Before the attacks, she was living away from home while finishing college. After her college town was overrun by people escaping the city, Katie and her then boyfriend Leo Burnett made their way to Bakerville. Leo is a K-State business graduate, construction worker, and Marine. He's now a Lieutenant in the Bakerville militia and a member of the elite security team. Katie is in training to join the medical team.

Alvin and Dodie Caldwell: Jake's parents. They're both in their seventies and fiercely independent. Before the attacks, they lived in nearby Prospect. Prospect has experienced many challenges, including the hospital burning to the ground. Happy to be in Bakerville, Alvin and Dodie now worry about Jake's brother, Robert, and his wife and children living in California. Have they been severely affected by these tragedies?

Doris and Evan Snyder: Neighbors and good friends of the Caldwells. Evan is a retired deputy sheriff, having been part of the county's Specialized Services Division. Evan is a member of the council and leads the elite section of the Bakerville militia referred to as the security team. Always thinking about how to keep Bakerville safe, he was the first to suggest moving to a more defendable location for the winter. Now most of the community is living on the mountain, while a portion remain in Bakerville proper. Doris is retired from both the Navy and a government job. She always insisted she wasn't a spy or anything. Turns out, that might not have been the truth. Doris's oldest daughter lives in Germany and is assumed safe. Her youngest daughter, Lindsey Maverick, was widowed only a few miles from Bakerville.

Phil and Kelley Hudson: Community members. Mollie considers Kelley one of her closest friends. Phil, retired Coast Guard, is a leader of the community. Kelley is a psychiatric nurse practitioner, retired from Commissioned Corps. Kelley's children, Sylvia and Sabrina, arrived in Bakerville with Lindsey Maverick and several others.

Belinda and TJ Bosco: Belinda, a nurse practitioner, is fourth generation Bakerville and related to the founders of the community. TJ is friends with Malcolm. Belinda was recently injured and her mom, Tammy, was killed by mentally ill Lydia. Lydia later took her own life . . . or did she?

Bill Shane and Aaron and Laurie Ogden: Grandmaster Bill Shane taught martial arts to Jake, Mollie, and Malcolm in nearby Wesley, Wyoming. Jake invited him to join them at the homestead if the situation deteriorated in Wesley. Bill brought Black Belt and secondary instructor Aaron Ogden as well as Aaron's then girlfriend, also a

Taekwondo Black Belt, when they escaped Wesley. Along with Evan and Cole Gunderson, Bill is one of the militia leaders. He's also a councilmember.

June and Sam Mitchellini: After fleeing from their small Wyoming town, they've been hiding out in Bakerville. They and their eight-year-old twins—Abigail and Willie—are now living under assumed names. Retired Navy doctor Sam and chiropractor June are an essential part of the medical team. Recently, Sam was shot by an unknown assailant. His injuries are substantial, especially without a proper hospital and the needed equipment and medicines.

Cameron and Vasquez Families: Recently escaped from the atrocities being committed in nearby Prospect, the two families and many friends have joined forces with those from Bakerville living on the mountain. Two other families from Prospect are living in Bakerville proper.

Chapter 1

Thursday, Day 163
Prospect Creek Dude Ranch, Wyoming

Mollie

"Mom? Mom!" Calley cries with a slam of the front door. "Shelby had her baby! It's a girl!"

Sarah, eyes filling with tears, puts a hand over her own swollen belly and asks, "Are they both okay?"

"Her grandpa Paul says they're fine, resting now. He hasn't seen the baby yet, but Shelby's husband told him she's perfect. What a Thanksgiving!"

Grant and Shelby Cameron, along with the rest of the Cameron family, joined our community at the end of September, having escaped the murderous reign of Richard Majors in the nearby town of Prospect. When they arrived in Bakerville, along with several neighbors and friends, most of the community was in the process of relocating to the nearby ski resort.

While my husband, Jake, and I hated the idea of leaving the homestead we'd spent years lovingly developing, the safety offered by the community—the safety our children and grandchildren needed— swayed us to make the move. Not everyone in Bakerville was convinced this was the right choice, and part of the community stayed behind.

Uncomfortable with leaving everything they owned, a few families even divided, sending most of the family to the ski resort while someone—usually the husband—remained to protect their property.

"It smells so good in here. Is the cooking going okay?" Calley asks.

"We're good," I say, wiping my forehead with the back of my hand. "How's the firepit?"

"The meat's getting close to ready. It also smells amazing. Do you think there will be a huge difference between Pamela Cameron's domestic turkeys and the wild ones Jake and Evan shot?"

"I think it'll be noticeable," I say with a smile. "Did Paul happen to know anything about Dr. Sam?"

"I asked that too. They kept Sam in the other room, on account of his fever and possible new infection, but he was able to verbally offer his expertise."

I nod my understanding. "Any change in the fever?" Dr. Sam was shot by a still-unknown assailant two months ago. The first several weeks were touch and go, but the last few weeks have been much better, to the point he's even started consulting with patients again. He's still unable to walk, or even sit upright, from the bullet that shattered his pelvis and did considerable internal damage. His doctoring is now limited to an advisory position, with his wife or one of the others on the medical team as his proxy.

Maybe, if we had an actual hospital—and an actual surgeon with unlimited supplies and resources—things would be different. But during the apocalypse, everything is finite.

Sam has already had several infections and used many of our antibiotics. There was some disagreement among the Bakerville council as to using so much medication for one person. Belinda and Kelley fought hard for Sam, saying they felt if they could get the infection under control, he had a chance. And as a doctor, his survival could mean many other people survive in the future.

"He still has a fever," Calley says. "Just low, around a hundred, like it has been for days. Belinda thinks it might be the same virus floating around. Are you feeling okay, Mom? You look a little . . . " She shrugs. "Your color's funny."

I wipe my forehead again. "Just hot from cooking."

"You sure?" Sarah asks.

I raise my eyebrows in response. "We're about an hour away from having all of the cooking done. Can you check with Kelley on the rest of the preparations?" I ask Calley.

"Kelley's at the clinic with Shelby and the baby. Doris took over setting up the dining area at the ski lodge, and Angela and Katie are doing the decorating. It's looking good."

"And Gavin?"

"Oh, he's helping, too, of course. You know how he is!"

I can't help but laugh, thinking of the antics of my almost three-year-old grandson as he "helps" his mom—Angela—and his aunt Katie with their duties. Probably better he's in there than outside at the firepit with his dad and uncles.

"Where's Malcolm?" I ask.

"With Tony and TJ, where else?" Calley says with a wave. "They're acting as runners, making sure everyone has what they need for the party. I still don't know why you volunteered our family to oversee the festivities."

"Not just our family," I say. "Kelley's and Doris's families are also taking part."

Calley nods. "A birth on Thanksgiving. That definitely changes the plans, but it's still amazing." She gives another wave and then tightens her coat and goes back outside.

I glance at Sarah and catch her wiping her eyes.

"You okay?" I ask.

"I'm so happy for Shelby," Sarah says. "And for Grant. She's been worried about the birth—you know, with not having a hospital and all."

"She has been. And I know you worry about it too. With the birth of Shelby's baby, it might be hard for you these next few days." Sarah tilts her head at me. I rush on with, "Seeing Shelby and Grant together, holding and loving their child, it might make you think of Tate more."

With downcast eyes, she says, "I think about Tate all the time. Seeing them with their baby won't change it. Besides, they'll be keeping the baby away from people until she's older. Belinda talked with me about doing the same when my baby arrives."

With a nod, I turn back to the corn casserole I'm assembling, when the tinkle of a bell sounds. "I'll go," I say, turning to leave the kitchen.

"No, Mom. Let me. I'll tell her about Shelby's baby being born. She'll—there will be tears."

Two months ago, my son-in-law Tate—Sarah's husband—along with his dad, went missing during a hunting trip in the mountains. A search party spent a week looking for them. With many snowstorms since, there's little chance Tate or Keith are still alive. Sarah and her adopted children—Marc, Sissy, and Andy—bore their loss. Her mother-in-law, Lois, hasn't done well with accepting the deaths of Tate and Keith—her husband of almost forty years. She still expects them to walk in the door at any time.

Unfortunately, during her time of mourning, she's taken to her bed, rarely leaving it, as she seems to fade away day by day. Sarah takes the children in to visit her each day. We know Lois loves this time, often reading to them or listening to their stories. But the visits seem shorter and shorter; she tires so easily. When she needs something, she rings her bell. Even that isn't too often since she doesn't wish to be a burden. Tate's sister, Karen, is Lois's main caregiver. But having come down with a cold a few days ago, she's keeping her distance, even sleeping on the couch in the great room instead of the bedroom they share. Lois is so weak, we're not sure her body could even handle a mild cold. Sarah and I have been taking turns during this time.

~~~~~

Calley was right about Katie and Angela's festive décor. The space is lovely. As we enter the building, the wonderful food aromas, combined with the joyous atmosphere and people laughing and talking, make it a truly wonderous occasion.

"Hello, Mrs. Caldwell," a young voice says.

"Well, hello there, Cheyre. I sure like those boots you're wearing."

"Mrs. Snyder found them for me. She said I needed some nice warm boots for winter. She also got me a pair of slippers. I love wearing slippers in the morning. They keep my feet toasty warm."

"I'm with you on that! I put mine on as soon as I roll out of bed. Are your mom and sister here?" I ask, glancing around.

"Both are. We're sitting at the Cameron table. Did you hear they had a new baby?" I give a nod as Cheyre rushes on. "Mrs. Cameron asked us to sit with them today. She's always so nice, and with my mom on the hunting crew now—well, she's not really on the crew, but she's in training. They have a special name for it that I can't remember."

"She's an apprentice?"

"Yeah, that's the word. She used to hunt before, when we still lived with my dad on our ranch, so they say she'll only need a little bit of training. I'd better go. I think Pastor David is going to do the prayer soon."

She gives me a small wave before bouncing off toward their table. It's great to see her so cheerful. She, her mom, and her older sister
~~~~~

haven't had it easy. Rochelle, her mom, did what she had to do to protect her children, but the emotional scars are still evident.

"Folks," David Hammer says loudly, "let's get settled down so we can enjoy this feast."

The Thanksgiving meal is truly a feast. While some of the dishes were made in my kitchen, and the meat was cooked in the firepits, Kelley's daughters used the smaller kitchen in the ski lodge to make the rest.

Like Karen, there are several people with sniffly noses in the community. Because of our close quarters here at the ski lodge, dude ranch, and surrounding houses, under Dr. Sam's guidance, Belinda suggested anyone exhibiting signs of illness forgo the group meal. Food was boxed up for those to enjoy in their own residence. Likewise, those on guard duty are taken a still-hot plate of food.

David Hammer leads us in prayer. He and Pastor Ralph have become our spiritual leaders. When our group broke up, Pastor Ralph chose to stay behind in Bakerville proper. David now leads a twice-daily Bible study, following breakfast and supper, allowing people to join as their schedules permit. Chaplain Rick, part of the group that arrived here from Prospect a few months ago, will sometimes assist David. But for the most part, Chaplain Rick acts as a counselor and confidant, which is a huge help to psych nurse Kelley Hudson. Living in the apocalypse, we need all the mental health help we can get.

I've just finished filling my plate when a gruff, nasally voice near my ear—too close to my ear—says, "Nice spread."

I close my eyes. I prayed he'd keep his distance today. I start to move away.

Slightly louder, he says, "I said this all looks great, Mollie."

"I heard you the first time, Brad," I say with plenty of venom in my voice. There's an immediate pain behind my right eye, a common affliction when Brad Quinton is near.

"The polite thing to do is acknowledge a person when they speak to you."

Turning, I face him full on and paste on a fake smile. "It's also polite to keep your distance from someone who wants nothing to do with you." I spin on my heels, making a beeline for the section my family is occupying. My husband's eyes meet mine, questioning, asking if I'm okay and what Brad wanted. I give a slight shrug and a nod.

"I've been looking forward to this meal all week," I say, with forced joviality as I set my plate on the table. "Did you try both turkeys, Calley? The domestic and the wild?"

"Yeah, you were right. Big difference. I'm sticking with the domestic."

"Probably not for long," Jake says. "The Camerons only brought toms they order in and raise each year. We've trapped a couple of wild females, but it's not likely they can reproduce naturally with the domestic toms. We need to trap a wild male so we can start our own flock, which hasn't proven easy."

"Please," Sarah says, raising a hand. "Can I not hear the details of this while I'm trying to eat?"

"What?" Calley's husband, Mike, says with a goofy smile. "You don't want to hear the details of breeding among turkeys?"

"Or how domestic tom turkeys need to use artificial insemination because they're too heavy and will crush the females?" Angela's husband, Tim, asks.

"Definitely not," Sarah says. "I never want to hear about that."

"So you definitely don't want to hear about 'milking' the toms?" Mike asks.

"Ewww. Stop," Sarah says. "Jake, I really wish you wouldn't have brought this up. Mike and Tim are like little boys any time they get an opportunity to tease." She turns to Tim and sticks her tongue out, causing everyone at the table to laugh.

It does my heart good to see Sarah acting a little like her old self again. *Thank you, Lord. Thank you for helping to heal Sarah's broken heart.*

Chapter 2

Wednesday, Day 176

Jake

"Happy birthday to you. Happy birthday to you. Happy birthday, dear Malcolm. Happy birthday to you!"

Mollie engulfs Malcolm in a hug, causing him to squirm, and then plants a big kiss on his cheek. The color creeps up his neck.

"Um, thanks, Mom," he says.

"How's it feel to be eleven?" Katie asks.

"About the same as being ten, except I think I have a mustache starting now. See?" Malcolm points to his lip, which looks the same today as it did yesterday, and every day before that.

"Hmm," Katie says, examining it closely. "I don't see anything."

"It's just because it's so dark in here. Wait until tomorrow, in the sunlight. You'll see it then."

"Oh, I'm sure." Katie laughs.

Her husband, Leo, joins in. "It probably won't be long. I was shaving when I was fifteen."

"Yeah, well, no one shaves now," I say, rubbing my own itchy beard. Shaving is one of the many things that have fallen by the wayside since the EMP. While we still have a small stash of safety razors, it just doesn't make sense to take the time to worry about being clean shaven. Plus, now that we're fully in winter's grip, it seems smart to have a little more insulation on our faces. I understand why Malcolm, who's now surrounded by bearded men, might be rushing his maturity a little.

"You get a sharp enough blade on your new birthday knife, and you could shave with it," Leo tells Malcolm.

"Don't give him any ideas!" Mollie says, throwing up her hands. "He's growing up fast enough already. He doesn't need to be shaving yet."

I feel my face fall slightly as I realize it's not just the beards but our entire life aging Malcolm quicker than he should be. While things are slightly more relaxed living in the mountains this winter, our days are still full. There's so much to do to keep our group going, from making sure there's plenty of wood for the fire to tending the livestock to manning the guard towers. The guard towers, originally thought to be only necessary for dangers of our fellow man, quickly became useful in avoiding wildlife encounters as well.

Living halfway up a mountain, in an area inhabited by both black and grizzly bears—along with wolves and mountain lions—has its dangers. We'd only been living here two weeks when the first bear was spotted. The sentry put out a call, which allowed time to get the livestock and people locked down. With the bears bedding down for their winter sleep, we hope to not see them again until spring.

Unfortunately, predatory animals and invaders aren't our main worries. We're almost positive there are people living among us who plan to do us harm.

Deputy Fred turned out to be a criminal. We also discovered Fred may not have been acting alone. Not a fan of the leadership of Bakerville, he was planning a coup. Around the same time, Dr. Sam was shot; his shooter has yet to be discovered. When Tate and Keith disappeared during a hunting trip, it was rumored to be related to Sam's shooting. Was it? I don't think we'll ever know.

"How big of a piece do you want, Dad?" Malcolm asks, knife hovering over his birthday cake.

"This big." I motion for a two-inch square. "And just one scoop of ice cream." While I could easily eat more, even on birthdays, we ration food and had to receive special permission for the ingredients. Next week my grandson, Gavin, will turn three. I'm not sure we'll be allowed the ingredients for another celebration, so Angela's working on a different plan.

Our years of planning so we could provide for our family took quite a turn. While it seemed as if we had rooms full of food and supplies—and we did—with more people living at our place than we had planned, and helping to contribute to those without, our stores depleted quickly.

When it was decided we'd join the main group of Bakerville that was moving up to the ski lodge, we didn't realize our remaining food and supplies were expected to become community property. That was almost a deal breaker for us. But the truth is, we weren't sure we'd be safe staying at our small homestead. All of our nearby neighbors moved up to the mountain. Those who stayed behind either lived directly on the river or relocated to be near the others.

My friend Evan Snyder now jokingly refers to Bakerville as the mountain people and the river people. When spring arrives, us mountain people will return to our homes so we can grow crops to get us through another winter. Now, in order to get the ingredients for a special dessert of cake and ice cream, we must either work additional duty shifts or somehow "make a deal" for extra rations. I admit, this bothers me. Especially since the goats providing the milk for the ice cream are owned by us!

"Karen, here's a nice piece for Miss Lois," Malcolm says. "Do you think she'll want ice cream?"

"Just one scoop, like your dad," Karen answers. The mild virus that went through a couple of weeks ago has passed, allowing Karen to once again be part of our group activities. We hoped Lois would join us tonight. Earlier in the day, she said it was a good day and she planned to leave her room for Malcolm's party. But by the time the party arrived, she was too tired. While Karen has recovered fully from her cold and mild fever, Dr. Sam has taken a turn for the worse.

"Thanks, Dad," Malcolm says as the party begins to break up. "I really like my new knife. Do you really think Mr. Vasquez will teach me how to make knives?"

"I think he will. He seemed excited about having a willing student. He'll teach you leatherwork, too, so you can learn to make your own sheaths."

"I don't know if I could make one as nice as this," he says, stroking the leather.

"I think you can." I ruffle his hair. "Let's tell everyone goodnight. It looks like they're getting ready to leave."

"You ready for bed?" Mollie asks as we finish cleaning up the kitchen. Mollie and I live in the lodge of the old dude ranch with Malcolm; our informally adopted children, Tony and Lily; my parents; plus Mollie's oldest daughter, Sarah, her three adopted children, and her mother and sister-in-law. It's crowded. And because of the running water and the large, mostly working kitchen, it's far from private.

There's a policy in place that allows the rest of the community to use the public facilities anytime they wish between 0600 and 2100. The two bathrooms on the main floor are community space, along with the kitchen and den. Most people are kind enough to knock and wait for us to answer. There are a few people, though, who just walk in and help themselves.

"Jake? You ready?"

"I told Art I'd go see him before bed. He thinks there might be something going on with the little blond-colored goat."

"Honey? From last year's kidding?"

"Yeah, from last year."

"Is she okay?" Mollie asks, concern lacing her voice. "Should I go with you?"

"I'll check her out. If anything seems off, I'll have Madison look at her." I walk to the hook for my coat.

"I'll wait up," Mollie says, raising her eyebrows slightly.

"I won't be long." I shove my feet into my heavy boots and put on a stocking cap. I'm only halfway off the porch before I start putting on my gloves. It's cold tonight. The old equipment shed housing the livestock is part of the original ranch, possibly before it was even used as a commercial dude ranch. Its driveway is off what used to be a county road, which ends not far beyond the turnoff to the ski lodge on the south and the dude ranch on the north, about a third of a mile walk on icy roads. Instead of risking the walk in the dark, I fire up the quad.

A curtain in the RV parked next to the lodge flutters slightly. Katie gives a small wave. I return her wave, and she holds up an index finger, asking me to wait.

She and Leo share the Class C RV with Laurie and Aaron, another newly married couple. Towing their RV up here, after the electronics were wiped out by a presumed EMP, was a challenge. Such a challenge, there's little chance the RV will ever move from its spot parked next to the lodge we're living in.

"Jake!" Katie sticks her head out the passenger's door. "Where're you going?"

"To check out a goat Art was telling me about. You need something?"

"Leo's on watch tonight. Can he ride down with you?"

"Yep. Is he ready?"

She sticks her head back in the RV, and a moment later says, "Two minutes? He's tying his boots."

"I'll wait." It's less than two minutes when the door opens again and Leo climbs out.

"Thanks for waiting," Leo says, putting on his well-laden backpack.

"No problem."

Instead of going straight to the livestock shed, I cross the county road and drive down the entrance to the ski lodge, crossing the large parking lot, then over the bridge. The final stretch to the ski lodge and the small shed next door, being used for the militia headquarters, is a steep hill. Too steep for my quad.

"You know your assignment for tonight?" I ask as I let off the gas and coast to a stop.

"I'm taking a regular militia shift, which won't start until 2200, but Cole—uh, *Major Gunderson* asked me if I could come in early."

"I call him Cole too. The whole rank thing seems unnecessary."

"Yeah, I agree. Evan, Bill, and Cole don't care, and neither do I." Leo's been given the rank of lieutenant. Evan and Bill are each a colonel. "But you'd be surprised how bent out of shape some of the sergeants and corporals get. They like to make a big deal about outranking people."

"Oh, believe me, I know," I say. "I had one of the sergeants get after me, until he realized I'm the same rank. Then he changed his tune. Personally, I can't stand it and wish they'd rethink the ranks."

"I'm with you on that. Oh, and to answer your question, I'm fairly certain I'll be in the uppermost tower on the west side. I'm glad we have the snowmobile to get to the top of the hill."

We're fortunate to have several snowmobiles in the community. Some were part of the equipment belonging to the ski resort, others were owned by community members. There are also a couple of snow grooming machines. While the EMP fried a few of the newer snowmobiles in Bakerville, even the ski resort owners' recently purchased machine still runs. We're not sure why, but one theory is because it was kept in a metal building, which may have acted as a Faraday cage. "All right, Leo. See you tomorrow."

Art, dressed in his winter gear, is sitting in a camp chair near the doe goat pen inside the livestock shed. Formerly used to house a variety of large equipment, the shed has been converted into several small pens to keep goats, sheep, and milk cows. The chickens and ducks also have a small area on one side, with a door to an outside pen. Art has made his home in a storage room connected to the livestock shed—his choice. He says he loves being with the animals and enjoys the solitude.

"What's going on, Art?" I ask as I bend down to pet one of the cats. Our three barn cats from our homestead live here now. One of them has become so friendly with Art, she curls up on his bed every chance she gets.

"Not sure, Jake. She seems better now, not crying like she was."

I spend several minutes looking her over. She seems fine, even running over, tail wagging, to take a few bites of hay after I'm done with her. "She's eating okay?"

"Yep, just cries out occasionally."

"Maybe she's coming into heat?"

"Hmm. None of the others acted like that. I suppose it's possible. I could put her with one of the bucks tomorrow and see what happens."

"If there's no trouble with her overnight, let's try it. The way she's wagging her tail makes me think that might be what's going on."

"Sounds good, Jake. Sorry to get you out here on this cold night."

"You still think you're going to be warm enough living in here? It's going to get a whole lot colder before winter ends."

"It's chilly in here, but not in my room. The little stove warms it up right nicely. I suspect I'll have it better than some of those living in camp trailers. Hard to keep those tin cans warm."

"I guess that's true. But seriously, you can always stay in the lodge if it gets too cold."

"Yep. Uh, I ran into Kelley Hudson on my way back here. Seems our doc took a turn for the worse. She was on her way to help Belinda with him. There's talk of opening him up again."

I let out a sigh. "To see if they can isolate the infection?"

Art shrugs. "Don't know. She was in a dither, and that's all I got out of her."

I nod. "See you tomorrow."

I slow the quad when I drive by the doctor's office—one of the duplex-style cabins set up for surgery, a patient room, and examinations. The lights are all on, and movement shows through the curtains.

Lord, please reach out to Sam with Your healing touch. Make him well and whole again. I ask these things in Jesus' precious name, amen.

Chapter 3

Thursday, Day 177

Mollie

"Mollie? You in the kitchen?"

"Kelley? We're in the laundry room. C'mon back."

I grab a towel to dry my hands, then offer it to Deanne, my daughter Calley's mother-in-law and my good friend. The front of my apron is also wet, one of the difficulties with doing wash by hand. I remove the sodden item while waiting for Kelley to reach us. Most washing machines, with their advanced electronics, were destroyed by the EMP. We have a small RV-style machine, which is a quite simple design, that was unaffected. We can use it for many things, but sheets, blankets, denim, and heavier items need to be handwashed.

"Hey," Kelley says from the doorway. "Hi, Deanne."

"Hey. What's wrong?" I ask, taking in her red-rimmed eyes.

"Sam—he's not . . . " She lets out a huge breath. "There's nothing more we can do," she whispers.

Deanne lets out a gasp.

My shoulders sag as I close my eyes. "The antibiotics?"

"Not helping. Nothing is helping. We can't get his fever down. And he's coughing now. We think it's pneumonia, on top of whatever else was going on."

"That's not uncommon when someone's confined to their bed, right? Isn't there special positioning you can do to help?"

"We're doing it. We've *been* doing it."

"What about the— "

"Mollie, we've tried everything. Sam knew days ago. He didn't want us to use any additional antibiotics or medications. There's nothing— " She covers her face as she dissolves into tears.

I go to her, wrapping my arms around her. Deanne joins us as we cry together.

We're now sitting in the kitchen, lingering over a cup of tea from our weekly rations. I've reused my teabag at least three times now; it barely tints the water. I'd prefer a cup of coffee, but it's not part of our personal rations. The little coffee still available is reserved for special events. Again, the coffee is nothing more than lightly flavored water since it's stretched as far as possible.

We purposely avoid talking about Sam during our teatime, instead discussing Shelby's new baby, Malcolm's birthday, Gavin's upcoming birthday, and Christmas plans. Several of the teachers are working on a program for the children to perform. I'm not sure of the details; my own children and grandchildren have been very secretive.

"Phil said Evan and Jake are talking about goose for the Christmas meal," Kelley says.

"Really?" Deanne exclaims. "We haven't seen any geese lately."

"They'll go down to Bakerville. Isn't this the time they usually goose hunt?"

I tilt my head. "Usually after the new year until mid-February when the season ends. With the elk and culled cattle, why bother with geese?"

"Don't know." Kelley shrugs. "But I do have to admit, I kind of like the idea. It'd be very traditional, give people something to look forward to maybe."

"And more variety," I say with a nod. "The little bit of fish we add into our diet is always popular."

"It sure is. And, I never thought I'd say this, but I miss venison," Kelley says, raising her eyebrows.

"I know. It's just enough different from elk to know we're eating something else."

"Right." Kelley laughs. "That's exactly how I'd describe it. Especially the whitetail."

"We can't risk it," I say, suddenly alarmed. "I know some people are still hunting deer for their personal rations, but as a community— "

"Oh, I know," Kelley says. "I'm completely with you on the deer risk. After we found those sick ones over the summer, we just don't know. I really think they had Chronic Wasting Disease. Based on everything I've read about the subject, they had all the clinical signs."

"Yeah, and even though CWD isn't believed to be a threat to humans— "

"Neither was BSE, but once it jumped from bovines to humans and became Mad Cow Disease, it was obvious the threat was real. I don't want our community to experience Mad Deer Disease." She gives a shake of her head.

"Agreed. I'm glad the council overruled Jon Dawson and stuck with only hunting elk and antelope for our food supply."

"And moose if they come down," Deanne says longingly. "Wouldn't it be wonderful?"

"It would be!" I agree. "So, back to the goose hunt. Would they take the horses? No way could they get down the road in a truck without a snowplow leading the way."

"They can take the snowmobiles," Kelley says. "That's probably a better choice, knowing Jake's apprehension toward horses."

"Definitely better. Jake insists the horses hate him," I say with a small smile.

"Do you think we're having a nuclear winter?" Deanne asks. "To me, it doesn't seem to be any colder or more snowy than I'd expect here on the mountain."

"I know that was a big conversation at breakfast," Kelley says. "After all, we've heard about the bombs being dropped on the east and west coasts—and Doris's daughter even saw the mushroom clouds—but I'm with you, Deanne. I don't think it's much different than a normal winter."

"What did Ellen and Zeb say?" I ask. As the owners of the ski resort, they'd know better than anyone if we're seeing normal winter conditions.

"They both agree it's slightly colder and slightly more snowy than they've seen in the last decade or so," Kelley says. "But they also think other places that don't see winters like we do might notice a change more."

"What was your husband saying about it?" Deanne asks Kelley.

"Phil thinks we may notice a cooler spring and summer, but it depends on how many ground detonations there were. From what we hear, there were five or six on the West Coast and around the same number on the East Coast. But you know how hard it is to get exact info from the radio."

We talk a little more about the Christmas meal, and Deanne, who's in charge of the menu, gives us insight into the food plans. While we'll still have a nice meal, it won't be too elaborate, since we have the rest of the winter to get through. There won't be a community gift exchange, though families can do as they wish. Jake and I have been working on gifts for our young children and grandchildren but won't have gifts for the adult children or each other.

Kelley says her daughters, Sylvia and Sabrina, are acting very secretive. She's sure they have something up their sleeves, possibly related to the children's pageant.

"What do you think they're planning?" I ask.

"I have no idea."

"What about the other children? Have you heard if the parents are able to give gifts?"

"Doris let people know there are a few things in the store available in exchange for extra duties, but I'm not sure how many people took her up on it. But, yes, it's an option. I prefer the direct exchanges, like you did to get Malcolm's birthday knife."

"Me too. I'm glad Judge Avery decided bartering was allowed."

"Who would've thought the idea of a simple barter system would have people so wound up?" Deanne asks with a small laugh.

I shake my head, remembering the meeting that almost came to blows. Two women had exchanged children's clothing. Someone else felt it was unfair that outgrown and unwanted clothing needed to be made available for community use instead of direct exchange or barter. I was surprised when nearly half the people at the meeting agreed with her.

"Maybe we should— "

The front door pops open. "Mom? Mom! Hurry, we need you!" Katie yells, sticking only her head in the front door.

I jump up so quickly, I knock over the kitchen chair. "What's happening?"

"Someone's missing. One of the Baker girls. We're putting a search party together." I'm at the door when she says quietly, "I think it's bad. They found . . . there might be blood. We're meeting at the livestock shed. Hurry!" She pulls the door shut.

I turn and look at Kelley and Deanne; both are up and moving toward the door. "You heard?"

"Not good," Kelley says, while Deanne shakes her head.

"Mom?" Sarah hollers down from upstairs. "Should I go?"

I meet her eyes, seeing the fear and memories there. "Stay, in case Lois needs you. You shouldn't be traipsing around in the snow anyway."

"All right, Mom. Karen heard too. She'll be right behind you."

Kelley is working her foot into her snow boot while I put on my coat. "Which Baker girl do you think it is?" Kelley asks.

"Not sure. I didn't think to ask. I don't really know any of them other than to say hello. You?"

"Phoebe. I know her. She's the one who snuck out to get help last summer when they were under attack."

I answer with a nod while putting on my stocking hat. "Ready?" I grab my small backpack, already loaded with a water bladder, snacks, extra cold-weather gear, and snowshoes bungeed on either side.

"I need to grab a pair of snowshoes," Kelley says as I open the door. "I'll see you there."

"Same here," Deanne says, sitting on the bench, lacing her heavy, fleece-lined, military-style boots. "As soon as I get these boots on, I'll run home and then meet you there." Deanne and the rest of her family didn't bring winter boots or clothing from Casper, expecting to only be in Bakerville a short time until the attacks stopped. Doris found these in our supplies. They're a men's boot, but Deanne is tall with larger feet, and after adding heavy socks, they fit well. She often complains about their main drawback being the time they take to get on and off.

I find several others, including Calley and Angela, on my way to the meeting place.

"You have your snowshoes?" I ask each of them.

They both turn so I can see their backpacks, shoes strapped on. My family had a collection of snowshoes and cross-country skis before the attacks. Snowshoes, clothes, and a few other items were labeled personal items that we could keep, instead of becoming community property. That also didn't happen without a fight.

"I sure hope they'll have some working radios for this," Calley says.

"That was the reason they put them up," I say. "Only the few people on guard duty use them now so we can save the batteries."

"I know, but you know how things seem to go," she says, making a noise of disgust.

She's not wrong. So many of the things we thought were happening are no longer. Sometimes, I wonder if the river people of Bakerville have these same issues.

I'm huffing by the time we reach the large group waiting at the livestock shed. The smoke hanging in the air from the multitude of woodstoves compounds my breathing difficulties. I've always loved the smell of a fire warming a home, but here, when wood is our only source of heat, the aroma's almost overwhelming.

Bill Shane, a retired Prospector County deputy sheriff, is already giving out instructions. Within a few minutes, I'm in a group of five—along with Angela, another girl around her age, a man slightly older than me, and another man slightly younger than I am—that will follow the county road down the mountain.

It's not expected we'll find anything since the blood trail—assumed to belong to the missing girl, Phoebe Baker, the same one Kelley says she knows—took off through the woods. The trail was discovered by a teen out for a walk. Retired detective Jesse Richardson is with the group—which Bill says includes Jake—investigating the blood trail to see if it really is blood. If it is, they'll try to reacquire the trail. While we're gathered around receiving our assignments, there's more than one murmur suggesting the boy who found the blood trail is likely the guilty party.

"Knock it off," Bill says. "There will be no assigning blame to anyone at this point in the search. Your only mission is to find Phoebe. You need to keep in mind, we still believe in innocent unless proven otherwise."

"Easy for you to say," someone murmurs. "You're an outsider too."

"What's that?" Bill demands, his voice booming over the crowd. I watch as several people cower in response.

Adding to the drama, and providing more tongue wagging, no one knows for certain when Phoebe went missing. She was at dinner last night, but her bed in the women's dorm was not slept in. Her roommates didn't think anything of it since she often stays in the cabin or apartment of one of her relatives. At fifteen, she's younger than most people in the dorm. It seems she was staying the summer with the rest of her family when the attacks happened. Her parents are divorced; she lives with her mom back east but spends summers with her dad and his new family in Bakerville. She begged her dad to let her stay in the dorms instead of crowding into the small cabin with them. Even so, she often stays over with her dad or with one of the other Baker relatives. None confirm having her stay over last night.

Angela and I got all this information in a quick, rambling stream from a lady named Tricia. When she finished her spiel, we were both exhausted just from listening to her talk and watching her gesticulate. For a moment, I feared she'd be on our search team; I'm not sure I'd be able to handle her for any length of time. Oh, she was nice enough. Just exhausting.

We fan out along what was once a blacktop county road. The snow in this area is packed down, thanks to the snow grooming machine that keeps all the roads and driveways usable. This part of the road is kept clear for travel between the lodges and a couple of houses down the road that we're also using for housing, making the walk somewhat easy and our snowshoes unnecessary for the moment.

"Be careful, Mom. It's slick in places," Angela says.

I answer with a nod. *When did I get so old my children started looking out for me instead of me looking out for them?*

We take our time checking the ditch and the drifts on either side of the road. A light snow started falling minutes after we left the livestock shed. Hopefully, it won't snow too much, allowing someone to find evidence of Phoebe and bring her home. If she was missing overnight, will she—I stop my thoughts. I'm not going there right now. This is a rescue mission. We're going to find her.

"The bridge is especially slick," the older man says, reaching out his hand to help a woman in our group. Though rather plain at first glance, the smile she offers him completely transforms her face. And with her warm smile, I'm led to believe they're more than friends.

As we cross the bridge, a cow in the dude ranch pasture lets out a deep bellow. While the livestock shed houses the smaller animals—goats, sheep, pigs, and poultry—the cattle and horses are in several large pastures on both sides of the road. When we made the move from Bakerville proper to the mountain, the cattle were the last to come up. Both Mick Michaelson and Barney Sanchez had small operational ranches before the attacks started, Mick having around four hundred pairs and Barney less than half that. There were also several people in Bakerville raising seasonal cattle or raising them for their own use.

When part of the community decided to stay behind, those with livestock kept what they owned. Mick and Barney each donated several cull head to help get them through the winter. The rest were moved up here in an old-fashioned cattle drive. The Cameron family had recently brought their small herd of cattle from Prospect in the same manner, adding their livestock to ours.

When we're close to the first house on the road, where six of our residents are living, we see the owner of the home, Rudy Wallace, at the driveway. "What's happening?" he yells.

"Someone's missing," the younger of the two guys yells back, in a voice much deeper than his small stature seems it should have.

"Need more help?" Rudy asks. He and his wife are both close to seventy; they retired up here twenty years ago. Before the attacks, they were talking about moving into Prospect or Wesley—the property was just too much for them. When we decided to move Bakerville to the ski lodge for the winter, they opened their home to two other couples that are even older than they are.

I don't really know Rudy, or any of the others living at this home or at the home farther down the road. Because of the distance to the ski lodge, where we eat our meals and have our community events, they only attend on special occasions. It's just too far between here and there for them to make the trek regularly. Instead, food is brought down every few days so they can have their own meals. I heard Rudy joked about it being the apocalyptic version of Meals on Wheels.

When they do come up, we send a vehicle for them. It's often the snow grooming machine, which has to make multiple trips because he can only crowd two in the cab at once, and he does the road at the same time. I don't think having any of them out in this weather, walking on the snow and ice, is a good idea.

"We're probably good," I say. "Especially with the snow coming in. But you might call on your radio and see."

"I'm surprised they didn't call you," the younger guy says.

"Our rechargeable batteries aren't holding a charge like they should. It's dead, and we didn't realize it until we saw you all walking down the road. My wife plugged it into the little solar thing. Not sure how much good that'll do with the snow starting."

"When we get back, I'll tell Doris," I say. "Maybe she can get you new ones."

"Humph," he says. The perfect answer for everything these days. He lifts his hand and turns back toward his house.

"What are we going to do about the battery issue?" Angela asks. "Especially next summer, how can we be so spread out on watch without a way to communicate?"

I shake my head. "I'm not sure. There's probably a plan floating around. I just don't know what it is."

"At least the ham radio still works," Angela says. "It lets us know a little about what's going on in other places."

"True." I choose not to say that, unfortunately, because of contact we made with the nearby town of Prospect, they know a little about what we're doing also. After that experience, we stopped reaching out to others, and we now only listen. Calley is one of the listeners, and she has a regular shift monitoring the radio. She isn't allowed to share what she hears; everything is filtered through the council, then we're given a weekly briefing. There is, of course, a rumor floating around that what we're being told in the briefings are watered-down versions of what they're hearing.

We plod on in silence until we reach the end of the packed snow where the last house for our group is located. No one greets us at the road, but a woman does wave from the porch. As far back off the road as the house is set, even if she is trying to talk to us, it's unlikely we'll hear her. My guess is their radio is still working and they're in the loop. Like the Wallaces, this is an older couple who've opened their home to other older couples. Also like the Wallaces, they're not good candidates for being out here plodding through the snow.

I glance up the hillside behind the house to our easternmost lookout. Most of our guard towers are part of the ski lodge. We've utilized the ski lift shacks—with their multitude of windows and commanding views of the slopes—to be able to see the entirety of the ski resort.

This lookout is a newly constructed log cabin built in a lean-to style. It has a pony wall along the eastern side, but the top part is open to the elements. There's a small woodstove to help heat the semi-open building.

The fact that most of the weather comes from the west or the north—which both have solid, closed in sides—is a plus. But even so, it gets cold in there. None of us are overly excited to have guard duty in the east lookout. There's a plan to bring up windows before next winter, but it works for now. And the partially open side gives an expansive view of the valley below. It'd be incredibly difficult for anyone to approach without being seen.

"Time for the snowshoes," the older guy says.

"Remind me of your name?" I ask him.

"Harry English. And this is my friend Annette." He motions to the woman. She says something, but with the wind blowing and her mouth covered by a scarf, I can't make it out.

"Heath Jefferson," the younger man says in a confident voice while extending his hand. His weak grip reminds me of a dead trout. "I was on Foxtrot Team. Your daughter is Katie, right?"

"She is."

"And your husband is Jake? Dot's my wife. They were on Alpha together."

"Oh, yeah, sure." I met Dot in passing a couple of times over the summer. Jake said she was a very capable member of their team.

Looking over Heath, I question if he's as capable as his wife. There's nothing overly impressive about him. He's slightly below average height and on the skinny side, with his brown beard frozen around his mouth. I glance to his waist and notice he doesn't appear to be carrying a sidearm. That's unusual on our mountain, especially considering the predators. Of course, he may prefer to conceal carry as opposed to open carry.

"This is my daughter Angela," I say.

Heath reaches for her hand.

"Hello," Harry says, as Annette gives a small wave. Then Heath shakes Harry's and Annette's hands too. Like Heath, Annette is also firearm free, but there is a wicked-looking knife on her belt.

"Well," Heath says, "I guess we should get the snowshoes on. I'm glad the ski resort had plenty as part of their rental stuff. We sure need them out here."

"I'll undo yours," I say to Angela, motioning her to turn around. Once I have them unhooked from her pack, I help her get them on. She returns the favor, then I assist Annette with strapping her shoes on. She has the kind with rubber strapping, which I know from experience, having had this exact style as my first pair, don't stay hooked well. "Have you used these before?" I ask.

"No," she says quietly. There's more to her answer, but I can't hear it.

"Make sure there's someone behind you," I say. "They can tell you if your strap's coming loose. Otherwise, you'll walk right out of it and might not know it—unless you're the one breaking the trail, of course."

Heath takes the first turn at breaking the trail. Unlike on packed ground, we'll stay in a line on the creek side of the road as our eyes search the surrounding area. We're to go down the road until we reach a popular picnic spot along the creek—at least, it *was* a popular spot back when our world was normal—then turn around. We'll break a new trail on the hillside on the way back.

With this fresh, unblemished snow, we'll be able to easily see any tracks. It hasn't snowed enough since Phoebe went missing for us to not notice a disturbance anyplace within our line of sight. The undisturbed snow is also going to be a workout for my legs.

Chapter 4

Thursday, Day 177

Jake

"Careful, Laurie," Toby says, offering his friend a hand.

"I'm good," she says, regaining her footing after sliding down a slight embankment.

When the Cameron family and their group showed up a couple of months ago, Laurie was shocked to discover her old neighbor, Toby James, among them. When they still lived in Wesley, Toby was severely beaten and transported to the Prospect hospital. When the fire started at the hospital, they assumed Toby was among the lost. Instead, he was one of many rescued by Chaplain Rick, who housed him until the mayor of Prospect and the city police were killed in a violent takeover. Rick and Toby then escaped to the Cameron ranch.

"It was just right up here," Toby says. "At first, I thought it was from an animal, but with Phoebe missing . . . " His voice fades off, and he finishes his statement with a shrug.

"Mm-hmm," Jesse Richardson says, furrowing his expansive forehead.

We continue through the snow, following the tracks Toby made earlier through the thicket of evergreens. After about fifty yards, Toby says, "Right over here. See it? You can see from my tracks I didn't walk over to it, but there it is. Or, uh, there she is." Toby points to a spot against a tree about twenty feet away.

"Yep," Jesse answers. "The rest of you wait here. Toby, walk with me."

My snowshoes depress slightly into the soft, unpacked snow. They help with keeping me on top of the snow when we're moving, but gravity still pulls me down when I stop walking. Evan, having the same issue with sinking, repositions himself, trying to find more solid ground. I look around the area, taking everything in. What I see doesn't seem like anything out of the ordinary to find in the forest.

"What do you think?" I ask in a whisper.

"Can't tell from here, not with any certainty. But my guess is we're looking at a crime scene."

Laurie gasps. I crease my forehead and look back over the area. What is retired SWAT officer Evan seeing that I don't see?

"Really? I thought . . . looks to me like those are rabbit tracks," I say, keeping my voice low. "And the blood over there goes with the bit of grey fur up against the tree. And I'm fairly sure those— " I point to a different set of prints " —are coyote."

"Like I said, a crime scene. Just not the kind where we can find the missing girl."

Jesse turns toward us, motioning us to move forward. Toby, red faced, turns also. "I think . . . I guess I was wrong," he says quietly. "Sorry to get you out here like this."

"Personally, I'm happy you were wrong," Laurie says, giving him a small smile and a nod.

"Why were you out here?" Jesse asks.

"No reason, really. I borrowed snowshoes and thought I'd practice with them. You saw the tracks we followed. Dax and Bryce Cameron said I need to be able to walk quietly in snowshoes before they'll take me hunting."

"I heard you were trying to get on the hunting squad."

"Right. Before Shelby had her baby, she taught me how to use the bow and arrow. And Paul Cameron showed me the crossbow. I already knew how to use a hunting rifle. But," he says with a shrug, "I'm loud and clumsy."

Laurie gives him a small smile. "You did fine while we were walking out here."

"The trail was already broken," he responds, completely dejected.

"So, Toby," Jesse says quietly, "when was the last time you saw Phoebe?"

With a shake of his head, he says, "I have no idea. She and I don't— you know we aren't really friends."

"She's a pretty girl," Jesse says.

As Toby's face colors again, I wish I were somewhere else.

"We don't talk or . . . or anything. We're really not friends. She's younger than me. I don't know her."

"She stays in the women's dorm. You stay in the men's dorm. You don't see her?"

"Sure, yeah. But, listen, I don't know where she is. Maybe I . . . maybe I need a lawyer or something."

"Do you need a lawyer?" Jesse asks evenly.

"I . . . I'm going back to the ski lodge. If you want to talk to me again, I want Chaplain Rick with me." Toby attempts a suave turn but stumbles over the tip of his snowshoe. He throws his arms out, unable to regain his balance. He lands in the snow with an *oomph*.

Evan and Jesse share a look. I catch a slight shake of Jesse's head. Laurie is moving toward Toby when Jesse says, "Let me help you up."

"No. I'm fine. I've got it." He clumsily untangles the shoes. Somehow, he's managed to get the cleats stuck together. He's finally up when he says, "I know you think you're doing your job, but wherever Phoebe is, it's not because of anything I did. And I don't know anything about it."

"Fair enough," Jesse says. "Let's head on back. Maybe they've already found her."

Toby leads the way, with Jesse right behind him. Laurie follows, while Evan and I hang back slightly. When they're out of earshot, I whisper, "Well?"

"I'd be surprised if he was involved."

"What about Jesse? He seems to think— "

"Nah, I don't think he does."

We double time to catch up with the others. Toby sets a brisk pace, making the walk back take considerably less time than walking out did. When we reach the livestock shed, Bill is still there. Toby keeps walking while the rest of us stop.

After giving Bill a brief synopsis of what we found, Jesse says, "I'll talk to the kid again, but I'd be surprised if he had anything to do with her going missing."

"Any news?" Evan asks.

"Nothing. We've got people in all directions and others going house to house. I haven't heard anything yet. Uh." Bill stops talking and stares at the man walking toward us. My face hardens. Brad Quinton—my wife's ex-boyfriend, and her daughter Sarah's dad.

"Hello, gentlemen, Laurie," he says in his smarmy way. "I heard someone's missing, thought you might need a hand."

"Yeah. We're just discussing our next step," Evan says.

"Say, didn't your wife go out with one of the earlier groups?" Bill asks.

Brad shrugs. "Maybe. I was napping. Had guard duty last night."

"Your son?"

"School, I guess. Where else would he be?"

A logical answer. All the children have school each weekday. There's even a nursery for the younger ones.

"We're probably fine. All the search teams have been sent out."

"So, what are you doing here then?" he asks, directing his sneer in my direction. "Taking some time off?"

I meet his gaze as Evan says, "Thanks for the offer to help, Brad. We're fine."

His glare focuses on Evan. "That almost sounds like I'm being dismissed."

Evan gives him a cold smile; Laurie looks down at her shoes.

"You people," Brad says. "It's almost like high school. You have your little cliques and anyone else, well, forget it. You treat us like scum." Brad turns and marches away. He makes it about ten feet before turning around and saying, "It's too bad about Dr. Sam. I know he was an important part of your little inner circle."

Evan starts moving toward Brad, but Bill grabs onto his jacket, yanking him back.

"Don't waste your energy on him," Bill says loud enough for Brad to hear.

Brad gives a scowl before once again starting his retreat.

When he's well out of earshot, I say, "Is there a new update on Sam?"

"Yes," Laurie says quietly.

Bill claps me on the shoulder. "Keep praying, brother. Keep praying."

Chapter 5

Thursday, Day 177

Mollie

We make it about two hundred yards before Heath asks in a ragged breath if he can swap with someone. It didn't take long for him to discover that breaking trail is hard work. He started at too brisk a pace and tired quickly.

"I'll do it," I say. "It makes sense with me being second in line, anyway. Do you want to step out and fall in at the end?"

"Yeah. Good idea. Then, when you tire out, your daughter can be next. We'll keep it up that way."

"Sure. Sounds like a good plan."

I start off much slower than he did. As the road begins to make a bend to the left, I glance around the corner. "Stop," I say, almost skidding to a halt.

Angela is too close and bumps into me. She grabs onto my coat to stop me from falling. "Mom?"

"The snow on the hillside—it's all messed up, like something was running down it."

"Probably an elk or a deer," Heath says in a bored voice.

"Only if he rolled down the hill." I adjust my jacket slightly, making sure my .40 Springfield Armory semi-auto is within easy reach.

"What do you want to do?" Angela asks.

"Keep walking, but everyone stays alert."

"Could be a bear," Heath says.

"Aren't they hibernating?" Angela asks with worry in her voice.

"Not exactly," Harry says in a kind tone. "They sleep, but it's not an actual hibernation. The sows should be bedded down, but it's possible for the boars to still be out. It'd be unusual, but not unheard of, to have one out in the middle of December. Like your mom said, stay alert. Are you still good leading, Mollie?"

"I'm good," I say, moving forward.

The snow, which has been falling lightly up until now, seems to increase in intensity, decreasing visibility. When we get closer to the disturbance, it's obvious something tumbled down the hill, ran across the road, and then went down the embankment on the other side. Within a few feet, it's also obvious it wasn't an elk, deer, or even a bear. The tracks on the road are human footprints, one barefoot.

"Not good," Angela says, her voice barely a whisper.

Following the tracks, I scour the embankment leading to the river with my eyes. "There," I say, pointing to a patch of blue against the white snow.

"What is it?" Annette asks in a barely audible voice. "Is it . . . blue jeans?"

"Someone needs to go back," Heath says. "Get the detective here."

"Annette and I will go," Harry says.

I watch for a moment as they take off at a moderate clip.

"We should probably go down. Check her for . . . you know," Heath says.

I look at the decline from the road to where the body is. It's steep where we're standing, but if we move over a few feet, we can weave our way down.

"So . . . we should go down," Heath says again.

"Angela, wait up here?" I ask.

"Absolutely." She shudders.

I take a couple of steps down the roadway and then begin my descent, making sure my snowshoes are gripping well.

"You need a hand?" Heath asks in an arrogant tone.

"No, I just prefer not to slide down the hill if it can be avoided."

"Humph."

I pick my way down, keeping an eye on my step and purposely avoiding the blue material waiting at the bottom. When I think I'm getting close, I look up to judge the remaining distance. A bare foot, blackened with frostbite, greets me. My eyes carry up the blue-jean-clad legs. The other foot, still wearing her athletic shoe, is bent awkwardly under her knee. Her bare hand, with black fingers, and her wrist are also showing. The rest of the body—and there's no doubt that's what I'm looking at—is obscured by brush.

"Well, I guess that's that," Heath says coolly. "The way her foot and hand look . . . do we need to check for a pulse?"

I swallow hard. Voice breaking a little, I say, "Probably not."

"Should we make sure it's her?"

I give him a hard look. "Are there other missing girls I don't know about? Feel free if you need to. I'm close enough."

He lifts a hand in response. I look up at Angela; at this angle, only her head shows above the embankment. Her eyes are filled with tears.

"You're sure, Mom?" she asks.

I give a nod. "I'm coming back up." I slowly make my way toward Angela.

Heath hesitates, taking a step toward the body, before turning around and following me.

At the top of the hill, I wrap an arm around Angela, hugging her close. "You should drink some water," I say quietly.

"You should too."

We sip our water as the snow continues to fall. It's not long until the rumble of an engine fills the forest. Two snowmobiles come into view a few moments later; Bill and Laurie on one, and Evan and Jesse on the second one with a trailer attached. At least one more machine is still approaching in the distance.

The sled is barely stopped when Laurie bounces off. "Does she need medical?"

I give a small shake of my head.

"You're sure?" she asks.

"We went down. Once we were close enough . . . yeah, I'm sure."

"Me too," Heath says boastfully.

"You're involved in this, Jefferson?" Bill asks Heath, voice dripping with animosity.

Standing tall, Heath says, "I'm on the search team that found her, that's all."

I look from man to man, wondering what I'm missing.

Bill's eyes are hard, drilling into Heath. Without looking in my direction, he asks, "Are you okay, Mollie? Angela?"

"Fine," I answer. Angela makes a small noise in response.

Finally breaking eye contact with Heath, Bill asks, "Do we need our snowshoes?"

"There might be footholds from us going down," I say. "Mind if I sit on your sled?" I'm suddenly feeling incredibly tired.

"Go ahead," Evan answers, clapping Bill on the shoulder. "Jake's behind us. He's on his quad. He thought you might need a ride home."

"That was nice of him," Angela says.

"Your husband is with him," Laurie says to Angela. "He thought you'd want a ride too."

The four of them take off, gingerly stepping down one by one.

"I guess it's too much to hope my wife is also with them," Heath says with a wry smile.

Even though I know he's trying to be funny, to lighten the mood, his humor is unwelcome. And there's something about him that grates on me. I'm too spent to even produce a courtesy smile.

It's several minutes before the quads come into view, creeping along in the tracks of the snowmobiles. They stop their machines, leaving the engines running. I stand on wobbly, exhausted legs.

"Are you okay?" Angela whispers.

"Just tired. Let's go talk to Jake and Tim."

"You found her?" Jake asks as we walk up.

I nod, while Angela says, "She's dead."

"Can you leave yet?" Tim asks.

"I'll find out," she says. "Mom, I'll ask if you can leave too."

"Please do." I turn to Tim. "I thought you were on watch?"

"Shift ended. I was talking with Jake and Evan when the call came over the radio."

"Thanks for coming and getting us. Even though I hate using our gas ration for it, I'm glad I don't have to walk back."

"Is that Dot Jefferson's husband? Does he need a ride?" Jake asks.

I shrug. "How?"

"Put Angela on with us, and let him ride behind Tim?"

Tim makes a face before saying, "Three on the quad? You think it's safe?"

"Not even close," Jake says. "But we can do it. Mollie can ride in front of me. Angela behind. It's fine at the speed we're going."

Jake motions to Heath. Angela is starting back from the edge of the hillside. When they both arrive, she says, "We can go, but they'll want to talk to us later."

We share the plan for riding back. Heath thanks Jake profusely, switching from the arrogant guy of a few minutes ago to appreciative. Angela says Jake had better not wreck. We load up and creep along the snow-covered roads. Between Rudy's house and the lodge, the other two from our search team are walking back toward the lodge, hand in hand.

"We can't fit them," Jake says. "This isn't a clown car."

The silly statement catches me off guard, causing me to laugh. We slow and I say to them, "They want to talk to us later."

"Yes, they told us over the radio," Harry says. "Should we meet somewhere?"

"I'm sure they'll let you know," Jake answers.

"Why don't you come to the lodge at the dude ranch?" I say. "That's as good a place as any."

When we get back to the lodge, the children are there. We were gone so long that school has ended for the day. Even though the older kids know about the missing girl, we don't immediately tell them we've found her.

"Well?" Sarah asks.

I give a small shake of my head and move my finger to my lips. She makes a silent *oh* response, then drops her head.

"Jake, can we light a fire in the den?" I ask.

"Sure, good idea," he answers.

We keep the den, with its own fireplace, closed off. It's not a room we use on a regular basis, and it doesn't make sense to heat it. There was talk at one time of turning the den into another sleeping room, but we ended up not needing the space when Belinda Bosco and her son TJ were able to get one of the small apartments in the ski lodge. The den is currently used for private meetings by the council. My guess is we'll have several people showing up here shortly.

Even though we live in the lodge of the old dude ranch, it's also considered public space. With the solar system for electricity and functioning hot water heaters—thanks to one being very old and surviving the pulse, and the second one being propane-only—that we moved up here from our home, we're one of the few places where people can have a shower.

Zeb and Ellen, the owners of the ski resort where many of our people are now living, also have running water and showers, but only when using a generator. Same with the two houses down the road. Finding functioning water heaters for those places was a challenge, but it was worth it.

The dude ranch had twenty-four guest cabins, ranging in size from small studio spaces to a single large bungalow with two bedrooms and two bathrooms. There are even several connected duplexes, a few with doors between the two in order to make one big space. While all of them were set up with electricity and fully functioning bathrooms, after the pulse took out the power grid, none of that worked. Now the cabins are dry—with drinking and bathing water hauled in. The lighting is provided by candles and lanterns, and heat's provided by woodstoves. Several people use camping showers or take sponge baths, reserving the actual showers for special occasions. But there are a few members of the community who still use the showers daily.

When it was obvious we'd still be short on housing, even with using the cabins and dorms constructed in the ski lodge, plus the camp trailers brought up, we converted the multitude of storage spaces used by the dude ranch into studio apartments. Many of the cabins had locked rooms off them that were chock-full of junk—or what would've been junk in our previous life. Now we try and use everything. And then reuse everything.

Angela, Tim, and Gavin are living in one of the former storage rooms, now turned into a studio apartment. It's attached to the duplex that houses Calley and Mike in a small studio and Mike's parents and sister in the connecting one-bedroom. We think the storage unit may have, at one time, been a bedroom for the studio since a door joins the two. It's even slightly larger than Calley and Mike's studio.

In addition to storage spaces being turned into housing, we've utilized every available outbuilding. Clark Thomas and his deputies have an old utility shed as their headquarters. The militia leaders have their own shed. There were a lot of questions as to why they couldn't share a space. It was finally decided the division between the two was necessary. We even have a makeshift jail in a section of Clark's headquarters.

Our radio room, where Neil Jonas set up his ham radio, is in an outbuilding near the ski lodge. Doris and her supply team have taken over the garage and a couple of outbuildings at Zeb and Ellen's house to store our necessary supplies.

We've really managed to turn this space into something safe and usable for all of us. The way it's spread out can be a hindrance at times. From our lodge to the ski lodge where we take our meals is about half a mile. With the roads kept clear, it helps. But it's still a long walk.

The hardest part is the last hundred yards. After crossing a bridge used only for foot traffic, snowmobiles, quads, and the grooming machine—never our full-size vehicles—there's a steep hill leading to the lodge. After a warm day with snow melt, then a freezing night, it's often an ice rink. We have a team doing their best to keep it safe for us, but it's almost a full-time job some days.

"Snack time," I say to the children. "Go wash your hands and then head into the dining room. Sarah, help me put it together?"

"Mom," Tim says to get my attention. When I look his way, he says, "I'm going to gather my things and then come back for a shower. Is there anyone here?"

"No one," Sarah says. "They've all been— " She tilts her head toward the door.

"Use one of the upstairs bathrooms," I say. "The public ones will probably get busy with the search over." This lodge was designed well for bathrooms. The main floor has two full baths, a his and hers, which are now used for the public. There's another bedroom and bathroom on the main floor, in what used to be the owner's quarters, with outside access. Jake's parents have this private space as their own. Upstairs are four bedrooms and two bathrooms, which is our family area, and, like Alvin and Dodie's room, it's not considered public space.

Tim nods, then gives Angela a quick kiss before heading out. I put my arm around Sarah while we walk into the kitchen, whispering quietly about the grisly discovery.

Angela, Sarah, and I join the children around the large table in the dining room while they nibble on their snack of elk roast and chunks of cheese. The cheese, based on the way it's waxed, is likely from our personal stores we contributed to the community. It's now part of the weekly personal rations we're allowed because of the children. Sarah, with her pregnancy, gets a few special rations also. Each of our main meals—breakfast, lunch, and dinner—are eaten together at the ski lodge. Extras, like teabags and snack foods, are allowed on a limited basis. Those of us with children do get a little more.

Thankfully, meat is plentiful due to the wild game and domestic livestock. We're even allowed to hunt on our own, outside of the official hunting teams, to add extra meat to our permitted rations. We're fortunate to have an ample supply of wild game, along with a small enough community so we're not completely depleting this resource.

Jake often brings up the book *Undaunted Courage*, a story of Lewis and Clark's journey, and how much meat they ate. When meat was plentiful, each man ate about nine pounds per day. While we're not as physically active as they were, and we do have other things we can eat, meat does make up the bulk of our food source.

Angela, sitting next to Gavin and encouraging him to eat his snack, gives me a look. I nod my agreement. She lightly points toward me.

I look around the table, catching Malcolm's eye. "What's going on, Mom?" he asks.

"You all heard that Phoebe Baker is missing?"

Malcolm, Tony, and Marc nod. The younger children are more interested in their cheese.

"We found her," I say softly. "She wasn't alive."

"She's dead like my mom?" my adopted daughter Lily asks. Her mom, Olivia, was kidnapped and killed in the early days of the attacks. Lily and her older brother, Tony, now live with us.

"And like my mom and Daddy Tate?" Sissy asks.

"Yes, sweetie," Sarah says, eyes glistening with unshed tears. She gently touches Sissy on the arm. These children have all had too much heartache.

"What happened?" Malcolm asks.

"We don't know yet, but until we know more, we're all going to be extra careful."

"Was it a bear?" Marc asks, eyes wide.

"No, honey. I don't think it was a bear."

"So why do we need to be careful?"

"Because we don't know what happened to her," Sarah says. "Grandma is asking you guys to watch out for each other. You all know the rule about not leaving the lodge alone?" Sarah makes sure each child gives a nod or says yes. Even Angela answers. "Good. It's especially important you stay together. I'm going to make sure I'm always with someone, and so will your aunts and your grandma."

"What about Uncle Leo?" Marc asks. "He's always doing his guard stuff alone."

"All of them do," Tony says. "Are they safe alone?"

"We pray so," I say. "And I suspect, soon, the council will be here to discuss this. When they show up, I'd like you all to go upstairs. You can play quietly in the loft area." I turn to Sarah. "Is Karen back?"

"Yes, she got here shortly before you arrived," Sarah says. "She was searching the outbuildings. They were excused from the search but not told anything. I should go and let her know." She slowly lifts from the chair as she says, "I think I can win at Crazy Eights today. See you guys in the loft."

"Can the doggies play with us?" Lily asks, motioning to Penny and Scooter sleeping on their beds in the corner. Scooter's tail starts beating a tune of excitement.

"They can watch," Sarah says.

"You win every time we play," Tony says. "It's not like it's even a challenge for you to beat us."

"I know. That's part of the fun." Sarah waggles her eyebrows. Even though she's trying to be upbeat, it's obvious Phoebe's death is very reminiscent of her own husband's disappearance. As sad as it is, at least the Bakers will have some closure. So far, Sarah doesn't have that.

Chapter 6

Thursday, Day 177

Jake

While the fire warms up the den, I give it a quick cleaning. As a family, we don't use this room. Instead, it's reserved for council meetings and other community meetings where privacy is needed. Even though there are people in and out a few times a week, and we keep the door closed when it's not in use, the dust has accumulated. My former job as a school janitor still comes in handy. Mollie's former job, mainly internet based, is completely useless in our new world. While we did bring some skills with us, we've had to learn many new things by learning from others and relying on our extensive preparedness library—the paperback books Mollie thought we needed reside in this room.

Angela sticks her head in the door. "Mom said to tell you Judge Avery and Jon Dawson are walking up."

I give a grim nod. Judge Avery is fine. Jon Dawson I could do without. But since he—along with the judge, Evan, Bill, Mick Michaelson, and two others—is on the council, I expected him. I follow Angela out of the room and head toward the front door.

"The children?" I ask.

"Just sent them upstairs. I'm going to join them. Tim's showering. We'll stay up there until suppertime."

"We might need you."

"Why?"

"You were with the ones who found them," I say patiently. "Dot's husband and the others should be showing up here shortly too."

She rolls her eyes. "Holler up if they decide they do."

"I might join you upstairs until I'm needed also," Mollie says before turning to me. "You were in the den for a while. Everything okay?"

"It was dusty," I answer with a shrug.

We walk to the door, hand in hand, opening it as Jon Dawson's hand is on the knob. Even though most people knock, Dawson believes knocking isn't necessary since the lodge is community property. He narrows his eyes at me.

With a laugh, Judge Avery says, "Good to see you, Jake. It's colder than—oh . . . hello, Mollie."

"Judge. Mr. Dawson," Mollie says. "Won't you both come in?"

"Planned on it," Dawson says with a huff. Mollie smiles sweetly in response.

As they remove their boots at the door, Dawson says, "Why don't you start some water for tea? Everyone will need a warmup."

"Sure, I'd be glad to," Mollie answers. "Did you bring teabags?"

"I'm sure you can spare them from your rations," he spits out.

"I'm sorry, Mr. Dawson, but you're mistaken. I'm happy to heat water for you, but anything additional will not come out of my family's allotment." Mollie turns and strides purposely to the kitchen. I can't help but watch as she walks away, a small smile on my lips. Sometimes I forget just how sassy my wife can be.

Dawson starts to say something, but the judge puts a hand on his shoulder. "Why don't you use your radio and see if Doris can send something over with Evan? Have her delve into those bags of apple cider and send enough for the children living here."

"What? No," Dawson says.

"Do it," Judge Avery instructs with a firm nod.

Dawson sputters for a moment before taking his radio out and making the call. His voice drips with bitterness as he puts in his request with Doris, who oversees supplies and rations. She has help from a few others, but she seems to know exactly what's what at all times. While she understands it's important to have the community coffers, like us, she's less than thrilled about losing most of their personal items also.

Dawson's barely finished talking to Doris when there's a light knock on the door. He pulls it open, greeting Mick Michaelson and councilmembers Rhoda and Jana. Our council had two additional members when we lived in Bakerville proper, but they chose to stay behind, thinking the small group on the river—where the winters tend to be slightly milder—would have an easier time.

When Dawson ushers them in, he makes sure to say, "No need to knock. This is a public place."

One of the councilmembers shakes her head. I start to tell Dawson what I think about his no-knock policy when Judge Avery says, "Personally, I think respect for the family living here should be put in front of the idea of this being a public place."

"Yeah, well, they knew people would come here to use the showers and the kitchen before they moved in."

I start to answer when the judge quickly says, "And so did the other families who already lived up here and graciously offered the use of their showers. I know you shower at Zeb and Ellen's house. I see you standing on their doorstep. You knock and wait for them to answer. Why is this different?"

"Well—that's their home! Of course I knock."

Judge Avery gives him a pointed look.

Finally, Dawson says, "Fine. Fine. Whatever you think, Isaiah. Jake, would you be so kind as to show us to *your* den?"

I feel my fingernails biting into the palms of my hands. Punching Dawson in the nose would be incredibly satisfying. Instead, I plaster a smile on my face and say, "Right this way."

As I'm closing the door to the den, I hear Dawson say, "I told you moving up here would be a mistake. We should've stayed in Bakerville like I wanted. But no, you had to go along with Evan Snyder and this crazy plan."

I've barely clicked the door to the den shut when there's a light knock on the front door. It's Evan, Bill, Laurie, and Jesse Richardson. The three others who were with Mollie when they found the body are starting up the walk.

Once all are inside, Bill says, "Brrr. Temp's really dropped."

"What's the plan?" I ask Bill.

"Who knows. Dawson and his cronies . . . " He clears his throat. "Why don't you all wait out here. Evan and I will see what's happening, then bring you in. Belinda should be here shortly also."

"Here's the care package Doris sent over." Evan hands me a well-used plastic grocery bag. "She put apple cider packets in, plus a jar of the homemade hot cocoa Sarah likes."

"Thanks, Evan. I'm sure Mollie has the water about ready."

"Give us a minute, 'kay?"

Jesse Richardson looks around the great room. "Can we sit?"

"Sure. Anyplace you'd like."

While they make small talk, I go in and check on Mollie. She's sitting at the kitchen table, staring at a water glass.

"Doris sent the goods," I say, setting the bag on the table.

"How does that Jon Dawson stand himself? I mean, really, doesn't he even annoy himself to no end?"

I can't help but smile. "Seems he would."

"Maybe we could ask to move somewhere else. I never wanted to live in this place anyway. Doris—she assigned us here. She was clear that since we had propane for cooking and hot water, plus the solar panels providing electricity—our *personal* solar panels, might I add— we'd be the main place for showering and cooking. But the way some people think they can just come in . . . " Mollie sighs. "And you know the ones who do have been encouraged by that . . . that man."

I pause a moment, waiting to see if she's finished or just taking a breath. She must be finished because she says, "Well? What do you think?"

"I think you're right."

"About moving?"

"About Dawson. He's an instigator. And ever since you let him have it at the meeting over the summer— "

"I didn't let him have it. I just . . . he was wrong, and I told him he was wrong. How could he not know about Chronic Wasting Disease? He really thinks it's some fake propaganda being spread by antihunters. And he still doesn't take it seriously. I heard he was boasting about the big muley buck he shot. Even though the community isn't eating venison, he's still feeding it to his family and friends. Don't ever take any jerky he offers you. It could be from a CWD-positive deer, and we just don't know if that's safe to eat."

Mollie has been passionate about CWD since before the attacks, insisting during our last hunting season we have our deer and elk tested. I give her a nod before gently asking, "So . . . is the water warm?"

"Of course." She motions to the thermos. "It's ready to go."

"Okay, thanks. I'll take the thermos in when they're ready. Do you want me to do anything special with the teabags and stuff?"

"Airpot carafe."

"What?"

"It's not a thermos, it's an—never mind." She gives a small laugh. "It doesn't matter. I'm being a sourpuss. It was nice of Judge Avery to order things for the children. But they should be getting ready for supper, so we'll save it for later. In fact, I need to run up and make sure Sarah knows how late it is." She stands up, stretches, then winces.

"Are you hurting?"

"I'm fine. Just a twinge. Lots of exercise today." She rises on her toes, giving me a kiss before putting the assorted teabags Doris sent over on a plate. She hands me the plate and then the hot pot of water.

I follow her out of the kitchen. She's at the base of the steps when the door to the den opens. "You can all come in," Evan says.

"I'll be right there," Mollie says. "I need to have Angela join us and have Sarah keep an eye on the time for supper."

"Yeah. We'll be a little late for that. Sorry." Evan leaves the door open as the others file in.

Mollie and Angela quickly reappear. "She'll be taking them all over shortly," Mollie says, putting her hand on my bicep. "Are you going with them?"

"Jake, you come on in with Mollie," Bill says from the den.

"Guess not," I mutter.

After Mollie, Angela, and I go into the den, Dawson says, "Shut the door. This is a private meeting."

"Yes, boss," I respond with a salute.

Mollie covers her mouth with her hands, attempting to stifle her giggle. The judge laughs loudly, not even bothering to hide his amusement. I'm surprised at my boldness. I'm not usually one to be disrespectful. I feel the color creep slowly up my neck as I softly close the door.

We find seats as Jesse Richardson says, "Belinda will be here shortly. Should someone wait for her?"

"She'll come in," Mollie says, then looks at Dawson before adding, "She's family."

"Okay," Jesse says. "So you all know we found Phoebe Baker. She was deceased. We, of course, won't be able to do any type of autopsy, but Belinda's assuming—and I agree—she died of hypothermia."

"Why was she out there?" Mick Michaelson asks.

"Not sure. She wasn't dressed for the weather."

"And that means . . . " Mick prompts.

"I think there's foul play involved."

"Humph," Dawson says. "I'd like to see the body, come to my own conclusion."

"That can be arranged," Jesse says, making a note on his pad. "Anyone else?"

Judge Avery rolls his eyes. While Mick and the others quickly say they aren't interested.

"Isaiah, don't you think we ought to make our own determination?" Dawson asks.

"You think I'd be able to tell more than Belinda or Jesse? You think *you* would? Evan, did you see her?"

"Yes, sir. I did."

"And you agree with Jesse?"

"I do."

"Yeah, well, he and Jesse also spread rumors about that Lydia lady," Dawson says. "And she *clearly* killed herself."

Jesse gives Dawson a hard look and very slowly says, "She did not kill herself."

"You don't know that. Just because Fred did some unsavory things— "

"Unsavory?" Mollie cries out. "He purchased Rochelle and her children. He held them captive against their will. *Unsavory* doesn't even begin— "

"Mollie," Evan says gently. "You're absolutely right. Unsavory doesn't even begin to cover what he did. And whether you believe it or not, Dawson, Lydia was murdered. Fred is the only one who could've done it. Phoebe Baker was also murdered."

"I suppose you're going to blame Fred for her murder too," Dawson says.

"Maybe so," Jesse replies. "We have no idea where he's disappeared to. Who's to say he isn't lying in wait, planning to pick us off one by one?"

"Ha! So he can lower our numbers to overthrow us like his crazy wife said he's planning? Sounds ridiculous."

Jesse, Evan, and Bill stare at him. Mick and the others on the council look at each other. Everyone else in the room, except Mollie and me, examines the floor.

"Truth is," Jesse calmly says, "while I do know for a fact Lydia was murdered, I am not saying it was Fred."

"Jackson?" Mollie asks quietly. Jackson Nicholson is a good friend of Deputy Fred and not a friend of hers. They were both on the same militia team over the summer and had a few issues. Those issues resulted in him being kicked from the militia. When Fred's wrongdoings came to light, Jackson was also investigated, but nothing further happened.

"Now hold on," Dawson says angrily. "You can't just go accusing people you don't like."

"Jackson would be a very likely candidate," Judge Avery says, flicking his index finger against his chin. "I can see that."

Another disagreement erupts, with all the councilmembers throwing their intense, and often ugly, thoughts around. Jesse Richardson watches them like it's a ping-pong match. When it finally calms down enough and there's a break in the action, Angela says, "I think you can argue without me in the room. I'd like to go have supper with my husband and son."

"You're quite right, Miss," Judge Avery says. "That was rude of us. Let's take your statement so you can be on your way. My stomach says it's suppertime also. Jesse, do you have questions for them?"

"We'll start with you." Jesse points at Angela, his small notebook and pen in hand. "Your name?"

"Angela Carpenter."

"You were with the group staying by the body?"

"Yes, but I stayed on the road."

"So, you didn't go down? Didn't see the body?"

"No way. I only saw what looked like a piece of material."

"Did you notice anything unusual?"

"You mean other than the body?"

"The one you didn't see?"

Angela furrows her brow. "I saw a piece of material. We all assumed it was a body."

Annette mumbles something I can't quite understand.

Jesse turns toward her slightly. "Hold that thought until I get to you, okay?"

She lifts one shoulder in response. I watch as Jon Dawson rolls his eyes.

"Angela?"

"The snow was all scuffed up. We could see—my mom noticed it, where someone had come off the hill. Then there were prints in the snow crossing the road and going down the other side. It wasn't too difficult to follow the trail in the snow to where the bod—I mean, material that looked like blue jeans was."

He scribbles in his notepad, then looks up and says, "Anything you'd like to add?"

"No."

"If you think of anything, you know where to find me?"

She shrugs. "I'm sure Evan or Bill do, and I know where to find them."

"Thank you. Have a good dinner."

Angela wastes no time getting up. She gives her mom and me a small smile before leaving the den. As soon as the door closes, the stairs erupt with my family plodding down them, on their way to supper.

"Must they be so noisy?" Dawson asks.

"Yes," Mollie says. "I'm quite sure they must."

"Disrespectful. The whole lot of you," Dawson mutters.

Judge Avery shoots him a look and puts his fingers to his lips in a shushing motion. I narrow my eyes at Dawson. He's acted like a blockhead since the first time I met him at one of our Bakerville meetings after the attacks started, but tonight his rudeness is unprecedented.

"Are you finished?" Jesse asks Dawson. "May I continue?"

"By all means," he says with a flutter of his hands.

Jesse stares him down for several beats before turning to the other woman on Mollie's search team. "Now you, Miss?"

"Annette." Her response is so soft, if I weren't watching her lips, I wouldn't have known she'd spoken.

"Excuse me?"

Slightly louder, she says, "Annette."

"Uh, okay. Your last name?" Jesse leans toward her, straining to hear. I notice everyone in the room follows suit.

"Harding. I have nothing to add."

"You went back to the house and called for help?"

"Harry and I did."

"Harry, do you have anything to add?"

"Nothing, Jesse. I didn't even really see the blue material. I just took their word for it, then Annette and I went for help."

Harry English and his friend Annette joined our community right as we were moving up here. They were part of Paul Cameron's group that escaped from Prospect. Harry had some sort of job with the city. When the elected mayor of Prospect was murdered, along with most of the police force and around a hundred civilians, Harry went into hiding until, with the help of Paul's grandson and granddaughter, he could find a way out of town.

They did as much damage to the people taking over the town as they could, in the form of guerrilla attacks, before heading to Bakerville. Harry, along with Jesse, the security team, and several others, is now part of the group planning for a springtime take-back of Prospect. Personally, I think we should just leave them be and protect our own people.

"If either you or Annette think of anything else, you let me know."

"Will do." Harry stands and offers a hand to Annette, who gives him a sweet smile before she stands.

"Now, Mollie and . . . "

"Heath. Heath Jefferson," he says in a confident manner. "We met at the Christmas sing-along at the community center last year. Remember?"

"Right. You two went down to the body? Why'd you do that?"

"In case she needed help. We didn't know she was . . . you know, dead. We couldn't see enough of her to know."

Bill lets out something like a snort. Heath glares at him in response. Jesse looks at both for a moment before turning to Mollie. "Is that right?"

"Yes. She wasn't moving, but we thought . . . I thought maybe . . . " Mollie finishes with a small shrug.

"You went down the hill, but did you touch the body?"

"You know we didn't," Mollie says evenly.

"How would I know that?"

"The tracks in the snow. You could clearly see where our snowshoes ended."

He gives her a smile. "I guess I did see that."

"So we could tell right away that . . . you know. I mean, I thought maybe we should check for a pulse, but Mollie said that with the way the foot looked . . . " Heath shrugs, then quickly asks, "We were right to not touch her?"

"About time you did something right, Jefferson," Bill mutters under his breath.

"You were right not to touch her," Jesse agrees with a nod. "Did either of you notice anything else?"

"Nope, not a thing," Heath says.

"Did you find her shoe?" Mollie asks.

"It wasn't with her body," Laurie says.

Jesse shoots her a look. "We'll be looking again tomorrow. We had to stop because of the snow and darkness."

"Will you be able to follow the trail tomorrow? After the snow?"

"Should be able to. We— " He's interrupted by a light tap on the door, then Belinda, looking worn and drawn, pushes it open.

"Sorry I'm so late," she says in an uneven voice. "Sam . . . Sam lost his battle."

Chapter 7

Saturday, Day 180

Mollie

"Thank you all for coming," June says, standing tall. "Sam would— "
She takes a deep breath. "When we first arrived in Bakerville, we were
warmly welcomed. We didn't meet any of you until after the attacks,
at a time when we were all scared and wondering what would happen
next. And you welcomed us, made us feel a part of the community,
even before you knew he was a doctor. That meant a lot to him. To
all of us.

"These last couple of months have been exceedingly difficult. It
was hard to see Sam . . . weak. As difficult as it was, I'm so incredibly
grateful—so grateful the children and I had more time with him. And,
oh, I miss him so much already. Talking to him, holding his
hand . . . but I know— " June puts a tissue to her eye. "I know I'll see
him again. Thanks to God's grace, we'll be together in heaven. When
we walk away from here today, let's celebrate, because Sam is where
we all need to be. He's with God."

June looks out over the crowd. She gives her children, sitting in
the front row, a small, sad smile. Then her eyes travel to the Baker
family. "To the Baker family, I'm so sorry for the loss of your loved
one—of Phoebe. Please know, my children and I have been including
you in our prayers each night. God bless you."

I close my eyes, attempting to stop my own tears. As June steps
away from the front of the room, one of Phoebe's relatives stops her,
pulling her into a hug. He then goes up and begins eulogizing Phoebe.
After he finishes, several others speak about either Phoebe or Dr. Sam.
This is a hard loss for our small community. A teenager, just barely
beginning her life and taken in such a violent manner, and our

physician—and friend—dying after being shot. Both murdered by a still-unknown assailant.

The memorial service was planned for 1100 so we could follow with our midday meal at 1230. All other activities for the day, except for guard duty, have been canceled. It's a day of mourning. Most of our community is at the service. The downstairs nursery, usually open for those in diapers, was made available for all children as desired by the parents. There are so many of them that they've spilled out into the hall, but it's better than requiring them to sit through the memorial. Dodie and a couple of other ladies are providing supervision for the kids.

After the service ends, I search out June and her children. The last several months have been difficult for her. Even before Sam was shot, she was facing her own personal issues. Things were finally balancing out for her when the shooting happened, throwing their world upside down.

"Mollie," June says, pulling me into a hug. "Thank you for coming." She pulls away slightly and then gives me a strange look. "Are you . . . are you okay?" she asks in a whisper.

"I'm just so sad for you. And for the Baker family. I'm just— " I pull her closer.

"No, I mean, are you feeling okay?" she whispers.

"Oh." I release her hold. "I'm tired. Nothing new there." I give a grim smile. I've been tired for so long. I don't know what it'd feel like not to be tired.

She nods. "I can relate."

"I'll be by tomorrow to take your laundry."

"You don't need to keep doing our laundry. Now, with Sam— " She sucks in a breath. "I won't be spending so much time at our little hospital. I can start taking care of my cabin . . . and my children. You and Jake have been such a help. All of you."

"I'll still help you with your laundry tomorrow. Maybe next week things will change." I hug her again before letting the line waiting to console her have their turn.

As I walk away, I realize how right she is. I am tired. But as I told June, tired is a common feeling these days. None of us get enough sleep. A few months ago, during an extreme spell of hot weather, I passed out. I'd had a bump on the head a few weeks before, which took me a long time to recover from and may have contributed to my fainting. Belinda examined me after my fainting spell and suggested I take a pregnancy test. I was fifty at the time. Fifty! Now, after another birthday and several months having passed, I'm obviously not pregnant. But I am still tired—tired all the time.

"Hello, Mollie."

"Oh, Mr. Richardson, hello."

"Please, call me Jesse," he says, giving me a broader smile than I feel is necessary. I didn't know Jesse Richardson before the attacks. His home was in a different section of Bakerville, and we didn't socialize. I'm not even sure I remember seeing him when things were normal. But to be truthful, he's incredibly average looking, without any features that particularly stand out. Like many his age, he has only a fringe of grey hair above the ears, wrapping around his head. He's average height and average build—really, nothing impressive about him. Evan has told us several times he was considered a brilliant detective wherever he worked back east. Now he's been retired over a dozen years. I wonder if part of his success was because he's so ordinary.

I glance across the room to where Jake's talking with Evan, Bill, Phil, and a few others. I catch his eye, and he tilts his head slightly. I smile in response, trying to convey my thoughts to him, *No, I don't know why Jesse Richardson is talking to me.*

"Do you have a minute?" Jesse asks.

"Um, yeah, sure."

"Let's step over to the edge, might be a little quieter."

I glance toward Jake again; he's watching as I walk away with Jesse.

"This should be all right," Jesse says. "It's still not quiet, but it's better. Are you feeling okay?"

Jeez, I must look awful if someone I barely know is asking me if I'm all right. "I'm fine."

"So, Mollie, how much contact do you have with your ex-husband?"

"My ex-husband? Do you mean Brad? We weren't married."

"Really?"

"Correct. He told you we were married?"

"When I spoke with him after Deputy Fred disappeared, he called you his first wife and the mother of his child."

"Humph. He's my daughter's biological father. That's the extent of our relationship."

"So your contact with him since he's been living in Bakerville has been . . . ?"

"As little as possible. Sarah wants him as part of her life. I do spend time with his wife and son, but not Brad."

"Even when he was living with you at your home down in Bakerville proper?"

"Like I said, as little as possible. They lived in the Tiny House, the same one they live in now. We didn't socialize unless it was for Sarah's benefit. Here, they're parked in the row of trailers closest to the county road, so I don't see him—any of them—nearly as much as when they were in my front yard. This is much better." I realize I'm rambling and shut my mouth so quickly I swear I hear the snap of my jaw.

Jesse gives me a long look, then lowers his voice. "And you haven't renewed your relationship in the last few weeks?"

"My relationship? With Brad?" His name comes out like a croak of disgust. Why is he asking about *him*?

"Right." He gives me a single nod.

"I have no relationship with Brad Quinton." My voice raises slightly. Taking a deep breath, I lower not only the volume but the tone. "The only reason he is here is because of my daughter Sarah and Brad's son, Victor. When we found out how sick Victor is, we couldn't just turn them away."

"I heard his son has cancer."

"Leukemia. Victor needs a stem cell transplant. They wanted to see if Sarah could be a donor. But then the EMP hit and, well, that's no longer an option. Dr. Sam— " I let out a sigh. "He had some ideas, but they were long shots. And now . . . " I shake my head.

"The boy seems to be doing well."

"Yes, and maybe that'll continue. Why are you asking me about Brad and thinking we have a relationship?"

"Someone said they saw you together."

I feel my forehead crease as I stare at him. "Not likely. Who said that?"

"Not likely? Does that mean they didn't see you together?"

"Whoever told you we were together is not giving you the truth. I avoid Brad."

"Where were you on Wednesday afternoon around 1600?"

"Are you serious?"

He gives me a hard look. *Oh, so that's how it is. Fine.* I stare back at him. I've taken several sales and marketing classes; I'm aware that in a negotiation the first to speak loses. While I have nothing to hide, he still hasn't told me who saw us together. And either *they* are lying or *he* is.

Finally, he clears his throat. "I am serious. Where were you on Wednesday?"

"I have no idea. Who said they saw us together? Maybe that'll help me remember what I was doing on Wednesday."

"Wednesday was the day before we searched for Phoebe, the day we believe she went missing."

What is going on here? *Does he think I had something to do with Phoebe's death?* What was I doing on Wednesday? I briefly close my eyes. *Wednesday . . .* "That was my kitchen day, lunch and supper. Both were prepared in the kitchen of the dude ranch lodge and then we transported them over here using the trailer."

"*You* transport them?"

"No, someone shows up and takes them."

"How many days a week do you have kitchen day?"

"One, sometimes two. Usually I have lunch and supper, but sometimes it'll be breakfast and lunch. There's a group of us with a rotating schedule—don't you know all of this?"

"I've heard. So, Wednesday was your kitchen day. Did you have an assistant?"

"One of my daughters, Pamela Cameron, and Alina—Brad's wife. We all work together."

"Brad's wife? Was Brad there too? Maybe he dropped her off or picked her up?"

"If he did, I didn't see him. Who said he and I were together? And what does this have to do with anything?"

"That's what I'm trying to find out. Thanks for your time."

I watch him as he walks away. He passes by Jon Dawson, who makes a point of catching my eye and giving me a smirk. What a jerk. Is he the one lying about Brad and me? I'm suddenly exhausted. So tired, I wonder if my legs will hold me up. I reach a hand to the wall, bracing myself against it. After a moment or two, I feel steady enough to make my way to a chair.

I've barely sat when Belinda Bosco appears, taking the chair next to me. "June said she thought you might be sick. What's going on?"

I look up and shake my head. "I'm fine, just tired."
She looks into my eyes and asks, "When did the jaundice start?"

Chapter 8

Sunday, Day 180

Jake

I watch as Jesse Richardson ambles away from Mollie. When Jesse walks by Jon Dawson, he gives him a nod. What's that about? Just a greeting? Something more? I don't trust Dawson. And I'm really starting to wonder about Jesse Richardson. There's something about him—something not quite right.

Based on Mollie's reactions during their discussion, things were tense. Her jaw appeared clenched, and her brow was furrowed throughout the entire talk. When I look back toward Mollie, she's got her hand on the wall and is looking at the floor. *Is she crying?* After a few moments, she drifts to a chair. Seconds later, Belinda sits next to her.

"What do you think, Jake?" Evan asks.

"What's that?"

"You think we should go down to Bakerville on Tuesday? Get us a mess of geese for Christmas dinner?"

"How long until Christmas?" I ask, trying to think of today's date.

"A week and a half," Phil says.

"We can head out Tuesday morning," Evan says, his voice full of excitement, "get there in time for a late afternoon hunt. Hunt all day Wednesday and then Thursday morning before heading home."

"We'll take the snow machines?"

"We'll take the one and hook the trailer on. I thought we could stay at your house while we're there, if that's okay?"

"Yeah, sure. I'd like to check the house out anyway."

"You mind checking mine while you're there?" Phil asks.

"We could do that on our way into town or on our way home." Evan nods.

"Jake?" Phil's wife, Kelley, says.

"Hey, honey," Phil says. "Jake and Evan are going to make the trip down to Bakerville for geese. They'll check out our place while they're there."

"That's great. Jake, Mollie isn't feeling well. Belinda would like to take her to the clinic and check her out."

"She's not feeling well?" I ask, confused. "She didn't seem sick this morning."

Kelley gives me a smile and a shrug. "If you want to join us, we're leaving shortly."

"I—yeah, of course. I'll, uh, see you later, everyone."

"Hope Mollie's okay," Bill Shane says. "I'll be praying for her."

"Me too," Phil and Evan say at the same time.

"I didn't even know she was sick." I shake my head. I feel like a heel of a husband. If she's so sick Belinda wants to examine her . . .

"Stop beating yourself up," Kelley says as we weave through the crowded room.

"What?"

"Stop beating yourself up, blaming yourself for not realizing."

"What's wrong with her? Is it the cold everyone had? She hasn't even had the sniffles."

"Let's wait until we can examine her. It might be nothing."

"Where is she?"

"Probably already making her way to the truck. Belinda said she'd wait for us."

We stop at the coat rack to retrieve our winter gear. I put on my hat and drape my coat over my arm.

"You'll want to wear that. My guess is you'll be riding in the pickup bed."

I slip into my coat as we go out the door. Kelley wasn't kidding. It's cold. Even colder than when we went in. My stomach growls. They were just setting up lunch when Kelley pulled me away. Mollie is probably starving too. *What's going on with her?*

We make our way down the slope from the ski lodge and then across the bridge. As we step off the bridge, I see the old lemon-colored truck—one from Phil's fleet of 1970s pickups. It's parked with the windshield facing the building. I figure, since Belinda had Mollie walk from the lodge to the truck, she must not be too sick. That's a good thing for sure. As we get closer, I can see Mollie sitting on the bench seat, shaking her head.

"She doesn't look very happy," I say.

"Oh, you know Mollie."

Yeah, I do. She's stubborn and often in denial. A couple of years ago, she had a terrible pain in her stomach. I wanted to take her to the emergency room in Prospect, but she insisted she was fine and knew just what it was. An ovarian cyst. By the next day, the extreme pain had decreased, but she was still a little sickly for a couple of days. Then she was fine.

Belinda opens the driver's door and says, "Hop in the back, Jake. Kelley— "

"I'll ride in the bed also," Kelley says, "let Mollie have some space."

Mollie gives a deep frown, shakes her head, and very loudly says, "I'm fine. This is ridiculous."

"Humor me," Belinda replies.

I get in and then offer my hand to Kelley.

"Whew, I always feel like a teenager again when I ride in the back like this. Of course, Oklahoma wasn't this cold."

"Yeah, neither was Northern California."

Less than five minutes later we're stopping in front of the clinic. As I climb out of the pickup, I realize I didn't tell any of our family where I was going. As usual, we walked over for the service and lunch. They'll probably just walk home afterward, but I still should've told them we were leaving. Mollie, with more energy than usual, bounces out of the passenger's side. I can't help but think she's faking the action.

"This is silly, Belinda. And, Kelley, I can't believe you went along with it. This is like medical kidnapping or something."

"Oh, yes," Kelley says, her lips twitching in a smile, "exactly like that."

"Let's just get this over with." Mollie stomps up the stairs.

Belinda unlocks the door and says, "After you," ushering Mollie in with a flourish of her arm.

"Humph," Mollie scoffs as she slips out of her snow boots.

I hold back a laugh at her antics. I'll be surprised if she's sick. My wife is too ornery to get sick. The room is on the chilly side. I walk over to the small woodstove and hold my hand over it; some heat radiates. I grab a couple of small sticks from the wood bin and add them to the hot coals.

"Thanks, Jake," Belinda says. "Now, Mollie, have a seat. Let's chat."

The cabin—a duplex that can be opened to make one big cabin—has been divided into sections. This half is separated into two areas with a curtain divider. The front section, usually a waiting area, has four chairs. Mollie chooses one and plops down. She gives me a look and rolls her eyes. That's when I notice something isn't quite right. Is she pale? Not pale, but her coloring is off.

"Jake, do you want to sit?" Mollie asks.

"Thought I'd get the fire going. Is that okay, Belinda?"

"Yeah. We'll get started. Kelley will take notes and start a chart for you."

"Humph," Mollie says again.

"Have you been sick to your stomach?"

"No."

"The cold going around— "

"I didn't get it."

"Any more fainting spells?"

"No."

"Dizziness or light headedness?"

"N— " I watch her as she bites her lip. Very quietly, she says, "I've been a little tired. Maybe a little lightheaded from that."

"Describe your tiredness."

"C'mon, Belinda. You know how it is."

"You're still on guard duty?"

"Yes. Once or twice a week."

"Kitchen duty?"

"Same." Mollie shrugs.

"You teach— "

"All of it, Belinda—kitchen, guard, teaching, greenhouse, firewood—same as everyone. And when I'm not on a community assignment, I'm trying to do our laundry, cook the kids' snacks, or clean up the bathrooms everyone uses and leaves a mess. I'm tired. That's all."

"I don't think that's all," Kelley says gently. "There's a yellow tinge to your skin and the whites of your eyes."

I take a closer look at her. That's exactly what it is: she's yellow.
How did I not notice this before?

Chapter 9

Sunday, Day 180

Mollie

I look from Kelley to Belinda and finally to Jake. His mouth is slightly open as he gawks at me. "You think so too?" I ask him in an accusatory tone.

He opens his mouth and then closes it, reminding me of a trout on a hook. With a nod, he says, "I notice it now that Kelley's pointed it out."

There's a hollow feeling in the pit of my stomach. Jaundice. What causes jaundice? I quickly think back to my time in medical assisting school and working in a doctor's office. Too much bilirubin in the blood. An issue with the liver? Malcolm had slight jaundice when he was born, but it cleared up in a couple of days.

"Okay." I let out a breath. "What are you looking for?"

"Anything that may be the culprit," Belinda says.

"With your advanced medical equipment?" I attempt a smile. *What is going on with me?*

"Let's go into the exam room," Kelley says, opening a curtain dividing the room. "Go ahead and put the gown on." She lays two gowns on the elevated wooden table posing as an examination bed. "Use the second as a robe. We'll have Jake get a nice, hot fire going. Once you're dressed, we'll need a urine sample. Everything is in the bathroom, just— "

"I know what to do. Thanks."

Kelley gives me a reassuring smile. "There are several things that can cause jaundice."

"That's right," Belinda says. "We'll figure this out."

Kelley slides the curtain shut. I lightly touch the material of the hospital gown. It's an unbelievably soft material in pale pink. The second one isn't nearly as soft, in light blue with yellow ducks on it. These are not ones from the supplies we donated to the medical team as partial payment when Angela and Katie were shot. Ours were all a minty green.

I peel off my sweater. It's not yet warm in here, and goose bumps immediately erupt on my arms. I replay Kelley's words in my mind— *there are several things that can cause jaundice*—as I continue to undress my top half. Once I have the pink gown on, I top it with the robe, then peel off my long underwear and pants. "My socks?" I ask through the curtain.

"You can leave them on for now," Belinda responds.

After folding and stacking my clothes on the chair, I go into the bathroom. The light provided by the window is dim. I turn on the battery-operated lantern and peer into the mirror. My skin color *is* a little off. I wouldn't have really thought it yellow, but my eyes certainly are. I never even noticed it when combing my hair this morning. Kelley's probably right, there's nothing to worry about. It's probably something as simple as dehydration. I know I don't drink enough water.

After producing the sample, I leave the toilet unflushed. *If it's yellow, let it mellow* is the mountain people philosophy. Water needs to be hauled from one of the lodges or snow melt, so we conserve our flushes in dry cabins like this. When it is flushed, the tank will be refilled. There was talk of having hot and cold running water in this duplex since it's used as our hospital, but a suitable hot water heater couldn't be found. Most of the cabins get their water for cleaning up from the river—thanks to a gravity-fed pump—and their drinking water from either the ski lodge or our place, provided by deep wells. But for the clinic, we only use well water, not wanting to risk any contaminations that might be lurking in the river.

There's hand sanitizer, which I use, and a thermos of warm water for proper washing. I noticed the big soup pot on the woodstove, most likely full of more hot water. I take my time, deciding a proper handwashing is in order. After leaving the bathroom, I open the divider curtain fully.

Belinda gives me an odd look. "Can you walk a few feet toward us?"

A shiver runs through my body; I pull the robe tightly around me.

"How much weight have you lost?" Kelley asks.

"Not much. I've managed to keep my weight up fairly well, even with the rations."

"Let's put you on the scale." She motions toward a bathroom scale.

I step on and watch the analog dial as it bounces a few times, until the pointer comes to rest. It reads a pound higher than the scale we have in the lodge, around twenty pounds less than I weighed before the attacks.

Kelley scribbles the results, then says, "Hop up on the table. We'll get your blood pressure and other vitals."

"I'll take care of the urine specimen," Belinda says.

While Kelley does her thing, Jake gives me a wink. I shake my head.

Kelley finishes with my vitals and Belinda returns from the bathroom, saying, "Your urine was a little dark."

"I'm probably dehydrated. My guess is, all of this is from me not drinking enough water."

"She doesn't drink enough water," Jake says. "Especially with the cold weather."

"Mm-hmm," Belinda says. "Let's have a look at your ears and throat."

While she does that, Kelley asks, "Any nausea or vomiting?"

"No."

"Are you drinking any alcohol?"

"Do we even have any here?" I ask. "What Jake and I had in our medical supplies and storage was required to be *donated*." I make air quotes around donated. I don't mention we did stash a few bottles in our underground caches back in Bakerville proper. I also don't mention there's a rumor of a still being set up in the forest west of the ski lodge, and we know from past history of other Bakerville residents that if I really wanted to drink, I'd figure something out.

"Right," Kelley says. "So when was your last drink?"

"I don't know . . . um . . . I had a glass of wine when my boss took me out for dinner while I was in Oregon. That was the night the airplanes went down almost six months ago."

Kelley nods, scribbling on her pad. "Do you smoke?"

"You know I don't. And there's no cigarettes around anyway. No chewing tobacco either." I give Jake a look and tilt my head. Quitting chewing was not easy for him, and unlike the booze situation, we've yet to find a way to cultivate our own tobacco products.

"Have you ever used intravenous drugs?"

"Like heroin?" I shake my head. "I hate needles. And I wouldn't anyway. So, no."

"Ever been diagnosed with hepatitis? Or cirrhosis of the liver?"

"No, nothing like that."

"Have you had any unusual bleeding?"

"What do you mean?"

"Nosebleeds, a cut that won't stop bleeding, things like that."

"I had some nosebleeds when we first moved up here, probably from the elevation change."

"How long did they last?"

"A week, maybe two. They weren't severe."

"Nothing recently?" Belinda asks.

When Belinda finishes looking up my nose, she touches me along my jawline. "You have a little swelling here. Any pain?"

"A little, probably TMJ. I've had it before."

"Are you experiencing clicking and trouble chewing?"

"No clicking, maybe a little trouble chewing. We do eat an awful lot of meat."

She continues my exam, eventually having me lay down so she can prod my stomach. "You have a bruise on your calf. And I noticed you look like you've lost weight in your extremities. They're thin."

"I'm not complaining about that." I laugh. "I've always held my weight on my thighs."

"And the bruise?"

"Who knows? There's one on my thigh too. I don't know how I got either of them, which isn't at all unusual. Tell her, Jake."

He clears his throat. "She's always had bruises. I'll ask her about them, but she won't know where they came from."

Kelley scribbles while Belinda nods. "Your stomach looks a little swollen. Any pain?" Belinda asks, poking me in a variety of places. She hits on a spot that causes me to jump.

"Does that hurt?"

"A little," I reluctantly admit.

"I'd like to take a look. Let's slide your gown up." Belinda grabs for a light sheet to cover me with. Shortly after she has me repositioned, she says, "Kelley, can you step over here?"

The tone of her voice causes my heart rate to accelerate. "What's going on?" I ask.

"Give us a minute," Belinda says. She pokes at me some more, causing me to jump again.

"I think I have a cyst or something," I say. It was bothering me a few weeks ago, but I think it's resolving on its own.

"Mm–hmm," Belinda answers.

"You didn't say anything about that," Jake says in an accusatory tone.

"Not an ovarian cyst. Like a pimple or a boil. On my *skin*."

"There is a slight discoloration of the skin," Kelley says. "Let me take your socks off for a moment."

"Go ahead."

She removes my socks and presses on my toes. Then does the same with my fingers.

After several more minutes of them checking me out, Belinda says, "Go ahead and get dressed. Kelley and I are going to step into the other room and compare notes."

"Can't you just do that right here, in front of us?"

"We'll just be a minute," she says, walking into the bathroom.

"Fine," I huff as she steps back out, rubbing her hands together to absorb the sanitizer.

Kelley gives me a small smile before also retreating to the bathroom. Belinda spends a couple of moments at the bookshelf by a small desk while waiting for Kelley. She soon slides off a large book, carrying it with her as they step into the room next door.

Once they close the door, I start to dress. As I'm putting my sweater back on, I ask Jake, "What do you think?"

"I think you should've told me you weren't feeling well."

"Oh, c'mon, Jake. It's not like I've been feeling terrible."

"I didn't realize your arms and legs are so skinny."

"They're not *that* skinny. Besides, with winter here, I'm always wearing layers."

"True. You even sleep in sweats, and we're both so tired we rarely— "

The door to the other part of the duplex opens. "Okay, good," Belinda says. "You're dressed."

"You finished your conferring?" I ask in a less-than-kind tone.

"Yes, and the truth is, we'd really love to be able to do more tests. As I said, your urine was very concentrated. The dipstick showed elevated protein. I also did a pregnancy test."

I snort. "That was a waste of a test."

"Yes, it was." She nods with a slight smirk. "It came up negative, but we had to rule it out."

I shake my head for the umpteenth time since we arrived at the clinic.

"You have some clinical signs that are concerning, so we want to run additional tests."

"What tests?"

"With the way things are, we don't have many options. But we can check for blood in your stool, which we'll do, and keep an eye on your urine and vitals. I'm going to take a small amount of blood from you to look at under the microscope."

"What will you look for?" Jake asks.

"White cells and red cells. We want to see if there's a normal amount of each and if they're shaped properly, while also checking the platelets. We'll look at your urine under the microscope also."

"Sounds delightful," I say, thinking how fortunate we are to at least have a few pieces of medical equipment. The microscope was from Kelley's supplies.

"Doesn't it? We also want to put you on a special diet to see if it makes any difference. And we'll be examining you often."

"What do you think is wrong?" Jake asks.

"We're not sure. It might be gallstones, or it could be something related to the liver or pancreas."

"Or it could be a whole host of other things, ranging from very mild to concerning," Kelley adds.

"Such as?" Jake asks.

Kelley and Belinda share a look. "We just don't know. Without imaging equipment, all we can do is read the signs and the symptoms using the knowledge we have and our medical books. We're both going to spend some time reading." She gives us a smile. "And in the meantime, Mollie will follow a very specific diet, including increasing her fluid intake, and she'll be on bed rest for a few days."

I roll my eyes. "Oh, that'll go over well."

"We won't make you stay in bed all day," Kelley says. "But you need more rest than you're getting now. You won't have any of your community duties. We want to see if we can reduce the jaundice or at least prevent it from getting worse. It really is very mild right now."

"Let's— " Belinda is interrupted by the radio on her belt.

"Clinic— "

She raises a finger to Jake and me. There's static over the radio and then, "Come in, clinic."

"This is Belinda. Go ahead."

"This is . . . we've got . . . on our way to you."

"What do you think he said?" Kelley asks.

Belinda shakes her head. Into the radio, she says, "Say again?"

"We've got an injury," the voice says slightly clearer this time. "We'll be . . . about thirty . . . out."

"Sounds like we're going to have company," Kelley says.

"Clinic's standing by to receive injury," Belinda says into the radio.

Jake and I stand up. "Go ahead and head home," Belinda says. "One of us will be over later with exact details of our plan. In the meantime, drink a big glass of water and take a nap."

I take a deep breath. I don't want to admit to them, or to Jake, I'm scared.

Chapter 10

Thursday, Day 184

Jake

"You're sure?" I ask, examining her face for any doubt, while at the same time checking her color.

"I'm sure," Mollie says with a nod. "With the kids here and your mom and dad fretting over me, there's no reason for you not to go."

"The jaundice looks better."

"I guess the goat's milk, ginger, and fish diet plus extra water is working." She shrugs. "Or it was a fluke and I'm fine."

"Yeah, I pray that's it." I give her a kiss on the nose. When we left the clinic after Mollie's exam, I was scared. Belinda and Kelley were both plenty concerned, but neither seemed to have any answers. I had some of my own thoughts and concerns, but I was too scared to even ask.

When Kelley showed up after dealing with the emergency at the clinic, I point blank asked her what she thought. She said we shouldn't jump to any conclusions; they aren't completely sure what's going on but will do any tests they can perform and will continue to look for options.

While the words were reassuring, there was something in the way she said it that didn't bring me full comfort. Yesterday, I breathed a huge sigh of relief when Belinda's exam showed the swelling in the jawline was reduced and Mollie's jaundice had noticeably improved.

Even her stomach, which was slightly distended before, seems to be flatter. And they've concluded her stool was normal—not that they can do any extensive tests to make this determination.

I feel like a terrible husband for not recognizing what was happening with her. I've vowed to pay closer attention to my wife, not just how she looks physically, but as my wife. Things have been so intense for so long, just being wrapped up in our day-to-day survival, that we don't take time to be a couple.

"And you'll keep with the resting? Not go back to overdoing it as soon as my back's turned?" I raise my eyebrows to let her know I'm kidding . . . sort of.

"Oh, you know me. Always the model patient."

"Yeah, I know you. That's why I asked."

"Are you fully packed?" Mollie asks, changing the subject.

"Yep. Evan should be here shortly. And we'll be back on Sunday."

"I expect you to be careful," she says, her eyes boring into me. "After what happened with the hunting team, we know it's not completely safe."

I give a nod. "I would've thought all the bears were denned up this late in the year. It could've been so much worse. Good thing the hunters were in pairs and— " I shake my head. "I forgot her name."

"Rochelle. Sounds like she was amazing, didn't even hesitate to take the bear out as soon as she had a clear shot. And it's fortunate it was a black bear and not a grizzly. PJ's injuries probably would've been worse."

"Right. And now we have bear meat."

Mollie makes a face. "I'm looking forward to the goose, but you can have my portion of the bear. Thanks for pushing your trip back a few days. I appreciate you being here." Mollie reaches for my hand, intertwining our fingers. "I get to start having meals with the group again today, provided everything looks good at my checkup. Of course, no red meat for the time being—even bear. But at least I can socialize again instead of feeling like a leper. I'm okay, really."

"Alright. I— " There's a light knock on the bedroom door.

"Jake? Evan's here."

"I'll be right down."

"Um, Doris is with him," Sarah says. "They'd like to talk with both of you. She said she could make it up the stairs if Mom doesn't feel well enough to come down."

"No," Mollie says, horror in her voice and on her face. "I'm a mess." She lifts her hands up to try and smooth down her wild hair. She cut it off over the summer, using the hair clippers, and has kept it incredibly short since then. Even so, it still pokes out at odd angles. "Besides, the stairs would be too much for her."

"How about you tell them we'll be down shortly," I say with a small laugh at my wife's shenanigans. While I know Doris would try and climb the stairs, and she could probably do it, her leg still isn't strong enough for bearing weight.

After we moved up here, Chaplain Rick suggested a knee scooter—a four-wheeled contraption she can rest her injured leg on. He'd used one after ankle surgery. Belinda and Sam agreed it was worth a try. Rick was going to try and build one and had put out word for the parts he'd need. But Zeb, the owner of the ski lodge, had used one several years earlier and stashed it in his attic. It works well for Doris and has given her considerably more freedom, but only on smooth surfaces. A few weeks ago, Rick came up with a second idea to give her even more mobility.

"I'll let them know you'll be right down," Sarah says.

"Thanks, Jake," Mollie says, climbing out of the bed. She quickly dresses; I watch as she puts her skinny legs in her long underwear. Is this only because of the rations, or is it indicative of something more sinister happening within her body?

She catches me gawking. "You need to stop," she says softly. "I'm fine."

I nod as she runs a comb through her hair.

She lets out a sigh. "I guess that'll have to do. Let's go see what our friends want. Then we'll get you on your way so you can bring home our Christmas goose."

Evan and I originally thought we'd go alone, but now we're part of a group of eight. The plan is to not only bring home enough for Christmas, but also to process the geese into jerky for the months ahead. While we do have elk and beef and we do some fishing, we're looking forward to other options. Evan and I are still taking the snowmobile and trailer, but the others are taking horses. They've likely already left; we'll meet up with them outside of Bakerville. At the top of the stairs, I offer Mollie my hand.

"Seriously? I can handle the stairs on my own."

"Can't a guy just want to hold the hand of his beloved?" I ask.

With a shake of her head, she relents, allowing me to hold one hand while she lightly grips the handrail with the other. Evan and Doris are in the great room. Evan, stocking cap in hand, is pacing back and forth. Doris is sitting on the edge of the sofa, shaking her head at him.

"Hey," Doris says, "you're looking better."

Mollie tilts her head slightly in response. Doris showed up Sunday shortly after Belinda and Kelley made their original assessment. She fawned over Mollie, assuring her whatever special diet and supplies was needed, she would do her best to provide them.

"What's up?" I ask, noting Evan's uneasiness.

"You know how Jesse Richardson was interviewing Mollie at the memorial service?" While the excitement of Mollie being sick took over most of that day, she did share with me Jesse's accusations of her being with Brad. At the time, I couldn't decide if I wanted to punch out Jesse, Brad, or whoever it is spreading lies. Now, I just simmer in silent anger every time I think of it.

"Of course they remember," Doris says to Evan. "Can you sit, honey? You're making me nervous."

He hesitates before sitting next to Doris on the couch. I lead Mollie to a padded rocking chair while I take a matching one.

"And?" I ask Evan once everyone is seated.

"And he did something similar to Kimba Hoffmann."

"To Kimba?" Mollie asks, while I simultaneously say, "What do you mean?"

"He told her someone saw her and Mick Michaelson together on Wednesday before Phoebe disappeared."

"Okay? So?" I ask.

"In a compromised position," Doris adds.

I watch Mollie as she furrows her brow. "That's . . . odd."

"And they weren't?" I ask.

"Nope," Evan says, while Doris exclaims, "Of course not!"

"Are you sure?" Mollie asks gently. "I know you had some issues with Kimba and felt she had trouble with the truth."

Doris starts to answer, then pauses a moment before saying, "That's true. But I believe her. She went straight to Rey about it and then they came to us, asking if Jesse or the council had a problem with them."

"Do they?" I ask. Kimba and Rey Hoffmann joined our community over the summer. They and their three children traveled from outside of Shoshoni, Wyoming, with Kelley's daughters. When they were camped in Meeteetse, they met up with Doris's daughter Lindsey and the group she was traveling with quite by accident. They finished the trip together, not realizing Kimba and Rey had a rather sordid past involving Doris. Seems they were all involved in some sort of clandestine government work. There was lots of drama for a time, but now I think Doris and Kimba are something resembling friends.

"Not to my knowledge," Evan says.

"So . . . what does this mean? I ask, not understanding what is going on.

"That's the question, Jake," Evan says, slapping his hand on the arm of the couch. "What kind of game is Jesse playing?"

"Who else?" Mollie asks.

"Pardon?" Doris replies.

"Is he going to anyone else with the same accusations?"

Doris and Evan share a look, one I can't quite decipher, before Evan says, "That's what we were wondering too."

"Why?" I ask. "What does he gain by this?"

"Another great question," Doris says. "Rey and Mick had some sort of a disagreement right after we moved to the mountain."

"I heard about that," Mollie says.

"What was it?" I ask, not remembering hearing about it.

"I don't really think it was much of anything," Evan says. "Just some chest banging on Mick's part."

"What does Mick say about this?" Mollie asks.

"Said it's a lie. Says someone is just trying to make trouble for him and his wife—thinks it's probably because he's on the council."

"Is this an investigation tactic?" she asks.

"Not that I'm aware of," Evan says. "Of course, I was only a knuckle-dragger not an esteemed detective."

"I've heard of something similar," Doris says. "But it'd be more likely to be used in a situation where you and Kimba or all four of you—husbands included—would be involved in a dirty deed."

I furrow my brow. "Jesse thinks we're in cahoots with Rey and Kimba? We don't even know them."

"Right. It doesn't make sense," Doris agrees with a vigorous nod.

"Well," Mollie says, "their children have spent time with ours, and I've had passing conversations with her, but that's all."

"Is Jesse just grasping at straws?" I ask.

"Could be," Evan says. "But I've always thought him to be more calculating than that."

"Calculating?" Mollie asks.

"Maybe that's not the right word. But we don't think you should speak with him alone. If he shows up here or corners you again, tell him you want Judge Avery present. Kimba is doing the same thing."

"All right." Mollie nods. "Does the judge know?"

"He does," Doris says. "We met with him last night. And, of course, Mick knows since he's involved, but we haven't told anyone else on the council."

"Bill?" I ask.

"Nope. We're keeping the circle small," Evan says.

I nod, but don't like it. I'd feel better if Bill knew about this also.

"You about ready to go?" Evan asks me.

"You still think we should?"

"Yeah, I think we're okay to go ahead with our plans. This is strange, but it's probably nothing more than that—at least right now."

"Give me a few minutes to grab my bags."

"Yep. I'll meet you at the livestock shed," Evan says.

"Do you want a cup of tea before you go?" Mollie asks.

"Nah, best hit the road."

Doris spends a minute putting herself together. Chaplain Rick's latest idea for her is a leg crutch with a removable crampon. It's kind of a cross between the knee scooter and a peg leg. She rests her leg on the platform—just like the knee scooter—and walks on the peg part. The crampon gives her extra traction in the snow. While she says it's plenty stable, Belinda insists she also uses a cane in each hand until she has better mobility. Once she's on her good leg and her peg is in place, she pulls Mollie into a hug, reminding her she's available if Mollie needs anything. After they leave, I ask Mollie if she wants to go back upstairs.

"I don't think so. It's nice to be out of that bed."

"You sure?"

"Mm-hmm. Yes."

I go after my bag. When I return to the great room, she's putting a log on the fire. She finishes, then says quietly, "I'll miss you."

"I'll be back soon," I say, enveloping her in a hug.

Chapter 11

Thursday, Day 184

Mollie

After Jake leaves, I make my way to the kitchen. A combination country and commercial kitchen, this large space is my favorite place in the lodge. It's not as inviting as my kitchen at home, but it's still plenty comfortable. As I put water on for tea, I wonder where Sarah is. She told us about Evan and Doris arriving, but I haven't seen her since. Likely, she's in with Lois.

Sarah's main duty for the community is as a seamstress, and she'll often do her work while visiting with Lois. The children are all in school. Dodie is helping with the preschoolers today, and Alvin is doing something in the armory, but Jake wasn't sure what, probably reloading or cleaning the guns. The quiet of the large lodge is almost unnerving.

I choose a spicy cinnamon tea. On one of Doris's recent visits, she said the teabags will be gone soon. Luckily, there's still a fair amount of loose-leaf tea from our salvaging trips and from mint, chamomile, and other herbs people were growing. When our community split, we also divided the salvaged goods and the harvest. While we're confident we have plenty of food to make it through this winter, thanks in huge part to a good harvest, I'm already wondering what next winter will be like. Without machinery to work the ground, will we be able to plant enough corn, potatoes, barley, and sugar beets to supply the calories we need?

The thought of sugar beets makes me shudder. While I will eat them, they're not my favorite. They're much too concentrated and sweet. Doris said one of the ladies thinks she can make a sugar beet tea to help extend our hot beverage choices. My response: ick.

I'm not even halfway through my tea when the tiredness hits. It comes on so hard and strong, all I can do is just ride the wave of exhaustion. I'm not sure my legs would even support me if I tried to get up to my bed. I put my head on the table, waiting for the fatigue to pass.

"Mom? Mom?"

"Mm–hmm?" I respond, trying to fight through the grogginess.

"Are you okay?"

"Sarah?" I sit upright, my neck instantly complaining from my strange position. "I . . . I guess I fell asleep."

"Um, yeah. Let me help you to your room."

"Yes, okay. Do you know what time it is?"

"About 0930. The lunch crew should be here anytime. When's Belinda supposed to be here?"

"Around 1000. Better get me upstairs before she sees me and I get a scolding." I attempt a laugh, which falls flat.

I stop at the bathroom on my way to bed. Sarah fusses over me, making sure I'm covered up and comfortable.

"I should be taking care of you," I say.

"I'm not the one who's sick."

"I know, but— " I shrug. "How are you feeling?"

"I'm good, Mom. The baby is active and seems to be growing well. Losing Dr. Sam was a blow to my confidence with the delivery. But Shelby said Belinda and Kelley were great. Sam wasn't even in the room, you know. He was just there if any questions came up. And several people have reminded me Madison has helped deliver cows and horses. How different can a little human be, right?" She gives a small laugh.

There's a considerable amount of noise in the kitchen as whoever oversees lunch arrives, their laughter carrying up the stairs.

"How's Lois today?" I ask.

"She seemed surprisingly good. The baby was moving, and I let her feel. I think if she can just hold on until she's born, it'll make a huge difference."

"She?"

With a small smile and a shrug, Sarah says, "I don't know, of course, but I think of the baby as a she. A really big she." Sarah pats her tummy. It's true, she's quite large. She still has almost two months left and is considerably larger than Shelby was right before her little

Hannah was born. Of course, Shelby is several inches taller than Sarah, so that's likely the reason; they carry their pregnancies differently.

"Thanks for helping me up to the room. I'm sorry you have me to worry about in addition to Lois."

"I just wish we would've noticed how unwell you were sooner." She gives me a slightly accusatory look.

I shake my head. "I honestly thought it was no big deal, just the usual from the busyness of our lives."

"Rest a bit before Belinda arrives," she says, walking toward the door.

I grab the book I've been working on since the start of my bed rest. Usually, I'm an amazingly fast reader, but these last few days, I fall asleep after only a couple of pages. This time, after my nap at the kitchen table, I make it through a couple of chapters before Belinda arrives.

She takes my vitals and checks my coloring and swelling before saying, "Sarah said you were tired this morning."

"I just— " I don't even try to hold back my large sigh. "I was having some tea, and the tiredness overwhelmed me. I fell asleep at the table."

"Okay. I want you to really pay attention to when it happens. If you feel the tiredness coming on, make sure you're sitting down. I'm also going to find you a bell like the one Lois has so you can ring it if you need help."

I roll my eyes in response.

"Now, don't be that way," she says. "What if you fell out of your chair?"

"Well, I suppose I'd get up off the floor."

"Mollie, this is serious. Overall, I'm encouraged with your progress. But you're not out of the woods yet."

"Okay," I say, dropping my eyes to the comforter. "I was really hoping I could rejoin society."

"I think that'd be okay. Let's start with one meal today at the lodge. Do you feel well enough for that meal to be lunch?"

My head darts up. "Yes, I do," I say with genuine enthusiasm.

"I've made arrangements to get you extra diesel rations for your truck. I don't want you walking such a distance, and you're not to be the driver, but you'll be able to take the truck back and forth. Start with lunch only today and tomorrow, then we'll go from there."

"Breakfast in bed still?"

"Breakfast in bed still. This remains where I want you spending most of your time. Pay attention to your body and give it what it needs. I'm going to check on Lois. I'll tell Sarah about your lunch plans?"

"Please do. And thanks, Belinda."

Two hours later, Sarah's helping me into the truck. Because it's a big step up from the ground, she puts a step stool in place. "You might need the stool also," I say.

"Oh, believe me, I've already thought of that. But I can't figure out how to use the stool and get it in the truck so we have it to get you out. I think I'll be fine with just the running board."

Lunch is my favorite meal at the lodge. The children have school in the same space we use for eating, so they're all enlisted to help with setting up and serving. It's wonderful to see them work together. After lunch, they help with cleanup also. While the children are all learning the scholarly basics, at an age-appropriate level, life skills are a big focus. Boys and girls all learn basic cooking and cleaning. They're also taught hunting and other outdoor techniques. Rotating teachers provides various focuses since all of us have different strengths and knowledge.

Sarah offers me an arm to walk into lunch. I shake my head. "I'm good."

"Sure you are, Mom," she responds with her own headshake.

Once inside, I head for a table. Even though I'm okay to eat here, Belinda doesn't want me standing in line for my food. Angela—who, along with Dodie, has the young kids today—sees me and waves. She and Gavin weave through the crowd to reach us.

"Hey, Mom." She pulls me into a hug. "So Belinda let you out?"

"For lunch only today and tomorrow. Then we'll go from there."

"You want me to get your plate?"

"I'll get it," Sarah says.

"Want me to keep Gavin here?" I ask.

"Sure. We'll be right back."

Sitting on my lap, Gavin is a little chatterbox, telling me all about the picture he drew this morning. As I listen to him, I glance around the room for more of my family. Malcolm and Tony are both in the serving line, dishing up lunch as people make their way through the line. The crowd is talking and laughing as everyone gets their food. A raised voice catches my attention. Two men, Barney Sanchez and another whose name I can't remember, are in the middle of the room. The one is poking his finger in Barney's chest.

"Hey, knock it off," Barney says. "You're mistaken."

"Oh, yeah? Well, I know you're lying," he yells at the top of his voice. A hush falls over the crowd as all eyes turn toward the altercation.

Barney shakes his head. "Listen, brother— "

"I'm not your brother!" he yells. There's a flash of movement and suddenly his sidearm is pointed at Barney's face. There's a rumble through the room; I quickly grab Gavin as we move to the floor. *Please, Lord, please intervene in this. Please protect Barney. Protect my family and all of us in this room.*

The room is completely quiet for many long moments. "Okay, okay," Barney says with a quiver in his voice.

"You admit it?" the other voice yells.

"I— "

"Daniel?" a new, very calm voice says. "Why don't you put that six-shooter down."

"Not until he admits he's been slandering my wife."

"C'mon, Daniel, let's move this outside," the calm voice, which sounds like Bill, says. "Just you, me, and Barney. We'll let everyone else get on with their lunch."

Gavin squirms in my arms. "Want up, Grandmo."

"Not yet," I whisper. Another child cries out in the room.

"Uh, yeah. I . . . I guess, that'd be okay," Daniel says. "I didn't— "

"You want me to take the handgun?" Bill asks.

"Oh, man. Yeah. I don't . . . man, I don't know what I was thinking," Daniel says, voice full of alarm. "Barney, man. I . . . oh, jeez." He makes a sobbing sound.

I hazard a look as Bill takes the gun from him, then passes it on to Aaron Ogden who is standing nearby. Bill wraps an arm around Daniel's shoulders before saying, "Go on back to your lunch, everyone. We're all good here." Then he ushers Daniel out the door. Barney and Aaron, along with a few others on the security team, follow behind them.

"They done now, Grandmo? Gavin eat?"

"Yes, I think it's done. We'll eat shortly." My heart is pounding in my ears as I think how close we just came to a shoot-out in the lunchroom.

"Mom?" Angela cries as she rounds the table. "Do you need help up?"

"If you can take Gavin, I think I can get up on my own."

My first lunch back with the group was way more exciting than it should've been.

~~~~~

Later in the evening, Alvin calls a family meeting. He wants to discuss what happened at lunch with Barney and Daniel. Alvin and Dodie seldom join the community for lunch, unless they have a duty shift that puts them at the ski lodge. They never miss breakfast and usually have supper with the group, but for lunch they choose to stay in our lodge and have a quiet meal together. I think part of it is the walk to the lodge three times a day is a little much. Today, Dodie was on teaching duty, so they were there when the near catastrophe happened. And Alvin seems pretty shook up about it.

"Could've been quite the mess today," Alvin says, looking around the room.

Deanne, Roy, and Sheila—who were all sitting at the table next to Barney—express their concern.

"I know Daniel," Mike says. "Or at least I thought I did. It surprised me that he'd do something like that."

"Isn't that what they always said on the news after someone was found to be a serial killer or something?" Calley asks, then in an elderly sounding voice says, "He was such a nice boy, always so polite."

"Yeah, they do that," Alvin agrees. "Did you notice what happened when they started yelling?"

There's shrugs and other indifferent responses.

"Nothing happened," Leo says. "Most people just stared at them. The people who reacted, like Mom— " he nods in my direction " — were few."

"That's right," Alvin says, slapping his hand on his leg. "Even when the gun came out, people just sat and stared. Most of you people too. Dodie and me, like Mollie, were on the ground. One of the people at my table even muttered something about us overreacting."
~~~~~

"Normalcy bias," I say.

"Yep." Alvin nods. "They were focusing on what was happening instead of the disaster it could become. We need to start thinking differently, start looking at what could happen and what we need to do to mitigate the danger. You've all been taking those self-defense classes, even continuing on your own. I think you should spend some time reacting properly to threats—even threats in places we think are safe."

Chapter 12

Friday, Day 185
Bakerville, Wyoming

Jake

"Wow, that was a good shot! How many is that?"

"Four for me," Evan says, a huge smile covering his face. "I've got you beat by one. What do you think? Another half hour until it's too dark?"

"Yep. And that's about right to get to Gabe Griffin's house for supper."

"It was nice of them to invite us."

"Even nicer they were willing to wait until after sundown so we could get our full hunt in."

"That's true too," Evan says with a chuckle. "I did half wonder if there might be some hard feelings. When we put up the handkerchief to let them know it was us, I had a moment of wondering if we'd be fired upon."

"You talked with Gabe about us coming down for goose hunting when we were finishing harvest."

"I did, but you know how things can be."

"It didn't hurt we brought elk meat along as a peace offering."

"They were happy about that since the usual herd hasn't been around. Most of them are wary about focusing their diet on venison."

"Yeah. After finding those emaciated deer over the summer, we're all leery."

"Gabe will be the first to tell you, he wasn't sure about it until he started seeing evidence of sick deer with his own eyes," Evan says. "He'd still eat it if his wife wouldn't have told him no way would she risk feeding a sick animal to her children."

We sit in silence for several minutes. My thoughts turn from emaciated deer to my own wife. I'm still surprised at how thin her arms and legs are. Her waist still holds some weight, but is it a healthy weight or something different? Evan interrupts my thoughts with, "Too bad about Gladys dying. She was a fine lady."

"Yeah," I agree. "I only met her a few times, but she was definitely the family matriarch. They seem a little lost without her. And Gabe said they've lost three others, all elderly."

"Maybe we should've encouraged one of our doctors to stay behind," Evan says. "I know they have people with some medical training, but not the knowledge we have."

"Who would you have stay?" I ask. "Sam was shot right when we were moving, and it took both Belinda and Kelley to care for him—and he still didn't make it. Madison and Leo—who are the next best medically trained—are both a part of our extended family, and they don't even know anyone who stayed behind. We left them with supplies and did what we could do."

"You're right, and I know it was their choice to stay here, which I do completely support. I guess I'm just feeling a little guilty since I fought so hard for us to move up the mountain so as many of us could survive as possible. Our move may have been a death sentence for some here. We're all just losing too many good people."

"Free will, Evan. They knew why you thought it best to move up. I hate that people are dying also."

We're silent for several minutes. "What do you think about the idea of nuclear winter?" I ask. "Does it seem like we're in it?"

Evan shrugs. "There's definitely more snow than we've had in the last couple of years. And it's a little colder too. But not as bad as the winter after we moved here."

"True, but that snow didn't start until mid-December, and then it stuck around until early March. Gabe said it's been snowing off and on since November and hasn't melted off."

Evan lets out a sigh. "Could be from the nukes, I guess. Who knows."

"Here they come," I say, pointing to a large flock in the distance.

When we're finished for the evening, we have ten geese—five each—and three ducks, our best hunt yet. This morning and last night combined were only nine Canadian geese and two Mallard ducks. Each of the other pairs of hunters did about the same. I'm excited to see how many they got tonight. Our mountain people are going to be eating good.

We clean up at my house. With everything usable taken to the mountain, or hidden, the amenities are few. We brought drinking water with us so we wouldn't have to haul a generator or hook up my cached solar system. For bathing and general cleaning, we hauled water from the river and heated it on the woodstove. Father and son Dusty and Dax Cameron are also staying at my place. Pete Fairbanks, who lives in the same neighborhood as Evan and me, is hosting the other three hunters at his house.

Everyone had a great hunt tonight, giving us a running total of thirty-eight geese and a dozen ducks. And we still have tomorrow and Sunday morning before we head home. I slap my hands together, rubbing them vigorously, thinking about finishing our hunt. It's going to be good!

Evan and I take the snowmobile to Gabe Griffin's house, telling Dusty and Dax we'll meet them there. When we get to Gabe's, it's obvious he invited all the river people. There are horses, ATVs, and snowmobiles pulling in ahead and behind us.

"You're sure they're all friendly?" I ask with a small laugh.

"Sure hope so," Evan says.

Gabe is in the yard directing everyone. He's motioning the horses over to a copse of trees while the machines are being parked on the other side of the yard.

"Jake, Evan. Glad you all could make it."

"Thanks for the invite," Evan says, shaking Gabe's hand. "Looks like all the river people are here."

"The what?"

Evan colors slightly, then clears his throat. "Um, we—uh . . . " He lets out a long breath. "You see, one day Jake and I were talking." He gives me a look.

"Oh no," I say, motioning with my hands. "This is all you, friend."

"Thanks for your help, Jake."

"Anytime." I laugh.

"We're the mountain people, you're the river people." Evan shrugs.

"Is that right?" Gabe asks.

"Yeah, but Judge Avery refers to you as Bakerville proper, so that's what many people call you."

"I guess both make sense." He turns to Dusty and Dax, who've ambled over after tying up their horses. "You came in with the Smalls and McCracken families, right?

"That's right. Dusty Cameron. This is my son Dax."

"I'm pretty sure we've met before, maybe at an outfitters event? And I know your dad and brother from working at the service station in Prospect. Might have seen you there a time or two also."

"Might have." Dusty nods.

"Evan told me about your brother running into a bear. Is he going to be okay?"

"Belinda says he will be. He's got a pretty good gash on his arm, is banged up a bit, and will be limping around with a sprained ankle, but it would've been a lot worse if he wasn't wearing a heavy jacket and several layers."

"Crazy. I've never run into a bear this late in the season. I'm glad it wasn't worse."

Dusty gives a nod. "Thanks for inviting us to your home."

"The whole town, all of us river people— " he gives Evan an exaggerated wink "— are happy to see you. The last bit of excitement we had wasn't nearly as welcome."

"What was that?" Evan asks.

"Our excitement? We had some trespassers."

"Oh?"

"Last week. Seems they might have been watching us for some time."

"What did you do with them?" Dax asks.

"They got away. We only caught movement on the butte over there." He points to a flat-topped mountain across the river. "By the time we were able to approach, they were gone. We found where they'd been camping, but they hightailed it before we could do anything about it. Beefed up our security for a few days, but we haven't seen them again. We're going to add our own watch tower on the butte, catch 'em before they get to us."

I feel myself paling. They were being watched. Surveilled. To what end? And would those watchers just move along after being discovered?

"That doesn't sound good," Evan says, worry painted on his face. "Have you looked around for a new camp? Seems to me they'd set up someplace similar."

"We've looked. Tracked them a ways too. The snow's at least good for something. But then they must have realized it, too, because they went straight to a game trail and scuffed their prints. We're keeping an eye out. We won't be caught unaware again."

Evan nods, but I don't think he's convinced.

"In some ways, it was a good thing," Gabe continues. "We might have been a little lackadaisical."

"Meaning?" Dax asks.

"With the snow and all, it's easy to think everyone is holed up in front of a fire. Those guys had to be there several days, even watching us during a blizzard that came roaring through a couple of days before we found them. That's some dedication."

"Do you think it could've been Richard Majors's goons from Prospect?" Dax asks.

Gabe gives a slow shrug. "Don't know. The McCrackens and Smalls, they thought so. I know what happened in Prospect to you all was bad, but it's possible there are others around that are looking to see what we have. 'Sides, we never got a look at them, didn't find anything other than a pocketknife one of them must have dropped. It could've been anyone."

"Yes, but we know— "

"They know all about it, Dax," Dusty says, dropping a hand on his son's shoulder. "They'll be diligent and watch for anything more."

Dax looks around the yard at the people; I follow his gaze. A group of children, bundled up against the cold, are running around playing an unorganized game of tag. Women are talking to each other. Men are standing around a big firepit, where the welcome aroma of meat is emanating. It's no different than it'd be for us on the mountain. Even though we have people on guard, just like they do, we're living and trying to enjoy our lives.

"We've got a good watch set up," Gabe says. "You guys really helped us out with tips on how we could make this work. Everyone living so close to each other makes a difference."

"How many of you are there?" Dax asks.

"There's eighty-two now, after my mom and the others died. Twenty-eight are from your Prospect group. They've been a good addition. I think we'll be fine. Now, let's go see how the food's coming along. My stomach says it's time to eat."

Chapter 13

Sunday, Day 187

Mollie

"This is not right!" Phil Hudson yells, interrupting the impromptu post-lunch meeting.

Judge Avery nods. "I understand how you feel. And I'm inclined to agree with you." He throws his hands up in surrender. "But we almost had a catastrophe here. This is a necessary step, at least for the time being."

"So your answer to *keeping us safe* is to check our weapons at the door? And if we come under attack while we're having our lunch?"

"Your concern has been duly noted," Jon Dawson says in a bored tone from his seat at his lunch table. "This decision has been made by the majority of the council." His wife, sitting next to him, touches his arm and gives a small shake of her head. He jerks his arm away from her as he stares straight ahead.

"Evan Snyder isn't here to vote," someone yells out.

"Doesn't matter. We had a quorum."

Sarah jumps to her feet, causing her large belly to sway. "We deserve a verbal accounting of who voted in favor of this."

I look at her, my eyes wide. Of my children, Sarah was always the most uncomfortable—to the point of almost being opposed—to our militia and self-defense methods.

"That's not happening," Dawson says.

Simultaneously, Judge Avery says, "That's fair."

"No," Dawson turns to the judge. "Council business does not need to be made public."

Still standing, Sarah very calmly says, "I seem to remember we, as a community, voted on who'd be on the council. We chose you as our representatives. I demand to know who is not representing me."

A proud smile crosses my face. Dawson turns red and starts sputtering. Judge Avery pushes his glasses up on his nose.

Bill Shane stands up and says, "I voted against this order."

"So did I," Mick Michaelson yells out.

After several beats of silence, Judge Avery says, "The rest of the council was in favor of prohibiting weapons at community events. I abstained from the vote."

"Thank you, Judge," Sarah says. "My understanding is you are the tie breaker, correct?"

"That's correct." He nods.

"And if Evan would've been present, he would've voted against this nonsense."

"You don't know that!" Dawson cries out.

"Really?" Sarah asks. "You believe he'd vote in favor of disarming citizens in direct violation of the Second Amendment? Especially at a time when one of our community members died under suspicious circumstances and another was attacked by a bear? We have a right to be able to protect ourselves."

"You'll be plenty safe while in these public places. And the Second Amendment has nothing to do with this," Dawson says. "You might want to read it sometime."

Sarah smiles sweetly. "Thank you, Mr. Dawson. I believe it says, 'a well-regulated militia, being necessary to the security of a free state, the right of the people to keep and bear arms, shall not be infringed.' In the past, I've done plenty of my own virtue signaling, without offering any real solutions or alternatives to perceived gun violence."

Sarah pauses for a moment while the crowd reacts to her statement. She takes a breath and continues, "And while I may have previously disagreed with the Framers' intent, I now believe it is always our God-given right to self-protection. Especially in public venues. And, as intended by the Framers, to protect us against a tyrannical government. Which seems to be our greatest need now."

"Well, you might think that," Dawson says, "but as far as this council is concerned, the Second Amendment has no bearing on our day-to-day decisions."

"Exactly what are you saying?" someone yells out.

"I'm saying we operate under our community bylaws," Dawson says with fake patience. "That was the decision we made months ago."

There's a rumble through the room. Even though I know the bylaws are our rule of law, I didn't realize the Constitution of the United States wasn't also considered when decisions were made.

Still standing, Sarah very loudly says, "I believe our bylaws allow for the community to petition when the council acts in a manner the majority believes is improper?"

"Quiet down, everyone," Judge Avery says. "Mrs. Garrett, can you please repeat your question?"

She clears her throat and asks again.

With a smile, Judge Avery says, "Yes, ma'am, it does. Any community member may call for a public review on the matter."

"Now just a minute," Jon Dawson says. "This is a right and just action. Do you not remember what almost happened here? We almost had a shoot-out!"

"Dawson," Judge Avery says, his voice laced with warning, "whether you think it's right and just or not, our bylaws do allow a community review. If Mrs. Garrett wishes to bring forth the review, she is well within her rights to do so."

"I wish to bring forth the review if she doesn't," a man in the middle of the crowd yells out.

A chorus of "me too" and "so do I" follow. I'm impressed Sarah knows this exists in our bylaws. I don't think I've ever read the full document, and I don't remember this being discussed.

"Well, I guess there's your answer," Judge Avery says. "I'll need to refer to the exact wording in the bylaws, but I believe we set up a series of three public meetings. In the first meeting, the council will detail how and why they took this action."

"Everyone already knows why we took it!" Dawson cries out.

Judge Avery shoots him a look. "Those on the council who were in opposition to this action will also have an opportunity to discuss their position. At the first meeting, the public is only observers gathering information. The second meeting will be a public forum. Any loose ends will be wrapped up at the third meeting, and a new public vote of the council will be called."

I watch as the councilmembers react. Those who voted in favor of the weapons ban all shake their head. Bill and Mick nod vigorously.

"Once I review the bylaws to make sure we're not missing anything, I'll announce the time of the first meeting. Be patient, folks. This will be a process."

"And in the meantime?" Sarah calls out.

"In the meantime, the council's orders stand."

There's much discord through the building. While many think the weapons ban is totally out of line, I do hear several agreeing with it, saying how bad things could've gone when Daniel pulled the gun on Barney. While I agree, things could've escalated to a point where someone ended up dead, I'd like to think this was an isolated incident. Though we still haven't heard what prompted the argument, both Barney and Daniel have been suspiciously absent from everything since that day. And no one has said where they are or what the consequences for Daniel will be for pulling the gun. The only thing we know is the rest of us are no longer allowed to wear our guns in public places.

I glance around the room; Deputy Clark Thomas is on the outskirts. He has a hard look on his face. When he sees me looking his way, he gives a slight nod. Clark oversees a group of five deputies. When things first fell apart, Deputy Fred enlisted Clark as part of his team. Things were never comfortable between the two of them, and when Fred brought on Brad Quinton—Sarah's dad—as a deputy, Clark quickly moved to a militia position. When Fred was arrested for his crimes, Judge Avery asked Clark, a retired Atlanta police officer, to head up a newly formed police force.

While our militia is charged with protecting our community from invaders, the police force, who we still refer to as *deputies*, is supposed to keep us lawful. Clark's most likely the one who dealt with Barney and Daniel.

A slight smile passes my lips when I remember the first thing Clark did when he was put in charge; he removed Brad from his team. There were some serious fireworks over that! When Calley told us about it, I expected Sarah to be upset. I know she had been incredibly happy, and proud, when Fred deputized Brad. Instead, she said, "I can see how my dad might not be a good fit with Clark in charge."

Brad wasn't as understanding; he went to the council about his dismissal. Jon Dawson sided with him, while everyone else supported Clark in his decision. Brad, like pretty much the entire community of Bakerville, is now part of the militia. Even that was met with some resistance.

Militia leaders Bill Shane, Evan Snyder, and Cole Gunderson all had reservations about Brad. Kelley was even asked to do an in-depth psych evaluation on him before they moved forward with putting him on the militia.

While I don't disagree with his need for a serious psychiatric evaluation, I don't know what prompted the extra scrutiny. Our usual practice for becoming a part of the militia is a physical exam and a short talk with Kelley to make sure we can mentally and emotionally handle what is expected of us. Those unable are excused and put on different work assignments.

All of us on the militia have it much easier here at the ski lodge than we did when we lived in Bakerville proper. There, we had twenty-four-hour shifts, and it was still a challenge to provide the security needed to protect our community. With our setup here, we take a four-hour shift during the day or an eight-hour overnight watch. Everyone breathes easier, feeling like we have an advantage based on our location. The ski lift shacks and the newly constructed lean-to that are being used as watch towers give us commanding views in every direction. It'd be difficult for anyone to sneak up.

Even so, the idea of not being armed bothers me. Yes, we're probably safe and would have plenty of warning in case of an attack, but in this crazy world we now live in, there are no guarantees. I carried a sidearm before things changed, choosing to conceal carry in my everyday life. I'm not willing to give it up.

As Sarah and I stand to leave, Clark Thomas is suddenly at our side. "You look like you're feeling better, Mollie."

"Thanks, I am."

"Sarah, good job speaking up. You were very eloquent."

"I was nervous."

"Couldn't tell. Jake and the others will be home today?"

"Yes, that was the plan," I say. I catch Sarah's eye. It wasn't long ago when her husband went on a hunting trip to never return. She bites her lip as tears fill her eyes.

"Okay, good. Listen, the new regulations specify no firearms in public places."

"I heard."

He gives a grim nod. "Most of the first floor of your lodge is considered a public place."

"You can't be serious," Sarah blurts out.

"This is not my doing. I was just specifically told to make you aware of it. The only first-floor space considered private is the bedroom and bathroom Jake's parents use."

I feel the heat traveling up my face. "Let me guess," I say, "Jon Dawson."

He tilts his head slightly. "The orders were written specifically to include the first floor of the dude ranch lodge. Even people living in the ski lodge aren't allowed to have a gun on them unless they're in their private apartment. Those in the dorms won't be able to keep their weapons with them."

"That's ridiculous!" Sarah exclaims.

He gives a combination nod and shrug. "All public places, including the supply shed, the greenhouses, the livestock areas, and the medical clinic."

"The livestock areas?" I say with alarm. "What if there's a predator attack?"

He shrugs. "Believe me, that was mentioned to no avail. And you should start praying for me now because I have to tell Doris she isn't allowed to carry her weapon when she's working supplies."

"Yeah, that's going to go over well. You do know Evan is going to do everything in his power to reverse this when he returns. I can't even believe they'd make a decision like this without his input."

"I have no doubt there will be some serious discussions resulting from this."

"So you're planning to enforce this?" Sarah asks.

A look I can't quite decipher passes over his face. "As far as if you have weapons on the first floor of your home, I'm sure I'll never see that happening. And if no one else sees anything, there should be no issues."

"What exactly are you saying?" Sarah asks.

"Um, Sarah," I say, touching her arm, "we should let Clark get on with his duties."

"I've delivered the message as required," Clark says with a slight nod.

When we exit the ski lodge, Toby James is waiting with the snowmobile and trailer, as he has been the past two days per Belinda's request.

"Hello, Mrs. Caldwell, Mrs. Garrett," he says, stepping off the machine. He offers me his hand to help me into the trailer. Sarah, with her girth, finds it easier to ride on the seat behind him. Once Toby's back on, Sarah climbs on behind and he gives us a ride down the hill and over the bridge to our pickup truck where the rest of the family is already waiting.

"Dr. Belinda says you can have all three meals at the lodge tomorrow," Toby says, smiling. "I'm on guard duty at breakfast time, but Bryce Cameron is on snow crew, so he'll help you up and down the hill."

"Thank you, Toby," I say. "Hopefully, only a few more days of this and I'll be fine."

"Those of us on the snow crew have several people we give rides to, any of the elderly that need it." He gives me a nod. I try not to take offense to being labeled elderly. "And it might be longer for Mrs. Garrett," he says, motioning to Sarah. "You know, we gave Shelby rides too during the final days of her pregnancy."

"I still have six weeks," Sarah says, her cheeks coloring.

"Oh? I thought it'd be much sooner than that. Anyway, see you at lunch tomorrow."

"Mom, what was Deputy Clark talking with you about?" Calley asks after Toby speeds off.

"Let's go to the lodge. We'll discuss it there." I climb into the passenger's seat of the truck. I'm doing so much better, I don't need the step stool to get up. I scoot to the middle, allowing Sarah to slide in next to me. Tim drives while the rest are piled in the bed.

After setting up the children in the loft with toys and games, we gather in the dining room to discuss what Clark told us.

"I guess I'm confused by this," Mike says. "If we can't carry a weapon in a public place, what about when we're outside? I take my sidearm and a rifle when I'm walking to guard duty. I see plenty of people on the way. Wouldn't that be public?"

"Of course it is," Sarah says. "The same thing that happened at lunch could easily happen while walking around outside."

"The entire thing is ridiculous," Tim says. "And after what happened to Angela and then to Katie and the rest of you when you were attacked— "

"If Mom and Sarah wouldn't have had their guns concealed, we'd be dead," Calley says.

"I think Clark was telling us we should still carry concealed," Sarah says, her tone low and cautious. "Don't you think so, Mom?"

Instead of directly answering *yes, that's what I think*, I say, "You know I carried concealed for years. No one knew I had a weapon unless I told them."

"You brought your holster collection?" Angela asks.

"Yes, I packed them with the rest of my clothes and things. I'm not sure I have concealed holsters that will work for all our weapons, especially the larger handguns you men are carrying, but we'll do what we can."

"I've got my .380 in my pocket right now," Mike says.

I give him a nod. Mike has carried a pocket pistol for years, keeping the small holster in his front pants pocket. I must admit, him carrying it that way freaks me out, but right now, I'm thankful for his foresight. I glance around the great room. We added a lock to the coat closet and turned it into one of our gun safes. There are several fully loaded and at-the-ready weapons tucked in various places on both the first and second floor. I have no intention of telling anyone about these hidden gems, but will Dawson insist on a search of our designated public spaces?

"Do you think Leo will be exempt?" Katie asks. "You know, since he's on the security team? They're always supposed to be ready at a moment's notice. Evan makes a big deal about that."

"They should be," Sarah says. "That's their job. And I should've thought to clarify with Clark, but I'm sure he and his deputies are exempt."

"No doubt we'll find out more in the next few days," I say. "But in the meantime, I think we should do what we can to protect ourselves whenever possible—even in our own home. Even if Dawson thinks this is a public space, I don't agree. And we need to keep quiet about it."

"We also need to continue the training you've started," Alvin says. "You've been teaching the children, young and old, about duck and cover," he says, looking around the table at his adult grandchildren and extended family.

"Right," I say. "We started yesterday. Leo?"

"Yes, sir," he says to Alvin. "We worked with the youngest children first, making sure they knew if there was any fighting or shooting nearby, they should move to the floor and make themselves small."

"It was good Mom took Gavin to the floor the day before," Tim says. "He seemed to fully understand the need for it, even explained it to Andy and showed him how to curl up like a ball on the floor."

"We also chose meeting places," Angela says. "The one for this lodge and our private residences are easy since we already had those set up in case of a fire. We're still meeting at the playground swing sets. For the ski lodge, they chose the tree along the fence line—you know, the lone tree on the way to the triple lift."

"That's a good spot," Alvin says. "Far enough away but easy to get to."

"And somewhat hidden," I add, thinking of the deciduous tree well away from the lodge. Malcolm knows this tree as a meeting place for when he was in a ski group. It makes sense he'd suggest it.

"Calley brought up a good point," Sarah says. "She mentioned hearing about a hostage situation on the ham radio. She said it reminded her of—what was it, Calley?"

"There's a television show—or I guess I should say there *was* a television show—about a family of police officers in New York. The daughter on the show, she's not a cop but a lawyer, is taken hostage. Mom, do you remember this one? We watched it together."

I shake my head, not sure what show she's talking about.

"You know it. She's got a gun to her head and her brother is talking to the bad guy and then he says, 'Please don't hurt my family,' which is a code they've worked out in the past. She knows she needs to get out of the way because he's going to shoot the bad guy."

"Oh, I've seen that," Deanne says. "Sheila, you and I watched it together. Remember?"

"I remember. I think it's a good idea. But I also like how Calley said they used the word 'fire' when they were attacked. It was from the self-defense class they all took together when the children were young."

"Right," Sarah says. "Mom took us on a weekend retreat after our dad died—after Jamie died. We learned then that, if we were attacked, yelling fire would attract more attention than yelling help."

"Yes," Katie agrees. "But for us, it became our battle cry. For a while, after the retreat, we'd practice what we learned at home. One of us would yell fire, which meant try and beat each other up." She gives a smile. "It had been a dozen years since we'd sparred together, but as soon as Mom yelled it out, we all knew what to do."

"Sounds smart," Alvin says. "But if you're going to have codes, they need to be simple. Those children are young. They're smart, but they can't remember much yet. Use the KISS principle. Keep it simple, sweetie."

Chapter 14

Christmas
Wednesday, Day 190

Jake

I've made a pig of myself, eating way more goose than any human should at one sitting. Mollie's feeling considerably better. So much so, she suggested we walk home. It was a good idea and is settling my stomach, at least from overeating.

My stomach has truly been in knots since returning from the goose hunt and discovering the heavy-handed gun control measures put forth by the council. To say I was angry would be an understatement. And my anger was mild compared to Evan's. He was shocked they'd move forward with something so drastic without his input, to the point he came close to quitting the counsel, only staying on because Bill convinced him his voice is needed. Bill's right. I can't even imagine how bad things could get without Bill, Mick, and Evan looking out for us.

"I'm glad the children did their pageant last night," Mollie says. "It was the perfect beginning to our Christmas celebration."

"Yep. And the sledding this morning was a huge hit." Kelley's daughters set up the magic carpet, the lift used for the bunny slope, on the solar system as a Christmas gift to the community. While skiing or snowboarding would be too dangerous—we can't risk a broken leg, or worse—riding up and sledding down was great fun for everyone. I took a few runs with the children, and we laughed more than we have in months. After eating, many people went back to the fun. I'm much too stuffed for sledding, but our family is still playing as Mollie and I start for home. "Did Kelley tell you they planned to do that?"

"I don't even think she knew." Mollie laughs. "She thought they were up to something, but we figured it'd be part of the pageant." She stiffens slightly and says, in barely a whisper, "There's Heath Jefferson. He looks awful."

I shake my head. "Well, he should. Sounds like Fred's wife beat the tar out of him. And rightly so."

"Oh, I'm not saying he didn't deserve it. It sounds like he's been harassing her for weeks. Remember, Rochelle doesn't like being referred to as Fred's wife."

"Okay . . . but she *is* Fred's wife," I say, not understanding.

"She was Fred's captive. She married him under duress, doing what she had to do to keep her girls safe. And now, for Heath Jefferson to attack her like that . . . "

"From the looks of him, she held her own," I say. With his black eye visible from a distance and his arm in a sling, he's looking the worse for wear. "Rumor is he told Dot he fell on the ice. Kelley was treating him when Clark Thomas showed up after getting the complaint from Rochelle."

"Oh, that's not just a rumor," Mollie says. "It seems to me he got what he deserved. Katie said she's not surprised. He was trouble on the militia team over the summer. He never bothered her, but he did bother a few other women. I guess that's why Bill was so cold to him that day at our lodge." She gives my hand a squeeze. "I don't want to talk about him anymore. This is a nearly perfect day. Did I tell you how much I enjoyed the geese you brought home?"

"They do make a nice addition to our diet. I'm looking forward to the goose jerky," I say.

"We're making soup tomorrow. And we'll boil down the carcasses, so we'll have broth as the basis for several more meals."

"Are you sure you're ready to return to kitchen duty?"

"I promised Belinda and Kelley I'd only do stuff while sitting. I can easily chop veggies from a seated position."

"Without falling asleep at the table?"

"Oh, puh-leeeze," she says. "That was a . . . a fluke."

"Mm-hmm." I stop walking and turn her to face me. "If that kind of fluke happens again, you need to tell Belinda. We're not going to let your health slide any longer. Got it?"

She narrows her eyes slightly. "It's obvious I'm pretty much normal now, right?"

"Normal, huh?"

"Hardee-har-har. You know what I mean."

I pull her close. After several moments, I whisper, "I'm serious. You are my— " I'm suddenly overcome with emotion. I pause to collect myself. "You're my everything, Mollie."

She pulls back slightly, searching my face, before giving me a small smile. "Ditto, babe." She lifts onto her toes, her lips connecting with mine, light as a feather. I can't help but pull her in close, kissing her hard.

When we release, she says, "Well, that was . . . something. And right here where people are around."

"We could take this back to the lodge," I say, my voice huskier than usual.

~~~~~

Later that evening, after a community sing-along at the ski lodge, our entire extended family gathers in our great room. As part of our rations for the week, we were able to get popcorn for tonight's festivities. In the past, we would've given the children their gifts to open early in the morning. But because of watch and meal schedules, we decided to hold off on our personal celebrations until evening.

Once everyone is gathered, my dad reads from the gospel of Luke. A year ago, we wouldn't have done this as part of our Christmas observance, at least not with all the children present. Mollie and I had only started returning to Christ after several years of mild rebellion and floundering. During that time, which started after the death of our good friends, we came incredibly close to divorcing. When the attacks started, we were doing better. Now, even though I know I'm not as attentive as I should be—as evidenced by my failure to notice Mollie's health crisis—we're good. Better than good.

Mollie's adult children were, at one time, Christians but faced their own crises of faith in varying degrees. Now, as I look around the room, as we listen to my dad read, I see not only interest but understanding and often emotion. Sarah, who during college declared herself an atheist, has tears in her eyes. Before she lost her husband, she'd begun to rethink her position. I wouldn't say she considered herself a Christian again, but she was searching for answers, for the truth. After Tate and Keith went missing, she really began questioning. A few
~~~~~

weeks later, she repented and asked God's forgiveness for her lost years. Now I see her putting God first daily and teaching her adopted children about Jesus.

At one time, Katie planned on becoming a missionary. She had started the process with a group at her college. Then she suddenly stopped talking about it. We found out later it was because of her relationship with Leo. Katie was feeling so guilty about some of the choices they made, she totally withdrew from church and God. Individually, both she and Leo repented and started anew, basing their relationship on Godly principles.

Likewise, Angela and Calley have developed a new closeness with Christ they didn't have before. Things are so different in the apocalypse. While we're busy—busier than we've ever been, in many ways—we have time for God and each other. Time we never focused on before. Sometimes, in my rare philosophical moments, I wonder if it was part of the plan, if God brought us to this time and place to purposely turn us back toward Him. Not just my family but all His children.

Looking around the room, I can't help but marvel at our new family. Even Lois is feeling well enough to join us. She brought her own Bible and follows along while my dad reads. Karen sits next to her, ready should she need anything.

I reach for Mollie's hand, lacing our fingers together. She leans her head on my shoulder. When my dad finishes reading, Sarah says, "That was beautiful, Grandpa Alvin. You know, I'm sure I've heard those passages before, but this time— " She takes a deep breath. "The meaning was so clear."

"Jesus loves me," Sissy says. "Da Bible tell me so."

"Yes, Jesus loves me," Marc sings out. With the next line, all the children join in. Soon, everyone is singing "Jesus Loves Me."

Mollie wipes at both eyes with her knuckles as she sings in a wobbly voice. I'm so choked up, I don't even try to join in. Such a simple song, sang with such heart and wonder. Several more songs follow and then we move into the gift-giving part of the evening. Because of our circumstances, we only have a single gift for each of the young children.

"Okay, who's first?" I ask, looking around the room.

"Gavin should go first," Malcolm says, motioning to Gavin sitting on Angela's lap.

Gavin gets a big smile and claps his hands. "Gavvy go first!" he cries out.

"See? He's excited. And since he and Andy are the youngest, we can keep it organized and go from youngest to oldest."

"Why not oldest to youngest?" Tony asks.

"That works, too, but I was hoping to keep the excitement up as long as possible. If we go oldest to youngest, I'm second and then my fun is over. Gavin's so young he won't care."

"I'm with Malcolm," Tony agrees. "Youngest to oldest."

"Do you want to go first, little man?" Angela asks, tickling his tummy. "Or should we let Andy go first?"

"How about we have Gavin and Andy open their gifts at the same time?" Sarah asks, hugging Andy to her. "Would you like that, Andy?"

He gives a shy nod.

"Good idea," Mollie says.

"I'll get their gifts," Lily says, jumping up and going to the sad Charlie Brown Christmas tree decorated only with small strips of paper, yarn, and string. Mollie calls it the Bits and Pieces Tree. And she said it's her favorite one that we've ever had.

"I'll help Lily," Katie says. She moves a large package aside to pull out the boys' gifts. Angela and Sarah sit them side by side. Gavin turned three earlier in the month. We don't know exactly when Andy's birthday is—it wasn't something we thought of asking his mom. We didn't ask about Marc or Sissy either. Marc thinks his own birthday is in September, and he likes the number eighteen, so that's when we celebrated him turning eight. He thinks Sissy's and Andy's birthdays are in the winter. We'll celebrate one in January and the other in February.

Angela helps Gavin untie the ribbon on his fabric-wrapped gift. He lets out a squeal of delight before the gift is even exposed. Sarah helps Andy with his.

"Oh, wow, that's cool," Malcolm says after both gifts are revealed. "Did you make them, Dad?"

"It was a group effort," I say. "Your mom and Sarah made the tool belts out of old apron material. Grandpa and I cut the toolbox and tools out of scrap wood. And Katie painted— "

"I have a hammer," Gavin says, raising it up to whack the floor.

"Not the floor," Angela says. "See these little wooden pegs? Those are your nails."

"Katie painted everything," Mollie says with a laugh. "The 'nails' are golf tees we were able to get from supplies. And the squishy stuff is florist foam."

"They're so perfect," Sarah says. Andy wastes no time, immediately picking up a small square of sandpaper plus a chunk of two-by-four and going to work on it.

"Am I next?" Lily asks in a very prim and proper manner.

"You are next," Katie says. "You and Sissy get to open your gifts together too." She scoots out the biggest box, wrapped in a hodgepodge of scrap paper—some Christmas, some other patterns—sealed with a prudent amount of masking tape.

"Is that for me?" Sissy asks, her voice full of disbelief.

"There's one big thing for both you and Lily to open and share, then a smaller gift for each one of you. But it all goes together. Okay?"

"Yes!" Lily says, ripping at the big box. "Sissy, help. This is hard work." Sissy tentatively pulls a piece of paper off. "What is it? What is it?" Lily asks.

"It's a dollhouse," Katie says. "See? There are rooms with furniture and even little curtains. Next, open this box. And here's a box for you to open, Sissy."

"I . . . I can't. It's so beautiful, I just want to look at it," Sissy says.

Lily unties the string on the small fabric-covered box. "People! It's our people, Sissy. Open yours and see!"

With Katie's help, Sissy's box is soon open. Each girl has a little wooden family of people, constructed to match the girl's hair; Sissy's family's hair is all brown yarn, and Lily's family is all yellow yarned.

"Wow!" Calley says. "I think I'm going to need to play with you. I never had a dollhouse like that."

I stand up and walk over to the tree. "Let's see . . . who's next?"

Marc shyly raises his hand.

"Yep. It's you, Marc. I think Grandpa Alvin has your gift."

"C'mon over here," my dad says to him.

When Marc is standing in front of him, he reaches to a spot next to him. "Merry Christmas, Grandson," he says, handing him a plain brown box.

Marc opens it and holds up a folding pocketknife. "My own knife?" he asks, scrunching up his face.

"That's right. Thought it was time you had one."

"Is it the kind for guys like us? For left hands?"

"Pocketknives work no matter if you're right or left-handed. You, Malcolm, and I can use the same pocketknife as your grandpa Jake. Be sure to keep a good blade on it. There's a whetstone in there also. Tomorrow, I'll teach you how to do it right. Keep the knife in your pocket. You never know when you might need it."

Marc throws himself at my dad, hugging him tightly. We talked about having Trey Vasquez make Marc a knife like he did for Malcolm for his birthday, but since he's never owned a knife before, a fixed blade didn't seem appropriate. This pocketknife was one my dad kept in his fishing tackle box, and he was happy to offer it to Marc.

Marc happily takes his knife and sits next to Tony, showing it off. Tony pulls his own knife out of his pocket: a butterfly version Evan gave him last summer. They look at each, comparing how the two open.

"So, Malcolm, I guess it's you next," Katie says.

"All right!" He jumps up. While he moves toward the tree, I step closer to the door of the den.

"Here you go, Buddy." Katie hands him a small box—the kind that would hold a necklace or similar piece of jewelry.

Opening the box, he lifts out a flat piece of plastic.

"What is that?" Lily asks. "It's so small."

With a wide smile, he says, "It's a guitar pick. There's two more in the box."

"Yep," I say. "And hold on just a moment . . . " I reach around the den door and pull out a guitar case. "Here's the rest of it."

"No way! You got me a guitar?" Malcolm rushes over, taking the case from me.

I meet Mollie's eyes. She was sure Malcolm would love the guitar. He loves to sing and used to play the keyboard. The keyboard, plugged in at the time of the EMP, no longer works. This acoustic guitar was one salvaged from the empty homes. Doris let me trade an extra hunting and woodcutting shift for it. An excellent trade, in my opinion.

"And Dax and Bryce Cameron have agreed to give you a few lessons to get you started," Mollie says.

"Thanks, Mom and Dad. This is a great gift." He opens the case and attempts to strum.

"The lessons are a good idea, Mom," Calley says, nodding vigorously.

"I think you'll play wonderfully, Malcolm," Deanne says, shaking her head at Calley.

"Okay, Tony," I say. "You're the last one. Ready?"

Katie hands him a box slightly larger than Malcolm's. It takes him only a second to pop the lid off. He holds it up and shakes his head. "I have no idea what this is."

Malcolm looks up from his guitar and says, "No way. Dad? Is this what I think it is?"

"What is it?" Tony asks.

"Hold that thought," I say, as I step into the den. I return a moment later carrying a compound bow.

"It *is* what I thought!" Malcolm says. "The trigger thing to help shoot! That's so cool, Tony! We can take our bows out together."

"That's right," my dad says. "A trigger release aid, helps with drawing and firing."

"Wow!" Tony exclaims. "The bow's for me?"

"It's for you," I say, handing him my old bow. I stopped using a compound bow several years ago after switching to a crossbow. "We'll need to adjust the draw weight and the peep sight. Paul Cameron has already checked it over and said it's still sound. He can make all the needed changes."

"Thanks," Tony says, gingerly taking the bow and admiring it.

"So, we'll be able to practice together?" Malcolm asks. "I can use the bow Grandma and Grandpa gave me last year. It's not as big as that one, but it's still good for antelope hunting."

Before I can answer, I'm distracted by a knock at the door.

"Humph," my dad says. "It's getting kind of late for showering. And on Christmas? Let me get rid of them."

"I'll take care of it," I say, feeling the irritation creep through my body.

I pull open the door to see Doris and Evan. "Oh, hey, Merry Christmas. C'mon in."

"We'd rather not," Evan says stiffly. "Can you and Mollie step out for a minute?"

"Uh, yeah. Is everything okay?"

"No. It's definitely not okay."

Chapter 15

New Year's Eve
Tuesday, Day 196

Mollie

Jake and I have been on pins and needles for the past week, ever since Evan and Doris arrived at the end of our gift opening on Christmas. When they refused to come inside, I thought they were mad at us. While I was putting on my boots and coat, I racked my brain trying to figure out what the problem might be.

When we went out, they were sitting calmly on the porch bench. Doris stood up, bracing herself on her leg crutch and the wall of the house, pulling me into an awkward hug. "You look so good," she said. "Rosy cheeks and all."

"So, what's going on?" Jake asked.

"That's a good question. We're not entirely sure," Evan said quietly.

"Pull the other bench over so you can sit close to us," Doris said, easing herself back onto the bench. "We can keep it down that way."

"Or we could just go inside our house," Jake said.

"Nope. Public space, and I am not unarming," Evan responded.

Jake and I share a look, wondering how we should reply. We were saved from needing to say anything when Doris said, "Once the holidays are over, they'll schedule the community meetings to discuss this. But— " she paused and looked pointedly at Evan.

He heaved out a loud breath. "But I don't think it'll make a difference."

"But . . . but Judge Avery— " I sputtered.

"Wait a minute," Jake said, scooting the bench over.

Once Jake and I were seated, the four of us leaned our heads together. In a whisper, Evan said, "It's not his doing. He isn't any more in favor of this than we are. There's something more going on. Something we all feared might really be happening."

"The coup?" I asked quietly.

They both nodded. "And it might go deeper than any of us can possibly believe," Evan said.

Calley interrupts my memories of Christmas evening, asking, "Are you making any New Year's resolutions?"

She's sitting at the table, cutting an onion to add to tonight's supper. The other two from our kitchen crew are working on the outdoor fire, getting it ready so we can cook the cornbread. We're doing a somewhat traditional New Year's dinner of beans and greens along with cornbread. Not black-eyed peas, since most of us Northerners don't keep those in our food storage or grow them in our garden. The greens are home-canned beet greens from last year's sugar beet harvest and will have small bits of goose added to them along with sautéed onions. The beans have been simmering all day and smell delicious. I can barely wait for our evening meal. I stir the beans, then return to mixing up the cornbread.

"I hadn't planned on it," I say. "You?"

"Mmm. Maybe. Not really a resolution."

I wait for more. After a minute, she says, "I'm glad we're adding in the new stuff when we're doing our self-defense training. The children really like the different scenarios everyone is coming up with. Some of the ones Malcolm and Tony think of are really out there."

"You mean like what do we do if there's an alien invasion or zombie bigfoot?"

"Right! How'd he even come up with the zombie bigfoot idea?"

"From one of my books." I laugh. "*Zombie Bigfoot.* I brought it up with me if you want to read it."

"Has Malcolm read it?" she asks with dismay.

"I don't think so. He just likes the name of it and the cover."

"Anyway, I think they're really learning a lot. The blinking fast to say 'I have a plan' was smart of Tony to suggest."

"And three slow blinks for 'I understand' was good too. But," I say, shaking my head, "I think Alvin's right. We need to keep it simple. It might be getting to be too much."

"I think pulling your ear for fight was smart. That's not too much. I wish we would've had a signal when Morse was trying to kidnap us. Sarah and I were kind of at a loss trying to figure out what you and Katie were planning. Of course, as soon as you yelled *fire*, we knew to move. But maybe, if we had a code then, it might have helped. Maybe I could've done something quicker and kept Katie from getting shot."

I stop my mixing and turn to look at her. "You feel guilty for that? You know it wasn't your fault."

"Sure. I know, but sometimes . . ." She shrugs. "I just think it's good we're having this training. Doris thinks it smart too. But she agrees yelling fire is the best way to say *go now*."

"You told Doris?"

"She and Kelley came over as we were finishing the other day, the day you had greenhouse duty. Don't worry, we swore them to secrecy. She saw the TV show, too, so she knew exactly what we were doing. And she agrees, for the children, 'please don't hurt my family' is important and they'll know to get out of the way. Of course, Malcolm and Tony both say they'll fight. Marc chimed in saying he would too."

"Malcolm's already proven what he'll do," I say, remembering when Lydia was in the middle of her mental breakdown and was coming at me with a scalpel.

"So, about the resolutions," she says. "Mike and I have been talking. We've been thinking about a baby."

I close my eyes briefly. While it's totally reasonable to want to have children, even in the apocalypse, it still scares me. Everything went fine when Shelby Cameron had Hannah, and I'm in continual prayer Sarah will be okay, but it's an unknown and scary thing. Calley isn't very tall, at only five foot. What if her baby takes after Mike's six-foot-plus large frame? All of Mike's family is tall, even his mom and sister. It could be a big baby.

"Are you going to say anything, Mom?"

"I do love grandchildren," I say quietly. "And I trust you and Mike will know when the timing is right."

"So, you wouldn't be mad if we did?"

"Mad? No. Why would I be mad?"

"You know, with the end of the world and all."

"I guess, when you put it that way," I say with a small laugh, "having a baby does sound kind of silly."

"I'm serious, Mom."

"No, honey. I wouldn't be mad. I love you and only want the best for you."

"Mom."

"Mm-hmm?"

"Mom, you should look at me."

I stop midway through greasing one of the cornbread pans to look at her.

"We're not really talking about it. We're going to have a baby!"

"You're already— "

"Yes! I'm not supposed to be telling you yet, but I just can't help myself."

I quickly set down my bowl and move to her side, bending to hug her as she sits in the chair. "You're going to have a baby," I whisper, tears rolling down my face.

Calley and I spend many minutes hugging and laughing before returning to our preparation duties.

"Mike isn't going to be happy with me, so you can't tell him you know. He wanted to tell his family and you and Jake at the same time, but . . . " She finishes with a shrug.

My emotions are all over the place—happy for a new grandchild, but also scared for my daughter.

~~~~~

The community room at the ski lodge is abuzz with excitement. Instead of ringing in the new year at midnight, we're having a late afternoon party. Doris liberated the last of the hot chocolate, along with a few other treats that we're having before our meal. I catch pieces of conversations as I move through the room; more than one person is sure this year will be better than last year. In many ways, this isn't an extremely high bar. Last year, our world flipped upside down. First with the physical attacks resulting in thousands of deaths across the nation, followed by the cyberattacks taking out our phones and electricity, then with the EMP shutting things down for the foreseeable future.
~~~~~

Over the ham radio, we've heard some places, mainly coastal areas, weren't as severely affected by the EMP. Unfortunately, those areas were often targeted by nuclear ground detonations, so they're still suffering. We're hearing reports from various areas about warlords, cults, or both—often fighting against each other. Some of it is exceedingly frightening. Can our world return to some semblance of normal in the new year?

Really, though, none of that matters much. What we're concerned about is here—our mountain community and the river community of Bakerville. And we're concerned for our county and nearby towns, and the violent overthrow of Prospect's legitimate town government last summer as well as what may be happening in our little group. When Evan and Doris said they feared Deputy Fred's supposed coup may be a reality running deeper than we know, it reminded us just how perilous things are. And to find out people we thought were for the good of Bakerville may be playing both sides . . . I stifle a sigh.

Evan was able to see Barney Sanchez. He and Daniel are both confined to quarters while the committee decides the next steps. Barney insists he's completely innocent in the altercation. Daniel attacked him, asking why he did it, why Barney lied to Jesse Richardson about Daniel's wife. Barney isn't entirely sure what Daniel thinks he was lying about.

But Evan has an idea. Could Daniel's wife also have been accused of being involved with someone? I know I wasn't with Brad the day before Phoebe disappeared. And Doris believes Kimba wasn't with Mick either. And Daniel's wife . . . I don't know who she was accused of being with, but is that also a lie? If so, why? And what, if anything, does this have to do with Phoebe's disappearance and death?

There's one common denominator in each case: Jesse Richardson.

A couple days after their Christmas night visit, Evan and Doris returned. That time, they were willing to come inside. The children were up in the loft, and we sat in the kitchen talking. It originally started with discussing the situation with Barney and Daniel but soon turned to other things. We finally ended up grabbing a deck of Pinochle cards. It turned into a fun evening.

Neither Doris nor Evan directly said it, but Doris dropped several obvious hints that she, too, refuses to be in a situation where they can't readily defend themselves.

Fortunately for Evan and his entire security team, Clark Thomas went to Judge Avery and wants their right to open carry fully restored. He said the edict allows for the police force to carry, and if he must deputize the security team, he will.

Judge Avery agreed and added an addendum to the new rule—in the form of something resembling an executive order—that allows the security team to be always armed. Only the security team, not the militia since that would negate the order, considering about 90 percent of us are militia members in some fashion.

A disturbance across the community room captures my attention. Another fight? I pray that's not what is happening. Seconds later, Bill Shane calls for everyone's attention. "Folks, I hate to break up this party, but it seems— "

"My sister is missing!" a young woman standing next to Bill cries out. "I can't find her anywhere."

There's a rumble through the crowd.

"Okay, okay," Bill says. "We're going to divide up. We have less than an hour until sunset."

Bill, Evan, and Cole put search teams together. Angela and several others are put in charge of watching the children while we search. Clark Thomas walks with the sister out of the lodge, likely taking her to the small lean-to shed attached to the ski lodge that he and his team use as an office. Will Jesse Richardson interview her?

This time, I'm on a team going through the ski lodge. My group of three starts in the women's dorm, where we're told Amy—the missing girl—and her sister sleep. The correlation between murdered Phoebe Baker sleeping in the dorm and newly missing Amy also sleeping in the dorm isn't lost on me.

"Do you know her?" I ask one of the ladies searching with me.

"She and her sister are part of the Prospect group."

"She's a Vasquez? Or a Cameron?"

She shrugs. "I think they're just school friends of one of the Cameron boys."

After checking every possible place in the women's dorm, we move onto the men's dorm and then continue to work our way through every space in the building. It's full dark by the time we've finished. Other searchers are making their way back to the lodge. Our New Year's Eve party won't be happening, unless someone has found Amy and she's fine, but people will still need to eat.

I move to the kitchen, where a couple people have already started putting things together for serving. We set everything up, and the children start moving through the line.

It's several hours before all the search teams return. There's no sign of Amy anywhere. The search will continue tomorrow morning at daylight. David Hammer and Chaplain Rick lead a quick prayer service while everyone finishes eating. *Please, Lord, please let us find her.*

Chapter 16

New Year's Day
Wednesday, Day 197

Jake

The sun has yet to crest the horizon as we start the search. After a night of heavy snow, it's cold. The analog thermometers scattered along the various ski lodge buildings, leftover from when this was an operating ski resort, vary between negative four and zero. The snow started to fall as we wrapped up yesterday, resulting in a good four inches overnight. It's still lightly snowing, but at least the sun is shining.

My group of ten, which includes my son-in-law Leo as our medic and militia leader Cole Gunderson, is heading up the face of the mountain. I'm part of this group because of my familiarity with the mountain. The last time I was on this slope I was on skis, heading back down after a leisurely ride on the triple chair all the way to the top. Malcolm was on the ski club, and he'd just learned to ski one of the black diamond runs; he wanted to teach me. He was great at giving me tips and pointing out obstacles, but I still fell many times.

Walking up isn't much easier than skiing down. We're spread out, fanning the area to look behind every tree and indention. We're avoiding the open expanses—what used to be the ski runs—since we'll be able to see between them but also because the snow isn't as stable there. The wide-open swath, great for skiing when properly groomed and tended, hasn't been maintained. Instead of walking on this unstable area, we're choosing to look for anything out of the ordinary from either side. Unfortunately, at these temperatures, we have little hope of this being a rescue mission.

"Tell me why we have to climb this hill?" Jackson Nicholson loudly asks for the umpteenth time. While it seems he's yelling—and he is—with the distance between us, we have to shout to be heard. Several people on the team are farther away, and I can't hear them at all, resulting in a game of grapevine to communicate. Unfortunately, Jackson is within shouting distance, so I hear most of what he says.

"Mainly so we can hear you complain," Cole answers. I can't help but snicker.

"I think we all know she isn't up here," Jackson persists. "She'd have to be nuts to walk up this mountain. How much farther are we going to go?"

"Hey, buddy," the searcher to my right says, "we've already been told. We're filling in the space between the top ski lift shacks." He told me his name before we started off, but I sure can't remember it now. Even in a small community, it's hard to keep everyone straight.

"What'd he say?" Nicholson asks.

"He said we're filling in the space between the top watch towers," Cole relays.

"I still think— "

"We all know what you think, Nicholson," Cole snaps. "Now button it before you bring an avalanche down on us."

I consider pointing out yelling doesn't change the pressure on the snow, so that's not likely to cause an avalanche, but I don't want to hear him either. Jackson Nicholson is a piece of work. He used to be on the same militia team as Mollie, and when they were responding to a hostage situation at the Baker ranch a few months ago, he tripped my wife—purposely and with intent. As I remember the incident, I clench my hands. What kind of lowlife purposely trips another person? A woman, at that—my wife!

When I heard about it from Evan and Bill, they prohibited me from confronting him. They assured me he'd be dealt with. Personally, I don't think it was dealt with. He was booted from the militia, but that was all. He needed the tar beat out of him. And I should've been the one to do it.

I give him a sideward glance; he's muttering as he makes his way up the hill. He's also strayed from the edge of the tree line toward the middle. While yelling might not cause the snow to give way, stomping through the open expanse could displace the snow slab.

"Jackson! You need to move back toward the trees and out of the ski run."

He gives me a look followed by an obscene gesture.

"Seriously," I say. "After last night's snowfall, the mountain might be unstable. You can see at least one old avalanche track." I motion to where a slide has occurred sometime in the recent past.

"Mind your own business," Jackson yells.

"This *is* his business," Cole says. "If you trigger an avalanche, we'd have to rescue your worthless— "

"Whatever, dude." Jackson purposely changes his stride to look like a ballerina on snowshoes and angles out of the center of the run more toward the edge. I shake my head, wondering why this guy was even put on our team.

The sun, shining so bright it's almost blinding, has reached its zenith when we finally arrive at the top. I remove my sunglasses and wipe the sweat from my face, then take off my wool cap, running my fingers through my damp hair. It's warmed up considerably, but with stopping our movement and the slight breeze rustling my wet hair, a shiver runs through my body.

"Told you this would be a waste of time," Jackson says.

"Now what?" the guy next to me asks. "Can we walk back down under the ski lift? It'd be easier with the snowmobile tracks in place."

"Nope," Cole says. "Same thing going back down. We might have missed something, and downhill will give us a different angle. Let's take a thirty-minute break. Eat your food and drink some water, then we'll get started." A huge gust stirs up the snow, blowing it into Cole's face. He grumbles somewhat good naturedly before wiping the snow from his goggles.

"It's going to be dark before we get back," Jackson whines.

"Going down will take less time and be easier," I say. "You've already put foot holes in place and won't have to stomp your steps in."

"I don't need a break," he snaps. "See you losers at the bottom."

He takes off, using his snowshoes and poles more like skis as he practically runs down the slope. He doesn't even bother to act like he's looking for the missing girl, just on a mission to reach the bottom as quickly as possible.

"Slow down," someone yells. Jackson spins around to deliver his favorite hand signal when there's a rumble and the snow blows up around him. With the explosion of snow, I can't see anything. Then I catch a glimpse of his red coat as he's being swept down the mountain on the wave of snow.

"He did it. That bonehead did it," Cole says, shaking his head in disbelief.

"As soon as it stabilizes, we can go after him," Leo says, putting his goggles back into place.

One guy, too far from me to hear clearly, yells something about his family.

"There's a flat area between here and there," Leo says. "It should stop before making it anywhere near the bottom." He must have asked if the avalanche will hit the lodge. Like Leo, I believe it'll stop well before then. We're quite a long way up the mountainside at the top of the ski area.

"Stay along the edge," Leo says. "Use your tracks to go back down. He's between Cole and me. We'll watch for any sign of him. When we see him, we'll have you move toward us."

"You done anything like this before?" Cole asks.

"Nope. I went to a mountain rescue seminar once. That's the extent of my knowledge," Leo answers. "Jake?"

I shake my head. "I went to a search and rescue meeting at a sporting goods store in Cody once."

"Great," the guy worried about his family says. "So you guys don't really know anything?"

"Just do it," Cole says. "Let's move."

While we move down the hill with more care than Jackson, we're still quick, knowing his life depends on us reaching him. My mouth is like sawdust and my vision narrows; I'm immediately stressed and focused on what's happening. The cold air makes it hard to breathe. Even though I don't think much of Jackson Nicholson, I certainly wouldn't wish for him to be swept away like that.

"Do you see him?" Cole hollers out.

"Not yet!" Leo answers.

I'm somewhat higher and approaching a slight knob when I catch movement out of the corner of my eye. I train my vision on the spot.

"There!" I yell. "Leo, you've gone past him! Cole, at your two o'clock."

"I see him," the guy next to me yells.

I attempt to double time to the spot but manage to trip and slide on my bottom, bringing snow with me. Thankfully, I'm in an area of powder, which doesn't set off a second avalanche. What were we thinking coming up here like this? I hate to admit Jackson was right;

it'd be very unlikely to find the missing girl up here, and we may have lost him in the process.

Leo, like me, has a small garden trowel, and Cole has a decent folding shovel. They start to dig, and when the others reach them, they use whatever is available to dig, too, including their own snowshoes.

"Is he there?" I ask as I reach the group.

"You saw his glove," Cole says. "It was lying on top of the snow, but Erik got ahold of something."

Leo chucks his trowel aside and starts pawing at the snow like a dog unearthing a bone. "Here! I feel something," he says.

"Keep going," Cole yells. "Uncover his nose and mouth. The rest of you, work on his body."

"He's facedown," Leo says. "We've got to get him out!"

"I've got his arm uncovered," someone says.

I'm at one of his legs; I keep digging.

"Let's go, let's go," Cole encourages us. "Get him out of the snow so he can breathe!"

I keep working on his legs while Erik, the one who was beside me on our trek, helps Cole remove the snow from Jackson's torso.

"It's clear!" Cole yells after a few minutes. "Can we roll him over?"

"Not yet," Leo says. "He's still covered by too much. Keep digging." It feels like forever but is likely only minutes until we are moving him out of his snowy coffin to a semi-flat area.

"Go for help," Cole says to the two youngest guys on the search team, while Leo quickly checks for vitals.

"Bring back the stretcher and the trailer," Leo yells after them.

"Anything?" Cole asks.

"Nothing," Leo answers. "Starting CPR."

Cole moves into place for rescue breathing, while Leo begins chest compressions. When Leo yells thirty, Cole gives two breaths.

"Jake, cover his lower half," Cole says. "Let's try and warm him up."

"That won't matter if we don't get his heart beating again," Leo says. After several minutes, he says, "I'm about spent. Who can take over?"

"I'll do it," I say, moving into position across from Leo. When he finishes his count and Cole gives his breaths, Leo quickly checks for a pulse and then I take over.

"Two-inch compressions," Leo reminds me.

I have a little hope when Cole gives a breath and there seems to be a response. I look to him to ask, but he shakes his head and says, "Keep going."

It doesn't take long before my arms ache. Erik takes over compressions just as the sound of an engine reaches my ears.

"Take over breathing," Cole tells me. Erik and I continue CPR as the snowmobile makes its way toward us. It stops on the edge of the trees and the two riders jump off. One stops to grab something out of the back as the other heads straight for us. As he gets closer, even bundled head to toe in full winter gear, I can tell it's Evan.

"Report," he barks.

"He was buried for about fifteen minutes," Leo says. *Fifteen minutes?* I had no idea he was under the snow for so long. Erik yells out thirty, and I give my two breaths.

"Let me in here," Belinda, the other rider on the snowmobile, says.

I slide back to give her room, while Erik stops compressions and leans back on his bottom.

Belinda does a few things before saying, "Resume CPR."

Erik restarts compressions.

"Jake, I'm going to take over for you," Belinda says. "I'll use my bag valve mask. Maybe . . . " She shakes her head.

"I thought maybe he was coming around," I say. "When Cole gave a breath, it seemed . . . " I shrug.

Leo's near my side and says, "It's like that, Jake. When Cole gave him a breath, it made his chest rise. It can seem like it's working, but . . . " He shakes his head, just like Belinda did.

They continue for several minutes with Leo taking over chest compressions for Erik as he tires. I start to wonder if I'm still needed or if I should begin walking back down the hill when Belinda says, "That's it. We're not bringing him back."

Chapter 17

New Year's Day
Wednesday, Day 197

Mollie

I'm on cleanup duty after lunch. This morning, my search team went through every nook and cranny of the ski lodge again and then started on the lodge's outbuildings, searching for Amy. We didn't find her or any clues as to where she might be. As people came in for lunch, their reports were the same.

About ten minutes ago, two people came awkwardly running down the ski slope as fast as their snowshoes would carry them. I recognize one guy in orange goggles as part of Jake's search team. A few minutes later, a snowmobile and trailer took off. I can only assume Amy was found. I pray she was able to find someplace warm to spend the night. We had a lot of snow overnight and low temps. Hopefully, she was dressed for the weather. I flashback to Phoebe in her blue jeans with a bare foot.

Emily, Amy's sister, was sitting in the eating area of the lodge when she saw the men come running down the hill. She wasted no time racing out to them. I'm wiping off the tables when she comes back inside. She flounces down on a chair and lets out a large sigh.

"They won't tell me anything," she blurts out, "but it doesn't sound like they found her. From the little I was able to pick up—" She sighs again and continues, "I think someone fell down the hill or something."

"Who fell?" I ask, instantly concerned about Jake.

"Don't know. Dr. Belinda wouldn't tell me anything, just said it wasn't about Amy."

I chew on my lip. "But they said someone fell?"

"That's what it sounded like. They took the stretcher too. Maybe it's a broken leg or something?"

Please, Lord. Please let Jake be okay. I instantly realize the selfishness of my silent prayer and quickly amend it to *please let all of the searchers be okay*. A laugh almost escapes me. God knows my true heart. He knows I already thought of Jake first. Jake's a part of me; my prayer for him may be selfish, but it is genuine.

"Do you think they'll find her?" Emily asks. "I mean, they won't just give up, right? I heard about the pregnant lady whose husband and father-in-law went missing. They just gave up, didn't bother to make sure they found them."

I move over to where she's sitting. "Do you mind if I join you?"

"I'd like the company," she answers quickly. "I feel like I'm all alone. My few friends are out with the searchers. I wanted to search, too, but Dr. Kelley said I should stay inside. I'm too emotional, I guess."

"I can understand that," I say. "It's hard not knowing."

"So will they leave me hanging like the other lady?"

"That's my daughter," I say softly. "My daughter Sarah's husband and father-in-law are the ones who went missing."

Her eyes go wide and her mouth forms an *O*, then she drops her head and starts crying. After a few minutes, she says, "I'm so sorry. I didn't know."

"With over 250 of us living here, it's hard to know who's who."

"I don't know your name."

"Mollie Caldwell. My daughter is Sarah Garrett."

"Your daughter, she's friends with Shelby. Shelby and I were at the Cameron ranch together. I just—I feel like such a fool. I'm so sorry if I caused you any extra pain."

My heart almost melts at the concern this young lady is showing during her time of worry. "You didn't cause me any extra pain. It is hard not knowing what happened to Tate and Keith. Even though we know they're likely— " My voice catches as I choke back a sob. "We still have a small hope they're holed up somewhere for winter. We have plans to search again in the spring."

"I guess hope is good," Emily says. "Phoebe Baker, her family knows she's dead. It's hard knowing someone you love is dead."

"It is," I agree. "But as believers, we do have the knowledge we'll see them again."

"Yes." She nods. "Our parents were killed, Amy's and mine. We watched it happen."

"I'm so sorry."

"We were in Prospect when Richard Majors killed the mayor and took over the town. They died that night. We went to Dax's place, thinking we'd be safe. We weren't safe. They attacked us, so then we escaped to Bakerville. And now, here we are. And Amy still wasn't safe." She dissolves into tears again. I sit with her, holding her hand while she cries.

We've been sitting for many minutes, alternating between talking and her tears, when I catch movement on the ski slope. I'm distracted, watching to see what's happening, when the door opens with a bang, causing both of us to jump.

"Oh!" Emily says.

I turn to see Clark Thomas and Kelley Hudson entering the ski lodge. From the looks on their faces, this won't be good news.

"Emily," Clark says.

"Um, excuse me," I interrupt, sliding my chair back to stand.

Emily pulls on my hand. "Stay?"

I look to Kelley, who gives me a slight nod.

"Do you mind if we sit?" Kelley asks.

"You found her?" Emily asks before they're situated.

Kelley puts a hand on Clark's arm, waiting to speak until she's settled. "Amy was found," she says gently. "I'm so sorry, but there was nothing we could do for her."

Emily nods several times, then says, "You found her, though, so we know for sure. She's— " Then she starts to cry again.

The noise of a snowmobile coming off the ski slope catches my attention.

"Mollie, can you sit with Emily?" Kelley asks. "I want to make sure I'm not needed."

"Do you know— "

"I wasn't there but was told it was an emergency of some sort."

"Jake was with the team going up the ski slope," I say.

Kelley nods. "I'll let you know. Emily, I'll be back shortly."

Clark stays with us. I hold Emily while she cries. After a few minutes, Shelby comes into the ski lodge.

"Emily, Shelby is here," I say softly. "I'm going to move out of the way so she can sit by you."

"Th-thank you for being with me, Mrs. Caldwell."

"I'm very sorry for your loss," I say, trying to keep my own tears at bay.

Shelby embraces Emily, who starts crying again. Clark mumbles his condolences and moves away when I do.

I need to return to wiping things down so we're ready for tonight. Did the people working in the small kitchen already finish? I didn't hear them leave the lodge. I debate between going in and checking out their status and going outside to find out who was hurt—to make sure Jake's okay. I look up the ski slope and see several people walking down. I squint so I can examine each one individually. I can't help but smile when I make out Jake's form with Leo walking next to him.

I quickly go to the kitchen to find the room empty. All tables and counters have been wiped down, and everything looks as it should. I'm surprised I was so oblivious to what was going on around me while talking with Emily. I don't usually experience such tunnel vision.

Slipping into my jacket, I go to the deck to await Jake's arrival. The sun, just beginning its descent, is warm and welcoming. I'm always amazed at how pleasant winter can be. Belinda and Kelley want me to sit outside in the sunshine every day, preferably with as much skin exposed as possible. I remove my jacket and roll up my shirt sleeves. I debate rolling up my pant legs, but the long underwear is unlikely to go up enough to make a difference.

When Jake is closer, I give him a small wave. He lifts his hand in acknowledgment, altering his trajectory toward me. I slide my sleeves down and slip back into my jacket before stepping off the deck.

"Hey, I heard— " My words are cut off as he pulls me into a bear hug. I feel his body shudder. "Jake?"

"In a minute," he whispers. It's many minutes before he tells me about Jackson being caught in the avalanche. He chokes up again when he talks about giving CPR and thinking it was working. "I didn't even like the guy, but I didn't want him dead. It was . . . it was awful."

Chapter 18

Thursday, Day 198

Jake

I squeeze Mollie's hand as we walk along the road. We watch our steps, avoiding the shiny spots in the packed snow. Falling would not be good. After a night of restless sleep, focusing on my steps is almost too much for my exhausted mind. Each time I'd try to close my eyes, Jackson's death replayed like a movie. At last night's supper, an announcement was made to show up an hour early for supper tonight for Jackson's and Amy's memorial. Even though Mollie and I were not friends with Jackson, and we didn't know Amy at all, we'll attend.

As of yet, the cause of Amy's death hasn't been revealed. Jesse announced the death was suspicious and is being investigated. Like Phoebe, she was found in the snow not far from where the county road ends, about a quarter of a mile past the driveways to the ski lodge and the dude ranch. Someone asked if it could've been a bear or wolf; Jesse was adamant we were not looking for an animal as the culprit. He didn't come right out and say she was murdered—or that Phoebe was murdered—but it's widely believed to be the case. There's a murderer among us.

Everything is such a mess right now. And, somehow, the argument between Barney and Daniel seems related. As we were leaving the evening meal last night, Jesse said he wanted to question Mollie. She smiled and, as Evan suggested, said she'd be happy to talk with him if Judge Avery was present. He tried to brush it off as unnecessary, saying, "There's another rumor about you and Brad. I'm sure you can put it to rest by answering a few questions."

"Not happening, Jesse," I said. "If you want to talk to Mollie, Judge Avery will be there and so will I."

Jesse gave me a hard look and said, "It's not like you to be argumentative. Makes me wonder if you have something to hide."

I returned his hard look with one of my own. "You can wonder what you want. Set up an appointment with the judge and you can talk to her. Until then— " I made a shooing motion with my hand " —leave her alone."

This morning at breakfast, the judge searched us out and asked us to drop by his place before lunch, which is where we're now headed.

"I just don't understand why Jesse's singling me out like this," Mollie says. I've lost track of how many times she's said something similar since last night—really, since he questioned her after Phoebe's death. I wonder the same thing. Why Mollie? Why Kimba? And what about Daniel's wife?

"Maybe we'll have answers today," I say, trying to be encouraging. I don't feel encouraged, though. I'm stressed. Stressed, exhausted, and discouraged. I'm not the only one.

There's a despondency over the entire mountain community. It's been there for weeks, probably starting around the time Dr. Sam and Phoebe died, but it's increased in severity with the firearm restrictions and the division that has caused. Last night and this morning, almost everyone appears to be in a fog. Two more deaths. Jackson's was an accident, but Amy's being suspicious has everyone even more on edge.

And now Mollie's being asked about her involvement with Brad, this time after Amy disappeared. Is Kimba also being questioned about being with Mick? How it all ties together is beyond me. And to be quite honest, I don't like Mollie being dragged into this. Keeping my cool over her involvement hasn't been easy. I'd like to give Jesse Richardson a piece of my mind.

"What's going on over there?" Mollie asks, gesturing toward a couple standing near the livestock shed.

"Looks like Dot and her husband are having an argument," I say.

"No kidding, Jake. I can see that," she snaps, jutting her chin in their direction.

I watch as Heath puts his finger up by Dot's nose, pointing it rapidly to punctuate whatever it is he's saying to her. She bats his finger away, but he grabs her by the collar. Mollie sucks in a breath. Heath utters several profanities and begins shaking Dot.

"Great," I mutter under my breath, as Mollie veers in their direction. I look around for Clark or one of his deputies, seeing no one. I take a deep breath. Shaking my head, I loudly say, "Hey, Heath. Hey, Dot. You two doing okay?"

Heath stops shaking her, rapidly putting his hands to his side and then into the pockets of his jacket. Dot quickly looks down and tries to discreetly wipe her eyes.

"We're okay, Jake," she says shakily.

"Nothing's happening here," Heath says.

"Just making sure," I say evenly.

Heath turns to me with fire in his eyes. "You ought to learn to mind your own business."

Mollie starts to say something, but I touch her arm. "No problem, Heath." I try to keep my voice light.

He turns back to Dot. "Is he the one?"

"What?" Dot asks, shock in her voice. "No! I told you, I would never— "

Quick as a flash, his hand smacks her across the cheek. She lets out a shriek as he grabs her by the hair with his left hand. I step in, grabbing his wrist and twisting his arm behind his back, then sweeping his legs out from under him while taking him to the ground. I hold him in a combination armbar and bear hug.

"Don't hurt him!" Dot cries. "He didn't mean to do it."

"Jake?" Mollie says in a wavering voice as she goes to Dot, putting an arm around her and practically dragging her away. Dot collapses into Mollie's embrace.

"He's okay," I say over the sound of my insanely loud heartbeat and Heath's crude protests. I take a deep breath, keeping pressure on the arm of the squirming man as he lets out a whimper.

"What's going on?" Art asks, stepping out of the livestock shed.

"He attacked me!" Heath screeches.

"That's a lie!" Mollie yells. "Heath hit his wife. Jake stepped in and stopped him."

"Go get Clark or one of his men," I say in a ragged breath.

"No need. He's on his way." Art gestures toward Clark, who's attempting to run up the long, snow-packed driveway from the ski lodge parking lot. There are at least a dozen people standing around, gawking and pointing. I take another breath, trying to calm my heart rate.

"Jake?" Clark says, standing back about thirty feet, hand on his service weapon. "What's going on?"

"He attacked me!" Heath yells again.

"Jake, I want you to slowly release him. Heath, you stay right where you are. Both of you keep your hands where I can see them as you separate."

I remove my hands from Heath, keeping them visible, as I put my feet under me and slowly take a duckwalk step backwards.

Heath starts to scramble when Clark says, "Easy now."

"You keep him away from me! He's a menace, attacking me like that."

Clark walks to Dot as she continues to cower in Mollie's arms. "Is that what happened, Dot?"

She responds by biting her lip and giving a slight shake of her head.

"Dot," Heath says, a warning in his voice.

"Let me see your face," Clark says softly. Dot turns her head slightly, hiding the side where he hit her. "I told you before, if he's hitting you, we have options."

"What options?" she asks, her voice barely a whisper.

Has Dot been hit before? Even though she and I were on the same militia unit when we were living in Bakerville proper, I don't really know her. But now that I think back, there were times she'd show up for training with bruises—after our three days off. She'd always have some good reason for the marks. Was he hitting her then?

"Hey!" Heath says, getting to his feet. "Whatever happens between my wife and me is none of your business."

Clark spins and quickly steps toward him, causing Heath to stumble backwards. His fall is caught by the wall of the livestock shed. "I'm making it my business. I've had trouble with you for the last time."

Heath gathers his footing and says, "I want to press charges against Jake Caldwell. He's attacked me for no reason."

"Not true," a small voice says from the edge of the crowd. A woman around Sarah's age steps forward. Her name escapes me, but she was with Mollie and Angela when Phoebe's body was discovered.

"I heard him yelling at his wife and saw him hit her," she says quietly.

Clark nods and tells her to wait a minute. "Okay, folks," Clark says loudly to the gathering crowd. "Show's over. If you witnessed the actual altercation, step forward. Otherwise, let's break it up. We all have things to do." He eyes the group. When few people move, he makes a shooing motion with his hands. "Unless you have something to tell me, go on." As the mass disperses, he turns back to us.

"Sorry I can't help you, Jake. I came out when that ninny" —Art points to Heath— "started screaming like a little girl."

Heath gives him the evil eye, which Art returns with a sloppy salute. I barely stifle a chuckle.

"Hey, Art," I say. "We're supposed to have a meeting with Judge Avery. Any chance you can run over to his place and let him know we're going to be late? Tell him we'll stop by and reschedule."

"Sure thing, Jake. He's parked next to the supply garage, right?"

I give a nod in response. Before he takes off, he gives Heath another look and a shake of his head.

"Remind me of your name," Clark says to the quiet woman.

I strain to hear her response. "Annette . . . " Her last name is lost in the breeze.

"All right. Let's all head over to my office," Clark says. "Heath, Jake, you're both on your best behavior, agreed?"

Heath grumbles a response. I give a nod. Like I'm going to start anything? I wouldn't be involved if it weren't apparent the argument was escalating into something more when he held her by the collar and started shaking her. And when he smacked her . . . that's not okay.

Clark's office is nothing more than a long, skinny lean-to storage shed attached to the basement section of the ski lodge. Outfitted with a folding card table as a desk and several folding chairs for seating, its accommodations are rather sparse. One end of the space has two small rooms: jail cells. Having our police force's office attached to the ski lodge is smart. The main level of the ski lodge, where we have our meals and meetings, is where most of the action is. The militia headquarters is in a freestanding shed nearby, also a useful location.

"Normally, if I suspected an abuse situation," Clark says, eyeballing Heath, "I'd have the couple separated. Dot, we've been through this before." He lets the statement hang in the air as Dot drops her head. "So let's hear it. Annette, what did you see?"

Her story is the same as what Mollie and I saw; Heath and Dot were arguing, then Heath grabbed her and started the shaking. Annette was going to help when she saw me step in. After she finishes, Mollie shares her story and then I share mine. Before questioning Dot and Heath, Clark tells us we can go.

Outside, in the crisp late-morning air, I turn to Annette. "Thanks for your help."

She leans in and says, "I'm glad you stopped him from hurting her. I've seen them arguing before. Maybe Clark can do something to help her."

"Maybe," I say while Mollie nods. We say our goodbyes, as Mollie and I begin the short walk to the judge's place.

"Are you feeling okay?" I ask.

"Me? You're the one who just got into a fight."

"I wasn't fighting— "

"I know. I should've phrased it differently." She grabs my arm and stops walking, forcing me to look at her. "Are you okay, Jake?"

I let out a long breath. "I'm okay. I'll admit, I wanted to punch his lights out. Taking him to the ground wasn't nearly as satisfying."

"Believe me, I know. I wanted to punch his lights out too."

"You ready for this?" I ask, motioning to the judge's camp trailer. He's one of many who brought up their own trailer, a small fifth wheel.

"Ready as I'll ever be," she says. "Let's just get it over with."

We quickly finish the rest of the walk. I knock on the door, which is promptly answered by Jesse Richardson.

"Sorry we're late," I say. "Do you want to reschedule?"

"No need," Jesse says, his demeanor calm and welcoming. "C'mon in and we'll try to make this quick."

The judge, sitting at the small dining table, invites us to have a seat on the sofa. Jesse pulls out a folding chair, putting it across from us. He takes his time adjusting and making himself comfortable before pulling a small notebook out of his pocket. The whole Columbo routine is slightly annoying.

"Before we start," Jesse says, "I understand your desire to have an impartial witness. Judge Avery is well respected, and we all know he can be trusted. I just think you're making a bigger deal out of this than needed."

Mollie smiles and says, "Maybe so, but this is how it's going to be. Anytime you want to talk with me, I want both Judge Avery and Jake present."

"Fair enough. So where were you on New Year's Eve around three o'clock?"

"At 1500? It was my kitchen day. I was in the kitchen."

"At the dude ranch lodge?"

"Yes, that's right."

"Who was working with you?"

"Calley. She and I were getting things ready. Pamela Cameron and one of the Vasquez ladies were also on duty. They were getting the fire ready to cook the cornbread."

"I do like the bread cooked over the fire," Judge Avery says. "The way you all use the Dutch ovens to make bread and rolls is amazing. The flatbread is okay, too, but the fire cooked is best."

Mollie nods. "Cooking in the fire is a lot of work. I'm only allowed to work in the kitchen right now."

"I heard you've been sick," Jesse says.

I narrow my eyes at him. Somehow, him saying my wife has been sick doesn't sit right with me. She was—and maybe still is—but I don't like him knowing about it.

Mollie shrugs. "Do you have any more questions?"

"Did you see Brad Quinton that day?"

"You know, you can just use his first name. As far as I know, he's the only Brad living on the mountain."

"Did you see Brad that day?"

"Not during the day. He was at the party. I saw him talking with Sarah before we broke up to try and find Emily's sister."

"So if I told you someone saw Brad coming out of the lodge around three in the afternoon . . . " He lets the statement hang. After several beats, he says, "Mollie?"

"Was that a question?"

He gives a humorless smile. "Yes, it was a question. Was he leaving the lodge around three?"

"The dude ranch lodge? Not that I know of. But you do realize people use the showers on the main floor anytime they wish? While some people knock and we let them in, not everyone does."

"You're saying he was at the lodge and using the shower?"

"I'm saying I have no idea."

Jesse nods several times, then writes something in his little notebook. "Okay, that's it for today."

"Don't forget," I say as we stand to leave, "if you want to talk with my wife again, it's with the judge and me in attendance."

"Unless Mollie decides otherwise," Jesse says with a smile.

"I won't," Mollie says firmly as she opens the door of the trailer.

Chapter 19

Friday, Day 199

Mollie

"All right, folks," Judge Avery says, trying to bring the somewhat rowdy crowd to order. Our usual dining space has been rearranged with the council at the front, sitting behind tables. The rest of us are in chairs, auditorium style. The meeting was scheduled to start at 1400; it's now 1430 and has yet to begin. Jon Dawson was late, having just arrived a few minutes ago.

When he, his wife, and two teenage sons finally turned up, they all looked awful. Jon's wife, always well put together, looks completely frazzled with red eyes and a puffy face. She chews on her upper lip as she finds her seat. His teenage sons, usually immensely helpful and polite, have scowls on their faces as they stare straight ahead and plop into their chairs, arms crossed.

And Dawson—oh my! He is a disheveled mess. His hair, normally in a well-organized combover, is stringy and hanging at awkward angles. Frequently resembling a politician on the campaign trail, shaking hands and working the room, he barely makes eye contact with anyone as he takes his seat at the council table.

I glance around, locating each of my adult children. Even though Malcolm and Tony both felt they should be included in these proceedings, Dodie is watching all the youngsters. Sarah and Katie are sitting in the same aisle as Jake and me. Angela and Tim are in the row in front of us, with Mike and Calley next to them. Leo is the only one unaccounted for because he had an extra duty shift. We suspect it's somehow related to this meeting. Since Phoebe's death, Jake and I have been extra diligent with knowing where each child is—young or old. And now, after Amy's death, fear for their safety is even more real.

This morning when we arrived for breakfast, Clark Thomas was at one door and a deputy was at each additional door. They were sending out the no-firearms-at-the-meeting reminder. Like we'd forget? We aren't allowed to carry our firearms anywhere. Why would the meeting be any different?

I guess I can see Clark's point of reminding. While the no firearms in public places rule has been in effect since before Christmas, there have been many times it's ignored, either accidentally or on purpose. Often, someone will come straight from guard duty to a meal. When on duty, we're required to carry our sidearms and rifles. And everyone is used to heading straight to their meal as opposed to going home. Those of us that live at the dude ranch have over a mile walk to get there and back. And those living in the ski lodge aren't even allowed to carry their weapons in public spaces, which really makes no sense considering some of the apartments are off the dining area.

All of it was quickly becoming unrealistic. Out of necessity, Clark set up a weapons storage area where the old ticket office was. Now, rifles and handguns are locked in there during meals and then returned to us afterward. Those living at the ski lodge leave them locked up until they are needed. Today, there were still a few people arriving directly from watch; all of them dutifully went to the locked room to stash their weapons.

Clark and his team were there again as we returned for the meeting, even having us lift our jackets to confirm we weren't carrying. At least we weren't patted down. I must admit, I started to get a little nervous when I saw what they were doing. While I'm being quiet about it, rules or no rules, I'm still protecting myself. My girls and I came too close to being killed to make the mistake of not being prepared.

"Okay, since we're late, we'll need to move this along," Judge Avery says. "As a reminder, this is the first of three meetings to discuss the new rules requiring no firearms in public places. At today's meeting, you'll hear from your councilmembers on why this rule was passed. You'll also learn how each member originally voted. But they won't tell you how they would vote today if this same issue came up. You are observers only and will not be permitted to ask questions or make comments.

"At the next meeting, which we'll hold on Monday and will start precisely at 1400— " Judge Avery gives Dawson a pointed look. Jon Dawson is writing something and doesn't even look up. The judge shakes his head and continues. "At that meeting, you can ask questions and bring up concerns in an orderly fashion. Let's get started." There's rustling while everyone adjusts into position. "Councilmember Evan Snyder was not at the meeting that passed this decree— "

"Excuse me, Judge," Jon Dawson says. "I must insist you call this a law. It was dutifully brought forth by the council and voted into law that firearms are prohibited from all public places in Bakerville."

"No," Evan says. "You are not correct."

"You weren't even there," Dawson says adamantly.

"Right. This was brought up when I was gone. But what is not correct is this is not a Bakerville decree." Evan looks at him pointedly, daring him to disagree. "This only affects the mountain."

"Not true!" Dawson yells. "They chose to stay behind, knowing full well our legal government was moving up here."

"True, but two of our councilmembers also stayed behind."

"Their choice," Dawson huffs. "Not my fault they didn't know what was good for them."

"You may remember, Jon, we added an addendum to our bylaws," Evan says calmly. "Our original bylaws specify we must have seven in attendance for a quorum, right?"

"Listen, Snyder," Dawson says, pointing at Evan. "We had a quorum, and the law is valid."

Evan straightens his shoulders. "Yes, you did. But under the old bylaws, you wouldn't have had a quorum."

"Doesn't matter. As you said, we added an addendum."

"Do you remember the details of the addendum?"

Dawson gives him a hard look. "Judge? What's he getting at? Is he trying to say our vote was invalid? Because he's wrong."

"No," Judge Avery says, pushing his glasses up his nose. "I think he's pointing out it's only valid on the mountain. Councilmember Harper made a point of having us clarify, within the addendum, the quorum and any new decrees brought forth are only valid for the time we're separated. Any decrees made while we're separated must be addressed again when we reunite."

"Fine, whatever," Dawson says. "Notwithstanding, this law is valid while we are on the mountain."

"As of today, this is true," Judge Avery says. "Evan, did you have anything else?"

"No, sir."

Judge Avery nods. "Councilmember Snyder is here as an observer only since he was not part of the quorum passing this decree." Dawson narrows his eyes at the judge. "There has also been a rumor going around that Evan Snyder will be able to vote at the third meeting. The bylaws specifically state only those who were present for the original vote will be allowed to vote on any challenges."

There are many shouts of anger over this ruling. I close my eyes and shake my head. I'd already heard about this part of the bylaws. I don't agree with it but know we'll follow it.

"Now, we'll start with Jana—oh, and one more thing, councilmembers," Judge Avery says, giving them hard looks. "There will be no speaking out of turn. I will call on you. You will share your thoughts that led you on your vote. There will be no discussion amongst yourselves." He then addresses the crowd. "And remember, no questions or discussions from the audience. Observe and take notes only. You'll have your chance in a few days."

Each of the councilmembers try to maintain a detached demeanor, relaying only the facts of their vote and keeping the emotion minimal—until it's Jon Dawson's turn. He's full of passion, sharing how gun control laws should've been enacted long ago.

"If Wyoming had a red flag law in place," Dawson says, "Daniel wouldn't even be able to possess a firearm. His wife would've turned him in long ago. He gets crazy jealous, as evidenced by— "

"Excuse me!" Clark Thomas shouts. "Bringing this up, since it is part of an open investigation, is not appropriate."

"I have to agree," Jesse Richardson says, standing.

"Sorry," Dawson says. "I'll retract the statement."

"Thanks a lot," Clark responds, voice dripping with disgust.

Dawson goes back to his tirade on gun control. I'm glad this guy never had a chance to be voted into public office. With the damage he's done in our small community, I can't imagine what he would've done to our county in the position of county commissioner, the office he was running for when the attacks started. His arguments aren't even very cohesive as he jumps from thought to thought. At one point, Dawson even confuses himself.

Jake and I share a look and a head shake. What is going on with Jon Dawson today? Usually, he's organized and put together. He's such a mess, I almost feel sorry for him. I search out his wife and sons in the crowd. She has her hand on her forehead. Both boys are looking at the floor. What is wrong with this poor family? Is this a situation like Dot seems to be facing with Heath? Is Dawson abusing them? But if he were, would that account for his own disorder and confusion?

When he finally finishes, Judge Avery takes over. "Well, Jon, thanks for sharing your thoughts—all of them." This gets a small laugh from the crowd.

I lean into Jake and whisper, "I think there's something wrong with Dawson. Like, seriously wrong."

"You think?" Jake mouths.

"Now everyone on the council who voted has shared their reasoning and thoughts behind their vote," Judge Avery says. "I've noticed many of you taking notes. What you do with those notes and this information between now and the next meeting is up to you." He looks around the room, purposely making eye contact with several individuals.

"You'll have the weekend to sort out your thoughts. The next meeting is Monday at 1400—and we *will* start on time." He looks at Dawson, who's examining his fingernails. "Jon?"

"Yeah? Uh, yes, Judge?"

"Any issue with starting at 1400 on Monday?"

"Nope. No problem."

Judge Avery shakes his head. "As a reminder, when we meet, you will remain organized. If you wish to speak, you'll be given a limited time to ask your questions and share your thoughts. In the interest of time and organization, you may wish to have a single representative for your group or family. As before, the directive of no firearms in public places continues."

A rumble follows the reminder. The judge raises his voice. "We have a little over an hour until supper. Let's clear this place out so the setup crew can do their work. Oh, and those of you in attendance, feel free to share what was said with the kitchen and guard teams that couldn't be here. They're a part of this too. You're dismissed."

As we stand to leave, Sarah says, "That was interesting. I can't believe how everyone was almost like a robot, except for Dawson. Did they plan it?"

"Why would they?" Jake asks.

"No idea. But it just seemed so . . . odd."

After supper, Jake and I are sitting by the fire in the great room discussing the meeting and the events from the previous days, when

Sarah comes in. With a big sigh, she plops herself onto the loveseat. "Today was exhausting."

"Mentally?" I ask.

"Yes, exactly. Just putting the children to bed was almost too much for me. I'm glad, when we met with Belinda and Kelley today, they assured me the tiredness is normal. It's even worse now than in the first trimester, I think. Calley and I are two peas in a pod, always wanting to nap." She gives a small smile. "You should nap more, too, Mom. You heard Belinda."

I make a conscious effort to not roll my eyes.

"What's this?" Jake asks.

"Mom, Calley, and I all had appointments this morning. We're all good, but Belinda's worried Mom is doing too much."

"Thanks, Sarah," I whisper.

"She's not wrong, Mom. You've been looking tired again. But anyway, Kelley let me use her stethoscope to listen to the heartbeat. It was amazing. Much faster than I expected. Then Mom and Calley got to listen also."

"It was very different listening with a stethoscope than a doppler," I say.

"Belinda said so too," Sarah says. "She seemed to have a hard time counting it, said it was almost like an echo." Sarah stifles a yawn.

"Why don't you go on to bed?" I ask, motioning to the staircase. "It's almost time anyway."

"I did lay down for a few minutes, but I'm just too restless. My mind won't shut down."

"Everything does seem absolutely insane now. It's hard to be still when there's so much uncertainty."

"I don't even know why this is so important to me, Mom. It doesn't make sense for me to even think about going against council rules."

"Why not?" Jake asks.

"Me, Jake. Me. You know how I was always— " She slams her lips together into a tight line.

"Against my gun ownership?" Jake asks.

"Well, no. Not really. I understood you liked hunting, and that was fine. I thought it was rather barbaric, but I'm exceedingly glad now that it's a skill you have—a skill so many people here have. But other than owning guns for hunting, I saw no reason for it. Did you know

I used to think the Second Amendment was only useful for that? For hunting? I mean, how could we need to defend against a tyrannical government when the government only wants the best for us?" She gives a humorless laugh. "I'm glad you and Mom brought some of your weird books up here."

"Weird books?" I ask, furrowing my brow.

"You know, the ones about the Constitution and Bill of Rights. Plus, those kid's books about liberty."

Jake turns to me. "Which books are those?"

"The *Tuttle Twins* series—you know, the ones about economics and civics. Sarah was reading one to Marc yesterday."

"Oh, yeah. The ones you had Malcolm do the verbal reports on."

I give a nod as Sarah says, "We ought to give those to Jon Dawson to read. They're simple enough even he could understand them."

"Um . . . you do know he's an attorney, right?" Jake asks.

"That doesn't mean he's smart!" Sarah says, this time giving a genuine laugh.

I give Jake's hand a squeeze. He clears his throat and says, "There's always been people like Dawson. I've never been particularly political, but watching from the sidelines, it does seem many were more vocal than they had been in the past—from both sides of the aisle. While I don't agree with much of what Dawson has said recently, I do believe we need to focus on what's happening here. We're getting limited information from outside of our little bubble. Some of what we do hear is concerning, but does it affect us? What they're doing in Prospect could very well affect us. But what we hear coming from the West Coast and the rumors of what's happening on the East Coast—I don't know if it matters right now."

I nod my agreement. "You're right, Jake."

"What does matter?" Sarah asks.

"Our family. Your mom's health, your health, your baby's health—all of us. Being able to protect yourself as needed—especially with Amy's and Phoebe's deaths."

"Murders," I mutter.

"That's what really scares me," Sarah says. "If they were murdered—and from the little we've been told, it sounds like they were—how can anyone think we shouldn't be able to carry a gun?"

"That's true." Jake nods. "I worry about that, too, and I'm glad we're making a decision to do what we think is right for our own safety, no matter what the council believes."

"But are we trusting God when we take these matters into our own hands?" I ask.

"Mom," Sarah says, a hint of exasperation in her voice, "if we weren't armed when Dan Morse tried to kidnap us, we'd be dead. I mean, your kung fu stuff was impressive, but Katie was still shot. I've come to realize a gun is an equalizer." Her voice gets quiet as she says, "Tate carrying a gun didn't bring him back to me, but— " She lets out a sigh. "Nobody should be able to tell me I can't defend myself or my children. Especially considering we have a murderer on the loose."

My eyes fill with tears. None of us want to do the things we've had to do, but we no longer have the luxury of standing on ceremony.

"We do need to do what is right in God's eyes," Jake says, his voice decisive. "When times are at their darkest and full of uncertainty, we need to be turning to the word. When you feel your heart sinking with grief for all that's going on, it's time to turn our eyes and heart toward the Messiah. That is where we need to look for answers."

Sarah bites her lip. "I'm not—it's all new to me, you know. And while I want to believe, sometimes it's still hard to."

"You need help overcoming your unbelief," I say with a smile.

"Yes! Exactly."

"We've been there, Sarah," Jake says. "For your mom and me, we found what we were looking for through scriptures and prayer. His word never returns void. Learning not to trust in our own understanding, but believing and having faith— "

"And praising Him through it all, which isn't always easy," I add.

"Yes, praising Him through the calm and through the storm," Jake says. "It's not easy, and sometimes I fail— "

" *We* fail," I say, squeezing his hand.

"We do. And that's when we know we need more of the word."

Sarah wipes a tear from her eye. "Sometimes I'm still so angry about losing Tate. It seems so unfair to have him taken from me like that. Then I think of God and how He gave up His own son. And Jesus, He was willing to be crucified. I mean, He did ask for the cup to be taken from Him, right? But He still allowed it to happen. He could've stopped His crucifixion at any time. He didn't. He went through the humiliation and the pain." She lets out a sigh. "I think you're right. I need to spend more time reading and praying. And I need to not let Jon Dawson get under my skin!"

"Amen to that!" I say. "He definitely has a knack for bringing out my worst thoughts also. But I do have to say, I kind of felt sorry for him today. His entire family seemed to be facing issues. We need to be praying for him instead of condemning him."

"Ugh," Sarah says. "I don't want to pray for him."

"Praying softens our heart," I say, not only to convince Sarah but to remind myself. "It helps us to let go of our own agenda and become more like Christ."

Sarah shakes her head. "I don't know if I can do that."

"It's not easy," Jake says. "Pray about it."

"Pray about praying?" Sarah asks with a smile.

"Exactly."

Chapter 20

Sunday, Day 202

Jake

"You're first, Tony," I say, encouraging him to step up to the line.

"Yes, sir," Tony replies.

Tony and Lily have been with us since June, when their mom was killed. We've tried to make them feel welcome and a part of our family, but neither refer to us as mom or dad—understandably. Tony usually calls me *sir* and Mollie *ma'am*, or sometimes *Mr. or Mrs. Caldwell*. Lily sometimes calls me *Mr. Jake*, like several of the other school children.

Before the attacks, I was the janitor at one of the elementary schools in nearby Wesley, the same school most of the young children in Bakerville attended. When I help at our simple school here on the mountain, those students who knew me still call me Mr. Jake. I can understand how Lily is comfortable with that.

She sometimes calls Mollie *Grandmo*, just like the grandchildren. Lily and Tony—all the children—have had a terrible time these last several months. We're happy to love them and provide the best we can for them now.

I watch as Tony nocks his arrow, taking extra time to make sure the white fletching is down and in the correct position. He's barely holding on to the bow, making him slightly awkward and clumsy. "Grandpa Alvin told me to always make sure to keep my three fingers down when holding the bow," he says by way of explanation.

"Yeah, he taught me that too," I say. "But when you're setting up, you can hold onto it so you don't drop it. When you get into position, you can adjust your grip. Did he tell you about a wrist sling?"

"The thing you wrap around your wrist so, if you're barely holding onto your bow, it doesn't fall and hit the ground?"

"Exactly."

"He couldn't find his, said maybe we could make them." He spends about a minute getting everything the way he wants it before drawing back his string.

"Okay, line up the peep sight with the top pin," I say. "Then drop it slightly below the bullseye. We're about fifteen yards, so you'll need to aim low."

He lets his arrow fly, barely catching a piece of the target on the top left side.

"Not bad," I say. "Try it again."

"Why is he aiming low, Dad?" Malcolm asks, while Tony sets up for a second shot.

"The top sight is set for twenty yards, the middle thirty, and the bottom forty. We're closer than twenty, so you'll need to manually adjust."

"Why don't we just move back to twenty yards?" Tony asks.

"We will, but let's get you comfortable with the bow first. I know you spent a little time with Grandpa Alvin the other day. He suggested starting at fifteen again so you can both get a feel for it, then we'll move back."

Tony finishes his three shots, improving with each attempt. "Okay, Malcolm, your turn. You remember what you've learned before?"

"I didn't remember much until Grandpa was helping us. It seems harder to pull back than it should."

"We might need to turn the draw down a little. We'll see how you do."

As he pulls back the bowstring, I say, "Find your nock spot. You want a good anchor."

His shot is high and skims over the top of the target. After two more, both on target, we retrieve both boys' arrows and shoot again. We try fifteen yards again, then both are doing well enough we move back to twenty. After three more rounds, I call it good for the day.

"You boys are doing great. Next time, we'll start at twenty and see if we can move to thirty."

"I could try thirty now," Tony says.

"Best not. You can hurt your shoulder or back if you shoot too much. Even though we have the draw weight on the low end, it's still a lot when you're new at this. Besides, I need to get a nap in. I'm tired after watch duty, and I'm going out on the hunting crew this afternoon."

"Don't you think it's going to snow?" Malcolm asks, looking at the sky. "Will you still hunt?"

"It does look like snow. We'll still go if it's not too much."

"Maybe we can be on the hunting crew soon," Tony says wistfully.

"You keep shooting like you are, and it'll be no time at all before you have your draw weight high enough and are accurate enough. But before you hunt, we want to make sure you can make a good, clean kill shot. There's a lot of responsibility with hunting."

"Can we practice on our own?" Malcolm asks.

I pause a moment to consider this request. They're both shooting great and being safe, and the practice area we've set up is close to the dude ranch lodge. "Let me or your grandpa—even your mom—come with you a few more times, then we'll see about you two practicing on your own."

"Mom never feels well enough to do something like this," Malcolm says with a pout. "She used to always want to do outdoor stuff, but now she likes to stay inside."

"She's doing better," I say, trying to convince not only Malcolm but myself.

He shakes his head. "But she always needs to rest. She's almost as tired as Lois."

I start to defend Mollie when Tony says, "Who's that?" He points to someone walking away from us through the woods.

"Not sure," I say. Looking again, I change my mind. "That might be Dot's husband."

"The guy who was beating up his wife?" Tony asks.

I give a slight nod, watching as Heath struggles through soft powder, his snowshoes giving him little leverage as he practically stumbles through the woods. He's heavily laden with an overly stuffed backpack and a tent strapped to it. Where is he going? This isn't exactly camping weather, and in today's world, none of us would think of going camping for fun. Especially not in the middle of winter when a new storm is blowing in.

"Where do you think he's going?" Malcolm asks.

"Not sure, Buddy. Let's head on back to the house."

Inside the lodge, Katie and Leo are in the kitchen with Mollie and Sarah. "Hey, Leo," Malcolm says. "You should've gone shooting with us. Tony and I both almost hit the bullseye."

"Yeah," Tony says. "We were really close."

"Is that right? I've never tried archery. Maybe when you two get good at it you can teach me."

"I can teach you now," Tony says. "Maybe you can take us later, after our arms rest up."

"That might work," I say. "But it'll depend on Leo's schedule."

"I'm off today," Leo says. "Maybe this afternoon? Katie, do you want to give it a try too?"

"Sure. Why not."

Mollie flashes me a smile, then gives me a long look before asking, "Everything okay?"

I shrug. "Probably. We saw Heath traipsing off into the woods."

"Okay? So?" she asks.

"He was carrying a big backpack," Malcolm says. "Like when we go on our overnight trips—you know, when we *used* to."

"Why would he be doing that?" Mollie asks, confusion painting her face.

"I'm not sure. I thought maybe I'd go see Dot, ask her."

"Jake . . . " Mollie pauses, chewing her lip. "Do you really think that's smart?"

"No, probably not."

"I mean, it's really none of our business if he wants to go camping in the snow."

"That's true." I nod. "So you think I should just let it go?" I hate the idea of letting it go, something just doesn't feel right about it. While I don't know Heath, having never spoken to him before the day he was with Mollie when they found Phoebe, Dot would often share funny stories about her city-raised husband, including his disdain for all things nature. And after what happened the other day . . .

Mollie shrugs. "What would you gain by going and seeing her? Maybe they had another fight and she asked him to leave. Do you want a cup of tea before you go lay down?"

I shake my head in response. "Maybe when I get up."

"Wake you for lunch?"

"Do we have any roast leftover? I can just have that and get in a good nap before I go out this afternoon."

"Okay, sure," Mollie says, giving me a smile. "See you later."

"See you later," I say, giving her a quick peck. Does she look pale today? Maybe a little, but at least she isn't yellow.

I make my way up to our room, feeling every bit of my almost fifty-two years. During the daytime, we have four-hour watch shifts. The overnight shift is a full eight hours, starting at 2200 and ending at 0600. While it makes for a long night, it's not terrible. And it's easier on everyone if we don't switch in the middle of the night. The overnight shift, unlike the day shifts, has two people in each location plus roving patrol. During the daytime, most lookouts are staffed with only one person and roving patrols. The only one continually staffed with two people is the far east lookout—the most likely location from which hostiles would approach.

I settle into bed. I should've suggested Mollie take a nap too. She's doing too much again. She's been better, but that could change. Belinda and Kelley made a big deal about her not getting too tired. I sigh and start to sit up. Might as well holler down and tell her to come up here and rest. My feet are on the floor when I hear noise on the stairs. A moment later, the bedroom door opens.

"Hey, Jake," Mollie says.

"Hey yourself. I was just going to see if you wanted to come up and rest. You look a little tired today."

"Yeah, a little. And I think I will . . . but I've been thinking about Heath taking off. Maybe it would be best to check on Dot. I think I'll go over there."

"I'll go with you."

"No, no. You rest. I can handle this."

"Honey, I'm going with you. I won't be able to sleep knowing you're doing something I should've already done."

She gives a reluctant nod and pulls another sweater out of her dresser. "Okay. Katie and Leo are going to stay with the children. He said he'd go with me, but" —she gives me a small, guilty smile— "I kind of figured you'd go if I mentioned it."

Bundled up against the lightly falling snow, we start toward Dot's cabin. We're wearing our backpacks with snowshoes attached. Somedays, the road is slick enough we need the cleats on the snowshoes to keep us from falling. Today isn't too bad, allowing our boots to provide us with enough traction. I reach for Mollie's hand.

Wrapping her fingers around mine, she lets out a sigh and says, "I should've just crawled into bed with you."

"You've been overdoing it again."

"Not on purpose. It's just— " She shrugs. "It's hard to remember to slow down."

"How are you feeling, other than tired?"

"Okay. And I'm not really that tired. Just sometimes. While I could sleep, or at least rest, I'm not bone weary, you know?"

I nod. "Once we talk to Dot, we'll both go home and take a nap."

"Sounds good, husband."

"Yes, it does, wife," I say with a laugh and a squeeze of her hand. Before we move onto Dot's porch, I turn Mollie toward me. "Seriously, you need to take it easy."

She nods and lifts slightly. I kiss her solidly before we step up to Dot's door. I give a knock. After a minute or so, I knock again.

"Not home?" Mollie asks.

"Maybe not." I knock harder this time. There's a slight rustling noise and then a tapping.

"What was that?" Mollie asks, a concerned look on her face.

"Dot? Dot, are you there?" We hear the tapping again, slightly louder this time. "Dot, this is Jake Caldwell. I'm going to open your door."

"Jake," Mollie whispers, "it might not be safe."

"Why wouldn't it be?" I ask in a low voice.

"I don't know. I just . . . " She shrugs.

"What do you want to do?" I ask, suddenly wishing we would've brought Leo along with us.

"I'll get Bill. His trailer is just past the next set of cabins. Be right back." She's off the porch and practically running before I can respond.

"Be careful," I say quietly. The tapping comes again from inside, this time sounding more urgent. I test the doorknob; it turns easily in my hand. I take out my sidearm, holding it by my thigh. I'm tempted to enter the cabin alone. We had training last summer on clearing a building, but I've never done it on my own. And really, with what I'm hearing, it's not likely there's a threat . . . right? I quietly release my breath. Best to wait and be sure. I step back from the door, putting the solid log wall between me and the interior while covering the entrance.

Nervous sweat is beading on my forehead when Bill and Mollie come into view. I watch as their labored breaths puff out in front of them. Bill motions me to go to them.

Several feet from the cabin porch, tucked slightly behind a winter-worn tree, he asks, "Do you know anything more than what Mollie told me?" When I shake my head, he rushes on with, "I should've known that rat Jefferson could do something like this. We should've taken it as a warning when he was harassing Rochelle and then when he smacked poor Dot out in public. Should have done something." He shakes his head.

"I didn't go in, but I did turn the doorknob and pushed it open a crack."

"So, the door was unlocked? Are you still hearing noises?"

"Nothing after I stopped making noise."

Bill nods. "This is one of the studio cabins. There isn't a back door, but there's a good-sized window one can go out if needed. Mollie, you've got the window. Put your paddles on. The snow's deep behind the cabins since no one goes back there."

Mollie gives him a blank look until he motions to the snowshoes hanging off her backpack. I remove one shoe from her pack, and she quickly slips into it as I undo the second.

"Jake, I doubt there's anything more than—well, I'm assuming Dot, or someone, is in duress. So I'll go in fast and quick. You'll follow me. Ready, Mollie?"

"Give me just a second. I'm hooking the last strap," she says. "There. Ready."

"We'll give you sixty seconds to get into position. Find a place you can cover the window while staying concealed. Don't shoot unless you have to."

She gives him a look that says *duh.*

He nods and says, "Just saying."

As Mollie leaves, I start counting in my head. I'm only at forty when Bill says, "Let's get going."

It takes us more than twenty seconds before we're ready to enter the cabin. Bill takes the lead. "Okay, Jake. You ready?" he asks in a low voice. I nod my response as he pops open the door and bursts into the room. I'm a step behind him. My gaze stops on the bed as Bill says, "Clear. Jake, go to Dot. I'll check the bathroom."

Dot is bound and gagged, one hand tied to the bed's headboard and a foot tied on a long rope attached to the leg of the bed. It's obvious she's been beaten. One eye is swollen shut, the other barely a crease.

"Hey, Dot," I say, feeling like a dork as soon as the words leave my mouth.

I'm working on the gag as Bill says, "The bathroom is clear." He knocks on the large window and yells out, "Mollie, come in here."

I've barely removed the muzzle from her mouth when, in a rough whisper, she says, "Thanks, Jake."

"Dot," Bill says. "Mollie's coming inside. I'm going to leave Jake and her with you while I go get one of our docs. Jake, you can untie her, but don't move her."

Mollie rushes in the door, looking around the room before her eyes fall on the bed. She's immediately by Dot's side, saying all the right soothing words.

"Be right back," Bill says.

I work on untying Dot's hand while Mollie comforts her. Dot's crying softly and whispers, "He left me for dead. He couldn't do it himself, but he left me to die. He said no one would miss me."

I'm grinding my teeth so hard my jaw is instantly cramped. As soon as I know Dot's okay, I'm going after that sorry excuse for a man.

Chapter 21

Monday, Day 203

Mollie

There's plenty of shuffling and scooting of chairs as everyone who wishes to speak forms a line at Judge Avery's request. Our family unanimously chose Sarah to represent us. I watch as she waddles to a spot in line. She looks beautiful but extremely uncomfortable. It's still five weeks until her baby is due around Valentine's Day. How much larger can she get?

I squeeze Jake's hand. He's had a rough several days—we all have. After Kelley arrived to take care of Dot, Jake and Bill formed a group to go looking for Heath. They were gone until nightfall, but even with the tracks in the snow, they couldn't find him. At some point, he must have realized how easy he'd be to follow and started walking in circles, messing up the snow as best he could. Yesterday, they went out again at first light, looking all day. They spent another several hours searching this morning, arriving just in time for lunch and the meeting. It's been decided to not pursue him further. The general opinion is to let the elements have him.

With temps below zero last night and, according to Dot, equipment that's summer weight instead of winter weight, he's likely having a rough time of it. He may have already succumbed to hypothermia. Jake would prefer to keep searching—not for any sort of revenge, but to keep Heath from his own stupidity. Jackson's death in the avalanche still disturbs him. I think Jake feels a need to save Heath.

Dot's doing okay, considering the beating she took. He'd assaulted her the day before and tied her up. She said he sat in a chair and watched her as she suffered. She hadn't had any water or food for over twenty-four hours when we found her. Our friend Madison, a veterinarian and part of our medical team, is staying with Dot while she recovers. Madison, single mom to Emma after being widowed early in the attacks, has her baby with her. Kelley said Dot asked if they could stay indefinitely. She'd love to be able to keep the small cabin, and if Madison and Emma were her roomies, it'd be good for all three of them.

Since we moved to the mountain, Madison and Emma have been living in the women's dorm. Emma will be a year old next month, and having more personal space makes sense. Emma's rapidly outgrowing the playpen she's been sleeping in.

Jon Dawson walked in exactly at 1400. While technically on time, we're still getting situated to begin the meeting. Dawson isn't looking any more put together than last week. His wife and children are not in attendance. I try to recall if I've seen any of them since the last meeting. Jake and I have been making a point to pray not only for Dawson but for our entire leadership council. We're reading 2 Chronicles right now, and a verse from Chapter 7 is really sticking with me: "*If My people, who are called by My name, will humble themselves and pray and seek My face and turn from their wicked ways, then I will hear from heaven, and I will forgive their sin and will heal their land.*"

There's no doubt our sins are many and our land most certainly needs healing.

"Everyone ready?" Judge Avery asks. Instead of mutters to the affirmative, there's a resounding yes. "Proceed," he says to Sally-Ann Hinkle, the first person in line.

She makes a statement against the new decree and then asks questions of Rhoda and Jana, trying to figure out why they voted as they did. Paul Cameron went to school with Sally-Ann, which is how the Cameron family and others from Prospect ended up here. When she's done speaking, Paul, standing a few spaces behind her in line, applauds loudly. She shakes her head, beaming. "You're a silly old man." There's plenty of laughter over her remark.

Following Sally-Ann, another lady—one who's lived in Bakerville for years and whose name is on the tip of my tongue—makes a statement in favor of the decree, which results in a staggering round of boos and catcalls. I watch as she straightens her back and proceeds with her thoughts. She then questions Evan as to what his vote would be, had he been there. Judge Avery stops her, saying Evan's opinion is not relevant to these proceedings.

"It most certainly is relevant," she says. "My understanding is the council is to deliberate again and we'll have a public vote at the next meeting. We deserve to know how Evan is thinking."

"So you can harass him?" Bill asks. "The same way you and your bunch have been harassing me and Mick?"

"What's this?" Judge Avery asks. "Shannon, care to elaborate?"

"We are not harassing them," the speaker, who I now remember as Shannon Decker, says indignantly. "We're lobbyists. We're doing nothing different than everyone in this line is doing. We are making our points known."

"That's right!" Shannon's husband says from his seat.

"Who are they?" Jake asks in my ear.

"The Deckers," I whisper. "Miles and Shannon. They live in Zeb and Ellen's guest house. Shannon's sister, Moira, and her family live with them."

Judge Avery taps his finger to his chin before turning to the seated councilmembers. "Jana, Rhoda, has anyone been talking to you about your vote?"

The two councilwomen share a look. Rhoda clears her throat and says, "Just Shannon, her husband, and Shannon's sister. They wanted to confirm I would not be changing my vote when these, I believe the word Shannon used was *shenanigans,* are over."

"Jana?" Judge Avery asks.

"Shannon and her sister had me over for tea," Jana says, smiling at Shannon. "They were genuinely nice and concerned. It wasn't a big deal."

"Thank you," Judge Avery says. "Shannon, Miles, and everyone else, you will not browbeat, harass, or otherwise intimidate the council. Whatever may have happened in political circles before will not happen in Bakerville. Shannon, I understand you may still harbor a grudge after not being voted as a councilmember— "

"That's not true, Judge— "

Judge Avery lifts a hand. "You are more than welcome to express your opinion to your councilmembers, they are here as your representatives, but I won't hear anything additional about harassment."

"Judge Avery," Shannon says sweetly, "I do not agree that any contact made with Councilmembers Shane or Michaelson was harassment."

"What about when you accosted me?" Doris yells, waving her hand to be recognized.

"I beg your pardon?" Shannon says, completely indignant.

"You stopped me on my way home three days ago. You badgered me about Evan— "

"I did not!" she yells.

"All right, all right," Judge Avery yells. "Doris, will you see me after this please?"

"If she's going to tell lies about me, I have a right to face my accuser," Shannon says.

"Fair enough. Both of you will meet me at Jake Caldwell's lodge after the evening meal."

"That is a community lodge," Dawson says, opening his mouth for the first time since the meeting started. "I object to it being referred to as Jake Caldwell's lodge."

"Give it a rest, Dawson," Judge Avery says with a sigh. "Doris, Shannon, we'll meet at Jake's at 1930."

"I insist on being there also," Dawson says.

"No. You will not be there. The council is not invited to this meeting. Doris, pick someone to join you—not your husband since he's on the council. Shannon, you do the same. And for the record and as a reminder, per our bylaws, Evan Snyder will not be allowed to vote at the next meeting, so there's no reason for anyone to lobby Evan or his wife. Only those originally in attendance will be asked to recast their vote."

A rumble goes through the crowd. I don't like this part of the rules. I think the meeting was purposely held while Evan was gone. Quorum or no quorum, the whole thing stinks.

"Now, Shannon," Judge Avery says, "do you have anything to add, or can we move on to the next person in line?"

"I'm not yet finished," Shannon says, then continues to talk and ramble on for several more minutes. I'm slightly reminded of Jon Dawson and his endless babble at the last meeting. Is this some sort of ploy both she and Dawson have hatched up? I take a good look at Shannon.

Before the attacks, I didn't know her, though Doris told me she's lived in Bakerville for well over a decade. The first I remember of her was when she was running for Bakerville council. At that time, she had a smart-looking short haircut, the kind that's angled in the front and clippered in the back. After she lost her bid for council, she threw a public fit about how the vote was rigged. At the time, Angela whispered, "Uh-oh, that Karen is going to ask to speak to the manager." I must have given her a funny look because she followed with, "You know, the Karen memes?"

Later at the house, the subject came up again while several of us were working on food processing. Sarah's sister-in-law, actually named Karen, really got into how Shannon is the epitome of the annoying phrase and memes. Our Karen is one of the kindest, most easy-going people around and doesn't fit the meme persona. Shannon Decker is a different story. While she still seems to be one to call the manager, she long ago lost her cute angled cut. Now her hair is pulled up into a tight bun, giving her a pinched, uncomfortable look.

My eyes move to Sarah; there are still three people ahead of her before she's to speak. She's shifting her weight from foot to foot. She's been having trouble with her feet swelling, not so much that Kelley and Belinda are concerned with it but enough she brought slippers along so she could remove her too-tight snow boots during this meeting. Her idea of bringing slippers was so brilliant, I brought a pair too—not because of swelling but for comfort. As I watch her shifting, I decide as soon as Shannon finishes, and before the next person begins, I'm going to get Sarah a chair. There's no reason she needs to stand while waiting.

"Jake," I whisper, "I'm going to get up. I want to get Sarah a chair."

"Good idea. I'll do it . . . as soon as this windbag finishes."

I look at him with wide eyes and raise my eyebrows. "Oh," he says sheepishly. "I meant *this child of God*. The other thing just slipped out."

I scrunch my face and shake my head. "It wouldn't slip out if it wasn't inside of you," I mildly chastise. I don't bother to tell him I agree with the sentiment.

He makes a face and lifts a shoulder. Shannon seems to be wrapping up, so Jake moves to the edge of his chair. As soon as Shannon says, "Thank you for your time," Jake is on his feet. Before the next person steps forward, he has a chair in his hand and is walking toward the line Sarah is in. I glance toward Judge Avery, whose eyes are following Jake.

"Just a moment, Paul," Judge Avery says to Paul Cameron, the next speaker. "Jake, good thinking. Your daughter is starting to look a little peaked. Sarah, do you feel okay?"

Sarah turns as Jake approaches. The few people behind Sarah move to the side, allowing him through. "Thank you, Jake," Sarah says. "I'm fine, Judge. But I do appreciate the chair. This baby seems to steal all my energy when I least expect it."

"I've heard they do that," the judge says. "Just wait until he's running around. At least you're young and should be able to keep up. 'Course, you already have the others, so you know exactly what you're in for."

"Yes, sir. I have a good idea," she says, gingerly sitting on the chair.

"Anyone else need a chair?" Judge Avery asks, addressing the line of speakers.

One of our more elderly residents shyly raises her hand.

"I'll be glad to grab you one," Jake says. "Anyone else?" Everyone else is fine, and once Jake has the second chair, Judge Avery asks Paul to proceed.

There's no more fireworks or surprises. When Sarah speaks—making sure she's standing tall and straight—she's eloquent and composed. I'm terribly proud of her. When finished speaking, Sarah returns to her seat next to Katie, two rows in front of Jake and me.

After everyone who originally lined up has spoken, Judge Avery asks if there is anyone else who wishes to say anything. There isn't, and the meeting is completed with a reminder that the final meeting, which will include a new council vote, will be next Monday. And another reminder, since Evan missed the original meeting, he will not be allowed to vote at this one. There's plenty of disagreement, but Judge Avery reminds them we will be following the bylaws as agreed.

Then he dismisses us to leave the area so the setup crew can get supper ready. I quickly get to my feet so I can congratulate Sarah. She's still sitting when I reach her row. Katie and her have their heads together, talking softly. "Sarah!" I call from the aisle.

"Mom!" She has a frantic look as she motions to her lap. The front of her dress is wet. My eyes follow to the hem, also wet, and to the puddle at her feet. "It's too early," she says.

I fight back tears. "Your baby must not think so. Stay right here. I'll find Belinda and Kelley."

Jake appears by my side and asks, "What's going on?"

"Sarah . . . it's . . . she's— " I point at her.

"Well, okay then," Jake says calmly. "Mollie, stay with Sarah and Katie. I'll find our doctors."

"Mom, sit here," Katie says, moving from the spot next to Sarah.

I slide in and put my arm around Sarah. "Is there any pain?"

"I don't know, maybe. My back has been hurting since before lunch, but that's normal. Standing in line, it seemed to come and go. Maybe those were contractions?"

"Maybe," I agree.

"It's too early," she says again.

"Only a few weeks. And besides, without an ultrasound, we don't know for sure. And both Kelley and Belinda have said you're measuring ahead. It's probably not too early, just with everything— " I shrug.

"Well, Sarah," Belinda says, causing me to jump. "You sure know how to give a speech. And now this big finale. Well done."

"It's too soon," Sarah says.

"You'll be fine," Belinda says. "Jake said you brought the pickup today. He's warming it up right now. I've asked Bill if he can grab the snowmobile to take you down to the truck. Let's give another minute for the place to clear out a bit, then we'll go outside."

"I think my clothes will freeze when I leave the building."

Belinda gives a small laugh. "We'll get you into a gown once we're at the clinic. Kelley is on her way there now. She'll have the fire going and you'll be cozy warm. Mollie, are you helping with the birth?"

"She is," Sarah says. "And my sisters. If Mom gets tired, one of them will take over."

"Okay. I'm not sure how that will work with so many people, but we'll figure it out. At least we have enough space in the hospital room."

Sarah moves slightly in her chair, a look of discomfort on her face. "My back's hurting again."

It's not long until Belinda and I are escorting Sarah to the waiting snowmobile. Katie stays behind, promising she'll be there shortly, but she wants to mop the floor first. Sarah apologizes profusely for making a mess, which causes Katie to laugh and say, "It's not like you did it on purpose. See you soon."

Sarah climbs into the attached trailer.

"Get in with her, Mollie," Belinda says. "I'll ride behind Bill. In fact, maybe we'll just have Bill take us all the way to the clinic so Sarah doesn't have to get in and out."

While finding Belinda, Jake told Calley and Angela what was happening. They're going to find others from our extended family to have supper with the children and then take them home for the evening. As we approach the truck, Jake's sitting in the driver's seat, a look of worry painting his face. I give him a thumbs up. Belinda hops off and tells him we'll meet him at the clinic.

We're soon walking Sarah into the clinic. "What should I do?" Jake asks, offering her an arm. "Boil some extra water or something?"

"Stay for now," Sarah says. "Is that okay, Belinda?"

"That's fine. Jake will know when it's time to leave."

"When the screaming starts?" he asks, winking at Sarah. She responds with wide eyes and a frantic look.

Jake stays in the waiting room section while the rest of us go into the hospital part, closing the door. We soon have Sarah changed into a dry gown and robe. Kelley offers her a pair of Depends undergarments, telling her it might help keep her clothing dry. "What?" Sarah asks appalled. "I'm not planning to wet my pants."

"No, but your membranes have ruptured. The amniotic fluid will continue to leak out. This will help save on laundry."

"Gross," Sarah says, grumbling the entire time she's slipping them on.

Kelley and Belinda are setting things up. I watch as they put out two baby blankets, two small homemade bassinets, two diapers . . . "Kelley?"

"Mm-hmm?"

"What's going on?"

Sarah turns slightly and lets out a gasp. "Am I having twins?"

Belinda softly says, "We don't know."

"And you're telling me this now?" Sarah's voice has risen an octave.

"We really don't know," Kelley parrots. "There's a chance. Or you just have your dates slightly off. You're measuring larger than you should be. You felt movement a little earlier than usual. And . . . it's possible we may have heard two heartbeats at the appointment before last. We just don't know for sure."

"And you didn't think to tell me about this before?"

"We didn't want you to worry," Kelley says. "Worry isn't good for you or the baby. And not good for your mom either."

"Or Calley," Belinda adds. "There's enough to worry about. This isn't something we can change, so" —she shrugs— "we made a medical decision."

I give them both a hard look. In the process, I realize they've probably done the same thing concerning my health. They suspect more about what is going on with me than they are saying. Kelley seems to interpret my look, giving me a slight head tilt. *We'll discuss this later*, her look seems to say.

Stomping on the porch indicates more arrivals. Hopefully it's family and not someone else in need of our doctors.

Chapter 22

Monday, Day 203

Jake

The door flies open, and Angela and Katie tumble in. "Is she okay?" Katie asks.

"I guess," I answer with a shrug. "She's changing into her hospital gown. I'm waiting here."

"Calley will be here shortly. She's making sure everyone knows to watch the children."

"That's good," I say.

Both girls remove their jackets and snow boots. "I wish I would've brought slippers to the meeting, like Mom did," Angela says.

"I'm sure there's time if you want to go and get a pair," I suggest.

"Sarah's got wet," Katie says. "I should grab her another pair."

They put their boots and jackets back on, telling me they'll be right back. I add another log to the fire before returning to my chair. As far as I know, it's not time for Sarah's baby to arrive. Malcolm was early, too, by two weeks. Sarah thought her baby would arrive around Valentine's Day, still over a month away. Do a few weeks make a big difference? I don't know enough about babies to know for certain what a few weeks earlier means. A small baby? A baby with problems?

Lord, protect Sarah and her baby. Keep them both healthy and well. Help her have an easy delivery. I've barely finished my internal petition when the door to the hospital section opens. I quickly finish with amen.

"Jake? You're alone?" Mollie asks, looking around. "We thought we heard someone else."

"Katie and Angela. They went back to grab slippers."

"Good!" Sarah says, "Mine are . . . not good. And Mom's feet are too small for me to wear hers."

"Shouldn't you be in bed or something?"

"Not yet," Belinda says. "We're going to let her walk around as long as she's able."

"They think I'm having twins," Sarah says, her voice monotone.

"Huh?"

"Twins, Jake. Two babies. They didn't want to tell me."

I look to Mollie, who nods.

"That probably would've been good to know," I say. "Make sure we have everything we need for two."

"Don't you?" Belinda asks.

I look to Mollie again, then say, "I guess so. We've got two boxes, and they made little blankets and stuff. Are there enough?"

"We'll be fine," Mollie answers. She has a strange look on her face, one I can't quite decipher.

Sarah gasps. "Oh! Something different is happening."

Belinda is by her side and lays a hand on Sarah's swollen belly. "That's good," she says. "Maybe the back labor will stop and the progress will start."

After Sarah straightens up, I ask, "Should I stay?"

"Might as well," Kelley says, "as long as Sarah wants you here."

Sarah and Mollie start walking around the room while Kelley and Belinda go into the hospital section. When I stand, I notice the two boxes—wooden crates made before Shelby had her baby. Dr. Sam had Art make them for him. He specifically asked for two instead of one, just in case. At the time, I thought he was being cautious, based on his military background and his fondness for repetition. Now, I wonder if he suspected Sarah may have twins even then. Losing Sam was a blow to our community. I have full faith in Belinda's, Kelley's, and Madison's medical skills, but Sam was special.

Thinking of his death reminds me of his memorial service, his and Phoebe Baker's. Which in turn reminds me of the service we held for Amy and Jackson. Between those two services, we also lost an elderly person.

Heath, who took off by his own accord, will probably perish in the wilderness. Dot will end up like Sarah and Lois, not knowing for sure if her husband is dead or alive. Even though I know death is part of life, and for believers we rejoice when people go to their Heavenly home, it's still sobering when it occurs. And in the case of Phoebe and

Amy, at someone else's hand. We believe there is a murderer among us, but we don't know who it is.

The stomping on the porch combined with laughter indicates the girls returning. I open the door for them, as all three of Mollie's other daughters hurry in. "Did we miss anything?" Calley asks breathlessly.

"Oh . . . maybe something," Sarah says. "You brought me slippers?"

"Yep," Katie says.

"Gi'me," Sarah jokes, holding out her hand. Then immediately she says, "Ahhh, it's starting again."

After Sarah's contraction ends and she has the slippers on, she says to her sisters, "I might have two."

"Two what?" Katie asks.

"Babies."

There's plenty of questions and excitement, which continues until the next contraction. I'm starting to feel out of place. I signal to Mollie I'm going to leave. She nods.

"Um, Sarah, I'll go check on the children," I say. "See you after this is all over, okay?"

"Thanks, Jake. Thanks for . . . everything."

"Sure. Yep."

As I open the door, I'm startled to find Brad on the porch. "I heard Sarah's here," he says.

I pull the door shut slightly and turn back to where Sarah is walking the room with her family. "Just a minute, Brad," I say loudly.

Sarah bites her lip and shakes her head slightly.

"You want me to get rid of him?" I mouth.

She starts to nod but then shakes her head. "Dad? You can come in for a minute."

Brad doesn't wait for me to open the door, just pushes on it, elbowing me out of the way. I take a deep breath to prevent reacting. Sometime, this guy is going to—

"Sarah! I heard your water broke in the meeting. You shouldn't have put yourself through the stress of speaking."

Sarah gives a small laugh. "I'm quite sure babies come when they want to. Besides, the meeting was important."

"No, it really wasn't," Brad says gruffly. "The council does what it wants to do anyway, no matter if you or anyone objects. Besides, you're backing the wrong horse on this."

"Meaning?" she asks.

"Never mind. We can talk about this later. How are you feeling?"

"I'm good. Mostly. Did you tell Victor he's going to be an uncle soon?"

"Not yet. I wanted to check on you as soon as I heard. What can I do?" he asks, looking around the room.

"Um, nothing." Sarah shrugs. "I can have Jake come and tell you after the baby is here."

"You can have Jake come and tell me after the baby is here?"

"Yes. He was just leaving. It's just, Belinda and Kelley are only letting my mom and sisters stay."

"Is that so?" he asks.

"Hello, Mr. Quinton," Belinda says, walking in from the other room right on cue. "I'm so glad you were able to stop in and check on Sarah. We'll likely have a long road ahead before her baby arrives."

I notice she says *baby* and doesn't mention the possibility of twins.

"My grandchild," Brad says, puffing out his chest.

"We'll be sure to send someone around to let you know. And would you do me a favor and tell Alina I may need to reschedule Victor's appointment? I'll let her know if tomorrow doesn't work."

Brad shakes his head. "Were you able to figure out how to use the cord blood to help Victor?"

"I'm sorry, Brad. That just isn't an option. We don't have the ability to do it. We've discussed this. I'm sorry."

"But it wouldn't hurt to try, right?"

"It could hurt. We don't know if the cord blood would be a match for Victor. It's more than just making sure the blood type is the same. We could hurt him if we did it wrong. And besides, we don't have the equipment or know-how needed. I'm sorry, Brad. This isn't an option."

"You do realize by not doing anything you are— " He sucks in a breath.

"Brad," Kelley says, "you know Belinda and I will do everything we can for Victor. This, though, it's not something we can do. And as we've discussed, he's doing very well. While we can't prove it, we believe him to be in remission."

Brad nods as anguish covers his face. I feel bad for him. I can't imagine the pain of knowing your child is ill and not being able to do anything about it. If he would've told Mollie what he wanted the first time he phoned her, a week or two before the attacks started, things might be different. But Mollie says when he called, he was secretive.

In the blink of an eye, he seems to peel off his sadness like a coat. He's back to being smug and arrogant. "Whatever, I can see there's no changing your mind. Sarah, how about a hug before I go?"

Sarah clutches her stomach and bends over slightly, her breathing becoming irregular.

"Off you and Jake go now," Belinda says in a cheery voice. "Women only moving forward." She catches my eye and gives me a small wink.

On the porch with the door closed gently behind us, I say, "Will we find you at your house or do you have duty?"

"Bite me, Caldwell," Brad says, stomping off.

"So . . . at your house then?" I ask with as much cheek as I can muster. He stomps away without acknowledgment. I can't help but laugh at his childish antics. What did Mollie ever see in this schmuck?

Chapter 23

Monday, Day 203

Mollie

Of course Brad would show up. I take a deep breath, trying to release the irritation I feel toward him. There was a reason he had nothing to do with Sarah for the first thirty years of her life. He didn't even know she was born, having dropped me off at the abortion clinic with cash for the procedure and bus fare home before speeding away. I had no contact with him until a couple of weeks before the attacks started.

When he called me out of the blue, it was unexpected and unwelcome. And when he showed up several weeks after the EMP with his wife and sick son, I was shocked. I understand Sarah wanting a relationship with him, but I still don't like it.

"Mom?" Katie asks gently. "Are you okay?"

"Uh, yes, I'm fine."

"You're pale. Do you need to sit down?"

"I'm fine. I can walk with you guys."

"Go ahead and sit, Mom," Sarah says. "Cheer me on from the chair."

I nod my agreement and make my way to the most comfortable of the four chairs. I notice Kelley watching me. I paste on a wobbly smile. The look she gives me implies I'm not fooling her; my weariness is evident. Just like she didn't fool me when she and Belinda gave their little talk about withholding medical info. *What aren't they telling me?*

"Mom?" Sarah asks. "Do you have your little Bible in your bag?"

"New Testament, Psalms, and Proverbs," I answer.

"Maybe you could read?"

"Anything specific?"

"Can you start with the Soldier's Psalm?"

"We almost know that one by heart," Calley says. "David Hammer read it so much over the summer. We don't hear it as much living on the mountain. I miss it."

I turn to the Psalm and begin to read, "*Whoever dwells in the shelter of the Most High will rest in the shadow of the Almighty. I will say of the Lord, 'He is my refuge and my fortress, my God, in whom I trust.'*"

A pain overcomes Sarah. I stop and wait for it to pass before continuing. After I finish Psalm 91, Angela gives a suggestion. While they walk, pausing as needed for Sarah, I read. After the sun fully sets, Belinda offers me an LED headlamp so I don't strain my eyes in the dimly lit room.

When there are footsteps on the porch, Sarah says, "If that's Brad, please don't let him in."

Kelley answers the door and then turns back to us, holding up a thermos. "Soup," she says. "Doris brought it. There's a box with a few more things."

"Can I eat?" Sarah asks.

"Yes, a little," Kelley says, grabbing the box off the porch.

Katie, who's been in training to be part of the medical team and seems to know where everything is, pulls a set of TV trays from a closet.

"Sarah, take it slow. It's possible you might feel sick during labor and vomit. I'd prefer you to focus only on the broth, maybe a little bread and cheese, and leave the more solid items behind." Belinda makes a face and we all laugh.

"Who was carrying the box for Doris?" Katie asks, grabbing bowls, plates, and spoons from a shelf along the wall.

"Her friend Kimba. They're going to your lodge for the meeting with Judge Avery."

"You mean the *community* lodge?" I ask, my voice dripping with sarcasm.

"Exactly," Kelley says with a laugh.

"Do you know what that was about, Mom?" Angela asks.

"I really— "

"Mmm," Sarah says, not because of the meal but to move through another pain. When she's finished, she says, "I didn't mean to interrupt you, Mom." This garners a laugh from everyone.

"I don't even remember what I was saying."

"Doris. What's going on with her and that lady?" Angela reminds me.

"With Shannon?" I shrug. "Today was the first I've heard of it. Doris has been busy doing some sort of supply inventory. I don't see her much."

Kelley and Belinda share a look.

"What?" I ask.

Kelley lifts one shoulder while Belinda says, "There have been a few . . . discrepancies."

"Discrepancies?" Calley asks. "With our supplies?"

"Are things missing?" Katie asks.

"Yes," Kelley says. "It's not common knowledge yet, but we expect it to be announced soon."

"What's missing?" Angela asks.

"Things from all the different storage places. Art hasn't said anything to you about this?"

"Art? My father-in-law? Why would he?"

"He's the first one who noticed we might have a problem," Kelley says. "It started with him noticing missing animal feed and a couple of chickens and rabbits."

"Missing livestock?" Angela exclaims. "Maybe it's a fox or something?"

Belinda and Kelley shake their head, and Belinda says, "Not just livestock, other things. Food, medical, basic supplies, and more."

"How much is missing?" I ask.

"Too much," Kelley says. She seems to want to say more but is cut off by a moan from Sarah.

Doris sent plenty of food, knowing we might have a long night. We save chunks of roast and most of the cheese for later, along with a second loaf of bread. After supper, the girls resume the walking and I resume the reading. After about an hour, Sarah says, "I think I'd like to rest."

"Will you check her?" Angela asks, remembering her own birthing time with Gavin.

"As little as possible," Belinda says. "We're so primitive, we don't want to do any more than necessary. We'll try to let her body do what it needs to do."

"So . . . no epidural?" Angela asks, raising her eyebrows and giving a funny face.

"Ha! I wish," Sarah says with a groan as a contraction overwhelms her.

After Sarah is recovered, Kelley brings a wooden rocking chair from the hospital room. "You want to try this?" she asks Sarah. "Maybe with a blanket on the back so it's more comfortable?"

"Without for now," Sarah answers.

Once Sarah's situated, I return to reading. She rocks and I read.

Chapter 24

Monday, Day 203

Jake

"That lady is really loud," Lily says, putting her hands over her ears.

"That she is," I agree. Judge Avery is having his meeting with Doris and Shannon in our den—or as Dawson insists, the *community* den. Shannon and her sister seem to take turns yelling about—well, I have no idea what they're so upset about. But as Lily said, they are loud.

"Jake?" Karen calls from the top of the staircase. "Any news?"

"Not yet. How's Lois? Anxious?"

"Very," Karen says with a big smile. "She's also dressed and has her hair combed."

"Really?"

"She says as soon as we know anything, she'd like to go see Sarah."

"All right. You know, if you wanted to go over there— "

"No. Sarah knows I don't do well with blood and stuff. It's better if I stay with Mother and keep her company while we wait."

"We're just getting ready for a story," Lily says. "Maybe Grammy Lois wants to listen?"

"She might. Let me ask her if she feels like coming and joining you."

Karen disappears into the bedroom she and Lois share.

"She won't come down," Lily whispers. "She never does anything fun with us."

"She's still sad," Sissy says. "Because of my daddy and grandpa dying."

"They might not be dead," Marc says. "Maybe, since they didn't find a body like they did for the girls who went missing, maybe they'll come back."

The hope in Marc's voice pulls at my heart. "I'd like to think so, too, Marc. It's true, we don't know for certain. Your uncle Tim talked to you about this, right? About how they looked everywhere?"

Marc's face falls. "He said they didn't want to stop, but the snow was too deep and there was no sign of them."

"They didn't want to stop," I agree with a nod. "There was no place else to look, and it started getting too dangerous for them to stay. And then the next week, when the snow stopped falling, Tim and a few others went back on their own, right?"

"Yes," he says softly.

A noise at the top of the steps causes all of us to look.

"Hello, family," Lois says, her voice surprisingly strong. "Karen tells me you're starting your story time. I'd love to join you."

Malcolm and Tony both jump to their feet. "We'll help you walk down," Tony says. I can't help but smile at my children's willingness to help.

"Well, thank you, gentlemen," Lois says.

We wait as they slowly escort her down the steps. She's a shell of her former self. Skin hangs loosely from her jawline; she teeters on unsteady legs. She's only left her room a dozen times since her husband and son went missing. Karen walks in front of her, telling her to put a hand on her shoulder if needed.

"Oh, there's no need, Karen. Tony and Malcolm will help me just fine."

When she reaches the bottom, she says, "Thank you both. Can I keep your arm, Tony, until I reach my chair?"

Once she's seated, she asks, "What are you reading tonight?"

"*Treasure Island*," Malcolm says. "The book belonged to my great grandma—my grandpa's mom."

"Such a wonderful book. And how nice that it's an heirloom. I just love old books."

"This book smells bad," Lily says, holding her nose.

"It's a smell I love. When I was a teacher, we had story time every day, and we used real books, not those computerized ones that were so popular in recent years."

"But the eReaders sure hold a lot," Malcolm says.

"Yes, they are useful for that."

"Of course, Mom makes us keep the eReader and other electronics in the Faraday cage in the crawlspace under the lodge when we're not using them."

"Just in case of another EMP," Tony says. "At least we can use them sometimes. Even without the internet, the computers have the flash drives with information on them. It's almost like having extra schooling."

"It is at that," Lois agrees. "Okay, Jake, I'm settled in and ready. Oh! Where's your dad? Don't I usually hear Alvin reading?"

"He's on guard duty tonight," I answer.

"I would think they'd leave that to the younger men while we're up here on the mountain."

"He insists on taking at least one shift a week."

"And he goes out with the hunting team too," Marc says, his voice full of pride.

Lois pulls in a sharp intake of air and, in a wobbly voice, says, "I hope he's careful."

I clear my throat. "Everyone ready?"

I'm on the second page of tonight's chapter when the door of the den opens. As Shannon and her sister stomp out, they make a point of staring straight ahead. They grab their coats off the hooks and open the door without taking the time to put them on. I take a second to wonder why Shannon brought her sister instead of her husband. What did Mollie say his name is? Miles?

Judge Avery's robust laugh helps soften the slam of the front door. "Oh, Kimba, that is quite the tale. You should write a book—all the stories you have."

"Who'd read it?" she asks. "The people living here have all heard my stories."

Karen gives me a questioning look. I answer with an exaggerated shrug. Kimba's stories are news to me, not that I've spoken with her many times.

"Judge, can Kimba walk home with you? I'd like to stay and visit with my second family." Doris gives the kids a small wave. "Seems like forever since I've seen these munchkins."

"Sure, sure. I'd be happy to escort her home. Maybe she'll share another story on the way."

"Kimba, will you ask Evan to come over here?"

"Sure, Doris. I'll send him right over."

Doris and Evan have a small one-room cabin. Kimba and her family live in Evan's fifth wheel trailer, parked next to the cabin. Like most of the trailers we brought up in the fall, it's unlikely we'll be able to haul it back down to Bakerville proper. Fuel is a precious commodity, and we can't afford to use it hauling trailers down in the spring and back up in the winter. Besides, there are several empty houses in Bakerville for people to move into.

Doris takes off her leg crutch, then gently lowers herself onto the floor next to Sissy and Lily, who immediately climb onto her lap. "Careful of her leg," I say.

"They're fine," Doris says with a wave of her hand.

"I wanna sit on Miss Doris," Gavin pouts.

"You can sit with me," Karen says.

"'Kay," he says, climbing on her.

"Is it okay if I finish reading?" I ask Doris.

"I'm here for the story," she says unconvincingly.

I'm at a good stopping point for tonight's reading when there's a knock at the door. It opens slightly and Evan says, "Hello, Caldwells. Mind if I come in?"

"Hey, Uncle Evan," Malcolm says. He took to adding *uncle* before Evan's name and *aunt* before Doris's shortly after we moved up here.

"Yep," I say. "We're just finishing up tonight's story. Kids, say hello to Evan and then it's time to get ready for bed."

After several minutes of greeting, I say, "Okay, that's enough. Let's get pajamas on and teeth brushed."

"Gavin and Andy are too little to do it on their own," Lily says, pointing to the boys. "And where will Gavin sleep?"

"Gavin's going to bunk with Andy tonight. His dad has watch tonight, and his mom's helping Sarah, so he's staying with us."

"I'll help them get ready," Tony says.

"But who's going to tuck me in?" Sissy asks.

"I'll tuck you all in," I say. "When you're ready, get into bed and I'll be up shortly." I attempt my calmest, most understanding voice. Malcolm gives me a look, which I interpret to mean *you're out of your league, Dad.* I agree with him. While I love having a house full of young children, tonight is overwhelming.

"But Aunt Sarah always tucks us in," Lily whines. "Maybe she can tuck me in after she gets home."

"How about I take care of tucking everyone in?" Karen asks. "Mom, I'll walk you back up first and then make sure everyone gets tucked in."

"Need a hand?" I ask.

"I'll help you up the stairs, Grammy Lois," Tony says. Malcolm and Marc both chime in with, "Me too."

"Thank you, boys," Lois says quietly. "I'm afraid going up might be slower than coming down was. Jake, I'm sure with your strong, young men, I'll be fine. You visit with your friends."

Evan helps Doris from the floor and onto the sofa. Instead of putting her leg crutch on, she uses him for support. She's still not allowed to bear any weight on the bone that was shattered.

I shake my head at the younger children as they stampede up the stairs. Malcolm, Tony, and Marc are all being very attentive and offering any help they can to Karen as she assists Lois. She's right about being slower; she stops several times before reaching the top.

Once it's quieted down, I turn to the Snyders and ask, "What's on your mind?"

"I can't remember the last time I saw Lois," Doris says. "She looks surprisingly good. Tired, but not terrible."

"Yeah. She's excited about the baby." I don't mention Kelley and Belinda had things set up for twins. Truth be told, I'm trying not to think about what that might mean for Sarah or for the babies. Will they be healthy?

"I think we're all excited about the baby," Doris says. "When Shelby had her baby, it really gave everyone a boost. But then Phoebe and Sam died, which deflated the community. And with Amy— " She shakes her head.

"They're not saying much about her cause of death," I say.

"No. It seems to be a state secret," Evan says. "I'm not even really in the loop. I don't think any of the council is being told the full extent of what Jesse and Clark have found."

"Clark's helping with the investigation?" I ask.

"Somewhat, near as I can tell. We do know it was foul play. And with the similarities of the investigation—you know, Jesse saying Mollie was with Brad and Kimba was with Mick—it seems suspicious."

"What are you getting at?" I ask.

Doris leans in closely. "We need to stay alert. There's more going on here than we're being told."

Chapter 25

Monday, Day 203

Mollie

After resting and rocking for over an hour, Sarah is back to walking. Calley, exhausted from her own babe within her, asks if she can rest on the exam table.

"There's cots," Katie says, "in case of additional patients."

"Right," Belinda says. "That should be more comfortable, and safer than that high wooden table." Angela and Katie help Belinda set up three cots. Calley is soon settled in and asleep.

"Mom, do you want to rest?" Sarah asks. "I think it'll still be a while, and I'll need you later."

"You're sure?"

"I think so. You should try and sleep," she says with a smile. "I'm sure you'll know if I need you. Is a cot okay, or do you need to go home?"

"The cot. I'll stay here," I answer, standing up to stretch. I've been sitting in one spot for so long, every part of me is tight. I hobble to the cot and carefully lower my stiff body to the low bed. I stretch out and then cover myself with the light blanket. With the warmth of the room, it's enough. I close my eyes, letting my mind drift. I'm somewhere between sleep and awake when Sarah's groan jolts me fully alert.

I open my eyes to see Kelley standing with her hand on Sarah's stomach. "This might go quicker than we thought," she says. I close my eyes briefly when Sarah lets out an anguished cry.

"It's happening again—already," she pants.

"Mollie, you might not get any rest after all," Kelley says. "I think it's time to move Sarah to the bed."

"We'll check her and then go from there," Belinda says as another wave overtakes Sarah, causing her to again cry out.

"Not sure we need to," Kelley says. "They're right on top of each other."

Belinda gives a solemn nod and says, "Angela, why don't you come in here. We'll get you into position first."

"Me?" Angela asks.

"Yes, c'mon now."

I go to Sarah as a questioning Angela follows Belinda. With the door open between the rooms, I watch as she positions Angela against the headboard. Sarah has another contraction before Belinda returns.

Kelley and Belinda walk her into the room while Katie and I follow. Calley stirs and groggily says, "Is it time?"

"Close," I say. She turns over and snuggles back into the cot.

It takes many minutes before Sarah is in position on the bed, using Angela as a backrest. "Is this supposed to help?" she asks.

"Angela will be your brace. It worked well for Shelby," Belinda says. "Just remember not to squeeze Angela's thigh. Grant probably still has a bruise from when Shelby did that."

"Oh, now you tell me," Angela says.

"Mollie, let's put you here," Kelley says, scooting a chair next to Sarah. "Katie, can you bring the rocker back in and another chair for Calley?"

"I think she's still sleeping," Katie says.

"I'm up! I'm not missing this," Calley says, coming into the room.

Belinda puts a basin of water within reach for both me and Angela. "Use the washcloth and the water to help keep her cool. It may help lessen the intensity if she's comfortable. I'm going to wash up and then we'll see where we're at. Kelley? Join me?"

Sarah breathes through another contraction.

"Tell me if you want the wet cloth," Angela says.

"Did it help with the pain when you had Gavin?"

"Are you kidding? I had an epidural right after I arrived at the hospital. But I'm sure the wet cloth will work just the same."

Sarah and Angela both laugh over that. Then Sarah is crying, saying, "I hope I can do this. It's so much more than I expected. Mom?" She reaches for my hand. "It's not too early, right?"

I blink several times before saying, "It's going to be fine, Sarah."

"Okay, Sarah," Belinda says as she and Kelley return from the bathroom. "Let's see where we are." She spends several minutes with her, poking and prodding.

After Sarah recovers from another wave of pain, Sarah asks, "Well?"

"Soon for sure," Belinda answers. "You're almost fully dilated." Soon turns into about an hour, until Belinda and Kelley are telling Sarah it's time to push.

"I'm too tired," Sarah says in a whimper.

"Sarah," I say gently, "it's time. All the work you've done up to now was to get ready for this. It's time for your baby to be born."

"You can do this, Sarah," Angela says. Calley and Katie echo Angela.

"I've got this," Sarah says, as a roar from deep within her is let loose. Time seems to stand still, until several contractions later when Belinda announces, "It's a boy!" followed by a soft cry, a whimper, and then a hearty wail.

"It's a boy," Sarah says in a dreamy tone. "Is he . . . is he okay?"

"He's perfect," Kelley says. "Big and healthy. We're going to leave the umbilical cord attached until everything is finished. Sarah, I'm sliding him onto your chest."

I wipe tears from my eyes as the full-size infant is positioned on Sarah's chest. No way is this a twin. He's at least seven pounds, and pudgy. How can he be five weeks early?

"He's so beautiful," she says, holding him next to her. "I love him so much already. Oh, I don't—it's happening again," she says between clenched teeth.

"Okay, Sarah," Belinda says. "Just relax a minute. Let me look."

"It stopped," Sarah says.

Belinda smiles. "I don't think there's a second baby. I think that was just a cramp as your body gets ready to expel the placenta. Just relax and let your body do its work."

"You're sure?"

"I don't think there'd be any more room in there." Kelley laughs. "This is a good-sized baby."

"Mom?" Sarah reaches for me. "Can you see him?"

"He's amazing," I say through my tears. "You were amazing."

After many minutes, the placenta is delivered. "Okay," Belinda says, tying a small string around the cord. "You look good, Sarah. I'm going to wash up and then check out your baby."

"Tate. His name is Tate."

Tears run down my cheeks. She and I had discussed names several times, but last I knew she hadn't chosen any. Naming him after his dad is perfect and heartbreaking.

"I'll check Tate after I'm washed up," Belinda says. "And Kelley can help you get up. I bet Angela is almost as exhausted as you are."

"Truth," Angela says, still acting as Sarah's backrest. Kelley and Belinda again disappear to the bathroom.

Little Tate is already moving around and making rooting motions. "Does he want to eat already?" Calley asks.

"Looks like it," I say—not adding that, at his size, he may already have a full set of teeth and be ready for an elk steak. I'm amazed at how large he is.

"I don't know what to do," Sarah says, her eyes filling with tears. "I mean, I read the books we have, but it's so different in real life. I thought I was ready for this."

"You'll be fine," I say. "It's always overwhelming."

"But what if he won't nurse? We have bottles but no formula."

"We do have a little formula," Belinda says as she returns from the bathroom. "But let's not worry about that yet. I'm going to give him a quick exam, Kelley will get you and your bed put back together, and then we'll get him some food—from you."

Kelley helps Sarah up, having her stand on one side of the bed. I move my chair to help Angela off the bed on this side. I grab for her as she immediately loses her balance. "My foot's asleep. I hate that feeling." She staggers around a little, trying to bring the feeling back, while Kelley helps Sarah into a new gown and robe.

"Calley, will you help me remake the bed?" Katie asks.

"Your baby looks perfect," Belinda says. "And while our weighing method is not exactly accurate, I'm estimating his weight at over eight pounds."

"How can he be so large at five weeks early?" I ask.

Belinda gives a soft laugh. "My guess is he isn't five weeks early. We estimated based on Sarah's last cycle, but she did say the cycle was abnormal. Right, Sarah?"

"Right. We were moving, and I thought it was just from the stress. Do you think I was already pregnant?"

"I'd say so. You definitely have a healthy, full-term baby boy. Here he is, Sarah. Put him right in against your chest," Belinda says, unsnapping the shoulder of the hospital gown and handing Tate to her. "Hold him for a few minutes and let him get acquainted with you outside of the womb. Then we'll get him eating."

"He's so perfect," Sarah says, once again dissolving into tears.

Chapter 26

Tuesday, Day 204

Jake

"Can we go see our new brudder after breakfast?" Andy asks as I finish lacing his snow boots.

"I think we'll be able to," I say. "Grandmo said your mom was asking for you. She can't wait for you, Sissy, and Marc to meet him."

"Grammy Lois gets to see him first," Sissy says. "Maybe he'll make her happy and she'll want to play with us again. I liked her being with us at story time last night." She lets out a big sigh. "Grandmo is sure tired this morning."

"She stayed up during the night to help your mom have your new brother. It's hard work having a baby, so Grandmo and your aunts are tired too. I'm sure your mom is very tired but still excited to see everyone and show off the baby."

"And we'll get to learn his name then?" Sissy asks.

I smile and give a small nod. Mollie told me the baby's name, but Sarah wants to tell Lois and the children herself. Naming him after Tate is the right thing to do but will probably cause many tears, especially when Lois and Karen learn his full name is Tate Keith Garrett, after his father and his paternal grandfather.

"Marc, will you run up and see if your Grammy Lois is ready to go?" Today will be the first time she's left the lodge since we moved in. While she has been out of her room a handful of times, she's yet to leave the building. I'm not entirely confident she'll be able to do so today.

Ten minutes later, I'm surprised to be helping Lois off the front porch. We'll take the pickup and drop Lois and Karen off at the clinic and then continue to the ski lodge for breakfast with the children. All but Marc, Sissy, and Andy will stay after breakfast for school. I'll take them to meet the baby and see their mom before returning them for classes. I'm working in the greenhouses today, so I'll head there after dropping off the children.

I help Lois out of the pickup and up the steps to the clinic. At the door, she says, "Are you going to come in and see our grandchild?"

"I'll see him later. You and Karen enjoy this time with him."

Lois pulls me into a hug. "Thank you, Jake."

The children and I have almost finished breakfast when I notice Evan, Bill, and Deputy Clark conferring in a corner. Bill's face is pinched and angry as he shakes his head almost violently. Evan puts a hand on his shoulder. Bill stiffens and shakes it off. My surveyance is interrupted by a question from Tony. When I look back, all three of them are gone.

I leave all but Sarah's children at the lodge for their school day. It's amazing how easily the large room converts from an eating space to a teaching space. All children out of diapers are welcome. The community teachers—residents who take turns acting as teachers— divide the children up into age groups. Those still in diapers are in a small nursery on the first floor of the ski lodge.

Like many, Mollie and I each teach a school day once per week. I helped Mollie with homeschooling Malcolm before, but being an actual teacher of multiple children is considerably different. A few residents used to be teachers—including Lois and Karen, who aren't helping currently—so they give most of the guidance, allowing me to be more of a helper. We do try and have a variety of subjects and life skills for the children to learn.

Malcolm used to want to be an engineer. I don't know if that will be a possibility for him in our new world. It might be many years before we look toward much but survival. And from what we hear on the ham radio, other areas aren't doing any better. As far as we know, there isn't any place in the United States that wasn't severely affected by the attacks, the EMP, or the nuclear detonations.

I've only just pulled out of the ski lodge parking space, heading toward the clinic, when I see Bill and Evan. "I'm going to talk with Evan and Bill. Won't take but a minute," I say to the children as I slow my truck and roll down the window.

"Then we see my brudder?" Andy asks.

"Yep. Soon, Andy." Then I call out the window, "Hey, guys. What are you up to?"

"Hey, Jake," Evan says. "You might as well know, too, since you've been a part of this. We think Heath was poking around their cabin last night."

"Really? I can't believe he came back. Where is he now?"

"That louse. I always knew he was bad news. I wish we knew where he was, but he's gone again," Bill says. "Madison heard a noise at the window, shined a light out but didn't see anyone. We gave her and Dot one of the radios—you know, just in case. She called it in. The roving patrols and one of Clark's guys went and checked it out. He didn't find anything, but this morning, in the daylight, there are new tracks all around the cabin."

"So . . . what are you doing about it?" I ask.

"We're going out again, see if we can pick up his trail. You want to go?"

"I do, but I'm on greenhouse duty starting at 1000. Sarah had her baby last night."

"That's right! Doris told me. A little boy—congrats, Grandpa." Evan turns to Marc and his siblings. "I bet you kids are excited about the new baby."

"I have a brudder," Andy says proudly.

"That's great," Bill says. "He's healthy?"

"Mollie says he is. I'm going to see him shortly."

"How's Mollie?" Evan asks.

"Tired. But happy and relieved. You heard Calley's pregnant?"

"I hadn't heard. When's she due?"

"End of June. Of course, we thought Sarah was due in February, so who really knows." I can't help but give a small laugh.

"So do you want to see if you can get out of greenhouse duty and go with us?" Evan asks.

"Yeah, I'd like to. Can you give me a minute to take the children to see the baby? Then I need to get Lois home."

"Yep. Leave in half an hour? We'll meet at your lodge."

"Should work. See you then." I roll up the window as we drive through the parking lot.

As I make my way up the driveway, the door to Zeb and Ellen's guest house opens. Shannon—the one who was meeting with Judge Avery in our den last night—her sister, their husbands, and their children live here. One of the men steps out, raising his hand in acknowledgment as he smartly strides by. A little too smartly. He hits a slick spot and momentarily loses his balance. After regaining his footing, he's much more cautious.

"You children wait here," I say, turning off the pickup. "I'll be right back, then we'll see the baby."

"Hey, Jake, you're early," Ellen says, giving me a smile.

"I wanted to see if you could spare me today. Looks like Dot's husband was poking around her cabin last night. I'd like to go out with the team to look for him."

"Did he hurt her again?" she asks, concern filling her voice.

"No, he didn't go inside. I'm not exactly sure what his thought was— "

"To terrorize her. Men like that, it's all about fear and control. You know he was harassing Rochelle and other women, too, but I had no idea about him abusing Dot. I should've . . . I should've seen it."

The way she says it makes me wonder if she's personally experienced domestic violence. Her husband, Zeb, seems like a good guy. But, of course, Heath didn't seem too bad either. Until right before Christmas when Rochelle put him on the ground. Then it came out he'd been hassling her and several others.

As if reading my mind, she says, "Not Zeb. He's wonderful. But my first husband, he used his fists to make a point."

"I . . . I'm sorry to hear that," I say, stumbling slightly over my words. Even during Mollie's and my darkest times in our marriage, I never once thought of being physically abusive. I don't understand that mindset at all.

"We'll be fine without you today, Jake. And Milena is doing better, so she should be able to return for her next shift. You're off the hook for greenhouse duty for now."

"Thanks, Ellen. You know, I do enjoy it."

"Oh, sure you do. I know you'd rather be out stomping through the woods any day."

"Well, you're right about that. But this isn't a bad job. I've always enjoyed our garden at home."

"Won't be long before we'll need to start our garden plants," she says. "I hope we've been saving enough seeds."

"You and Zeb will be moving down to Bakerville proper for the summer?"

"We're not sure yet. We might stay behind to help guard what we've got up here. I'll keep the greenhouses going so we can keep our food supply up. I just pray we can grow enough crops without the aid of machinery."

"We do have the one tractor they got going. Plus, there's a plan to use the quads to help with plowing."

"Yes, and did you hear Aaron Ogden suggested figuring out a way to turn the two snow groomers into plows?"

"I haven't heard about that. Will it work?"

"I don't know how, and we'd still have the fuel issue. There's probably enough fuel to get through planting and harvesting this year, but next year . . . " She shakes her head.

"I've got to get going. Sarah had her baby last night. We're going to meet him before I head out."

"That's wonderful! Both mom and baby are healthy?"

"As far as I know, yes. See you later."

I knock on the door of the clinic, waiting until I hear a "come in" before entering.

A tired looking Kelley greets us. "Hello, children. Lois was just saying you should be here anytime. She's loved her visit but needs a rest."

I nod. "Can we see Sarah and the baby first?"

"Send them in," Sarah calls from the other room.

"There's your answer," Kelley says with a smile. She lowers her voice and says, "They're doing fine."

"Hi, my sweeties," Sarah says from her bed. She looks radiant holding her son. Exhausted, but totally happy. "Jake, thanks so much for bringing them over."

"Hey, Sarah. You look good."

"Take a look at him. He's amazing."

"His name is Tate," Lois says proudly.

"Like my daddy?" Sissy asks.

"Yes, just like your daddy," Lois says, her eyes filling with tears.

I nod as I look him over. "He looks good. Big."

"You want to hold him?"

"No. He's not *that* big. I'll wait."

"I want to hold him," Andy says. "He's my brudder."

"He is your *brother*," Sarah says, gently correcting his pronunciation. "But not yet, honey. When he's a little older and we're back at home you can hold him. Today, you all can just look at him."

"You're feeling okay?" I ask.

"I feel good, better than I expected. And he's eating, which makes me happy."

"When will you come home?"

"Tomorrow. They want me to rest here today."

"Sounds good. I need to get going. You ready?" I ask, directing my question to Lois and Karen. "I need to take the children back to the ski lodge for school. I can pick you up on my way back by."

"I think we're ready," Karen answers, looking toward her mom, who gives a weary nod. "When they come home tomorrow, we'll have plenty of time to spend with him."

"Oh, I do hate to leave," Lois says, leaning in to kiss baby Tate's head.

After dropping off the children and then helping Lois to her room, I check in on Mollie. She's still asleep. Instead of waking her, I leave a note telling her I'm going with Evan and Bill to look for Heath. On my way out of the bedroom, I grab a few things to add to my pack. I'm ready to go when there's a knock.

"Right on time," I say, opening the front door. Instead of Bill and Evan, it's Jesse Richardson.

"Oh, hey. I was expecting someone else."

"I need to talk with Mollie again," he says.

"She's sleeping. Our daughter had her baby last night, and Mollie was up helping her."

"It can't wait."

I look behind Jesse to see Evan and Bill striding up the walkway along with Aaron Ogden, Lindsey Maverick, and a couple others in the community.

"Jesse?" Bill says as they approach.

"Bill, Evan," he says, nodding at the others.

"Ready to go, Jake?" Evan asks.

"Not sure. Jesse says he needs to talk with Mollie. And it can't wait."

"Is that so? You set up an appointment with Judge Avery?" Evan asks.

With a smirk, Jesse says, "I thought we could skip that nonsense this time. It'll only take a minute."

"No can do, buddy," Evan says in a friendly tone. "Even the judge made it clear that if you want to talk to Mollie, both he and Jake will be present. And Jake is needed elsewhere right now."

Jesse narrows his eyes at Evan before turning to me. "Maybe you can help me, Jake," he says evenly.

"What's on your mind?"

"Lydia lived at your house, right?"

"Well, sort of, yes."

"What does *sort of* mean?"

"Hey, Jesse," Bill says quietly, "you know the condition she was in. The poor lady was so messed up, she never even left the basement. Not until— " Bill clears his throat.

"Not until after she killed Tammy and stabbed Belinda," I finish for him. "Then tried to attack my daughter, son, and wife. That was the only time she left the basement. She was sick—first detoxing from whatever she was on and then with whatever mental problems she was having."

"How much contact did you have with her?"

"Me? None."

"Bill?" Jesse says. "You lived there. Did you have any contact with her?"

"No, she had a problem with men, so the women took care of her. It was better that way."

"So, if I showed you a piece of jewelry, you wouldn't know if it belonged to her?"

"Jewelry?" I ask. "I'd have no idea."

Bill says something similar.

"What's this about, Jesse?" Evan asks.

"Would Mollie know?"

"I doubt it," I say. "She wasn't one of her caregivers. She'd sit with her on occasion, but Belinda and Tammy were the ones taking care of her. Sometimes Kelley too."

"All right. I'll leave Mollie be, for now, and check with Belinda and Kelley."

"What's this about?" Evan asks again.

Jesse pauses while giving Evan a long look. Then he looks to the rest of us standing around. He shakes his head and says, "This place and the rumors. I guess you'll hear soon enough."

We all look at him, waiting for him to say more.

"Jackson Nicholson's wife was cleaning out his dressers, putting clothes together for the community." He stops talking, giving each of us a long look.

"And?" Evan prompts.

"And she found some jewelry. We've identified two of the pieces. There's half a dozen more pieces we're trying to figure out."

"Okay, so? What does this have to do with Mollie? Why did you want to talk to her?"

"I think Jesse might believe one of the pieces belonged to Lydia," Bill answers. "And, unless I miss my guess, the two pieces he's identified belonged to Phoebe and Amy."

Chapter 27

Wednesday, Day 205

Mollie

"You look good, Sarah," I say, tapping her on the arm. We're sitting on the couch, watching baby Tate as he sleeps in his box. As part of our preps, Jake and I purchased a couple of Finnish Baby Boxes.

Modeled after the boxes given to expectant mothers in Finland, these are stuffed with things a new baby needs and then the box becomes the baby's bassinette with the addition of the included mattress. I have another new one for Calley. We'll then reuse the box and as many items as possible for any future babies in the family.

Surprisingly, we were able to include the baby boxes as personal items instead of community property when we moved to the mountain. Mainly, I believe, because there are so few people of childbearing age, considering Bakerville was predominantly a retirement community.

Many of the few younger women already had children, and they were able to keep any baby goods they had on hand as their own personal items also. Items found in empty homes went in the community coffers. Before Shelby gave birth, we had a shower for her, most of the gifts magically appearing from the supply shed. We were planning a shower for Sarah, but Tate had other plans.

"I feel good. Much lighter." Sarah laughs. "I just wish— " She chews on her lip as her eyes fill with tears. "It's hard, Mom, hard not having Tate here to share this with me."

I put my arm around her shoulder as she lays her head on mine. We spend many minutes like this as she cries. Finally, she says, "Enough of that. While this isn't how I want it, it is what it is." When I cringe, she says, "Oops. Sorry, Mom. I forgot how much you hate that phrase."

"It's fine," I say with a wave of my hand. "I guess, in many ways, the phrase fits much of what's happening. Our circumstances are fact, and we need to accept them. But we don't know what will happen tomorrow. I've always been one for planning." I pause and raise my eyebrows at her.

"No kidding, Mom."

"Yeah, and when Jamie died, all my plans—our plans—went out the window. Trying to develop a new life wasn't easy. And in some ways, it was even more difficult than the life we're now living in."

"Why is that?"

"I tried to do it all then. Tried to keep you girls happy, tried to not be too sad for you while you all were grieving. But I was doing it alone. I didn't have the Lord to lean on then. No, that's not the right way to say it. I didn't *know* I had the Lord to lean on. Now, things are . . . I don't even know a good word to use. Uncertain? Scary? But I have a different kind of peace than I did then. Don't get me wrong, if it was possible, I'd go back to the way our world was in an instant. But there are good things now."

"Marc, Sissy, and Andy," she says quietly. "I love being their mom."

"Yes, and I love being a mom to Tony and Lily—even though I feel more like Grandmo to them most days. Lily often calls me that. Tony still usually calls me ma'am." I raise my eyebrows at her. We've discussed his formality with both Jake and I several times. I can't even imagine the hurt both he and Lily are feeling. "And you, Sarah. If our world wouldn't have fallen apart, you may not have gone back to the Lord."

She's quiet for several moments before she says, "I wouldn't have. There would be no reason for me to. Things were good for Tate and me, and we were doing fine on our own. Plus, it was all over social media and the news how Christianity is full of hate and bigotry. I believed what I learned in college, that I'd been brainwashed as a child to think there was a God or Jesus. But once I opened my mind—and my heart—I realized there was something missing." Baby Tate lets out a squeak and squirms. "Do you think he's hungry already?" she asks.

"Wouldn't surprise me. It's been almost two hours. Do you want me to get him for you?"

"Do you mind? I'll get everything positioned." She grabs the u-shaped pillow she made before Tate was born. Angela told her this type of pillow was a lifesaver when she was nursing Gavin. She positions the pillow, wrapping the open part around her waist, then gets everything else ready. "Okay, let's do this," she says, opening her arms for her baby. I can't help but kiss his downy covered head before I hand him off.

It takes a couple of minutes for the two of them to get everything working. Finally, she says, "That's something about Jackson."

I shake my head in reply.

"At least we have answers as to who killed Amy and Phoebe," she says.

"And Lydia," I say. "We know it wasn't a suicide and he was behind it. Though, how he had the opportunity—I still think Deputy Fred had to be involved somehow. After all, the makeshift jail was at his house."

"I heard Jesse interviewed Rochelle."

"Yeah. She said in the early days Fred had them at his house, he didn't let them outside. She didn't even know about the jail. Eventually, she was allowed in the backyard, and after she agreed to marry Fred, the girls could go outside too. But they never even looked in the jail or any outbuildings."

"I didn't know Lydia wore a toe ring."

"Me neither. But both Belinda and Kelley said it was hers. I wonder if we'll ever know who the rest of the jewelry belonged to."

"Does anyone know of any unsolved murders around here?"

"Bill said there was one a few years back up in Pryor, a young girl around Phoebe's age, but" —I lift my hand— "who knows."

"I feel bad for his wife," Sarah says. "To find out you've married a monster . . . no wonder him and Fred were friends. They were really very much alike."

"And it was suspected Jackson knew what Fred had done—you know, buying Rochelle and her girls from that place—but it couldn't be proven," I say, nodding vigorously. "Tamra, Jackson's wife, insists she knew nothing about the murders or the situation with Fred."

"Do you think Jackson is the one who shot Dr. Sam? Maybe Sam suspected him of Lydia?"

"I think if Sam suspected him, he would've said something. But maybe . . . maybe Jackson *thought* Sam knew something. I don't know if we'll ever know who shot Sam, but it would make things a little less concerning if it was Jackson."

"Because then we'd know for sure all of the murderers were dealt with?" Sarah asks.

"Right. But we don't know where Fred is, and while not a murderer, they still haven't found Heath." Jake and the search team are out looking again today. I think they're impressed with his ability to evade them. Frustrated, but impressed.

"Do you ever wonder how so many—I don't even know the word . . . criminals? Bad guys? How are there so many depraved people in one small community?"

"I have wondered! I've also wondered how we have so many retired law enforcement officers, government agents, and military personnel in Bakerville."

"I'd rather have them than the bad guys," Sarah says, giving me a questioning look.

"Oh, me too. I'm just commenting about the interesting makeup of Bakerville. We definitely could do without the bad guys." As I say it, I'm suddenly struck with an image of Brad. When I knew him, he had a job working as an enforcer for a guy who owned several questionable businesses. I can't imagine his morals have improved much over the years, especially with the few things he has done while he's been here. He and Sam got into a small argument shortly before Sam was shot. It wasn't much of a disagreement, and certainly not worth shooting Sam over, but . . .

"Lois looks good," Sarah says. "I was so surprised when she showed up at the clinic yesterday morning. And she was visiting in my room early this morning. I wouldn't be surprised if she comes down soon. She said she was going to rest for a bit, but I think this will be a turning point for her."

"I pray so," I say. "If she gets better, it will be a relief for Karen too. Even though we all offer to help— "

"Right. She insists on being Lois's main caregiver. I think it's part of her own grieving process, but I have a suspicion she'd love to be able to do more things in the community. Both have been talking about helping at the school."

"We've been fortunate the council approved Karen acting as Lois's caregiver and not making her take duty shifts also. But if she and Lois could be part of the teaching team, they'd certainly be an asset. And maybe adding one or both into the rotation would get Jake out of his school day," I say with a small laugh.

"Ah, Jake likes school day. And the children love him. Haven't you seen how some of the younger kids flock to him? 'Mr. Jake, Mr. Jake, will you read us a story next time you're at school?' Apparently, he does voices and everything."

"Oh, I know. I've heard his voices. Where is Karen?"

"Said she was going for a walk. She's been gone a while. Maybe I should go up and check on Lois."

"We'd hear her bell."

"That's true." We sit and talk about nothing while she finishes feeding Tate. Everything feels so normal, it's hard to believe we're living during the apocalypse.

"He's asleep again," she says, tapping him lightly on the back. "Is it bad that I just want to sit here and hold him instead of putting him back in his baby box?"

"Not bad at all. But you might want to take a rest also. I can carry the box upstairs for you."

"Can I just stretch out on the couch? Would you mind?"

"Sounds like a great idea. Here, I'll put him to bed, then grab you a blanket out of the chest."

The door opens as I'm laying Tate in his bed. Cheeks rosy from the cold, Karen comes in, the scent of the outdoors wafting after her. "Ah, I was hoping to catch him with his eyes open," she says as she starts taking off her coat.

"He wasn't awake very long," Sarah says. "Fell asleep as soon as he ate and burped. Mom convinced me I should rest while he does."

"Smart idea. It was nice of Doris to have the kitchen crew work out of the ski lodge for a few days. That will help keep it a little quieter here."

"It'll be crowded for them," Sarah says.

"It's fine," Karen says with a flick of her hand. "They're using the firepit also and seem to be having fun. I stopped by to visit, that's why I'm so late. I think, if Mother continues doing so well, I'll see if I can get on the kitchen crew as a backup."

"We can always use backups," I say.

"What are you doing today, Mollie?"

"Nothing. Since Belinda and Kelley gave me three mandatory rest days, I'm just doing stuff around the lodge. Officially, they're worried for my health, but I think they were just being kind and allowing me to help Sarah."

"I'm extremely glad they did that. I can use the help. But they're not wrong, Mom," Sarah says gently. "While I'm so glad you were with me, I can see the toll it took on you. Are you still following the special diet?"

"I am," I say with a sigh. "Other than fish since they haven't been biting lately. I think many of us are missing those."

"Not me," Karen says. "Those boney trout are something I can do without. I always manage to almost choke on one of those thin little spears."

I give a soft laugh. "They can be a nuisance."

"I'm going to go up and check on Mother. Then I'm having a cup of tea. You two want to join me?"

"I'm still thinking a nap sounds good," Sarah says. "But maybe after I get up."

I sit in the easy chair while Sarah settles into the couch. I hate to admit that Belinda and Kelley are right. I have been exhausted since the night Tate was born. I was tired before, but being up and emotional for such an extended time really did affect me.

I've scheduled an appointment with them for Monday. I'm going to ask all the questions I now have about the secrets I think they're keeping from me. When I told Jake about the game they seem to be playing, he simply nodded and said, "Doesn't surprise me. I kind of thought they were only giving us the condensed version of what they think."

I guess, deep down, I've known. And I do see their point; why worry about something of which we have no control. They were wrong about Sarah. She wasn't pregnant with twins, just one healthy, full-term boy.

"M-Mollie," Karen says quietly from the top of the staircase. "Can you go find Belinda?"

I jump to my feet. "Is Lois sick?"

"N-no," she says, choking back a sob. "She's gone to her Heavenly home. She's with my dad again."

Chapter 28

Thursday, Day 206

Jake

Instead of a service at the ski lodge for the entire community, Karen wanted to have a smaller memorial for Lois at the dude ranch lodge with only our family and close friends in attendance. She said it didn't seem right to have everyone there when Lois spent her last months in self-imposed confinement. And with Sarah just having her baby, it's much easier for her. Since baby Tate is so young, he's staying upstairs during the gathering, with us taking turns watching him. We're doing our best to prevent him from being exposed to too many germs. In our current situation, we want to take all precautions necessary for his and all of our health. Sarah did introduce him from a distance and let everyone get a quick look.

Belinda, who came to know Lois very well when she was living at our homestead and in the months she's been caring for her after Keith and Tate went missing, is the first to speak. "When my mom, son, and I moved to the Caldwells' basement on the day of the EMP attack, we barely knew them. We only went because it was a safe place we could care for our injured. Lois was one of the first people to go out of her way to make us not only feel welcomed but loved. My mom made a point of saying, 'The light of Jesus shined through Lois.' It was a completely true statement. She had a way about her that made everyone feel special.

"When my mom— " Belinda pauses for a moment, taking a deep breath. "When Mom died, Lois was there for me and TJ. She would sit with me and hold my hand while I cried. When I recovered from my injuries enough to sit upright, she'd hold me and let me talk, sharing as many memories as I wanted. She did the same for TJ. She encouraged us to talk about our loved ones. I encourage you to do the same thing. Talk about Lois, about what a wonderful mother she was to Karen and Tate. How she was an extraordinary grandma to not only Marc, Sissy, Andy, and baby Tate but to all the children living here—whether she was related to them or not. Lois loved kids and made sure they knew it. Talk about Keith and Tate also. Remember the ones we've lost so we can keep their memories alive.

"Lois was able to help others through their grief, but she wasn't able to help herself through hers. As the doctors of the community, we did what we could to bring her out of her depression. She was so excited about the birth of her grandchild. I honestly believe that's what kept her going. And when she knew baby Tate was here and healthy, her heart simply stopped beating. As Karen has said many times, she's gone to her Heavenly home and is once again with her beloved husband. While I'll miss her, I'm also extremely happy for her."

Belinda sits down and other people take their turn. Even Malcolm spends a couple of minutes talking about how nice Lois was to him and how much she loved to share her "teacher stuff." Even in the months we've been up here, the children were welcome to come sit by her bed for a short story. He makes sure to say how wonderful it was when she joined the group for reading time on the night we were waiting for baby Tate to be born.

When Sarah speaks, she says how hard it will be to not have Lois to help share memories of Tate and Keith with their baby. And how she'll need everyone's help telling baby Tate how wonderful his grandparents and dad were. There's not a dry eye in the place when she finishes.

We scheduled the memorial between lunch and supper so a meal wouldn't be necessary. Even so, we do have both hot and iced tea and a few snacks. When delivering the invites from the list Karen and Sarah made, Kelley went around and asked people to bring what they could. According to Kelley, a memorial service without snacks is just not done. Deanne must have agreed because leftover meat and cheese showed up in the form of a deli tray. There are even wedges of flatbread included.

"Hey, Jake," Dot says. While she didn't know Lois, her new roommate Madison became part of our large family after Mollie rescued her and baby Emma from murderers. Madison used to live in the bunkhouse on our homestead with Lois, Keith, and Karen. Instead of staying at home, Madison encouraged Dot to join us. It's her first venture out in public after Heath left her for dead. Her face, still bruised and swollen, leaves no doubt to the severity of the beating she survived.

"Dot, I'm glad you're here," I say.

"Me too. Lois sounds like a wonderful lady."

"She was genuinely nice, but she really had a hard time when Tate and Keith went missing. We never had a memorial for them. She . . . she said it'd be too final. Sarah and Karen say that when we bury Lois at our place in the spring, we'll do something for all of them."

"That makes sense. I must admit, I thought it was creepy Doris insisted on a small shed as a morgue, but with all the snow and the frozen ground, there isn't anything else to do."

"Right. We'll each bury our loved ones on our land. The Bakers offered to bury Amy on their place next to Phoebe. Makes sense since they were friends in the dorm and their deaths were so— " I grasp for the word I'm looking for "—similar." I shrug.

"I was shocked when I heard about Jackson's wife finding the jewelry he took. I guess that makes him some sort of a serial killer?" she asks, eyes wide.

"Something like that, I guess. But Jesse made a point of saying they only know for certain about Lydia, Phoebe, and Amy. The other pieces of jewelry could be something else. I don't think he honestly believes that, but you know how it is."

"Yeah, it's not like there's some crime database he can access on the computer now."

"Nope, we're completely old school again," I agree. "I heard Madison's all moved into your place."

"She is. Doris was able to find someone with two twin beds who wanted to swap for my queen. And she had a crib for Emma. We're all set. Madison said there's a problem with our supplies—some things have disappeared?"

"Seems so. They made an announcement at breakfast. Doris and her team have done a full inventory. Depending on what it is, there's up to 10 percent of the supply missing. Of course, some things were hard to know for sure on, like all the sugar beets and other bulk items."

"Where'd they go?"

"That's the million-dollar question. That, along with who took them. They're adding more security to prevent anything else from walking off."

"Belinda will let me return to guard duty next week."

"You think you'll be ready?"

"I don't look too pretty yet, but I'm ready now. I need to do something other than feel sorry for myself."

"You should come visit Sarah. Mollie's returning to her duties the day after tomorrow. I'm sure Sarah would welcome the company and help for a few more days."

"You think?"

"Sure. Go over and ask her, but my guess is absolutely."

"Thanks, Jake. I'll do that."

After Dot walks away, I scan the room. Losing some of our supplies is a blow. The hope is, now that we know about it, we can prevent the loss of any more. Ten percent is a lot, but we're hopeful it won't be too detrimental. At least not this winter. But we all know our future survival could be impacted by this.

This year's sugar beet, potato, barley, and corn crops were amazing—more than we could've hoped for, considering we harvested by hand. This spring, we'll also be planting by hand. Can we do as well as was done last year without the convenience of modern machines?

Even our personal gardens are likely to suffer without modern conveniences. And did we save enough seeds to plant what's needed to get our community through another winter? Last summer was challenging with keeping the garden growing and then processing the harvest, while also on guard duty and the multitude of other things needed to prepare our community to survive the winter. At least then we had the advantage of the garden already being in and a considerable stockpile of food. Now the stockpile is gone, other than some we've stashed for emergency needs, and our garden needs to be enlarged. We had a very generous garden for three people but not nearly enough for the current size of our extremely large extended family.

My eyes fall on my beautiful wife. I know she's sick. She knows she's sick. She's scheduled an appointment with Belinda and Kelley for Monday to, as she puts it, "Get to the bottom of it." But last night, as she lay in my arms crying over the loss of Lois, our conversation turned. It turned to the reality of her own health. When she went to retrieve Belinda after Karen found Lois, she became so winded she had to sit in the snow before she could continue. Mollie must feel my eyes on her; she meets my gaze and gives me a wink and a smile. Always sassy, that woman of mine.

It's too easy to get bogged down in thinking about the days to come—worrying about Mollie, worrying about our food, about being in the middle of an apocalypse. Undoubtedly, I'm not spending nearly enough time with my Bible and in prayer. I need to remember there's no peace and comfort in the world; I'll only find it in the word. I smother a sigh. Too often, that's easier said than done.

Chapter 29

Monday, Day 210

Mollie

"Sarah said Karen's going to watch baby Tate while she goes to the meeting this afternoon. That still the plan?" Belinda asks as she looks in my ear.

"It is. She has no intentions of missing it."

"It feels like a lot has happened in the week since the last meeting— a new life and a death. But that's the way of the world, I guess," she says.

While Belinda continues my examination, Kelley takes notes. Jake sits awkwardly in the chair. He's stressed and nervous, afraid of what they're going to tell us. In some ways I feel the same, but mostly I just want the truth.

"So tell me about the day Lois died. What happened to make you need to take a rest in the snowbank?"

I give a small shrug. "Like I told you when you found me, I just got tired. I was starting to feel better when you came running over."

"You were almost to the clinic, only fifty feet away. You couldn't finish that distance?"

I chew on my lip while I give a slight nod of my head. I feel tears prickling my eyes. No, I couldn't finish the distance. Even though it was only fifty feet, I couldn't take another step. I'd never felt so exhausted in my life, like everything inside of me had gone to jelly. To Belinda, I simply say, "No."

"Were you running?"

"Ha!" I scoff. "Not running. Walking fast, maybe."

"And since then?"

"It's happened a few more times, not quite as bad but still there."

"Have you fainted?"

"No, I've been able to sit down—even if the nearest spot is a snowbank—and rest until it passes."

"Kelley, do you have any questions for her or feel we need to look at anything else?"

"I'm okay with Mollie dressing and then we can talk."

"And you'll be telling me the truth this time—all of it?"

"Scouts honor," Kelley says with a small smile.

"You were never a scout," I say, narrowing my eyes at her. "Seriously, Kelley. I want to know what you know."

"Get dressed and we'll sit in the chairs. I brought a thermos of tea."

"You think a tea party will help?" I ask testily.

She pats my arm and whispers, "Get dressed, Mollie." With a small smile, she closes the curtain.

As I put on my multiple winter layers, I can hear them rustling around. There's no conversation, just stirring sounds. Feeling a wave of exhaustion beginning, I sit on the wooden chair to put my sweater on. Whatever they tell me, at least I'll have the knowledge needed to move forward. Not knowing is hard. Once we have the information we need, Jake and I can make plans. I'm not going to lie; I expect it to be bad. I'm expecting some sort of cancer or other terminal diagnosis. Nothing else would make sense.

In some ways, I'm jealous of Lois—jealous she passed away peacefully. Yes, she hadn't been well for months, but it wasn't a physical illness as much as an emotional one. We all hoped after baby Tate was born, she'd return to us as her usual robust self. I pray, if what they tell me is too bad, God will spare me from the worst of it.

I slide open the curtain and do my best to flounce into the room; it's not easy to fake not being exhausted. I choose the seat next to Jake, reaching for his hand as soon as I'm settled.

Kelley hands us each a mug before sitting down with her own. Belinda brings a couple of large medical tomes over with her, placing them on the coffee table. She's without a cup but doesn't seem to mind. "Okay, Mollie. You asked for the truth."

"Yes, that's what I want."

"The truth is, we can't give you the truth. We don't have the answers we need to be able to tell you exactly what's going on." She pauses for a moment, letting the info sink in before continuing. "If we were in a hospital with access to testing equipment, we'd know for sure. But here, on this mountain, we're primitive. Kelley, Madison,

June, all of us are doing what we can to keep people healthy and alive. Sometimes, like with Lois, we fail."

"We don't blame you for Lois dying," Jake says quickly.

"Oh, we know you don't. But we do feel some blame on our own. We wonder if we missed obvious signs. You asked for the truth. Truth is, even if there were obvious signs Lois was having trouble with her heart, we wouldn't have been able to do anything about it. We lost the sickest people in Bakerville before we moved up to the mountain, one after we moved up. Gladys Griffin's passing came shortly afterward, along with—what? Three others in the river community?"

"That's right," Jake says.

"In the early 1900s, you and Mollie—Kelley too—in fact, most residents of Bakerville would be considered elderly. The life expectancy wasn't much past the age of fifty. At forty, I'd be bordering on old age," she says with a small smile. "Pharmaceuticals are one of the main reasons people live well into their eighties."

"But my grandma only died a couple of years ago," Jake interrupts. "She was in her late nineties and didn't take any medication."

"Sure," Kelley says. "There's always been a few people like that, but for most people, it's the medications keeping them going. We've tried to find alternatives, and some of those alternatives are helping. We have a few people on special diets and herbs who are thriving. And many people that have lost weight are doing considerably better. We'd hoped Gladys Griffin would be one of those people because she seemed to be doing very well when we moved up here."

"And what does all of this have to do with Mollie?" Jake asks, furrowing his brow.

Belinda looks at her lap. "The bottom line is, we're not sure what's wrong with her." She looks up, meeting my eyes. "Most likely, you have some sort of cancer."

I feel tears well up. Even though I expected this, it's still hard to hear. Jake's hand tightens in mine. "And?" I ask, choking out the word.

"And there's nothing we can do about it."

Chapter 30

Monday, Day 210

Jake

"Nothing at all?" I ask. Even I can hear the whimper in my voice.

Belinda shakes her head.

"What about surgery? Can you remove it?" I can't bring myself to say it out loud, to say cancer.

"We've talked about it," Kelley says, her own voice is wobbly and there's tears in her eyes. Mollie and Kelley have been friends since we moved to Bakerville, one month after she and Phil arrived here. "Surgery is just so risky."

"Do it anyway," I say.

"Where's it at?" Mollie asks. "The cancer, where is it?"

Belinda nods. "I should've told you already. Sorry. We believe we've felt three separate masses— "

"Well . . . " Kelley interrupts.

"Right. Full disclosure. When we first saw you, the jaundice was the first clue something was wrong. At that time, you had an enlarged gallbladder. It was so large, we could palpate it. This is called Courvoisier's law, and we're taught when we find a palpable gallbladder combined with jaundice that we're looking at a malignancy."

"I have cancer in my gallbladder?" Mollie asks. "If that's the case, then I'm with Jake. Just take it out. People get their gallbladders removed all the time."

"True, and we could. But again, surgery here is risky. Sam— " Belinda lets out a sigh. "Sam survived surgery but didn't survive the infections following. If you got an infection, we might not be able to save you."

"And if I have cancer? I'll die too, right?"

"It probably wouldn't be cancer in your gallbladder," Kelley says. "It's more likely to be cancer in your bile ducts or possibly your pancreas."

"Her pancreas?" That's what killed Michael Landon. And didn't he get diagnosed and die only a month or two later? *No. Not Mollie.*

"We don't know, Jake," Belinda says. "That's the trouble. We know there's something wrong. We knew it the first day. We've examined her several times since then. The gallbladder is no longer enlarged, so that's a good thing. But we do feel three separate masses in her abdomen."

I glance at Mollie as the hand not holding mine moves protectively to her stomach. She's staring straight ahead as the tears travel down her cheeks.

"And those masses?" I ask quietly.

"Likely tumors. We have no way of knowing if they're cancerous without a biopsy. All we can do is look at the symptoms. And the physical symptoms tell us something is seriously wrong. Is it cancer? Maybe. We don't know for sure. But we assume it is based on what we know and what we're observing."

"How long?" Mollie asks.

"How long have you been sick?"

"How long until I die?"

Kelley lets out a loud breath. "We don't know. If it's cancer, it might be a few months. It could be years. There's also a chance you don't have cancer and have a condition causing tumors. We found a reference to an autoimmune condition which can mimic cancer."

"Not cancer. That's possible, right?" I ask.

"It is." Kelley nods vigorously. "We just don't know. She also had bilateral swelling along the jawline, which is sometimes an indicator of the autoimmune condition."

"We'll take more blood from you before you go," Belinda says to Mollie. "So far, we haven't seen anything concerning when looking at your blood, urine, or stool under the microscope."

"That's good, right?" I ask, giving Mollie a nod.

"Definitely," Belinda agrees.

"So, what do we do?" Mollie asks.

"There's not much we can do, other than the things we've started," Belinda says. "We're encouraged with how well you've been responding to the dietary changes and rest. You've increased your amount of ginger and garlic?"

"I have," Mollie answers. "It was nice of Ellen to harvest a little of the fresh from the greenhouse. I'm glad that's part of the greenhouse plants, much better than the powdered ginger."

"You're mixing the ginger and garlic together like a tea? Then drinking it?" Kelley asks.

"Right. It's so delicious," she says.

"Oh, I'm sure it is," Belinda responds. "Doris said she returned all your ferments to you. You've added those into your meals?"

For several years, Mollie has done what she calls natural pickles. Based on the same idea as traditional sauerkraut, she puts vegetables—and sometimes fruit—into a saltwater brine and allows them to pickle until soft. Some, like the sauerkraut, are surprisingly good. Some are a little weird. But she swears by the health benefits of these and says the fermentation process produces lots of beneficial organisms, and by keeping it raw, all the good stuff is preserved.

When we found out we had to donate all of our food and many of our nonfood supplies to the community for the privilege of moving up the mountain, Mollie made sure I stashed some of her sauerkraut, which was fermenting in a clay pot, in one of our buried caches. She said that after the long winter, we'd need the nutrients the kraut provides. Sure, we stashed several other things, too, but ferments were a well-thought-out item. The rest of the fermenting she and our children did last summer were donated to the community coffers, as required. Mollie gave Doris specific instructions to make sure to keep the ferments cold to preserve them—we store ours in the refrigerator or root cellar at home. Doris found a cold closet but is too weirded out by the fermenting process to feed any to the community, for fear of food poisoning.

"We've only taken a few jars to the lodge," I say. "Doris has a good place to keep the rest of them."

"Okay, that's fine," Belinda says. "I'll be honest, I'm not sure about the fermented stuff, but Kelley thinks it's a good idea. She's shown me some of her books about it, and— " Belinda lifts her hands in a display of surrender. "I don't think it'll hurt, provided they're safe to eat. Kelley says you'll know when you open one up if something's wrong with it."

"I'll know," Mollie says. "It'll smell spoiled."

"Then have at it," she says with a smile. "Ideally, I'd like you only eating fish and eggs as your protein since they are easier to digest, but until the fish start biting again, try and focus on rabbit and chicken. I talked with Doris about getting you either a chicken or rabbit each week as part of your rations—and maybe Jake or the boys can snare wild rabbits. Try and go easy on the elk and beef. I heard there's a couple of goats ready to butcher?"

"That's right," I say. "Five goats. We'll butcher them in the next few days."

"I'm not sure I've ever had goat," Belinda says. "But I'll give it a try."

"It's very similar to venison," Mollie says, wiping her eyes with a handkerchief. "These are young, neutered males, so they shouldn't be gamey."

"Anything else we should know?" I ask.

"You should, of course, continue to pray," Kelley says. "When we tell you we don't know, we're being truthful. But God, He knows. He knows exactly what's wrong, and He's a God of miracles. Believe in that, Mollie, Jake. Believe in his miracles."

Chapter 31

Monday, Day 210

Mollie

Jake and I hold hands, the big medical books tucked under his other arm, as we walk back to the lodge in silence. Unlike the day Lois died, I can make the short trek without any problems. We'll take the pickup truck to lunch and stay there for the final meeting as the council re-votes on the gun issue. We were, again, given a slight diesel increase for while Sarah is in recovery, even though she's not taking meals at the ski lodge. Doris said, since we needed to haul food back and forth, it made sense. I wonder if our ration will stay increased once it gets around that I may have cancer.

Pancreatic cancer, even. While Jake mentioned Michael Landon, the actor who played Charles Ingalls in the *Little House* television show, I can't help but think of Patrick Swayze from *Dirty Dancing* and many other movies where he was a heartthrob. I remember researching pancreatic cancer at the time and reading it was a painful way to go—painful when the world was normal and narcotics for pain relief were plentiful. Here, we only have a spattering of pain relief medications we salvaged from empty houses. When we moved up to the mountain, we shared what we had with those staying in Bakerville proper.

Once we're in our bedroom, we fall into each other and cry. After a few minutes, I pull back and say, "Enough of that for now. While it sounds bleak, they said they aren't sure, right? It could be the other thing."

"Are you going to read through the books they gave us?" Jake asks, motioning to the two tomes he sat on our dresser.

"I will. They put sticky notes on the sections for us to focus on. I'll read through and then let you read the stuff I think you'd want to know about."

"I'll probably want to know all of it," he says, kissing my nose. "We need to leave in about fifteen minutes."

"I'll be ready. I'll wash my face and hopefully won't look like I've been bawling my eyes out."

"You're still beautiful."

"Ha. Go on with you."

After lunch, we stay and help set up for the meeting. Unlike the other meetings where the children go downstairs to the nursery, today they're taken to the lodge for an afternoon of games. Dodie suggested it, saying the extra space might be nice. Our full-time teacher agreed. Karen will keep baby Tate upstairs in her bedroom. We do expect this meeting to be quick, but Sarah was able to express enough milk for a feeding if needed.

As the council comes in and takes their seats, I take a long look at Mick Michaelson. He looks pale and shaky. Is he sick? When Jon Dawson arrives with five minutes to spare before the meeting begins, he's back to his well-composed, put together self. He's even dressed up for the occasion, wearing a sport jacket and slacks. Why even bring those things up the mountain? Maybe I should've brought an evening gown? I smile at my internal quip.

"Hey, Sarah, you look good today." I close my eyes as I hear the voice. Hazarding a glance in Sarah's direction, Brad is smiling brightly.

"Thanks, Dad. I feel good."

"Thought you might bring my grandson with you so I could hold him."

"There are too many people here—germs and all, you know." She says with a smile.

"Well, I guess. Why don't you and him come over for a visit? Alina and I are both off tomorrow."

"I'm not really taking him out right now. But you can come by the lodge if you'd like."

Brad looks toward me. "Will that be all right with your mom?"

I don't bother to tell him that Alina and Victor visit often and are always welcome. Him, not so much. Instead, I plaster a smile on my face. "I don't believe we've ever prevented you from visiting Sarah." I do make a mental note to notify both Jesse Richardson and Judge

Avery of his intention to stop by and see Sarah and the baby. I don't want there to be any doubts about his motives.

He gives me a curt nod. "We'll stop by after lunch, maybe even take Victor out of school and bring him along."

"I'd like that, Dad," Sarah says with a smile. "Where's Alina today?"

"She was out with the firewood crew this morning, decided to stay home and rest instead of attending this circus."

Sarah's smile fades slightly as she says, "Please give her my best. We'll see you tomorrow."

Brad nods as he moves forward a few rows to an empty seat.

"All right, folks," Judge Avery says at exactly 1400. "Today is the final meeting on the issue of carrying a firearm in public spaces. To recap, we heard from each of the councilmembers as to why they voted the way they did at the original meeting. That meeting was not a public venue, and even though Evan Snyder was not in attendance, it did meet quorum requirements. Because Councilman Snyder was not at the original meeting, he will not be voting today."

The usual rumble of displeasure makes its way through the crowd. Judge Avery raises his voice as he continues. "Last week we heard from you, residents of Bakerville, as to why you do or do not support the public weapons ban. Today, your council—minus Evan—will vote again. Before we get started, are there any questions about the process?"

Shannon—the one who, according to Jake, threw a fit at our house during the discussion with Doris and Judge Avery last week—raises her hand and quickly stands.

"Shannon, is this about the process? This is not the time to express your opinion on the vote."

"I make a motion to leave the vote as it stands."

"Seconded," Moira, Shannon's sister, cries out as the group erupts.

"Enough!" Judge Avery cries. "Your motion is out of order. There will be a new vote today. Now pipe down so we can get on with it."

It's several minutes before everyone is settled and again quiet. I look over to Sarah, her mouth in a tight line.

"Jon Dawson, you're first. How do you vote?" Judge Avery asks.

"I vote to leave the law in place."

"What a surprise," someone from the back says in a stage whisper.

"None of that," Judge Avery says in reprimand. "The audience will hold their opinions—and their tongues. Jana, what's your vote?"

"I vote in favor of the law."

"Bill, what's your vote?"

"I vote against the rule."

It doesn't escape me that Bill refers to it as a *rule* instead of a *law*.

"Rhoda, what's your vote?" Judge Avery asks.

Rhoda looks down at the table, then clears her throat. "Opposed."

There's a huge rumble through the crowd. Sarah grabs my hand and whispers, "Mom, we're going to win!" Judge Avery tries unsuccessfully to quiet everyone. Finally, Phil Hudson lets out a whistle, which quickly brings silence.

"When I said I wanted you to hold your opinions, I meant it," Judge Avery says harshly. "Now, Rhoda, I want to make sure I heard you correctly. You're voting against banning firearms in public places? Which will, once again, allow people to carry as they choose?"

"That's correct, Judge," Rhoda says, lifting her head. "After listening to our constituents, it's clear the majority are not in favor of a ban. I was elected to represent the people, and I am choosing to do so."

I look to Jon Dawson. He's examining his fingernails and doesn't seem at all concerned about losing the vote of one of the councilmembers.

"Okay, Rhoda. Your vote against the ban has been recorded. Let's wrap this up. Mick, what do you say?"

I can feel the smile on my face. Mick voted against the firearms ban. We've got this. We're going to be able to open carry again. We'll be able to protect ourselves in a legal manner instead of having to conceal it.

Mick Michaelson scans the audience; I follow his gaze as his eyes rest on his wife. Her face like a stone statue, she gives a single nod. He moves his head slightly, maybe looking at his children. Unlike most of the community kids who are at our lodge, all but Macie, their oldest and only daughter, are sitting next to his wife. I don't remember her being at the lodge when we left, but at thirteen, she could've chosen to stay in their camp trailer. I look back to Mick as his eyes drop to the table. My stomach gives a lurch.

"I'm voting in favor of the ban," Mick says, his voice void of emotion. Once again, the crowd loses control. There's some cheering from Shannon and her group but mostly boos and calls as to why. Even a few who yell out traitor.

Instead of immediately stopping the outcry, Judge Avery lets it go for a few minutes. He has such a shocked look on his face, I'm led to believe he's attempting to gather his own thoughts before trying to rein everyone else in. Finally, he brings the group to order before saying, "Mick? I'm not sure I heard you correctly."

Mick looks back toward the crowd to the section his wife is sitting in before saying, "You heard me correctly. I'm changing my vote to be in favor of the ban."

Chapter 32

Thursday, Day 213

Jake

Since the firearms ban was upheld, things have been tense. To say that Mick changing his mind and choosing to keep the edict in place was a surprise is an understatement. We feel betrayed. All we can figure is somehow Shannon Decker and her group got to him.

"Okay, boys. Let's wrap it up," I say to Tony, Malcolm, and Marc. "One more round each is enough for today." The day before yesterday, my dad said he thought Marc was feeling left out. He suggested talking to Malcolm about letting Marc learn on his youth bow and Malcolm could have my dad's old compound bow. Since Marc is left-handed, like my dad and Malcolm, it's a good swap. Malcolm loved the idea of a full-sized bow. When we talked to Marc about it, his face lit up.

Paul Cameron checked the string and made the adjustments needed for both Malcolm and Marc. I must admit, I felt a little like a heel for not realizing Marc was being left out. "You did good today, Marc. You're definitely a natural."

"You think so?" he asks, beaming.

"Better than I was the first day," Tony says.

"Me too," Malcolm agrees. "You know, Dad, I was thinking about the other bows I have, the ones for kids. Do you know where they are?"

"Still at the house, I guess. We only brought up stuff mandated by the community and personal stuff we thought we'd need for the winter. We secured the rest of the things in the cabinets in the basement."

"Yeah, they're probably there. You know how they're only regular toy bows? Not special bows for left hands?" I get in a quick nod before he rushes on, "Maybe Sissy and Lily will want to use them to learn how to shoot, you think?"

"It's a good idea," I agree. "They can start learning how to hold them and be on target. You have a couple of traditional bows and the small compound. We'll talk to your mom when we get moved back."

As we're walking back to the cabin, I raise my hand in greeting and holler out a hello to Harry English and his lady friend. Once again, her name escapes me.

"Hello, Jake," Harry says. "You boys been out practicing?" he asks, motioning toward the bows.

"Yes, sir. Dad or Grandpa take us out a few times a week," Malcolm says.

"Is that right? Good for you to learn the skill. Did you hear our news, Jake?"

"What news is that?" I ask, wondering what's going on now.

"Annette's agreed to become my wife," he answers with a broad smile. "The wedding will be a week from Saturday. I hope you and your family can make it."

"Wow, congratulations." I reach out my hand to him. When I offer my hand to Annette, she laughs and pulls me into a hug.

"I've been waiting forever for him to ask me," she says in her quiet way.

"Who would've thought she'd want to marry an old guy like me?" Harry asks with a shrug.

She gives him a smile and shakes her head. "It'll be an outdoor wedding at the gazebo by the river, so dress accordingly. The wedding's at 1130, and we'll have our regular lunch afterward."

"Sounds good. Where will you live?"

"That's being worked out," Harry says. "Right now, I'm in the bachelor trailer and Annette is in the women's dorm. One plan being discussed is Jackson's widow and kids moving in with Deputy Fred's wife and kids. We'd move into the other half of their duplex."

"Is their cabin big enough?" I ask.

Harry shrugs. "It's a one bedroom. The women say the four girls could sleep in the bedroom and they could have a daybed with a trundle in the main room. Tamra, Jackson's wife, already has a daybed that was in the cabin when they moved in, so they could move it over. They'd leave the queen-sized bed for us. It's a work in progress for sure."

"The Lord will provide," Annette says, and Harry answers with, "Amen!"

"Congrats," I say again. "We'll be happy to celebrate with you."

"How's your new grandbaby?" Harry asks.

"Growing fast. He's already losing that new baby look."

"It's smart your daughter is keeping him away from the group. Shelby and Grant did that, too, waited until Hannah was a month old before showing her off. I know it was hard on Shelby to feel like she was outside of the community, always isolated at home, but with our limited medical abilities, it's best to keep the babies isolated as much as possible."

"Belinda says a lot of doctors recommended it, even when our world was normal," I say.

"Yep. I've heard that too. Say, do you ever wonder why we don't have some sort of phrase for when things changed?" Harry asks.

"Meaning?"

"I finally got to read *Alas, Babylon* from the community library. Have you read that book?"

"A couple of years ago," I say with a nod. "It's one of my wife's favorites."

"Is that right? Oh! That's right. You and Mollie were— " He gets a strange look on his face.

"Preppers?" I ask.

With a guilty smile, he says, "That's the rumor I've heard. Many of the things we have up here are thanks to you, the Hudsons, and a few others."

While I'm sure it's meant to be a compliment, the statement leaves a hole in the pit of my stomach. The things we brought to the mountain were meant to be for taking care of our family and loved ones. We never planned—or prepped—to care for the entire community.

"Yeah, I guess the rumors are abundant around here. Even without telephones or radios, the Bakerville grapevine is alive and well. Anyway, what about the book?"

"They call it 'The Day' when the nukes hit and their lives changed. Here, people don't do that. We might say 'before the EMP' or 'prior to the attacks,' but we don't have a fancy buzz name for it."

"Okay. And?" I ask, not understanding where Harry is going with this.

"And nothing, really. I just found it interesting. I do have to say, though, other than the lack of the buzz word, so much in that novel—written before you and I were even born—is accurate today."

"That's true. Maybe we'll have a helicopter come flying in one day and tell us this is all coming to an end and things will soon return to normal."

"From your lips to God's ears," Harry says. "We'd better get going. It was nice chatting with you. Keep up the practice, boys. It's an important skill to have."

After they walk off, Malcolm says, "A wedding sounds nice."

"Yep, everyone likes weddings," I say.

When we get back to the house, Mollie and Sarah are both in the great room while baby Tate sleeps in his bassinette. The little box is fine for now, but with as fast as he's growing, we'll need a real crib for him before too long. Doris says she has another playpen, similar to the one Madison's baby sleeps in, but I'm thinking of trying to make him a crib. We'll have to see if my woodworking skills are enough.

"Hey, honey, boys. How'd practice go?" Mollie asks, setting the material she's sewing in her lap. Sewing is not her strong suit, but Belinda and Kelley have again taken her out of any physical duty stations, allowing her to do only kitchen duty if she's careful. So she's now helping Sarah with the mending and sewing for the community.

There are several other women, and even one man, who also do seamstress work instead of the more physical duties. When things need to be used and reused, you do what you can to preserve them. We even have a team who handles the recycling, making sure every item gets used until it falls apart.

"Marc did great," I say, ruffling his hair. "He's a natural. And Tony and Malcolm both hit the bullseye one time."

"Wow, guys! That's amazing," Mollie says.

Sarah chimes in with, "That's wonderful. Did you like it, Marc?"

"It's fun! But harder than I thought it'd be. And this bow is small. Right now, it isn't even set for hunting. But maybe, if I practice enough, I'll be able to hunt antelope when we get back to the homestead."

"Keep practicing," Mollie says. "When I started archery hunting, I could only draw to thirty pounds, but at least forty was the legal string draw for antelope and deer. I was able to work up to that. The bow

goes to forty-pound draw, so you could certainly use it for antelope."
She gives Marc a smile and a nod.

Like me, she has a compound bow and a crossbow. Where I preferred to hunt with the crossbow, Mollie had been focusing on her compound bow. The season before the attacks, she took it out a few times but wasn't successful. That whole winter, she used a target set up in the garage so she'd be ready for the hunting season. Now, we hunt almost daily for our food. While she's gone out with the hunting crew a few times, she isn't participating on it now. When we first moved up here, bows worked well because of the trees. We set up a few tree stands in heavily traveled areas and harvested several elk. But the herd has moved farther from our compound, so the crew is rifle hunting.

"I'm going to get a nap in," I say. "I'm on the new sentry team today."

"Did they get the kinks in that rotation ironed out?" Mollie asks.

"Seems so. Who would've thought we'd have to have guards to protect the food and supplies we need to keep us alive?" I ask, my voice laced with disgust. The look Marc and Tony share makes me wish I would've watched my words. "I mean, it's—look, boys. I didn't mean it quite like that."

"Sure, Dad," Malcolm says. "I think we understand that we'll be fine, but the group still needs to make sure we don't lose anything else. Are Leo and the security team still looking for the missing stuff?"

"As far as I know."

"Will they find it?" Marc asks.

"I'm not sure about that. But like I said, even if they don't, we'll be fine."

Chapter 33

Saturday, Day 215

Mollie

I roll over and reach for Jake. His side of the bed is cold. Did he have watch shift this morning? As I roll to my back, the night before comes rushing back. We had an argument. While he did sleep in our bed, knowing Jake, he's up early fretting over our disagreement.

I shake my head. The whole thing was a tad ridiculous, especially considering how upset we each became over it. Truth is, we'd both had a bad day—me because Brad spent several hours visiting Sarah and baby Tate. They were in the great room, and I stayed up in the loft working on my sewing. When I could no longer stand the sound of his voice carrying through the lodge, I moved to my bedroom. Even from there, I'd hear his occasional pompous laugh. He's so slimy and fake.

I don't fault Sarah for wanting to know him, but I do hope she's becoming aware of what kind of person he really is. With her newfound relationship with Christ, I pray she's listening to the Holy Spirit and is practicing discernment. For me, I can't really be around Brad without a headache starting.

Like me, Jake was also on edge. There was another sighting west of the ski lodge believed to be Heath, so he and the team went looking. While they were out, one of the searchers slipped off a slight slope; he landed wrong and injured his leg. The rest of them took turns helping him back. While his leg wasn't broken, the knee was swollen to cantaloupe size.

When Jake was helping him, he hurt his shoulder—or I should say, he *reinjured* it. Several years ago, he was picking something up off the floor and managed to tweak it. Turned out to be an incomplete rotator cuff tear. It was treated passively with rest and ice, followed by six weeks of physical therapy to get his range of motion back.

He was in considerable pain when he returned yesterday. So much so, when I hugged him, he made a yelping noise. He sheepishly told me about the injury. When I asked him what Belinda thought about it, he admitted to not seeing her, figuring it'd be fine in a few days. I lost it—completely and totally lost my mind. I didn't even bother keeping my voice low enough so the rest of our house didn't hear me having a hissy fit.

Jake gave me a single nod, turned around, and went to the coat rack. "Where are you going?" I demanded.

"To have Belinda or Kelley check it out."

"Good! I'll go with you."

"No need," he said. The door shut much harder than usual. It was several hours before he returned. By that time, with Brad spending the day here and my tiff with Jake, I had a raging headache and had gone to bed.

Jake came into the bedroom. Even though I wanted to know about his shoulder, I acted like a child and pretended to be asleep. Jake, usually extremely quiet when entering or leaving our room while I'm sleeping, made plenty of noise to wake me up. I finally rolled over and said, "And?"

"You're still mad at me?" he asked softly.

I let out a huge sigh. "No . . . I'm not. I wasn't *really* mad at you, just— " I shrugged.

"Scared?"

I gave him a timid nod. "You were in so much pain the last time you hurt your shoulder, and the recovery took so long. I just wanted to be sure that didn't happen again. Or something worse."

"I'm fine. Madison was in the clinic. She said it's likely a strain."

I furrowed my brow. I love Madison, and she's part of our family, but she's a veterinarian. Is she the best person to determine Jake is fine?

"I know what you're thinking. But I agree with her."

"In your vast medical experience?"

He gave me a kind smile. "It's not like the last time. It hurts, sure. But different. She gave me a couple of anti-inflammatories while I was there—sent me home with a small bottle also. It's already feeling better. I'll be fine. And I do have to follow up with Belinda or Kelley in a few days just to make sure. Okay?"

"Okay," I reluctantly agreed.

Now, I check the clock. I have breakfast duty this morning and need to start cooking at 0530, an hour from now, so we can start serving at 0730. That's enough time to visit with Jake beforehand. I climb out of bed, wrapping myself in my robe. With slippered feet, I pad down the stairs. Jake's in front of the fire, sitting on the edge of the rocking chair.

"Hey."

"Hey yourself," he says, giving me a small smile.

I plop onto the couch. "How's your shoulder?"

"Not bad. It was hurting me some, made it hard to sleep, but a couple of the pills helped."

"Maybe we should start you on turmeric."

"Madison mentioned it. Said they're trying to put people on it long term, but the ibuprofen will work for an acute injury. Did you know Kelley grew things like turmeric and ginger in her garden?"

"Yes, she gave starts—which she calls rhizomes—to Ellen. Ellen already had a small patch of ginger. That's what she's harvesting now. She'll have much more for next year. There's still more growing in pots in Kelley's cabin. And not just those but a few other herbs for medical purposes."

"We should've added those things."

"Kelley said she has several roots that need divided. I'll get those and a few other things."

"That'll be good. The more people growing those, the better. We're in need of alternatives."

"About last night," I say quietly.

Jake shakes his head. "You were right."

"Well, maybe so. But I was not right to raise my voice like that. I thought I'd matured past the point of that kind of outburst. I thought that was something God had helped me with."

"He has definitely helped you with your temper. Oh, you do still get a little snippy with me sometimes, though." His smile softens his words.

I give him a small shake of my head. "Snippy, huh? Well, last night was well beyond snippy. I'm sorry, Jake."

"You were right to be angry. Sometimes I forget, with the way things are, I need to be more aware. Just like you, how you need to learn to pay attention to what's going on with your body. I need to do the same thing."

"I can't have you ill or injured too," I say. "One of us has to be whole for the children."

"You're whole, honey." He moves to the spot next to me on the sofa. "You're still giving our children what they need."

Even though I don't agree with him, I give a small nod. "So you're on limited duty?"

"I'm just off the firewood crew for a few weeks. I can still take guard and teaching duty. So about Brad, Sarah said him being here yesterday was hard on you."

I give a slight shrug. "I don't know why, but every time he's around, I feel physically awful. That's no excuse for how I behaved toward you."

"Hey, you've apologized. We don't need to dwell on it. Was there something specific Brad said yesterday?"

"No, not really. Oh, other than telling Sarah she shouldn't go to Annette and Harry's wedding. Sarah's been working so hard on Annette's dress. She really wants to go. And she plans to take Tate, even though it's still a week shy of Tate's thirty-day quarantine. Belinda said she thought they'd be fine to go if she wore him in the baby sling and didn't socialize too much. She doesn't feel there would be much risk of him catching a cold or anything."

"That sounds reasonable," Jake says with a nod.

"Brad didn't think so, which was surprising to me since he kind of balked at Sarah asking him to wash his hands before holding the baby."

"Maybe he's not worried about his germs infecting his grandchild, just everyone else's."

I let out a snort. "Maybe. Sarah's been so good about it, making sure everyone washes before holding him. And maybe Brad is right, maybe it's a risk not worth taking."

"What does Sarah think?" Jake asks.

"Sarah will do what she thinks is right, whether Brad agrees or not. Even whether I agree or not," I say with a smile.

"She does have a mind of her own. They all do."

We sit in silence, staring at the fire. What kind of life will baby Tate have? Will the world return to normal before he's an adult?

Malcolm and Tony often talk about how things used to be. They both miss friends from before, ones who lived in nearby Wesley where

Tony went to school and Malcolm was in a homeschool co-op. Are their friends well? Have they found a safe place to hunker down for the winter and make it through these difficulties? Will we ever know how Jake's brother, Robert, and his family are doing in California?

And what about Ben and Bart, my bosses in Oregon? They said they'd made provisions for the two of them plus Ben's wife and son to escape the area if things got too bad. I had hoped they'd show up at our place, but they never did. I pray, wherever they are, they're safe.

"Do you have sewing to do today?" Jake asks.

"Kitchen duty first, then I'll work on the mending so Sarah can concentrate on the wedding dress. In fact, I'd better get going. I've got breakfast today."

"I saw the box of beets on the counter last night. I wondered who was responsible for them."

"Yep, I'm the one. Another batch of everyone's favorite sugar beet porridge."

Jake gives a visible shudder. "I'll stick with the elk roast. Speaking of, they're going ahead with butchering those goats today. That'll give us something new."

"I saw goat stew on Deanne's menu for Tuesday's lunch. I'm almost looking forward to it."

"And let me guess," he says, "the next day borscht is on the schedule."

"No surprise there," I say with a chuckle. "At least since Alina has taken over the borscht making, it's not terrible, even though it's made from sugar beets instead of red beets. She's using her mom's traditional Ukrainian recipe, but even that can't solve all of the issues with our beet soup."

Jake nods. "And as you've said before, it's a good use for broth made from the bones and scraps."

I make a slight face. It sounded like a good idea a few months ago, but now the sugar beet soup is less than appealing. "You have a four-hour guard shift this afternoon?" I ask.

"Nope. I'm completely off today. I'm going to take the boys out to practice with their bows. Other than that, I'm free. Want me to help you with the porridge?"

"No, Pamela Cameron is on duty with me. We'll be fine."

"Would you like to pray with me before you get going?"

My heart leaps to hear him ask. There was a time when we didn't pray together; Jake was uncomfortable praying out loud. Now, when we hold hands and share our petitions, it feels so right. "I'd love to."

He reaches for my hand before bowing his head. "Our Dear Heavenly Father, we thank You for the many blessings You've given us—a warm fire, good friends, and even sugar beets." I can't help but laugh when he says this. He gives his own chuckle before returning to our prayer.

"Our world seems so uncertain now. We do our best to get by each day, not knowing what tomorrow will bring. We want the best for our family, and we trust in You to guide us each day toward that end. It's sometimes hard for me to remember to put my faith in You and You alone. I'm still learning, Lord, still learning to lean on You through times of darkness. If it's Your will, please put your powerful hands on Mollie and heal her. Please help all those in Bakerville who are ill or suffering. We need Your miracles."

Jake squeezes my hand, letting me know it's my turn. Overwhelmed with emotion, I clear my throat. "Dear Lord, I don't need to tell You I've had some dark days. I've tried to put on a strong face, to not show how overwhelmed I am by everything. Please put Your healing touch on Jake's shoulder. I thank you for this time with my husband, to be able to come to You as a couple. I believe, no matter what struggles we face, if we keep praying together, You'll help us through them. Thank you for Your blessings, Lord. Thank you for allowing us to be together and for all our children to be with us. We pray these things in Jesus' holy name." I pause a moment so we can echo amen together.

Jake gives my hand another squeeze. "I was reminded of a Psalm while you were praying. I think it's 146. 'I will praise the Lord all my life; I will sing praise to my God as long as I live. Do not put your trust in princes, in human beings, who cannot save.' I'm going to read the entire chapter tonight before story time."

A smile covers my face. Jake's knowledge of scripture is something new. Where the Bible was something we turned to in times of need, now it's a part of our lives. He reads it in his spare moments, even taking notes and writing down passages to memorize.

"Sounds like a good plan. I'm going up to get dressed. See you in a bit."

Chapter 34

Friday, Day 221

Jake

"You sure you don't mind, Jake?" Cole Gunderson asks.

"Roving patrol's fine with me," I say, and truly mean it. On the night shift, roving patrol is a lot easier for staying awake.

"That shoulder won't give you trouble?"

"It's feeling better. Besides, I sling my rifle on my left shoulder, so it shouldn't hurt any more than sitting in one spot staring out a window would."

"All right, then you're roving with Dax. Here's your radios. Be sure to do your check."

Dax and I each have a specific pattern to follow. I'll start at the ski lodge and weave my way around the grounds to Zeb and Ellen's place, checking the greenhouses and other outbuildings. From there, I'll go down the main road to the two outlying places and then work my way back, stopping at the livestock shed, then over to the dude ranch section of our community. Dax will start at the dude ranch and work in the opposite direction.

Even though I enjoy the roving patrol, tonight is somewhat miserable, with a brisk wind making the cold even colder. I pull up my neck gaiter to cover my mouth and cheeks, leaving only my eyeballs exposed beneath my hat. If the wind doesn't lessen, I'll need to put on a pair of snow goggles. With the gaiter covering my mouth, I know it will be filled with condensation and then it—along with my beard—will freeze in a matter of minutes. My nose will be warm for a bit, but then I'll have to take the mouth covering down so I can thaw out. I'll repeat the process throughout the long night.

I'm more than halfway through my shift. The wind finally died down to a breeze, but the cold is still biting. On each round when I get near the militia headquarters, I pop in and warm up by the fire. The warmth makes it hard to go back outside, but at least the heat from the woodstove melts my beard and helps the rest of me thaw out slightly.

I catch a glimpse of something along the eastern tree line past all our housing. Not sure what I'm seeing, with the moon partially obscured by a cloud, I stop moving. I let my eyes relax, not looking at a specific spot but watching for motion. I let out a slow, steady breath, willing myself to remain patient and wait. When I'm about to give up, I see it again, a shift in the shadows.

I slowly move against the large tree nearest me and squat. After many moments, what was merely a motion becomes a form—a human form—not walking like someone who has a purpose, but instead using the trees to hide his intent.

I check my location. I'm on the eastern edge of the dude ranch section of our compound. Dax should be near the ski lodge. I give my radio three clicks, the indication to be on alert. Not only will Dax hear it, but so will everyone in each of the guard stations and whichever deputy is currently on duty, along with anyone else who happens to have a radio turned on. With our battery shortage, that's precious few these days.

I stay hunkered down, waiting to see what the mystery man—or I guess it could be a woman—does next. My gut tells me this really isn't a mystery man, and it's not a woman. It's Heath, coming back into the community to spy on Dot. Or worse. He slowly moves out of the trees, looking both ways before stepping out into an open area. Where he's at is the opposite side of the compound from Dot's cabin. We've always thought he'd gone west when we were tracking him, since that's the direction the boys and I saw him heading the day he beat her. We spent precious little time looking on the east side of the dude ranch.

Just as he steps out, the moon reappears and catches his face. It's little help. Wearing a full beard and his hat pulled down, he could be anyone.

Speaking softly into my radio, I say, "There's someone along the eastern edge of the trees. He came out from the forest." To help with noise, I have an earbud for receiving.

"Copy," Dax says. "I'm where the driveway to the dude ranch meets the main road.

"I'm just leaving HQ," Cole Gunderson says. "Clark's with me."

"Who else do you need?" a new voice asks. I can't tell if it's Bill or Evan.

"Do you know who it is?" Cole asks.

"Negative," I say.

"Is it Heath?"

"Unknown."

"Let's go with the assumption it is," Cole says. "Evan, you're close to Dot's cabin. Who on your security team is on standby?"

"Leo and Kimba. Copy, Leo? Copy, Kimba?"

Leo responds immediately. It's about ten seconds later before Kimba answers. Both say they need five minutes and they'll be ready.

"Copy," Evan says. "Lindsey's staying with us tonight, so she'll be with me." Former San Jose police officer and Doris's daughter, Lindsey Maverick has been a valuable addition to Evan's security team.

"Jake, do you have eyes on him?" Cole asks.

"Affirmative. He's still in the same spot. I think he might be waiting to see if the moon goes back behind the cloud."

"Slow and easy, folks," Evan says. "Don't spook him. I'm tired of chasing this numbskull all over the mountain and not finding him."

"He's moving," I say, "making his way toward the first line of cabins. He's quick and almost at cabin twenty-one . . . uh, I can't remember who lives there." While the name of the occupants escapes me, I know it's twenty-one since the numbers are prominently on each cabin and I've memorized them each time I'm on roving patrol. And I know better than to get too close to this cabin. Right on cue, the small dog living there sounds the alarm. The intruder quickly moves away from the cabin to the one next door.

"Copy," Evan and Cole reply at the same time.

"Dax," Evan says, "how close are you to Dot's place?"

"I'm at the firepit," he says. "I can see the front of her cabin from here."

"Go around to the back. Get in the cove of trees and stay low. We need eyes on the back window where he was lurking last time. Lindsey and I will cover the front. Cole, you and Clark have the south side. Leo and Kimba have the north. Jake, keep eyes on him. Follow as you can, but don't be seen."

"Affirmative," I say. The little yappy dog from twenty-one is once again silent.

When I lose sight of him, I move to the side of a shed—now turned into housing for a small family—where I think I'll be able to see him again. As soon as I poke my head around the edge, there he is, stealthily making his way toward the west side of the dude ranch. I hope this goes smoothly. The last thing we need is a shoot-out. All these cabins filled with sleeping people . . . I don't even want to think about how bad that could be.

I stay in the shadows, using buildings and trees for cover, keeping distance between us.

"Report," Evan says. "Everyone in position?"

Everyone responds they're ready, then Evan says, "Jake, eyes?"

"He's at the outer hedge surrounding the playground, up against one of the small spruce trees." As soon as the words are out of my mouth, his head whips in my direction. Did he hear me?

"Copy," Evan responds.

I'm statue still as the mystery man slowly scans the area. Dressed in a dark grey jacket and matching insulated pants, I should be invisible in this brush. If he spooks now, we could lose him again. It's many long seconds before he seems to relax and again starts to move. I wait until he's out of view before whispering, "He's on the move, out of view at the moment, at the edge of the playground when I lost him." I'm moving again, trying to get to a new location where I can see but not be seen.

"I've got him," Dax says. "I can just make out his shape. He's heading my way."

"Everyone, be on alert," Cole says.

I once again have eyes on him. As I'm watching him move through a second row of trees lining the playground, something seems off. He's too tall. This guy sneaking around is my height of almost six foot, maybe even slightly taller. Heath is shorter than me by several inches. Heath's also on the scrawny side, and this guy looks to be well developed. *Who is this?*

"I don't think this is Heath," I whisper into my radio.

"Say again?" Evan responds.

"He's too tall, too big," I say.

"I agree," Dax says. "This guy doesn't look like Dot's husband. I can't make out his face, but I'm with Jake. It's not him."

"Then who is it?" Cole asks.

"Unknown," I say.

"We have a visual," Leo says. "Agree, it's not Heath."

"Keep eyes on him," Evan says. "Let's figure out who he is and why he's sneaking around our community."

"We could be under attack," Cole says. "This might be a scout or a diversion. All sentries stay on high alert. I have a visual."

"Who's your runner tonight?" Evan asks.

"I am, sir," a small voice, almost overrun by static, replies.

"Are you in the radio shack? Wake everyone up at the ski lodge. Do it quietly without adding any extra lighting. We'll wait on waking up the dude ranch side until we get this guy handled. He's in the thick of us right now."

My heart drops to my stomach. Did my assumption it was Heath just put us in danger? Put Mollie and my family in danger? I shake it off as I finish moving. I'm in a spot I can watch the intruder as he approaches the playground. Dot's cabin is in the next section. If I'm wrong and this really is Heath, we should know shortly.

I take in a deep breath, immediately regretting it as the cold air hits my lungs. I force myself to hold back a cough. Failing miserably, I move my elbow to my mouth to stifle the noise. In the still of the night, even the muffled sound travels. He drops to the ground, landing almost prone, and fumbles at pulling out a sidearm.

"Security team, go! Go now!" Cole says.

I stay in my spot as the security team converges on the man. "Stay down! Drop your weapon!" Cole demands, as rifles point at the man. As Cole's loud voice disturbs the quiet of the night, several dogs begin to bark, followed by cabins lighting up as the dogs' owners try to figure out what's going on.

"No problem," the man says as he tosses his pistol into the snow and raises his hands. He's in a completely awkward position, after having thrown himself on the ground, with his hands and head raised. I move in, closer to the security team. I see Dax and Clark also stepping up.

"State your name and your business," Cole demands.

"Uh . . . you know me. I'm Miles. Miles Decker."

Miles Decker? Is this the husband of the lady who was accused of harassing people to change their vote? And considering Mick did change his vote, she was successful in her harassment.

"What are you doing out here?"

"N-nothing. Just out for a walk."

"Sneaking around in the woods?" I ask.

"I just needed some air. And I wasn't sneaking. I was . . . just being quiet so I wouldn't wake anyone."

"Why are you out in the middle of the night?" Evan asks.

"Couldn't sleep," he says with a shrug. "Can I get up out of the snow?"

"Leo, frisk him," Evan says.

"Hey! I'm one of you guys!" Miles cries out, as Leo pushes him back onto the ground and starts patting him down.

"Roll over," Leo says. Miles grumbles as he complies. Leo finds a pocketknife but no other weapons. "He's clear."

"There's no reason for this," Miles says with a whine. "The wife and I had a thing. I just needed to get away for a bit. You guys have no idea what it's like to be stuck in a house with relatives always around. My wife's sister, her loud-mouthed husband—have you ever had a conversation with Roscoe? He's nothing but a blowhard. And her kids, all they do is whine. That's the reason Shannon and I never had kids. They're a nuisance. It gets old never having any privacy."

I force myself not to nod in agreement as I remember Mollie and I having our own thing a few days ago when I hurt my shoulder. She was so upset, she lost it in front of everyone. It's not easy never having privacy.

"Can I get up now?" Miles asks in a quivering voice. Previously, I assumed he was frightened. Now I think he's cold from being face down in the snow.

"Yeah, let him up," someone says. It's at that moment I realize we have an audience. There are several people standing nearby or on their porch.

"Go ahead," Cole says. "Slowly."

"You've already searched me! What do you think I'm going to do? Tackle you?" Miles asks indignantly as he gets to his feet. "How about putting the guns down?"

Cole motions with his hand and all of us move our weapons to low-ready position.

"Miles, you're on the militia," Evan says. "You shouldn't be at all surprised by us wanting to know why you're sneaking around."

"I wasn't sneaking! Besides, I'm one of you. Why would you hold me at gunpoint?"

"Why did you drop to the ground and draw your weapon when I coughed?" I ask.

"You . . . you scared me! I thought you were a bear or something."

"Uh-huh," Dax says. "Sounds legit."

"It's true," Miles says with a huff. "Now, are you going to give me back my things so I can go home?"

"Leo, Kimba? Can you walk Miles home?" Evan asks.

"Give me my gun," Miles demands.

"Nope, sorry," Clark says, speaking up for the first time. "You'll get it back at your house. No firearms in public places."

"We're outside!"

"Surrounded by innocent civilians," Clark says, motioning to everyone gawking at us. "And, Miles, if I remember correctly, your wife was a huge proponent of our new gun laws. Seems you were by her side throughout."

"Oh, I see. So that's what this is about? You thugs attacked me because of that?" He points his finger at Evan. "Your feelings are hurt over losing?"

"Put your finger down," Evan says evenly.

Miles complies, withering in the process. He straightens slightly, then says, "Fine. I'm leaving now." He starts to stride confidently away, then catches a slick of ice and flails wildly before regaining his footing. Dax snickers. The others remain composed but shake their heads. Clark hands Miles's pistol to Leo and then motions for Leo and Kimba to follow Miles.

Cole motions for the rest of us to move in closer. To the gathered crowd, he says, "Show's over, folks. Everything's fine."

"What was that all about?" someone yells out.

"We'll have an announcement at breakfast," Clark says.

Into his radio, Evan says, "Runner, let the ski lodge know it was a false alarm. Everyone can stand down."

In our tight group, Cole says, "Jake, c'mon in for a debrief. Lindsey, can you take his patrol until we're finished?"

"Absolutely. Good job, Jake," she says, patting me hard on the shoulder—my sore shoulder.

Chapter 35

Saturday, Day 222

Mollie

Unable to sleep, I've been rocking by the fire, holding a book. I fell asleep immediately when going to bed after Jake left for his watch. But about an hour ago, I awoke with a start and have been in the great room ever since. I started with attempting to read, but my mind was too scattered. Is it because Jake is on sentry duty tonight? Or is it a culmination of everything?

I've been missing Lois today. Even though she hadn't been well since Tate and Keith went missing, her presence was still felt in this home. Baby Tate was making such cute noises and faces tonight, I know she would've loved experiencing them.

Deanne and Sheila, my daughter Calley's in-laws, were here this morning. Calley and Mike's baby was our main topic of conversation. It's the first grandchild for Deanne and Roy, and they're understandably excited and nervous. Sheila said she can't wait to be the crazy auntie who spoils the baby rotten. They examined the baby box we have for Calley so they can start putting together other items that may be needed. And since Tate will be almost six months old when Calley's baby arrives, there will be hand me downs.

Brad also stopped by again yesterday. He was, once again, insistent Sarah does not attend the wedding—it's too soon to take the baby out. I hate that I find myself agreeing with him. But as the mom, it's ultimately Sarah's choice.

She politely, but firmly, told Brad she's been looking forward to the wedding and that they *will* attend. She'll be careful with keeping Tate from getting too close to people. And with the wedding outside, the risk of him catching anything is minimal. Fresh air is good for babies, she insists. While she hasn't been taking Tate in public, she does take him on walks around the area, even going over to the archery range to watch the boys practice.

I should exchange the fiction book for my Bible. Instead of sitting here agonizing over what might happen, I should be turning to the word. While I may worry about what will happen tomorrow, God already knows. His plan for me, for Sarah, for my entire family, has already been determined.

I adjust the solar light, angling the arm slightly so I'll be able to read better. We're fortunate to have a complete solar system to power the dude ranch lodge. I'd love to be able to use the table lamp, but when checking our battery charge earlier, it was low. Yesterday and today were both overcast, not allowing the battery bank to fully charge. And with our ration on regular batteries, we rely on solar lights, oil lamps, or candles when we can't use the solar-powered electric. Keeping our collection of solar lights for personal use was another battle we almost didn't win.

I really should just go to bed. Harry and Annette's wedding is tomorrow—or today. I guess, since it's 0300, the wedding is today. Maybe a few minutes of reading His word will relax me. As I reach for my Bible on the coffee table, a shout shatters the stillness of the night. It's hard to make out the words clearly, but it sounds like "*stay down,*" followed by something else. A cacophony of barking dogs follows.

Are we under attack? I'm quickly on my feet and heading toward the locked closet housing many of our firearms when I hear another muffled shout. I'm fiddling with the lock when a voice booms behind me. "What's going on?"

I spin around. "Jeez, Alvin! You scared the life out of me."

"Dodie woke me up, said someone's yelling."

"I don't know," I say with a shake of my head. "It's outside."

From behind Alvin, Dodie says, "I told you it was outside, Alvin."

"Mom?" Sarah, holding Tate, asks from the top of the stairs.

"I don't know what's happening. I'm going out— "

"I'm going outside," Alvin says. "Dodie, you go upstairs. Stay with the youngsters and help Sarah and Karen. I'm going to get the 30.30 for you." He walks back toward the bedroom. Dodie shakes her head as he goes by.

I've barely retrieved my rifle when Alvin is back. "Here, Dodie." He hands her the old family rifle. He has his new AR-15, purchased in the early days of the attacks, in his other hand. I'm carrying a similar model, but in tan, purchased on the same day.

"Mollie, you up for this?" he asks, looking me up and down. Neither of us are really dressed for going outside. I'm in sweatpants and a t-shirt, covered by a fluffy robe. He's wearing lounge pants and a sweatshirt.

"I'm ready." I nod.

"Let's go then. Sarah, you and Dodie watch the kids."

Alvin and I put on heavy coats and snow boots. Rifles in hand, we look out the small window in the door.

"Looks quiet," Alvin says. "You stay behind the wall. I'll open the door and go out. If I don't get shot, follow me."

"That sounds like a terrible plan."

"Yep. Let's do it anyway."

I can't help but roll my eyes. When he opens the door, the voices are much clearer. While no longer shouting, they are loud and tense. He steps onto the porch and quietly says, "Sounds like they're over by the playground. Too bad we can't see what's happening from here."

I'm halfway out the door when I hear a low, "Grandpa?"

Alvin continues moving forward.

"Katie?" I ask quietly.

"I'm here," she says from the side of the lodge. "Aaron and Laurie are with me."

"Alvin," I say, touching his arm. He jumps slightly before looking at me.

"What?" he hisses.

"Katie is at the edge of the porch." I motion in her direction. His hearing may be bad, but his eyes are perfect. He immediately walks toward her.

"What's going on out here?" he asks.

"There was an intruder," Katie says, motioning in the direction of the playground. "Leo was called to help. He said we should be ready to protect the kids."

"So what are you doing lurking out here? Why didn't you come in and wake me up?"

"Well, uh, in case it was a false alarm." Katie shrugs.

"All that ruckus over there doesn't sound like a false alarm."

"That's true," Katie says with a nod. "But there isn't any shooting, just some yelling. And it sounds like only one guy."

"Who attacks a place with only one guy?" Alvin asks.

"It sounded like he said he lives here, sir," Aaron says.

"Yeah," Katie says. "We think he said he was out for a walk."

"At three in the morning?" Alvin asks, disgusted. "What kind of idiot does that?"

"Maybe one who couldn't sleep," I say quietly. "So you think everything is okay?"

"Sounds like they're wrapping it up," Aaron says. "There's enough of us out here." He gestures toward the line of four cabins and several camp trailers toward the ski lodge. Each has at least one person outside, and everyone has a dim light on.

"So I guess we can go back inside," I say, suddenly feeling like I can sleep.

"We'll wait a few minutes and make sure everything's okay," Aaron says.

"Mom," Katie says, "Jake's the one who saw him, saw the guy sneaking around."

"Jake? He's tonight's rover?"

Katie shrugs. "Must have been. I heard him call it in. Leo was on call, so the radio sounded when it happened and woke us all up." She motions to Aaron and Laurie, who respond with a nod.

"Nothing happened? He wasn't hurt or anything?" My stomach tenses as I remember his already injured shoulder. It's improved but still pains him.

"Didn't sound like it," Aaron says. "If you'd like, I can walk with you to where we can see."

"Thanks, Aaron. I'm okay to check it out on my own."

"Mom," Katie says, a slight warning in her voice.

"Let's go see what's happening, Mollie," Alvin says, taking a step off the porch.

I shrug at Katie as I take a quick step to catch up with Alvin, tapping his arm. When he turns, I ask, "Are your hearing aids in?" I point to his ear.

"Ah, nope. Too rushed."

We walk down the road toward a pathway that heads to the playground. We're almost to the path when a guy, dressed in insulated bibs and a heavy jacket—covered in snow—with an ear flap hat pulled low to the point of covering his eyes, comes out, walking slightly stooped. A penguin walk—it helps to keep balance when walking on ice. It's not slick on the road, but maybe the path is. There's something off about him. Something I can't quite place. I know he's one of the mountain people, but I can't remember his name or how I know him. That's not like me. I'm great with names and faces.

Steps behind him are Leo and Kimba, using a normal confident stride. Leo sees me and gives a small hand signal, one which means wait. I reach for Alvin and stop him also. Leo nods and continues to follow penguin guy.

I'm still trying to figure out who he is when Alvin says, "What's the commie's husband doing over here?"

"The commie?" I ask.

"Huh?"

I look at him and say, "Who's the commie?"

"You know, the one fighting with Doris. She convinced Michaelson to turn traitor."

"Shannon Decker?" Now that he says it, I'm sure he's right. "Oh, yeah. That's her husband."

"Sure enough."

"Okay. That's a good question on what he's doing over here. They live by the greenhouses."

"Huh?"

"Never mind." I tap his arm and point. "Here comes Evan and Cole."

"There's Evan," he says.

"Right."

"Jake's behind them," Alvin says. "He looks fine."

"Mollie, Alvin, sorry we woke you," Evan says.

"I was awake," I say with a shrug.

I look past Evan and catch Jake's eye. He gives me a small smile and a single nod.

I mouth, "You okay?"

He nods again, then rubs his shoulder, putting up his finger and thumb in a gesture of a little bit, then says, "Evan, I'm going to talk to Mollie for a minute. I'll be right behind you."

"Hey," I say, reaching for his hand.

He pulls me into a full embrace. "Hey yourself," he whispers.

"Everything okay, son?" Alvin asks.

"Seems to be."

"Huh?"

"He forgot his hearing aids," I say.

Jake partially releases me so he can turn and face his dad. "Yeah, I think it's okay."

"What was he doing over here in the middle of the night?" Alvin asks.

"Said he needed some air."

"Humph. I say he's full of it," Alvin says passionately. "Finish hugging your wife so we can go home. These pants aren't meant for standing in the wind."

Jake and I look at each other, a smile playing on our lips. He kisses me again. "Get some sleep, Mollie. I'll be home soon." He turns back to Alvin. "See ya later, Dad."

"See ya, Jake." Alvin raises his hand and turns to walk back. I give Jake another kiss and quickly follow.

At the lodge, Katie, Laurie, and Aaron are sitting on the porch benches. Most everyone in the other cabins and trailers have gone inside, and many lights are once again extinguished as the community settles back down for a few more hours of sleep.

"Looks like it's all over," Katie says, standing and stretching.

"Seems to be." Even as I say the words, something doesn't feel right. Maybe, after I talk to Jake and have more info, this will make sense.

"I'm going back to bed," Alvin says.

"Me too," Aaron and Laurie say simultaneously as they stand up.

"Do you want to come in," I ask Katie.

"I already went inside to tell Sarah and Dodie everything's okay," she says. "I used your bathroom too. You know how I love being able to flush."

I give a small laugh. Katie's RV, like all the travel trailers and cabins, is dry—no running water. The original cabins all have flushable toilets by adding water to the tanks. But the RV, camp trailers, and storage sheds turned into cabins are not hooked up to septic. And the fear of frozen lines led everyone living in those to not have incoming or outgoing water lines. They keep water in jugs for drinking and washing up and use a compost toilet system or something similar.

Most living in recreational vehicles or makeshift cabins use one of the public toilets, or a friend's bathroom, as much as possible. Katie and Leo removed the toilet that came in the RV and replaced it with a newly built compost toilet. They can put the original toilet back in when—*if*—things return to normal.

"Did Leo say how long he'll be?" Katie asks.

"We didn't talk," I say. "Sorry."

"That's okay, Mom. I'm going back to bed. You're okay?"

"I'm fine, why?"

"You look . . . " She pauses for a moment. "Actually, you look good. Cold maybe, but good. I'll see you in a few hours. I'm excited for the wedding. We needed something like this, a celebration." She pulls me into a hug before saying goodnight.

Inside the lodge, I hang up my coat and take off my boots. My robe must have skimmed the snow somewhere because the bottom edge is covered in ice. After stoking the fire, I turn down the damper, taking the solar reading light upstairs with me. I should've grabbed the book but decide against going back for it. I have another by my bed I can read if my mind isn't settled enough to fall asleep.

There's something odd about tonight. I understand not being able to sleep; I was in the same boat. But why go out in the middle of the night for a stroll, especially in the cold and wind? I give a shrug. He was certainly dressed for it. Maybe that's all it was.

Thinking of Shannon's husband reminds me of Mick. Since his vote upholding the gun ban, we see little of him or his family. The children no longer attend school with the others, and they don't join us for meals. Either Mick or his wife picks up food and takes it back to their trailer. The rumor is they're keeping to themselves out of fear of retaliation. Both Mick and his wife still show up for their community duties, but they seem to only be going through the motions. I really should go by and visit his wife, make sure she knows there's no hard feelings toward her or the children. I don't want to be angry at Mick either, though I'm having a harder time with that. I'd like to believe he did what he felt was right. Even if it doesn't make much sense.

Similarly, Barney and Daniel, both finally off house arrest, tend to keep to themselves. Daniel and his wife have even separated, with Daniel now living in one of the bachelor quarters.

After hanging my robe in the shower to allow the hem to dry, I check the clock: 0345. Jake is scheduled to be off at 0600, the same time I need to get up. I'll certainly need the wind-up alarm sounding its bell. Part of me thinks I should just stay up, but the other part wins out. I don't even realize I've fallen asleep when the alarm makes its racket. I'm tempted to stay in bed a few more minutes. But for fear of falling back to sleep, I slowly stretch and then roll out.

I'm dressed and waiting for the children when Jake opens the front door. "Good morning," he says loudly.

"In the kitchen," I reply from my spot stooped down by the cabinet.

"The children?" he asks.

"Should be down any minute. I've awoken them all. The boys were dressing, and Sarah was getting the girls and Andy ready. Are you going to breakfast with us?"

"Yes," he says, stepping into the kitchen and heading toward a chair at the table. "I thought I'd stay up, go to the wedding, and then just sleep like a normal person tonight."

"That's going to make a long day for you."

"What are you doing?" he asks as he slides a chair out from the table.

"Straightening the cupboard. By the time the cleaning up is done, we're all exhausted and tend to toss things in. I have a minute, so I thought I'd organize it. Any more news on last night?"

"Nothing else. His story was he was out for a walk. I told Evan and Cole everything I knew. My guess is they'll talk to him later today, see if they can learn anything else."

"And he was just walking around? You saw him and called everyone in?"

"No, it wasn't like that. He came out of the forest behind the easternmost cabins."

I straighten and lean my forearms on the counter. "He was just walking in the woods?"

"Seems so," Jake says with a nod, leaning back in his chair. "That's his story, anyway."

"He wasn't wearing snowshoes," I say, scrunching up my face as I recall his awkward penguin walk.

Jake blinks several times before he leans forward and smacks his hand on the table. "You're right. He wasn't wearing them when he stepped out."

"How could he walk in the woods without them?" I ask. "Is there a trail over there?"

Jake shakes his head. "Not that I know of, but I guess it's possible." Jake stands up. "I'm going to talk to Evan. I'll meet you at breakfast."

He pauses at the opening from the kitchen to the great room. "Unless you need my help getting everyone out the door?"

"Nope, we're good," I say, my heart filling as I'm again reminded what a good husband and father Jake is. "We'll see you at breakfast."

Chapter 36

Saturday, Day 222

Jake

"Jake? Is everything okay?" Doris asks, cracking open the door before rolling back her wheelchair and ushering me inside. Even though she uses the walking crutch or knee scooter when out and about, she still relies on the wheelchair at home. She says it's just easier and gives her a rest. The small cabin is toasty warm, thanks to a roaring fire in the woodstove.

"Not sure. Is Evan around?"

Evan steps out of the bathroom wearing basketball shorts and a t-shirt, towel-drying his hair. "Just finishing up a spit bath," he says. "What's up?"

"Mollie was asking me about last night. She brought up something interesting none of us thought of."

"And that is?"

"You know how it was just movement in the forest that caught my attention?"

"Right," he says with a nod. "I got that in your statement."

"Then it was a minute or two and I saw movement again before he stepped out."

"Uh-huh." Evan nods again.

"He was in the forest. He came out of the forest wearing boots. How was he walking around in the deep snow without snowshoes? Has someone shoveled a trail?"

"Wow!" Doris says. "That's a good point."

With a shake of his head, Evan says, "There's only a trail if one of the community members put one in as a personal project."

"Maybe some kids?" Doris asks.

"Welp, now I'm curious. Want to go with me to find out?" Evan asks me.

"Evan, Jake should sleep after being on patrol all night," Doris says.

"I planned on staying up today anyway. Besides, it shouldn't take long." I shrug, then ask Doris, "Are you going to breakfast?"

"You want me to tell Mollie where you went? Get you both a doggy bag?"

"You know, let me give Evan a minute to get ready. I'll go talk to her and be right back. I need to grab my backpack anyway."

"Let's meet at the spot we had Miles on the ground," Evan says. "We'll backtrack from there. Ten minutes?"

"Yep. That'll work."

Back at our lodge, Mollie and Sarah are getting the children into their outerwear.

There's a wonderful chorus of greetings from the children. Not wanting to remove my boots, I stay on the mat by the front door and return their hellos. "Where's Karen?" I ask.

"Helping serve this morning. She's already gone," Sarah says. "Angela should be here shortly to help Mom take everyone to breakfast."

"You're taking the truck, right?" I ask.

"Yep," Mollie says. "I'm still following doctor's orders."

"Would you mind bringing me something back?" I ask Mollie while I slip into my backpack. It's still damp from wearing it last night, as is the outerwear I've yet to remove after last night's watch. "Evan and I decided to go find out why Miles wasn't wearing snowshoes."

"Just the two of you?" Mollie asks, her voice full of alarm.

I give her a questioning look.

"I just—something doesn't seem right," she says quietly, giving me an urgent look. I know she's not saying what she really wants to say because of the children.

"We'll be okay," I say, keeping my voice light. "You know Evan. If there's anything hinky, he'll call in the cavalry."

"So you'll have a radio?" she asks, zipping Lily's coat.

"Most likely. Never known him to leave home without it."

"All right. Be careful."

"Always. See you all later." I exit to a chorus of goodbyes.

Evan has yet to arrive when I reach the spot where we cornered Miles. As I'm looking at the indentation in the snow where Miles was lying, I notice a slight discoloration. Either a dog used the same area as his bathroom or . . .

"Hey, Jake, been waiting long?"

"Nope, just arrived a few minutes ago."

"So, let's follow his tracks, see what we see."

It's not terribly difficult to follow to the edge of the woods where he came out. There's a small path behind the easternmost row of cabins, weaving through the trees. A few feet farther and we're both surprised to find a well-packed trail going into the dense forest.

"Well, I guess someone did put a path in," Evan says. "You feel like seeing where it goes?"

"We've come this far," I say. A few hundred yards later, the trail opens to a good-sized clearing, also well used and packed.

"Kids must have been playing back here," Evan says.

I turn slowly, taking in the tree line surrounding the clearing. While this forest is mainly assorted pine trees, such as lodgepole and white bark, there's also a good amount of spruce and fir, along with a few deciduous trees—mainly aspen—plus a spattering of shrubs and brush. On the northeast side, there's an opening between a couple of evergreens where the snow has been disturbed.

I start walking toward it when Evan says, "Whatcha got, Jake?"

"Might be nothing." When I get to the area, I change my mind. "Or it might be something."

Evan hustles over as I examine the spot. "That's interesting," he says. "Someone shoveled snow here to hide another path. Good find, Jake. Now, where's the shovel?"

"Might have been a trowel or something small enough he had it on him," I say.

"Leo would've found it when he frisked him."

"Good point." I start walking to a nearby juniper shrub. Evan goes to a similar one on the opposite side of the new trail.

"Well, well, well," Evan says, pulling out a cinch sack. Opening the top, he says, "Snowshoes." He bends back over the bush, then stands up with a folding shovel.

"What now?" I ask.

"Now we get some help. Then we find out where this trail someone was trying so hard to hide takes us. You up for it?"

"I'm in."

"Okay, then. I want you to stay and watch. Hole up over there." He points to the north side of the clearing. "Make yourself a blind of sorts. Here. Keep my radio. I'll grab another. And if anything happens, call it in. Do you happen to have your earbud?"

"Yep." I unzip my parka to reach into an inside pocket.

"I'll be back, but it may be a while. We'll probably form a plan before returning."

"A plan for what?"

He gives a shrug. "Whatever."

"Any chance you can let Mollie know? Tell her I might miss the wedding."

"Yeah. Maybe we'll wrap it up before then. But I'll make sure she knows."

He claps me on the shoulder before taking off. At least it wasn't my sore shoulder.

Chapter 37

Saturday, Day 222

Mollie

"Mollie, can I talk to you for a minute?" Clark Thomas asks. I must give him a look because he says, "Nothing big. Can we step over here?"

I nod my agreement as Angela says, "I've got the kids."

At the edge of the community space, Clark quietly says, "Evan wanted me to tell you Jake's going to be longer than expected. They found something. They're going out to investigate."

"Investigate what?" I ask, furrowing my brow.

"I can't really say."

"You can't say because you don't know? Or— "

He shakes his head. "I don't know, and if I did . . . " He puts his hands up in a *what can I say* type motion.

"Is Jake in danger?"

"Everything should be sorted out soon." He pats me on the shoulder. "Try and enjoy the wedding."

"Mm-hmm," I mutter as he walks away.

Back at the table, Angela quietly asks, "Everything okay?"

I give a slight shrug. "Should be. They found something. I'm not sure what, but Jake's helping with it." I let out a large breath. "Let's finish up. Whoever didn't have a shower last night needs one before the wedding today."

"I'm pretty sure I don't need a shower," Malcolm says.

"I'm okay too," Tony adds.

I give them each a look, raising my eyebrows slightly. "I don't remember either of you showering last night."

"Fine," Malcolm says with a sigh that must have originated at his toes.

"Malcolm, you'll take one of the upstairs bathrooms. Tony, you have the other. And remember, there's probably going to be community people wanting to shower downstairs. Be quick so everyone can get ready."

With a small laugh, Angela says, "I suppose Gavin will be like that soon enough. At least Sissy and Lily like showers."

"Don't be so sure. Each of you older girls went through your own 'I hate showers' phase. At least they were somewhat short lived."

"Really? I don't remember. I only remember you telling me to hurry up and get out of the shower. I'd stay in until the hot water ran out."

"That's true too. Okay, is everyone finished eating?" I ask while wiping Andy's face. "We need to get a move on it."

As we're driving up the road to our lodge, I see a couple people from Evan's security team waiting at his door. After we moved up on the mountain, the regular militia training was decreased. But we're encouraged to remain physically fit and have required range time every other week. As a family, we've done our best to continue with martial arts training and regular stretching. I stifle a sigh. I say we, but I'm not really doing any training, nor am I on the militia. I've been sidelined for my medical issues.

Even though the regular militia is somewhat soft, the security team has continued the intense training schedule they had before. When we moved up, two of the security team members stayed behind with their families. But we added additional members—militia who had shown promise—and now it's larger than when we were in Bakerville. Probably a good thing, considering the fitness level of our militia.

While the older boys take their showers, I go back to work on organizing the cabinets. As I'm squatting down, I suddenly feel lightheaded. So much so, I end up sitting completely on the floor. I lean against the cabinet bank, trying to gather my wits. Is it happening again? Or am I only tired from not sleeping last night? I take several deep breaths. After a couple of minutes, I'm fine. Not so fine that I go back to working on the cabinets, but well enough to move from the kitchen to the great room where Sarah is feeding Tate.

"I'm almost finished," Sarah says. "Then I'll get him and the girls dressed. Is it weird for me to be so excited? The idea of getting out and seeing people, especially for a happy occasion, is almost too much for me." She lets out a giggle. "What a goof I am."

"Not weird at all," I say. "You've always been a social person. After Tate and Keith went missing, you— " I pause a moment while I search for the right word.

"Holed up?" Sarah offers.

"I wasn't going to say it like that. You were in mourning. Sure, you went to meals with us and did what was needed, but your heart was broken. It wasn't in what you were doing."

"My heart's still broken, Mom. But it's . . . it's different. I miss Tate, but I now feel like . . . " She shrugs. "I'm ready to start being a part of the community again. I know keeping little Tate away from people is the best thing for now, but going to the wedding shouldn't be an issue. And I hate to admit this, but I'm thinking of staying for the meal." I start to object, but she puts up her hand. "I know what you're going to say. And I heard it all from my dad yesterday. But it'll be fine. I'll keep him in his sling and not let people fawn over him. We'll stay with the family when we eat. Honestly, what's the difference?"

"What does Belinda think?" I ask.

"I'll ask her or Kelley at the wedding. They both plan to be there, that's why Katie's covering the clinic. And I did talk to Katie about it. She thinks Belinda will be okay with it, especially since you all are around the community every day. Any germs are already brought home—it's more the germs that pass through contact. There's a name for them, but I can't remember it. Anyway, it's the same as everyone needing to wash their hands when they come in the house before they touch Tate."

I tilt my head. "You have a good argument. And you are Tate's mom. It's your job to make the best choices for him and you. Your dad may be upset. I may be upset—I'm not in this instance, but I'll possibly be at other times." I give her a wink. "But you're still the mom. Your choices are what matter for your children. Now, what's he wearing today?"

"The Denver Broncos snowsuit Doris found for him." She makes a face and then laughs. "He'll be totally styling for the wedding in it. Just a onesie and a pair of those soft pants underneath. Inside, he'll be plenty warm in the sling, or being held, so that will be enough. I'll tuck a few blankets in his diaper bag also."

"Sounds perfect," I say. "I'm going to go up and make sure all the boys are dressed, then dress myself. Do you want me to lay out clothes for Lily and Sissy?"

"I've already done that. They're supposed to be putting them on."

"From the giggles I keep hearing, I'm not sure they're following through," I say. "I'll get them going. We need to leave in about forty-five minutes."

"Maybe Jake will be back before then," she says. Sarah was also concerned about Jake going with the security team. I'm doing my best to trust Evan will remember Jake isn't as trained as the others. And I'm doing my best to put my trust in God to keep Jake safe.

Chapter 38

Saturday, Day 222

Jake

I've found a good place to be able to see the clearing and the start of each path without being visible myself. As I settle in for my wait, my stomach rumbles. While easy snacks, like commercially made granola bars, are now a thing of the past, we're given jerky and other rations for guard duty. I check my pack and find a slab of pemmican and a couple chunks of corn and barley hardtack. I picked up the pemmican—a paste of pulverized jerky and fat mixed together and then formed into bars—before last night's shift. Traditionally, pemmican would also have dried berries, but that's something we have little of, so it's not added.

Doris and her supply team work with Deanne and her kitchen team to make sure there's pack food available for the militia and security team. They also provide meals to anyone on shift who's unable to get away and eat in the dining area of the ski lodge. The hardtack is from last week. While the hardtack is edible, it's not my favorite. Rumor is, since we're starting to run low on wheat flour, we'll all be eating a lot more corn and barley creations before winter ends.

I hate that I'm missing today's wedding feast. Deanne told Mollie they were doing a few special dishes, thanks to two elk brought in a few days ago—the first in two weeks—and a Rocky Mountain bighorn sheep. Our hunting crew had to go on an overnight trip a little farther south. The elk herd was in a small, protected bowl, staying out of the weather. They stumbled across the sheep herd on the way back.

Maybe they'll do a couple of roasts in the firepit. I heard there might be enough lettuce in the greenhouse for a salad. Gosh, I hate to miss that. Mollie is making sure our entire family has some of the fermented food each day, and it does help satisfy some of my vegetable cravings, but I miss abundant fresh vegetables.

While we have had a few green salads, the production hasn't been enough to enjoy on a reliable basis. We originally planted too little. When it was realized, they increased the amount by planting most of our seeds. Then we had to let some of the lettuce flower so we could save the seeds. It's been a long process to get a salad. And since the lettuce isn't terribly high in calories or nutrient dense, some say it's a wasted process.

I settle in to wait and watch. At one point, I find my head dropping to my chest. I reposition to a less comfortable stance. It wouldn't be good to fall asleep while I'm supposed to be on watch.

A few minutes later, a slight rustle of brush puts me on high alert. I quickly realize it's coming from the wrong direction to be Evan and his team. I bring the radio close to my mouth so I can alert them someone is coming out. While I have an earbud for receiving, I still need to speak into the radio to transmit.

The rustling stops for a full minute and then restarts. Even though I'm confident I'm hidden and I'm in no danger, my heart is pounding. I catch a glimpse of movement on the concealed trail. I can't help but smile when two deer step out. As they step into the clearing, four more join them. All amble and browse without a care in the world.

A minute later one stiffens to alert, ears forward, head high, and eyes in my direction. Even though I'm hidden, I think she's scented me. The others also stiffen before the lead doe turns and bounces back in the direction they came.

I love watching wildlife. As a lifelong hunter, I've had people assume when I look at a deer, I only see steaks. It's not like that. While I do hunt for food, the beauty of wildlife still amazes me.

It's only been about fifteen minutes since the deer took off when the forest comes alive again. This time, the sound is different—obviously not deer or other wildlife—and it's coming from the dude ranch. Even though I assume it's Evan and his team, I hunker down to make sure I'm hidden, just in case it's someone else.

It's not long until Rey Hoffmann from Evan's team steps out, followed by several others including my son-in-law Leo and Rey's wife, Kimba. Evan is the last one in the clearing. "Jake?" he says softly.

"Yep," I reply before standing.

"You're with me. Everyone know what they're doing?"

There are several replies of affirmative as his team breaks into three groups. Two members stay with Evan. Leo and three others move toward the eastern edge of the clearing. Rey, Kimba, and two more move to where I was hidden. Each group stops and puts on their snowshoes. "Let's get our paddles on," Evan says to Atticus, Lindsey, and me. "Since Miles left a pair stashed, I'm guessing we might need them."

While we're getting ready, Evan quietly gives me an overview of the plan. "We've got just about everyone on this," he says. "We've kept eyes on Miles since last night. One of Clark's guys is monitoring him now. We've doubled up on our militia guards—a few of them weren't too happy to be missing the wedding." He gives a *what can we do* shrug. "I have my entire team out here. Two of them are near the beginning of the path."

"For . . . ?" I lift my hands.

"For whatever," he says. "Something feels wrong about this. We looked at the map, and it seems we can approach from the trail and at least two other directions."

"Approach what?" I ask.

"That's the question, isn't it? We can only assume there's something out there, something worth concealing, based on how things are scuffed up so we don't easily find the trail. The other two groups will stay even with us as we make our way."

"We'll take the trail, and they'll go through the forest?" I ask.

"Right, to make sure we have more coverage."

"Okay, I'm ready," I say, standing after attaching my snowshoes. "You want your radio back?"

"Keep it. I picked up another one, and you might need it." Evan motions with his hand, and the other two teams take off.

"Nice and easy," Evan says. "Atticus, you have point."

Atticus Dosen was added to the security team after we moved up the mountain. He and his twin brother Asher, his younger brother, his mom, and his aunt were new to our community, arriving when Doris's daughter Lindsey did. Atticus was part of the militia, on Echo Team with Mollie. And even though he's in his late teens, Atticus impressed Cole Gunderson so much he recommended him for the security team.

Lindsey is also in our group, falling in behind Atticus. Evan motions for me to go next and then he takes the final spot.

The trail is well packed, to the point we don't really need the snowshoes but keep them on anyway. Occasionally, I catch a glimpse of one of the other teams as we make our way toward . . . whatever. They don't have the advantage of a trail and are not able to move as quickly.

Evan slows us in order to keep us together. As we walk, I catch a hint of fire in the air. Is it from the community? With woodstoves burning twenty-four hours a day, seven days a week, the air always smells of smoke. I didn't notice it while I was waiting in my spot near the clearing, which isn't unusual since it's always around and I've grown accustomed to it, but I do notice it again as we walk.

We've gone about half a mile when Atticus lifts a hand in a stop motion, then quickly leads us off the trail and into the cover of the trees. As soon as we're in a somewhat hidden spot, Evan clicks his radio to stop the other two teams. From our concealment, I catch a glimpse of a roof. And there's a curl of smoke coming out of a chimney pipe.

Chapter 39

Saturday, Day 222

Mollie

"Let's stay at the back," I say to the children as we unload from the pickup. "There won't be chairs, so you'll need to stand."

"Why do we have to stay at the back?" Lily asks. "I won't be able to see her pretty wedding dress."

"You'll see her when she walks by," Sarah says.

"Or I'll lift you up," Tony says.

"Didn't you see my mommy helping make the wedding outfit?" Sissy asks. "It's not exactly a dress."

"Oh. I forgot," Lily says, scrunching up her adorable face. "Why is she getting married without a dress?"

"She wanted to be warm since it's an outside wedding in the middle of winter," Sarah says, as she slips baby Tate into the sling. He's asleep and barely stirs with the movement. "But wait until you see her. She'll be beautiful."

"What about the pictures?" Lily asks. "My other mom always had her picture in her wedding dress set up in the living room." The phrase *my other mom* catches my attention and breaks my heart.

"There won't be any pictures," Tony says. "Remember? Cell phones and cameras stopped working."

As he says that, I feel a wave of sadness. Katie and Leo were married over the summer, and I would've loved to be able to take photos. I wish we would've thought of having an instant camera as part of our preps.

"Ready?" I ask Sarah.

"Yes, he seems snug," she says, planting a kiss on baby Tate's forehead. "Let me just get his hat on him."

A few minutes later, we join Angela and Gavin at the back of the group. Katie is covering the clinic while Belinda, Madison, June, and Kelley all attend the wedding. Calley has radio duty, so she won't be here either. I look around for Leo, Mike, or Tim and see none of them.

"Hey," Angela says. "You guys are almost late."

"It's not easy getting our crew out the door," I say. "You should've ridden over with us."

"Gavin likes to walk." She drops her voice so only I can hear. "Did you know Tim, Mike, and Mike's dad are all on watch? They've added extra people, and Leo's team has gone out. Something's going on."

I move my head in a slight sideways direction. "I didn't know about Tim, Mike, or Roy. But I'm not surprised about Leo. You know Jake's also in the middle of whatever's going on. How'd you find out about Leo?"

"We stopped by to see Katie on our way here, that was after Mike came to get Tim. Rumor is, Cole doubled up all of the watch and even has roving teams. Teams, Mom. Not just one or two guys like usual. And based on the people not here, I'd say that's accurate. It sounds serious."

I look around the gathered crowd. She's right. There are several militia members missing, not just men but some of the women militia too. And I don't see anyone from the security team nor the police force. I shake my head. "I'd like to think that if it was anything too serious, the wedding would be postponed."

Angela shrugs.

"What are you whispering about?" Sarah asks.

"Go ahead," I tell Angela with a nod. She motions Sarah to move closer and shares what she knows. After she's finished, Sarah looks at me with raised eyebrows. I respond with a small shrug. I told her about Jake and seeing some of Evan's team at his door, but to find out the regular guards are increased . . . that's news to both of us.

"I think it's getting ready to start," Malcolm says, nodding in the direction of Harry and several of the Cameron men coming out of the ski lodge.

"Where's the bride?" Lily asks, straining to look.

"She'll be the last one to come out," Sarah says. "Remember Katie's wedding? All the men came out first, then the bridesmaids, then you and Malcolm, and finally the three brides."

"I wish I could be a flower girl again," Lily says longingly.

"Maybe someday," I say. "I don't even think Annette is having a ring bearer or flower girl." I look to Sarah for confirmation.

"No," Sarah says. "Just the attendants."

The ceremony site, mostly natural so we can enjoy the beauty of the space, has an aisle down the middle leading to the gazebo. During ski season—when things were normal—church services were held here every Sunday. Two large white baskets filled with pink painted twigs are on either side of the entrance to the gazebo. Two small tables covered in pink cloth holds several candles and oil lamps. Paul Cameron steps up into the gazebo, stationing himself between the tables. He's performing the ceremony.

In today's world of no government offices, we don't have marriage licenses, driver's licenses, passports, death certificates, or any other official papers. Judge Avery does handle very minimal paperwork for marriages, births, and deaths, thinking it might be nice to have accurate records when society returns. Of course, we have no need for passports or driver's licenses, so we don't even worry about those.

Harry walks up with Paul, joined by groomsmen Dusty, PJ, and Grant Cameron. The men are dressed in denim jeans, western boots, and western vests with long-sleeved shirts. Harry's vest is topped with a leather jacket. Dusty and PJ are wearing well-worn cowboy hats, while Harry has some sort of fedora looking thing on his head. Wedding attire in the apocalypse is considerably less matching than before.

Bryce and Dax Cameron, each on guitar, begin playing "Canon in D." A minute later, the door to the ski lodge opens and Shelby Cameron steps out. She's in a calf-length full blue denim skirt with western boots and is wearing a white long-sleeved button-up shirt topped with a sheepskin vest. Behind Shelby is Kirstin Lewis—another person who escaped Prospect—dressed similar but wearing a long sheepskin jacket. The women walk to the front and take their places on the gazebo.

The music changes to "Shubert's Ave Maria." All eyes turn to the door of the lodge. Milena Maynard, also from Prospect and Annette's best friend, steps out first. Her denim skirt is knee-length with lace along the hem. Her boots are fashion boots with a chunky heel instead of cowboy boots, and her button-up white shirt is a flowy version that reminds me of a pirate shirt. Instead of a sheepskin coat or vest, she has a suede jacket draped over her shoulders.

Milena is not only the Maid of Honor but also walking Annette down the aisle. With a smile to the gathered crowd, she holds the door open for the bride. There's a collective gasp when Annette steps out. The wedding attire Sarah helped her create is nothing short of glamourous. The original tea-length dress is now seeing its third wedding in less than a year.

Annie MacIntyre was married shortly after the first attacks, on the day the cyberattack took out power and stopped our phones from working. I missed that wedding; I was trying to make my way home from work in Oregon. Laurie Esplin, married in a triple ceremony with Katie and Leo, was the second to wear it. Laurie added a purple ribbon to coordinate with the other wedding dresses. With Annie's blessing, dramatic changes to the dress were made for this wedding. With these alterations, I question whether it can be transformed for a fourth wedding.

The white dress, covered in lace, had little cap sleeves. Doris produced coordinating lace to transform the short sleeves into long sleeves. The purple sash was removed, and the tea-length skirt opens at the waist—thanks to a piece being removed—to show off a pair of slim-fitting white leather pants, turning the skirt of the dress into more of a train. Pink cowboy boots and a faux fur pink cape finish the look. The boots are at least a size too large and stuffed with cotton in order to fit. The cape—designed for a child—had a piece added to the front so it would button.

When I first met Annette, I thought her plain. But today, with a light touch of makeup and a wholesome beauty, she's anything but. With her trendy dress and trim figure, she's reminiscent of a runway model. I'm so impressed with Sarah's ability to turn the simple, sweet dress and a few miscellaneous odds and ends into something so spectacular.

When Annette first came to Sarah, saying she thought she should wear pants for her wedding, Sarah agreed it was a good idea and got to work. This is so much more than I'd imagined they'd come up with.

Watching Harry's face as Annette walks toward him, he too is mesmerized by her. The ceremony doesn't take much time but is incredibly heartfelt. Harry and Annette share their own vows. Harry begins to joke about how a beautiful young woman like Annette could ever fall for a broken-down old guy. Annette doesn't even let him finish. She puts a finger to his lips and says, "God gave you to me and me to you." Then she kisses him—well before the declaration of husband and wife.

Paul Cameron laughs and says, "You're supposed to wait for that part."

A few minutes later, they're declared husband and wife. The guitars play "All You Need is Love" as everyone cheers.

Sarah lifts a hankie to her eyes to wipe them. "I can't believe how lovely it was," she says.

"Her dress . . . " Angela says, putting a hand to her chest. "You should've been a fashion designer."

"Oh. Well . . . " Sarah shrugs. "I think I can only remake things. I do love how Doris was able to help me come up with all the pieces. The pants were definitely a find."

"Who do they belong to?" I ask, trying to remember if I'd ever seen anyone wearing tight leather pants in Bakerville.

"Not sure. They were found in one of the vacant homes—someone on vacation when the attacks started. Doris said she almost didn't bring them up the mountain but decided they might work for riding horses."

"Um, as tight as those things are, I can't imagine climbing on a horse wearing those," I say.

"Exactly!" Sarah laughs. She looks down at baby Tate, still sound asleep.

"Shall we head inside?" Angela asks. "I think Gavin is getting chilly."

"Not Gavvy," he says. "Gavvy likes snow. But Andy gets cold." He points to Andy.

Andy nods and says, "I'm ready for inside."

I lean over to pick up Andy. Sometimes, the difference in speech between Gavin and Andy surprises me. Gavin is always a little chatterbox but still uses a lot of baby words and speaks in third person. Andy doesn't say much, but when he does talk, his pronunciation is typically good and he uses pronouns. There are a few words he struggles with, but not nearly as many as Gavin.

"Carry Gavvy, too, Grandmo?" Gavin asks.

"I'll carry you," Angela says. "Grandmo has her hands full with Andy."

Gavin lets out a big sigh. "Don't want Momma to carry me," he grumbles.

"How about your uncle Malcolm carries you?" Malcolm asks, reaching his arms out.

Gavin gives Angela a cheeky look before letting Malcolm pick him up. It's not going to be long until she has her hands full with him.

"Still planning to stay?" I ask Sarah.

"Definitely," she says with a smile. "It won't be a problem for me to keep Tate away from the crowds. Especially with so many of the militia missing."

Chapter 40

Saturday, Day 222

Jake

"What do you think?" Lindsey asks Evan.

"I think we found what we were looking for."

She gives him a *duh* look before saying, "And what are you thinking we should do about it, boss?"

"How about I go knock on the door?" I ask. I blink rapidly a few times, wondering why in the world I'd even suggest that.

Evan tightens his mouth and gives a slight nod of his head. "Not a terrible idea."

"You can't be serious," Lindsey says.

"We'll get into position first. Then Jake and I will walk right up to the door like we own the place."

I feel myself pale. It was a stupid suggestion. We don't know anything about the cabin or who is in it. It sounds like a great way to get shot.

Evan clicks the radio one time, then looks toward the east. Leo moves enough from the trees for Evan to see him. They do a couple of quick hand signals before Leo disappears again. He clicks the radio two times, then looks in the opposite direction until he sees Rey. He repeats the hand signal process and Rey, too, disappears.

"Okay, we'll give them a few minutes to get set."

"They'll know what to do?" I ask.

"They'll know to surround the building and provide perimeter cover. Lindsey and Atticus, you two set up from this side. I want you on us, ready for anything."

"Yes, sir," Atticus says, as he and Lindsey move through the trees.

"Well, Jake. You ready?" Evan asks.

"Uh, not really. I wasn't— "

"I know. But knocking on the door makes sense. That's what normal people would do, right?"

"You mean if I were walking out in the woods—in the middle of nowhere—it would be normal for me to knock on the door of the only house around? No. I'd avoid the house and keep walking."

"Yeah, well. It's as good a plan as any. Let's do this. First, let's take off the paddles. If we need to move quickly, it'll be easier without the snowshoes on. Oh, and remember, if they start shooting at us, make yourself small as you zig and zag."

"Thanks for the tip," I mutter as I remove my snowshoes.

My heart is pounding in my ears as we begin our slow walk toward the house. It's in a slight bowl, so we have a downward trek. The packed trail has slick spots, and I could use the traction the crampons on the snowshoes would've provided. As the house comes into view, it's obvious it's more of a cabin—or even a shack—than any sort of actual home. It appears to have originally been constructed out of logs but now has plywood on one complete side. What was probably a window near the door is also a piece of plywood. There's still a small window on the other side of the door, with a strip of duct tape likely covering a crack. A rickety porch leads to a well-used door. There are three outbuildings near the cabin, in about the same state of disrepair.

"What about the other buildings?" I ask. "Will your team have eyes on them?"

"They'll cover us. You ready for this?" Evan asks as we move out of the trees and into the open.

"Guess so," I mutter, my heart still beating much harder than it should be. I half expect gunshots to greet us as we make our way the twenty or so yards to the door. As we approach the steps to the porch, Evan motions me to go up the right side. He takes the left, each of us staying close to the wobbly handrail. When we reach the door, I move to the right, where there's some protection from the original logs of the cabin. He steps to the other side, between the door and the duct-taped window, before giving me a nod. I nod back as he lifts his hand to knock.

There's a shuffling noise and what may be a whimper, before a harsh voice demands, "Who's there?"

Evan gives me a bewildered shrug and calmly says, "Evan Snyder."

After a pause, the man says, "Go away! This is private property."

I tilt my head. The voice sounds vaguely familiar. Evan scrunches up his face, then mouths, "Who is that?"

I shake my head.

"Yep. I'm happy to go away as soon as we have a quick discussion," Evan says. I watch as pieces of the door blow out, the repercussion of a shotgun follows. There's a scream from somewhere as I throw myself to the porch.

"Go," Evan hisses as he motions me to move off the porch. I duckwalk to the railing and bail off the elevated structure. Staying low, I use the porch as protection. I peek around, trying to find Evan. He's also on the ground, on the other side of the steps.

There's a loud crash as the door flies open and the man yells, "I told you to go away!" Then he pumps the shotgun and fires again. A single shot answers. An *oomph* is followed by a thump and scream. Still hidden by the porch, Evan yells, "Stay down! Stay down or you'll be shot again!"

"I'm down, man. I'm down," the man says with a whimper.

"Jake, go to the side. Stay low. When I say now, you pop up and cover me." Into his radio, he says, "Keep us covered."

I move to the edge of the porch, staying low as instructed. Handgun at the ready, I take a deep breath.

"Who else is with you?" Evan demands.

"I'm, uh—there's just me and, uh . . . "

"You, in the house!" Evan barks. "Throw down your weapon."

"I'm not—I don't have anything," a young female voice responds shakily.

"Step out where we can see you. Keep your hands in the air."

"I'm Macie. Macie Michaelson," the girl says. "Thank you for coming for me."

A moment later, in my earbud I hear, "She's clear. No movement from any of the other buildings."

"Now, Jake."

I pop up, making sure to keep as much of my body as possible at the side of the house. Evan is also up, using a post holding up the roof of the rickety porch for cover. The groaning man on the porch is clutching his shoulder as he writhes around.

"Well, Heath, we've been looking for you," Evan says. "Macie, I want you to step behind him and walk over toward Jake."

"How did you know I was here?" Macie asks as she walks toward me.

I'm so confused by why she's here, I just shake my head. "Can you get off the porch?" I ask. "Are you hurt?

"No, they didn't hurt me."

"They?" Evan repeats, voice full of alarm.

Chapter 41

Saturday, Day 222

Mollie

As the group moves inside, we hang back to let the crowd thin. As soon as we enter the lodge, the aromas of the special wedding lunch cause my mouth to water. While I didn't help with the meal prep, Deanne went over the menu plan with me while we were having tea yesterday.

To go along with the elk roast and stewed sheep, we have mashed turnips, cooked pumpkin, and fresh greens from the greenhouse—and not a sugar beet in sight! It's too bad Jake is missing this. He'd love a salad.

Our usual table arrangements have been altered to provide a wedding table for the bride, groom, and their party. Their table's even been decorated for the occasion.

Though there's fewer people than there usually are at meals, thanks to the absence of many on the militia and security team, most of our group is still here. Rudy Wallace, his wife, and those living in his home and the house next door have all made the trek up for the occasion. There are several other seniors here who often have their meals delivered.

Dodie and Alvin are not among those attending, which isn't much of a surprise. The quiet of the lodge likely held much more appeal than a party.

"You still okay with staying?" I ask Sarah, gesturing to the full room.

She gives me a smile and a nod. "I still think it's fine."

"Are you going to check with Belinda?"

"I'm not." She raises her eyebrows at me.

I give a shrug in response.

"Okay, folks," Judge Avery says, and the room quiets down. "We've got quite a feast to enjoy. And I believe the Cameron brothers will keep the music going during the meal?" He looks over to where Dax and Bryce are setting two chairs at the edge of the room.

Dax gives a single nod.

"Good, good. Paul will bless the food and then we'll let the bride and groom go through the chow line first. Paul?"

Putting his hand on Harry's shoulder, Paul says, "Let us pray," then bows his head. "Dear God, thank you for this blessed day. Thank you for bringing Harry and Annette together, for allowing them to see Your love reflected through each other. We ask that You bless their marriage, their family, and all their relationships. We, as their family and friends, lift them up to You today and all days.

"Thank you for Your blessings on us as we navigate through a world in which none of us are familiar. In these times of trouble and uncertainty, we realize we need You and Your word more than ever. Please help Harry and Annette—help all of us—to remember to put You first in not only our marriages but our lives. Please bless this food and the hands which provided it. In Jesus' name we pray, amen."

"I'm going to get the children to the table," Angela says, as she starts moving them toward an empty one near the other exit door— the table we've taken to sitting at for meals. While there isn't assigned seating, most of us have tables we prefer. Today, with things rearranged slightly, it's obvious many are confused as to where to sit.

I give a wave to Kelley as she moves toward a table at the front. Like many, Phil's also missing, and I assume he's on militia duty. Doris, Deanne, Sheila, and several others are already seated. I'm surprised to see Tricia, one of the women from the Cameron group, at the table. While she's currently a part of the militia, she's been campaigning to be added to the security team. Of course, she is a close friend to Annette and Harry, which may be why she's here instead of with the militia. She's wearing an incredibly colorful Bohemian crinkle skirt. I owned something like it twenty years ago, only more subdued.

I smile as I watch her flamboyant hand gestures, which seem to match her skirt perfectly. Tricia is quite the talker and always has lots to say—about everyone. I almost laugh out loud when I realize she's chatting with Nina Rose.

Nina joined our community over the summer, arriving with Kelley's daughters and Lindsey. She's an aunt to Atticus Dosen, who was on the same militia team as me. I've tried to get to know her, but she's terribly quiet and withdrawn. Certainly not one who is known to gossip. She's also not one who I'd imagine would say much during a conversation with someone like Tricia. My guess, it's a fully one-sided conversation. Poor Nina.

I'm considering going over to rescue her when Sarah lets out a large sigh. I look to her and see the source. Brad is making a beeline toward us. I didn't see him at the ceremony and assumed he was one of the many called to extra duty. I guess I was wrong.

"Sarah," he says, "how about I make you a to-go plate?"

"No thanks, Dad. I'm going to sit at our usual table, and Mom or Angela will make sure I have what I need." She gives him a brilliant smile.

"Suit yourself." He spins on his heel and heads back toward a group of others. Jon Dawson is part of the group he joins. I look around the room, trying to find Alina and Victor. When I saw her yesterday, she told me how excited she was for the wedding. While I don't see them, I do see something unusual.

Clark Thomas is back by the kitchen. I only catch a glimpse of him as he pops his head out and then quickly yanks it back. What kind of weirdness is happening with that? I shake my head and turn to Sarah, asking her if she knows where Alina and Victor are.

"I don't know. Alina should've been here. You heard her yesterday say she couldn't wait to see Annette in the outfit. She wasn't at the wedding either."

I wish I would've realized she was missing before. I would've asked Brad if Victor is okay. He's been doing surprisingly well, with no apparent recurrence of his symptoms. Kelley and Belinda assume he's in remission and hope it will continue.

"Ready to get a seat?" I ask as I start moving toward our table. As we reach the table, Angela says she's sending the older boys up to start through the line now that the bride and groom have gone through and the rest of the people are lining up, as is our process. Marc will fill his own plate while Malcolm and Tony will get their plates plus plates for Lily and Sissy. Angela and I will go up when the boys return and get our plates as well as plates for Gavin and Andy. With Sarah here today, I'll manage a third plate for her. It's been a long time since I waitressed, but I can handle it. It'd be easier with one more adult, but we'll make it work. To see the smile on Sarah's face at being part of the community, it's worth it.

As the boys walk away, Sarah asks, "Mom, will you keep Tate? I'd like to go through the line. I can get some visiting in."

"Sure. Like I'd turn down a chance to hold my grandbaby?"

"Angela, wait for me?" Sarah asks as she gently removes Tate from the sling and takes the snowsuit off, wrapping him in a blanket before placing him in my waiting arms.

"Gavin, you stay with Grandmo," Angela says. Then she looks at the other children. "All of you stay here and don't move from your chairs. Grandmo doesn't need to be trying to keep you all rounded up while she's holding the baby."

Lily looks at Angela and, with plenty of cheek in her voice, says, "She's not my Grandmo. She's my mom."

I smile as tears of joy fill my eyes. Even though Jake and I have unofficially adopted Tony and Lily, we haven't made a big deal about them calling us Mom and Dad. With their mom dead and their dad missing, we're just happy to provide them a home and give them our love.

Angela, knowing the situation, says, "Sorry, Lily. You're absolutely right. You be good for our mom by being the helper you always are."

Lily beams as she gives a nod. "I'll help our mom. I know the little kids will be good."

Angela and Sarah head toward the line, stopping at the wedding table to visit before taking their place. The guitars are playing softly in the background as people talk and laugh. It's really a wonderful wedding reception, so very much like it would've been before the attacks, before the EMP took out our power grids and stopped many of our cars, before we had to join forces with the residents of Bakerville and move up the mountain. I study the children around the table. Gavin and Andy are having some important conversation about snowmobiles—at least, I think that's what they're saying.

Sissy and Lily are talking about Annette's wedding dress and what kind of dress each of them will wear for their own weddings. Lily catches my eye and gives me a sweet smile before she declares to Sissy her need for a pair of pink cowboy boots and a pink jacket for just her shoulders. Sissy tells her that her mom can make the jacket, that her mom can sew anything. I lean in to hear more of their conversation when a scream shatters the festivities.

Chapter 42

Saturday, Day 222

Jake

"What do you mean *they*?" Evan asks evenly. "Is there someone else in the cabin?"

"Not now," Macie says. "There were people here yesterday while they were making their plans, but the last ones must have left after I went to sleep."

"Heath, what's she talking about?" Evan asks. Into the radio, he says, "I want a perimeter and four with me, double time."

Heath moans in response. "Keep pressure on your arm," Evan says. "As soon as I know you aren't lying to me, we'll take care of you so you don't bleed to death."

"I'm not lying to you. There's no one here," he says through clenched teeth.

"He's telling the truth. Don't let him die," Macie says. "They brought me here a couple of weeks ago, to make my dad vote with them."

"Who brought you here?" I ask.

"You know, Jon Dawson and the others who wanted to get rid of the guns, but— " She takes a deep breath and, in barely a whisper, says, "They wanted to get rid of the guns so they can be in charge."

"What'd you say, Macie?" Evan asks. Before she can answer, his attention is diverted by his team emerging from the forest. Leo is the first to arrive, still in his snowshoes, as he asks, "Clear the house, sir?"

Evan gives a nod. "Outbuildings first. And move Heath over there so he's out of the way." He gestures to where I'm standing.

Leo has his snowshoes off as Rey and two more from the security team arrive and follow suit.

"Jake, cover us," Evan says, then into the radio he repeats the request for Lindsey. Leo and Evan quickly and unceremoniously remove Heath from the front porch and put him on the side of the house where I am. After checking him for weapons, Evan says, "Put a bandage on him, stop the bleeding." He turns to Leo and his team. "Let's check that shack first." He points to the closest outbuilding.

As they begin clearing the buildings, I take one of our homemade Israeli-style bandages out of my backpack for Heath's arm. When I move his arm, he lets out a moan.

"Try not to hurt him," Macie says. "He . . . he's been nice to me."

"Nice to you?" I ask.

She shrugs. "He's not a bad man. I don't think he's even a part of what they're planning."

"Is that right, Heath?"

With a grimace, he nods. "I was just out here, uh, camping."

"Save it. We know about Dot. We found her after you beat her up."

"That's not what happened! We just— "

"Don't," I say, putting more pressure on the bandage than necessary.

He lets out a scream. "Fine, man. Whatever you say."

"Is everything good, Jake?" Evan asks as his team comes around the house.

"Yep. Just dandy."

"Okay, then. We'll clear the house. Wait until we tell you what we found in the outbuildings," he says before going inside.

"There are chickens and rabbits," Macie says. "Plus, lots of other supplies. Heath said they probably took them from our storage buildings."

"Heath?"

He gives a shrug, quickly realizing that isn't a good movement after having been shot in the arm.

"How did you end up here?" I ask as I secure the bandage. I'm no doctor, but from the looks of it, only Heath's bicep was hit. It's low enough not to have damaged the shoulder, but it may have still broken the bone. "Last we saw of you, you had a backpack and tent heading west. Why are you here?"

"I found this place. They were taking turns watching Macie. I made a deal with them. I stay here, they don't tell anyone where I'm at. After the— "

"Takeover," Macie says quietly. "But I think it's really a coup. I learned about those in school."

I nod my understanding. "Who all is involved?"

Heath lets out a low moan.

"Are you okay?" Macie asks him, holding his other hand.

He gives her a small nod. "See, I said you'd be able to go home today, just not quite how it was supposed to work out."

"He said you could go home today?" I ask Macie.

"Yes, today's the takeover," she says, giving me an odd look. "Isn't that why you're here? Did you win?"

I start to yell for Evan when a garbled message comes over the radio.

"Say again," Evan demands.

There's silence for a minute when Lindsey says, "I couldn't make it out. Did anyone copy?"

Another voice comes on and says, "This is Alpha One, still near the start of the path. It sounded like 'we're under attack.'"

Chapter 43

Saturday, Day 222

Mollie

The first scream is followed by several gunshots and complete chaos. "Get on the ground!" I yell to the children, as I pull Andy—closest to me—off his chair, knocking it over in the process. As he's been taught, he curls into a ball, covering his hands over his head. I move for Gavin, finding him and both girls already on the floor. I lift my head, looking for Malcolm, Marc, and Tony. Before I can find them, a voice calls out, "That's enough. Everyone, quiet down and no one else will get hurt."

My eyes search for the voice. As I find him, my heart drops to my stomach. It's Jon Dawson standing near the serving line, with his arm around Malcolm's neck. Next to him is Miles Decker, holding Tony in a similar manner. I look for Marc but don't see him. There are several other children being held hostage. Miles's wife, Shannon, has Rochelle's young daughter Cheyre. Her sister, Moira, Jesse Richardson, and Brad are also holding children. Sarah and Angela are at the wedding table, standing only a few feet away from Brad and the mayhem next to the seated bride and groom. *Why are they not on the ground?*

Where's Clark Thomas? Is he still lurking in the shadows? Why didn't he stop this? My stomach drops as it occurs to me—he could be a part of this. Jesse Richardson, that skunk, is one of the conspirators. Maybe Clark is too.

As Dawson tells everyone to quiet down again, I slide over by Lily and Sissy. Whispering, I tell them the baby needs to lay between them. I move his sleeping form into the slight space available.

Lily lifts her head and says, "I'll take care of him, Momma."

Shifting slowly, I remove my prohibited handgun from my belly band holster. None of the conspirators seem to be looking in my direction. Walking slightly hunched, I cautiously move to put space between me and the children. As I'm moving, I notice Dax and Bryce Cameron. They're slowly putting down their guitars.

"Hey!" Dawson yells, causing me to freeze. "Guitar boys, you just hold on to those. Stay right where I can see you. No one needs to think about being a hero here. These kids don't need you to try something foolish like that." Dax lifts his hands. Bryce follows. "Good. I can see we understand each other."

Deciding I'm far enough away from the children, I stay put. Unlike the time when Barney and Daniel got into the argument and no one moved, this time many are sitting or lying on the floor. I guess the guns firing moved people into action. Even so, there are a few people still in chairs—one person's holding a hand over her blood-soaked arm. Laying in a heap on the floor is Judge Avery, a large pool of blood surrounding him. Four more people are on the ground, covered in blood. One man is squirming in pain, but the other three—one I'm sure is Tricia based on the vibrant, flowy skirt—are completely still. A pair of military-style boots, with both legs at an odd angle, poke out from under the table Doris was sitting at. My eyes linger on the boots.

An order from one of Jon Dawson's men brings me back on alert. I'm now on one knee with my other foot flat on the floor. I'm ready to move. Malcolm and Tony are both statues with tense jaws.

I watch for a moment as only Malcolm's eyes travel the room. He starts at our table, then slowly moves them in my direction. When he sees me, he gives a slight lift of his eyebrows. I blink my eyes rapidly several times—our signal for wait. He blinks three times: his response that he understands. I look to Tony, who is also staring at me. I repeat the blinking, and he responds with three blinks.

What options do we have with so many of the traitors holding our children? I take a quick look toward Doris. She's sitting on the floor staring at Dawson, her left hand pulling her earlobe. My heart skips a beat. She's saying, "We fight." Kelley is next to her, hand on her earlobe too.

"I want all of the men to go over by the guitar boys," Dawson says. "Everyone keep your hands where we can see them, and understand we *will* shoot the kids if we have to. The cute little blond girl will be first." He points to a girl of about eight, sobbing wildly while being held by Jesse Richardson.

As he's talking, I look again for Sarah and Angela. They're still at the wedding table and still standing. I want to give them a motion for "sit down," but that wasn't one we made a code for. Brad's even closer to Sarah now, having taken several steps near her. Is he talking to her? I guess the reason he didn't want her at the wedding is now clear.

"It worked out amazingly well with so many of the militia and the entire security team and police force gone today," Dawson says. "I couldn't have planned it any better." He lets out a laugh, and those in his gang join in. Except Jesse Richardson, he stares straight ahead, stone faced, a tight grip on his captive.

Brad takes another step toward Sarah. I want to yell at him to stay away from her, to tell him he never gets to be around her again. Sarah looks at me and uses her left hand to tug on her right ear, her right hand behind her back out of view. My eyes dart to Angela, whose hand is on her own ear. Instead of tugging it, she's holding up four fingers. Does that mean they have help? Annette, Harry, Kirstin, and Milena are all right there with them. Are they ready to fight?

We can move now, and Malcolm and Tony will know to also move, to dive to the ground as soon as I give the signal. But what about the other children being held? Four of them won't know what to do. I'm too far—with too many people in the way—to act as anything other than a diversion. I don't have a clean shot. But if Sarah and Angela have the help of those still at the wedding table, and Doris and Kelley are ready to fight . . . I shove my gun in my pants at the small of my back and quickly stand up.

"Jon Dawson," I say loudly. "Please, please let my little boys go." All movement and noise stop as all eyes are on me. I hear one lady— not one of Dawson's crew but one of us, a hostage—tell me to sit down and shut up.

"Oh, that's right. This is your kid, isn't it?" Dawson says in a saccharine sweet voice. "I just grabbed the nearest brat I could find, but I'd say that worked out right well. Don't think I've forgotten what a troublemaker you are, Mollie Caldwell."

I try to soften my face. "What is it you want?"

"What do I want? I'm sure you know. As of today, things are going to be different here. Judge Avery didn't have what it took to lead this community. He forced us to move up here and then allowed anyone who didn't want to join us to stay back—even giving them a portion of our provisions. What kind of a leader does that?"

I keep my face passive, wondering how in the world he thinks this can end. Even though they struck when our militia and security team are gone, he must know they'll come back and rescue us. Evan, Bill, and Cole are experienced. While the militia has decent training, those three and the entire security team are well-trained operatives. Dawson can't honestly believe his few ragtag conspirators and one former police detective are any match for them.

Dawson looks around the room with cold eyes. Scared eyes meet his. His face contorts into something resembling an evil grin. "Avery and his cronies are fools. Isolating us up here, not even letting us contact Prospect. We know they're thriving there, taking control of the situation and turning Prospect into the hub of the region. Moira has heard plenty of wonderful things happening there during her ham radio shifts. But did the judge allow you to know about those? Nope. He made sure that information never got out."

"What are you saying?" a familiar voice asks. I keep my eyes on Jon Dawson as he glances toward the speaker.

"What I'm saying, my dear Dr. Belinda, is critical information is being withheld from you. You all blindly took the word of Paul Cameron and his people as to the situation in Prospect. They lied to you."

Chapter 44

Saturday, Day 222

Jake

"Who was transmitting?" Evan asks into his radio as he barrels out the front door of the cabin.

Lindsey, still in her perch, relays the question in case Alpha One isn't receiving clearly.

"Might have been Clark Thomas," Alpha One replies.

"Leo, I want the other three from your team to stabilize Heath, then take him and Macie to the clinic," Evan says, both into his radio and for those of us nearby. "Atticus, keep them covered from your perch. Everyone else, let's move. Jake, you stay here and help with Heath."

"Not happening," I say, already standing and taking a step up the trail.

"Fine," Evan snaps. "No time to argue. Let's move, people."

Leo, Evan, and I hotfoot it across the snowy trail, picking up Lindsey at the top of the hill. When we reach the open meadow, Kimba, Rey, and their team members emerge from the forest. "We're right behind you," Kimba says, removing a snowshoe. Evan nods as we continue our sprint.

My beard and mustache are frozen, and my lungs are burning from the exertion and cold as we approach the trailhead. Rey and his team have no trouble catching up to us. "Alpha One, stay on watch," Evan says with a ragged breath. "Alpha Two, you're with me."

"Where do you think they are?" Lindsey asks, barely even winded.

"The wedding?" I ask with a croak.

"They're likely inside by now, starting the reception," Evan answers. "Hold up. Let's make sure there's no one waiting for us to come busting out of the forest. Kimba, Rey." He motions with his hands as each one moves off one side of the trail and through the snow. Even without snowshoes, they're light on their feet, practically floating above the white powder.

A few minutes later, Rey's slightly British voice quietly says, "You were right, boss. One tango down."

Kimba chimes in with, "Make that two tangos. Mine's still breathing."

My eyes go wide when I look at Evan.

"Ambush?" he asks into his radio.

"Right-O," Rey says. "Two of our own militia sharpshooters were set up to take us out as we exited the woods."

"Kimba, did your guy say anything?"

A scream of pain and terror carries through the radio and the wilderness, as Kimba calmly says, "Let me ask him again." After another scream, she's back on the radio. "Nothing more than we already knew. They've got them at the wedding luncheon. He says they're using the kids to control the adults. Oh, and it's Dawson leading along with five others." My heart falls. "My kids are at the wedding, boss," she says. "We need to move."

"Did he say anything about any other traps?"

"Nope. He's taking a break from talking at the moment."

"Restrain him. We'll deal with him later."

"I've already got him tied to a tree."

I'm surprised she had enough time to find him, tie him up, and torture him for information. It's only been a few minutes since she and Rey left the rest of us.

"Let's move," Evan says, as we once again begin our brisk pace. Rey and Kimba join us as we reach the second string of cabins. Even as we quickly advance through the dude ranch property, we're cautiously looking for additional ambushes or other hazards.

Evan's team acts as a well-oiled machine, each anticipating the others' moves as they make their way. I stick with Evan and pretend I know what I'm doing. I can see now why he didn't want me to go with them, but no way was I staying behind when Mollie and my family may be in danger. Fear once again grips my stomach. I shake my head to try and alleviate the sensation. *Please, Lord, please protect my family.*

As the quick petition floats through my head, peacefulness washes over me. Part of a verse I've been working on in Isaiah comes to mind. *"Fear not, I am the one who helps you."*

We're near the clinic when Leo holds up a hand to urge us to an immediate halt. He flutters his fingers, and everyone takes cover.

"What's happening?" Evan asks quietly into his radio.

Before Leo answers, a voice calls out, "It's me! It's Katie Burnett. I'm alone. I'm not a threat."

"Step out, Katie," Leo says to his wife.

"I'm coming out," she says as a hand appears along the side of the cabin, followed by the other hand and then Katie.

I let out a breath as my daughter partially steps into view.

"We're clear," Leo says into the radio.

"Keep watch," Evan says. "Leo, Jake, you're with me."

Leo is quickly at Katie's side; Evan and I are there a moment later.

"What can you tell us?" Evan asks her.

"Not much. I was outside getting more wood when I heard screaming and shooting from the ski lodge. My radio" —she motions to the clinic radio on her belt— "sounded, and Clark Thomas whispered they were under attack."

"Why are you outside?" Leo asks.

"If we're under attack, I thought I'd have better mobility outside than stuck inside," Katie says with a shrug.

"You're armed?" Leo asks.

Quietly, she says, "We keep a rifle locked in the closet of the clinic. I left it propped against the building. And I'm carrying." She touches under her left arm. Most likely, she's wearing one of Mollie's concealment tanks and has a little .380 tucked in the armpit holster.

"Good thinking, Katie," Evan says. "Stay here. We'll— " Evan's interrupted by a loud scream.

Chapter 45

Saturday, Day 222

Mollie

"That's right, folks," Dawson says with a sick smile. "You've been played. They've been keeping the truth from you to further their own agenda."

A rumble of gasps and noises of disbelief run through the room. Out of my peripheral vision, I see Bryce and Dax Cameron stiffen. At the wedding table, near Dawson, Annette visibly pales. While she and Sarah were working on the wedding outfit, she shared some of the terrible things that happened in Prospect. When Mayor Stringer was assassinated and the owner of the local newspaper—Richard Majors—took over, it was nothing short of a bloodbath. To say Majors sounds like a nut would be an understatement.

"I don't understand, Jon," Belinda says calmly. "Can you elaborate?"

Dawson lets out a large sigh. "You've been duped, Belinda. You all have. Judge Avery never liked Richard Majors. When Paul Cameron and his throng showed up, Avery was only too happy to believe what he was told. So much so, he removed the ability for us to converse with Prospect—or anyone—by having the ham radio rigged so we could listen only, not transmit. But I know Richard Majors. I know he's a good man who loves Prospect, loves his country. He's a patriot. I also know Paul Cameron. He's none of the things Richard Majors is."

"You've got that right," a voice booms through the room. "Richard Majors is a murdering coward. My dad is the one who is the patriot."

Jon Dawson darts his head in the direction of the voice. "Ah, PJ. Don't think I've forgotten about you."

He raises the gun in PJ Cameron's direction. One of the ladies sitting at a table nearby screams at the top of her lungs and dives under the table.

Dawson shakes his head at her, then says to PJ, "Not to worry. I have special plans for you, your dad, and the rest of you liars. You think your little guerrilla tactics are something to be proud of? You think killing good men makes you heroes? You're wrong. Avery might have been impressed, but I know you're nothing but murderers."

I quickly glance toward the Cameron table. PJ, like the rest of them, has a fierce look on his face. Sitting next to PJ is Rochelle; her eyes are on her daughter being held by Shannon. Cheyre, like Malcolm and TJ, is standing calmly, a determined look on her face.

"Now, let's get back to business," Dawson says. "All the men go over with the guitar boys—and yes, I know they're Camerons also. They'll be dealt with accordingly."

"Jon," I say loudly, "can you—would you please let the children go now?" I pause and take a deep breath, controlling my facial expressions. "What you've said, it makes some sense. We don't—we should reach out to Prospect, see if we can band together for mutual aid."

"Don't believe her," Brad says. "She's a liar."

"Oh, I know that," Dawson says. "Mollie Caldwell's one of the biggest bootlickers around. I think I'll be holding on to your kids for now."

As he says it, I flash back to the day Dan Morse and his hoodlums tried to take me and my girls hostage. Dan called me a bootlicker too. A burning deep in my belly takes over my body. My heart rate slows, and everything becomes clear. I straighten my back. "Please, Jon," I say. "Please don't hurt my family."

With a sinister look, Dawson says, "Try and stop me."

Chapter 46

Saturday, Day 222

Jake

"Let's move," Evan says for the umpteenth time today. "Stay here, Katie. Make the clinic ready."

"Are we under attack?" she calls out as we takeoff.

"Not by outside forces," Leo responds.

From the clinic, it's almost half a mile to the ski lodge. Thankfully, the main road between the two is kept well-cleared by our snow grooming machine. I continue my petitions to God to keep my family safe. Like Katie, Calley is also on duty and not attending the wedding, but as far as I know, my other children, grandchildren, extended family, and my wife are all at the wedding. They've all been looking forward to this bright spot in our lives very much.

"Stay alert," Evan says as we approach a cluster of camp trailers.

The words are no sooner out of his mouth when someone yells out, "Stop. We have you surrounded."

Evan stops so quickly I bump into him. Here we are in the middle of the road, fully exposed. "Not good," I hear someone from Evan's team say under his breath.

"Boss?" Lindsey asks quietly.

"Wait!" a second voice says. "It's our security team."

"How do we know they're not with them?" a new voice asks.

"Because my brother-in-law's on the team," a voice I now recognize as Angela's husband, Tim, says. "And Jake's with them."

"Bill and Cole told us to hold the line," the first voice, who told us we were surrounded, says.

"Call it in," Evan says sternly.

"We don't have a radio," Tim says. "Roscoe, we need to let them pass."

"Roscoe?" Evan says quietly. "Lindsey, what's Miles's brother-in-law's name?"

"Pretty sure it's Roscoe," she whispers.

"Great," I mutter, as I wonder how we can avoid being sitting ducks.

"Not happening," Roscoe says. "I want each of you to put your weapons on the ground. We'll let Bill sort this out."

"What are you doing, Roscoe?" one of the guards asks.

"Boss?" Kimba asks quietly.

"We know all about it, Roscoe," Evan says evenly. "We found the hideout. We found the girl. Your buddy, Heath, is bleeding in the snow. We even found the sharpshooters."

"I don't—I'm not sure what you're talking about," he says, a slight quiver in his voice. Then he loudly yells, "Put your weapons on the ground. I'm not telling you again."

"Whoa, whoa, whoa," Tim says. "Take your weapon off them, Roscoe. Stand down. You need to stand down."

"Don't even think about telling me what to do," Roscoe screeches. "I outrank you. You—all of you—will follow my orders."

"You don't outrank me," Evan says. "Stand down. Stand down now."

There's an *oomph* and the sound of a scuffle. All of Evan's team immediately goes to one knee, rifles at the ready. I mimic their moves, even though I think staying in the middle of the road could be suicide.

"Stay down," Tim demands.

"You're going to regret this," Roscoe scoffs.

"Tim, status," Evan says.

"He's unarmed and covered."

"How many are with you?"

"There's five of us, including Roscoe."

"The rest of you, lay down your firearms and step out, hands visible. Tim, you stay where you are and keep Roscoe covered."

It's mere seconds before the other three militiamen step out of concealment. Each are holding their hands up and looking bewildered.

"I'm not sure what's going on, sir," David Hammer's youngest son, Noah, says.

"Over here, Noah," Evan demands. "All three of you."

Noah gives a nod as he and the others move toward Leo, where he quickly frisks them.

"Rey, Kimba, help Tim."

They quickly and cautiously move toward where we heard the scuffle. "We've got him," Rey says.

"Tim, leave your weapon and step out here."

"Hey," I say, "you know him."

"Can't be helped," Evan answers.

Like the others, Tim moves out from behind the camp trailer, hands clearly visible. "Roscoe's working with them?" he asks.

Evan's shoulders barely move as he shrugs his answer. "Is he clear?"

"He's clear," Rey answers.

"Treat him as a hostile," Evan says.

There's a slight whimper as Rey hustles the zip-tied man out while Kimba keeps her weapon trained on him. While I couldn't picture who Roscoe was before, as soon as I see him, I recognize him. The first time I met him, he gave me a hard time for not respecting him since he was a sergeant and he assumed I was a corporal. Once we cleared up the minor misunderstanding, he was fine, and I thought him nice enough. He keeps his eyes on the ground and looks defeated.

"Noah, Tim, the rest of you, stay here." Evan turns to the lady he was earlier referring to as Alpha Two. "You've got Roscoe. If you have any trouble— "

"I'm not going to give her trouble," the man says softly. "But you'd better hurry if you plan to stop this. Dawson won't go down easily."

"We'll take him down," Evan says. We start to move when the crack of gunfire fills the air.

Chapter 47

Saturday, Day 222

Mollie

I barely have time to register Jon Dawson's sneer. "FIRE!" I yell at the top of my lungs.

Dawson's face clouds with confusion as Malcolm drops to the ground. Dawson bends over, trying to make a grab for him. I watch Dawson's mouth form an *O*—Malcolm's knife is sticking out of Jon's arm. With no clear shot from where I am, I bend at the waist and start moving toward the mayhem, pistol held by my leg. I lose track of the number of gunshots, the yelling, the complete bedlam. I'm halfway toward the front when the little blond girl—the one Jesse Richardson was holding—runs into me. She lets out a yell, pivots, and runs toward the kitchen.

"Clear!" a voice calls out. Four others repeat the word.

"Are they all down?" someone yells out. There are several people crying, including at least one baby. I look to the table my children and grandchildren are hiding under. Lily, holding baby Tate, is scrunched over and attempting to rock him.

"They're all down," someone answers. "We need the medical team."

"Quiet! Quiet down," Clark Thomas says. "I want everyone not injured to exit out the door nearest you. Go. Go now."

I quickly look for Sarah and Angela. Neither are where they were moments before. My eyes dart to Malcolm. He and Tony are leaning over, helping Marc to his feet. I rush back to the young children.

"Lily, you did so great taking care of baby Tate. Can you and Sissy help me get Gavin and Andy? We need to go outside."

"Go to our tree?"

"Exactly. We'll go to our meeting tree. Grab your coats but don't take time to put them on."

A minute or so later, we're outside, the cold biting into us while Tate is screaming his head off. I wrap the blanket and my jacket tighter around him. As we left, I grabbed my coat, the diaper bag, and my daypack but left the baby sling. "Where's my mom?" Sissy asks, looking around.

"She'll be here shortly." *Please, Lord. Let it be so.* "Lily, Sissy, put on your jackets and then help Andy and Gavin with theirs." While I speak, my eyes are frantically searching, looking for the rest of my family. I let out a breath when I see Malcolm and the other boys exit the building near the kitchen. Tony is between Marc and Malcolm, limping as he walks.

"Lily, I need you to hold the baby. Sit down right here," I say, taking a crinkly emergency blanket out of my daypack and laying it on the snowy ground. I leave it partially folded, while still allowing enough space for all the children. "Sissy, you sit next to her. Andy, sit on Sissy's lap. Gavin, can you sit here?" I ask, patting a small space between the two girls. "Save room for the older boys."

"Okay, Grandmo," he says, his face streaked with tears. I plant a kiss on his forehead; I didn't even realize he'd been crying. I hand baby Tate to Lily, securing the blanket tightly around him. Once he's in her arms, I drape my coat over the top.

"Can you reach in the diaper bag and get out his hat?" I ask, setting the bag next to her. "In a minute, we'll put his snowsuit on him. I just want to get the other boys first." I turn to look for my older boys. They're about a quarter of the way to our meeting tree, moving slowly. "Don't move," I tell the younger children. "I'm going to get the big boys."

"Here!" Lily says, thrusting a coat in my direction. "I grabbed Tony's. I . . . I didn't think to get Malcolm's or Marc's coats."

"Smart thinking," I say. "Hold onto it. We'll get him here and get it on him."

I run toward them, feeling a wave of dizziness sweep over me. I slow my pace slightly. "Tony?"

"I'm okay. It's just my ankle," he says.

"Marc, I'll help him. Can you run to the tree? Stay with the younger children. We'll be right there."

"Where's my mom?" Marc asks.

"She'll be there shortly. Keep the kids calm, okay?"

"I think she might have been hurt. Aunt Angela too," Marc says in a wobbly voice.

Tears fill my eyes. I blink rapidly, then say, "Take care of the little ones, okay?"

He gives a nod and runs off to the tree. "Tony, can you keep going?"

"Yes, it hurts, but . . . " he finishes with a shrug.

"Don't put any weight on it. Lean on Malcolm and me."

"Mostly on me," Malcolm says. "I can hold you. Mom, you don't look too good."

I give a nod. My breathing isn't right, and the dizziness keeps coming in waves. Tony grits his teeth the entire way. When we reach the tree, I put my hand on the gnarled base, trying to catch my breath.

"Are you okay?" Lily asks her brother.

"Yeah, squirt. I'm okay," he says with a shiver.

"I got your coat for you." She gives him a smile.

"Malcolm, can you help Tony into his coat? Then get a baby blanket out of the diaper bag for you and Marc."

"Are you okay?" he asks me while helping Tony.

"I'm better, just got winded. Tony," I say, taking a deep breath, "sit on the mylar blanket and let me check your ankle."

"Can you—let's wait." He gives me a look. Barely in a whisper, he says, "You need to find Sarah and Angela."

I give him a nod. "I'll send Belinda out and bring your coats back," I tell Malcolm and Marc. "Sit close to Tony."

"You want me to go with you?" Malcolm asks. "You might need me."

"I need you to watch the children, okay?"

"Mom, it's— " He lets out a breath. "Tony and I, Marc too, we used our knives. They're still—you know." Malcolm drops his head and begins to cry. Tony gives a grim nod as tears fill his eyes.

I drop to my knee. "You all were great. Everything we talked about, you did exactly as you should. Those men—and the women— they weren't thinking right. They could've hurt someone else."

"They killed the judge," Marc says. "And my mom might be hurt." His crying intensifies. As much as I want to go inside and find Angela and Sarah, I know I can't leave the children right now.

"Mom? Mom?" a voice cries out. "You're all okay?"

"Calley," I say, pulling her toward me. "Tony hurt his ankle. The rest of us are fine. I need to go back inside. Stay with the kids?"

"Where's everyone else?"

"Sarah and Angela are still inside," Malcolm says. "Mike's mom and sister were at the wedding—I don't know where they are now. They were sitting with Doris."

My eyes meet Calley's. Her eyes go wide, then she gives a nod. "I'll stay with them."

"Okay. Can you get Tate in his snowsuit?" I ask, as I bend down to give Tony a quick hug, then one for Malcolm and Marc too. "I'll be right back."

Chapter 48

Saturday, Day 222

Jake

We're near the parking lot when Lindsey says, "Look."

My eyes follow her hand. People are spilling out of the ski lodge.

"All right," Evan says. "Let's be cautious. It might be hard to determine exactly what's happening. And as we saw with Roscoe, we might have hostiles intermingled."

We slow our pace as my eyes scour the area, looking for Mollie and my family.

"Hold up," Evan says. We're well inside the large parking lot with over a hundred yards to reach the bridge. From the other side, those escaping the ski lodge are beginning to cross. More than one person has blood on them or is helping someone who is bloody.

"Chaos," Rey says. "Complete and utter chaos."

"You've got that right." Evan nods.

"What's the plan?" Lindsey asks.

"Make a beeline for the right side of the bridge," he says, motioning with his arm. "We cross one at a time, providing cover to get each of us across. Got it?"

As I nod my head, I see three children exiting the lodge. I squint slightly, trying to focus. I can't help the smile that covers my face—Malcolm, Marc, and Tony. Tony's limping, with the other two helping him, but they look fine otherwise.

I'm looking again, trying to find Mollie, when Evan says, "Jake, time to move."

With a nod, I fall in behind him. When he said beeline, he apparently meant sprint. I struggle to keep up with the well-conditioned team. Many people are now coming off the bridge, moving for the safety of their home or to receive treatment at the clinic. I'm starting to wonder how we're going to cross the bridge with so much traffic on it. Just as we reach it, the stream exiting the bridge stops.

"Lindsey, Rey, you're first. Make sure it's clear and then we'll all come up."

The two cautiously go up the slight incline of the snow-covered bridge. "Clear," Lindsey says. The rest of us scurry up behind them. I lose my footing, catching myself after sliding backwards several feet. On the other side of the bridge, Phil Hudson and a few others from the militia have stopped people from coming across.

"C'mon," Phil says, waving us forward.

"Stick with the plan," Evan orders. "Lindsey, go!"

She hurries across. Once on the other side, Rey follows. "You're next," Evan tells me as Rey is almost across. I take a deep breath. "Go! Go now," Evan orders.

On the other side of the bridge, with my lungs burning, I fall in next to Lindsey as she watches toward the ski lodge. Rey's focus is on the bridge and the parking lot on the other side. Phil and his team continue to keep the bridge clear, as the people looking to escape to safety wait impatiently. I join Lindsey in watching the ski lodge. I can't help but continue to look for my family. My eyes search out our meeting tree. With the ski lodge and the tree on higher ground than the bridge, all I can see is the icy top. Is my family gathered around it waiting for me?

As soon as the security team is across, Evan tells Phil to let the residents go. Then he calls him over. "Status," he barks.

"Not sure," Phil says. "Bill had the three of us patrolling together, then things went nuts. We heard the shooting, and Bill came over my radio saying there's an attack at the ski lodge. I still don't know what's going on."

"You didn't hear Clark on the radio?" I ask. I take several steps away, wanting to get to the lodge, to my family.

"Clark?" Phil gives me a quizzical look.

"Militia is on the alternate channel today," Evan says. "I didn't want their traffic interrupting our operation. I didn't— " He shakes his head. "It was a mistake."

"We're heading up to the lodge," Phil says. "We only stopped to help your team get across."

"I need you to get a couple of people you trust to the first row of trailers. They're holding Roscoe there. He's part of them. The team he was with needs to be interviewed."

The way Evan says interviewed doesn't sound right to me. "Evan," I say, "Tim and Noah aren't a part of this. We know them."

"Yeah, we do, but . . . " He shrugs. "Make the call, Phil. Then hotfoot it to the ski lodge."

As we take the final stretch to the lodge—a snow-packed hillside—the people coming down slows to a trickle. As we crest the hill, I look to our barely visible tree, the tree we told the children we'd use to meet up if there was ever an emergency at the ski lodge. My young children and grandchildren are there. So is Calley, holding Tate. My eyes scour the surrounding area, trying to find Mollie, Angela, Sarah, and the rest of our family.

"Jake?" Evan catches my attention. "Are you coming in with us or going to your family?"

"He's going to our family," Leo says. "Right, Jake?"

"Mollie— "

"I'll find her," Leo says.

I give a nod. "Find her for me, Leo. Sarah and Angela—I don't see them either."

"We'll find them," Evan says, clapping me on the shoulder. "Now go."

I resume my hustle, running toward my children. I hear a chorus of "Dad!" and "Grandpa!" being yelled out. Baby Tate emits a loud yell as Calley says, "Where've you been, Jake?"

"Where's your mom? Your sisters?" I look over my children and grandchildren. Tate, huddled in Calley's arms making fussing noises, is in his snowsuit and wrapped in a blanket. Marc is wearing Mollie's coat, and Malcolm is wrapped in a baby blanket. The rest all have on their jackets and are sitting on an emergency blanket. Tony has his leg stretched out in front of him.

"Mom was here. She went back inside."

"She's okay?"

Calley nods. "She went after Sarah and Angela. Deanne and Sheila are missing too. I don't know where they are."

"Okay. Evan and his team are clearing the building. As soon as they're done, I'll go inside and get them."

Chapter 49

Saturday, Day 222

Mollie

The metallic smell of blood causes my stomach to lurch as I step inside the ski lodge. Standing at the front door, I have my sidearm by my leg. There's crying and frantic voices. With my heart pounding in my ears, it's hard for me to make out what's being said.

I take two cautious steps, stopping where I can view the room. Our dining table is just a few feet away, the boys' jackets still draped over their chairs. I should grab them and hustle them back out to the boys before continuing. I look toward the wedding table, the last place I saw my daughters. Kelley's kneeling on the floor, working on someone. My heart drops. It's Sarah.

I weave past the tables and overturned chairs, re-holstering my pistol as I quickly make my way to her side. "Sarah?" I say tentatively.

"Mollie!" Kelley says. "Quick! Put on gloves. I need you to put pressure on her thigh. It's a through and through, so one hand on each side."

"Mom?" Sarah says weakly. "Are my children okay?"

"They're fine. They're all at the tree," I say, struggling to get the gloves on. "I have a bandage in my pack."

"I've got one, just not enough hands."

"Angela?" I ask, as I snap the second glove in place and move my hands into position.

"She was hit too," Sarah says. "Kelley checked her first."

My heart seems to stop as I raise my eyes to meet Kelley's. She gives me a small smile. "Just a flesh wound. She's leaning against the far wall." I nod as my tears well up.

"Okay, Sarah, we'll get the bleeding stopped and then patch you up as quick as we can. This is not an arterial bleed, so . . . " Kelley lets out a long breath.

I give Sarah a smile. "Kelley, have you seen anyone else from my family? Deanne and Sheila didn't come out—at least, I didn't see them where we were supposed to meet. They were sitting at your table, right?"

"Um, let's talk later," Kelley says.

"Mom," Sarah says quietly. "Deanne was shot when Dawson took over, right as he grabbed Malcolm. He . . . he just shot her."

"What? No." I close my eyes as I think back to the scene. I didn't see Deanne on the ground, but I did see a pair of boots—her boots, the well-worn men's lace-up ones she's been wearing all winter.

As Kelley tightens the bandage around Sarah's leg, she lets out a moan. "I'm sorry, Mollie," Kelley says. "There wasn't anything we could do for her. Sheila is still with her. I don't— " She clears her throat. "I don't think he meant to shoot Deanne. I think he was aiming for Doris, but . . . " She shakes her head.

Deanne has been a vital part of this community and has become a dear friend. I didn't know her well before the attacks, but we've become remarkably close. How will Sheila, who suffered an almost debilitating depression in the early days of the attacks, handle the death of her mother? And her husband, Roy, and their son, Mike—they are all extremely close.

"Is Doris okay?" I ask, holding my breath while I await the answer.

"She may have reinjured her leg, but she's fine otherwise," Kelley says. "There are several injured, and she's not severe, so it may be a while before we treat her."

"Who?" I ask.

"Annette," Sarah says. "She had that wicked-looking knife she carries in her boot. Jesse Richardson—can you believe he was with them?"

"No," I say. "You know, maybe. Some of the stuff kind of makes sense, considering he was a part of it. What about Annette?"

"She used the knife on Moira, then she got shot. I think it was Jesse who shot her, but I don't really know. Everything was so crazy."

"She's a priority," Kelley says. "Belinda's getting ready to move her. She and Madison will be doing any surgery. We'll be taking Sarah to the clinic—or more likely your lodge, since we'll have too many in the clinic and its overflow space. I don't think Sarah will need surgery. As soon as we finish stabilizing everyone, we'll move her. Do you want to go see Angela? You can all sit together." Kelley peels off her gloves and grabs a wet wipe. I remove my gloves, putting them in the plastic zipper bag Kelley offers, then roughly wipe my hands. "I'll be right back with her," Kelley says.

Leaning in, I plant a kiss on Sarah's forehead. "I'm so glad you aren't hurt worse."

"It was bad, Mom. When he—when Dawson and *my dad*— " She says his name in disgust. "I killed him, you know."

"What? Who?"

"Brad. He's the one who shot Angela. I was too slow. I tried to stop him before he pulled the trigger."

"Hey," Angela says, as Kelley helps her sit. I go to hug her but stop for fear of hurting her. "Yeah," she says. "Probably better you don't touch me. At least I can sit this time." She gives a small smile while motioning to her shirt sleeve cut off at the elbow and her bandaged forearm. "You're okay?" she asks Sarah.

"Kelley says I should be fine. It went through. Mom says all the kids are okay. They're outside."

"Have you seen Tim?" Angela asks me.

"No, sorry."

"Did you hear?" she asks quietly. "About Deanne?"

I bite my lip, trying to keep the tears from falling as I give a single nod. "I'm so glad you two are okay. That you were able to— " I give a shake of my head as tears overwhelm me.

"It wasn't just us, Mom," Angela says. "Doris, Kelley, and Belinda, they knew what you were doing when you created the diversion and then used the code words."

"Belinda?" I ask. "I knew Doris and Kelley were aware of our training, but not Belinda."

"That's my fault, Mom," Sarah says quietly. "At one of my baby appointments, we were talking about Barney and Daniel. I didn't even think. I just blurted out how we had a plan so the kids would know what to do. I think that's why she interjected herself in the conversation, to help with the diversion. And Belinda must have told TJ, because when you said 'please don't hurt my family' I saw him move. And then when you yelled out fire, he tackled Shannon."

My jaw drops open. "Is he okay?"

"Kelley said he hit his head, has a goose egg. Shannon had Cheyre. She dove to the ground when the confusion started—she's a smart girl. She wasn't injured."

"And Shannon?"

Sarah shrugs. "I don't know. All our children were amazing. I'm just so proud of them." She takes a deep breath and closes her eyes.

A new noise catches my attention. My hand moves to my sidearm. I look up, fearing the worst. I let out a sigh of relief when Evan and Lindsey appear from the kitchen area.

"There's Leo," Angela says, pointing toward the entrance near the gazebo. "And more of the team is coming in the other door."

"I guess the cavalry is here," Sarah says, eyes still closed. "Better late than never."

I look for Jake. Where is he?

Chapter 50

Saturday, Day 222

Jake

"Dad," Malcolm says, voice wobbly from tears, "Marc, Tony, and I . . . we had to use our knives. Maybe you can get them back for us?"

I must give him a strange look, because Marc jumps in with, "Those guys grabbed them." He points to Malcolm and Tony. "When Grandmo yelled, they dropped and then stuck them with their knives."

I shake my head.

"I don't really know what happened either," Calley says. "I'm only getting bits and pieces. But I think Tony has a broken ankle from it."

"Tony?" I drop to my knee and gingerly reach for the foot stretched out in front of him. His black boot is unlaced, and his ankle is swollen and discolored.

"It's pretty sore," he says, "but the cold seems to be helping it."

I get into my pack and fish out two anti-inflammatory pills—the last of my supply for my shoulder injury. I hand Tony the pills and my water bottle, then grab a plastic zipper bag and fill it with snow.

While I'm making an icepack, Malcolm says, "We were in line to eat. The next thing I knew, there was an arm around my neck and a gun went off right by my ear. I still can't hear too good—I mean, too *well*."

"Same," Tony says.

"There were guns going off everywhere," Marc adds. "But no one grabbed me. As soon as the shooting started, I went to the ground and pulled out my pocketknife. Will you get it back for me?"

"Did you drop it?" I ask.

"No!" Tony says. "When Mom yelled fire, Marc stuck his knife in the leg of the detective."

"Jesse Richardson?" Calley asks, eyes wide.

"Yeah, that one. Marc was awesome."

Marc shrugs and says, "Tony put his knife in the guy holding him, and Malcolm— "

"He was being held by Jon Dawson," Tony says. "He got him good. Right in the arm. I don't know what happened after that, but with the shooting— "

"Yeah," Malcolm says. "There was a lot of shooting."

I shake my head. "The little kids?" I ask, gesturing toward the others.

"We were at the table," Lily says. "I held baby Tate while Mommy talked to the bad man."

Mommy? That's new. I suddenly realize, when I was hustling over here, Tony's voice was one calling out *Dad*.

"It sounds like you all did exactly what you were supposed to do," Calley says.

"You weren't in there, right?" I ask, turning toward her. "You had radio duty?"

"Right. But Bill had Aaron and Laurie in with me, along with the runner. He said there was too much going on—the militia and security team went on separate channels. When I heard someone say they were under attack, I tried to leave—to go help—but Aaron wouldn't let me. Once everyone was rushing out, then I left. Look!" She points to the lodge.

I follow her finger. One of our snowmobiles with the trailer attached is pulling up to the kitchen door. A moment later, two people carrying a stretcher exit, followed by Belinda. White material blows in the breeze. My heart drops as I realize the person on the stretcher is Annette—the bride. They carefully position the stretcher across the trailer. Belinda jumps in, holding it in place. With the injured leaving, I can only assume Evan's team has finished their business.

"Yeah," I say. "I'll find them and get someone out here to help Tony with his ankle. You kids wait here. I'll be right back."

"With my mom?" Sissy asks.

"I want my mommy too," Gavin says, then starts to cry. Andy joins him in his tears.

I look to Calley. "Go," she says. "They'll be okay."

With a nod, I head toward the ski lodge. As soon as I walk in, the smell is almost overpowering. Blood and other bodily fluids, along with food odors—not a good combination. I blink several times after entering the space lit only by windows. As my eyes travel the room, I see Leo. I make a beeline toward him. I can't help but smile; he's standing over Mollie and Angela. My smile quickly fades as I see Sarah laying on the ground, a fair amount of blood around her.

"Mollie?" I say tentatively as I step close by.

"Jake!" Mollie jumps to her feet. She loses her balance, but I reach out and grab her, pulling her close to me. Looking over her shoulder, my eyes meet Sarah's. She lifts a hand, giving me a thumbs up.

As I release Mollie, Angela asks, "Have you seen the children?"

"Just left them. They're okay. Tony needs a doc. Leo, can you go check him? I think his ankle's broken."

"Broken?" Mollie says with a gasp. "I didn't—I should've checked it better."

"He'll be fine," I say.

"Give me a minute and I'll go," Leo says. "It looks like they're starting to transport the injured to the clinic. Might get a little crowded there."

"How many?" I ask, looking to Sarah with an Israeli bandage on her leg and Angela with a self-adherent cohesive bandage wrapped around her arm—what we call vet wrap. Put gauze under it and wrap, and the whole thing sticks to itself.

"Preliminary reports indicate— " Kelley hollers for Leo, interrupting what he's saying. "I'll check on Tony shortly. If you get there before I do, take him to the lodge. I'll treat him there."

"There are several dead," Mollie says, looking at the ground. "Deanne, she's . . . she's dead."

"Deanne? How?"

Mollie shakes her head.

Leo walks back over with TJ next to him. "Mind if TJ stays with you? His mom's pretty busy. And with him being a hero and all, he needs someone to be with."

"TJ, you were amazing," Angela says. "I heard you hit your head."

"Yeah, it hurts. Leo says I need to go to your lodge. That's where they'll be taking care of people who are only a little hurt."

"That's right," Leo says. "I'll go check on Tony and we'll get everyone situated. Might be a long night—a long couple of days, even."

Chapter 51

Wednesday, Day 226

Mollie

The number of dead from the attempted coup on Saturday is now thirteen, with one more expected to succumb to injuries. Seven of the dead are part of Jon Dawson's crew—including Jon himself. The guy Kimba secured to the tree didn't survive. Belinda thinks it was less a situation of his injuries being too severe as he had an underlying health issue.

The only one directly involved in the takeover at the ski lodge who was not killed was Shannon. She, Roscoe, and Heath are now locked up in a makeshift jail.

Judge Avery, Deanne, Tricia, and Nina Rose—the lady Tricia was talking with—were all killed at the beginning of the takeover. Judge Avery was targeted, but Deanne, Tricia, and Nina are assumed to be poor aiming or collateral damage. As little consolation as it is, we know they didn't suffer. Two other community members died within a day of the shooting.

Sally-Ann Hinkle, who's been an integral part of the Bakerville community for many years, is still suffering from her wounds. Our docs have done all they can for her with our meager supplies. Now they're simply keeping her comfortable as best they can with their limited ability. Annette is also still at the clinic. Belinda believes she'll recover, but it'll be a long time before she's healthy and well.

Sarah, Angela, and Tony are recovering well. Angela stayed at our lodge, which is being used as an overflow hospital for the minorly injured, for the first two days after the shooting. Kelley wanted to make sure she was nearby in case it was worse than what they thought. She's now at home with Tim doting on her. Tony is currently in an air cast. In a few days, he'll move to a walking boot. The final injured community member staying in our lodge left earlier today, so it's once again just our family.

While Sarah's leg is healing, her mental and emotional health are suffering. We're sitting together in the den, her leg propped up on an ottoman, as we watch the fire and I burp Tate after his feeding. She's sleeping down here since the stairs are too hard to navigate.

"Is it always going to be like this?" Sarah asks.

"Like?"

"Always a threat, always people being killed. Losing Lois was sad, but at least she went peacefully in her sleep. Deanne was *murdered.* And . . . " She lets out a sigh as her voice fades away.

I continue patting Tate's back, the cadence adding a rhythmic comfort to the silence.

After more than a minute, Sarah continues. "I know I did what I had to do, but I killed my own father. It's like something out of Shakespeare." She pauses, then quickly says, "He really gave me no choice. When you screamed, he loosened his grip enough that the little girl was able to squirm away. He reached for her, and Angela shoved him. He turned on her, and even though she had her gun out, she didn't fire. I know now it's because the little girl was still in the way. But then . . . " She shrugs.

"Everything was slow motion as he raised the gun," Sarah continues. "I . . . I don't even really remember squeezing the trigger. I had my gun behind my back, and the next thing I knew" —she shakes her head— "he was on the ground. Angela was also on the ground, bleeding. I bent to reach for her. That's when Brad shot me. My own dad shot me. I should've made sure he was . . . you know . . . dead."

She's quiet again. I'm trying to form a good response when she says, "Double tap. It's not just for zombies. I should've learned from the movies. Then I wouldn't be laid up worrying about infection."

"Your wound looks good. Kelley and Belinda are both incredibly pleased with it."

"I know, but *infection,* Mom. I never would've thought something so minor could now be so scary. The lack of pain pills isn't great either, but the fear of infection . . . " She lets out a long breath.

Tate, who's now asleep, wiggles slightly. I adjust him so he's cradled in the crook of my arm.

"I feel terrible for Alina and Victor," Sarah says. "I know she's glad Brad forbade them from attending the wedding. She wouldn't have wanted Victor to see his dad doing what he did."

I give a nod. Even though Brad was—as far as I'm concerned—a terrible person, his love for Victor has always been obvious.

"I'm glad they want to move in here with us," Sarah says. "It'll be better for them. And I'm glad they aren't mad at me. I know Alina wishes she would've known what he was up to—what they were all up to—so she could've stopped him."

"Looking back, I can't believe we were all so naïve," I say. "We knew they were planning something. We should've stopped it."

"Did you know who was planning it?"

"Well, not exactly. But we figured Jon Dawson was involved. We should've just locked him up."

"Lock him up before he did anything? Wouldn't that go against the Fourth Amendment?"

"Who cares?" I ask, feeling the anger rush through my body. "If we would've taken him out of the picture, Deanne would still be alive."

Sarah slowly nods. "*If* Dawson was the ringleader. Just because he was the one shouting out orders and making speeches— " She shrugs. "He might not have been the brains behind the operation."

"I don't care. We should've done it anyway."

Reaching out, she touches my arm. "You remember when I spoke at the gun meeting? The first one where I said, in the past, I didn't have much use for the Second Amendment?"

"Of course. You were amazing. You really put Dawson in his place."

"It wasn't just the Second Amendment I had little use for. The entire Constitution and Bill of Rights, I thought they were outdated and no longer functional. I thought we needed to rewrite the entire thing to work for today."

"Mm-hmm." I nod. I remember a long email conversation Sarah and I had while she was in college about this.

"But after we moved up here, and I actually read the Constitution, I changed my mind."

"You formed your previous opinion without reading it?"

"Well, I formed it based on what my college professor told me and several articles I'd read. My professor hated the Founding Fathers, said they were flawed racist slave owners and we had no business listening to them in today's world." She shrugs. "Anyway, now I think differently. And I think, if we're going to be strongly in favor of the Second Amendment, we also need to support the entire Constitution and Bill of Rights. Even when we don't like it. And I really wish we could have the support of the Third Amendment. Because I think our lack of privacy here is a direct violation of it." She gives me a cheeky smile.

I hate to admit it, but I'm having a hard time even recalling the Third Amendment. Instead of asking about it, I say, "I know you're right. But I still can't help but think we could've prevented this."

"Do you believe Dawson's family? That they didn't know either?"

"His wife seemed pretty convinced he was having some sort of a breakdown. Both Heath and Roscoe say she wasn't involved. Just like they made it clear Alina wasn't involved either. Shannon, as you know, isn't saying anything."

"Yeah, I think the fact TJ tackled her, knocking her out, is still a source of embarrassment."

I give her a slight smile. "She probably doesn't realize he saved her life." Sadly—according to Heath, who is happy to share everything he knows—she's convinced they were in the right and the deaths of Judge Avery, Deanne, and the rest were justified while her husband's and sister's deaths were murder.

"I don't like that anyone died," Sarah says quietly. "I'll never understand why Brad joined them. Or why they tried to take over in the first place. What were they hoping to accomplish? It's not like we could do things much differently. And the whole gun ban, it was just so we'd be sitting ducks, right?"

I give a combination nod and shrug. According to Roscoe and Heath, that was the plan. I guess they didn't realize we're a group of rebels. In addition to Sarah, Angela, and me being armed, there were many others, including Doris, Belinda, and Kelley.

Dax and Bryce Cameron each had a handgun in their guitar cases. Their dad, grandpa, and uncle had little revolvers in their boots. Like me, they were too far away, with too many innocents between us and the bad guys to use their weapons.

Doris killed Dawson after Malcolm stabbed him. Similarly, Tony stabbed Miles and then Belinda shot him. Jesse Richardson had Marc's pocketknife in his ankle. The gunshot wound that killed him was self-inflicted. The assumption is he chose his own death over the consequences of being part of the failed *coup d'état.*

His betrayal of the community has created a new concern. Jackson's wife, Tamra, is now questioning whether her husband was responsible for the deaths of Phoebe and Amy. Could Jesse have planted the jewelry? And if so, why? According to Roscoe, Jackson was not a part of their group. He said Deputy Fred, when he was still in Bakerville, was one of the main instigators and wanted Jackson included, but Jesse Richardson put the kibosh to that, saying Jackson gave him the creeps and he couldn't be trusted.

Though Tamra has her doubts, the consensus with the community is Jackson was a serial killer. We'd all love to have more information as to how and why. Phoebe's family and Amy's sister would especially like to know how he lured their loved ones to their death. It's a mystery we're likely to never solve.

There was an argument over the memorial service. Some people thought we should hold one service for everyone—even those responsible for the attempted takeover. There are many people who are under the same impression as Jon's wife: he and the others had a mental breakdown that drove them to do awful things.

In the end, there were two services. One for Deanne, Judge Avery, and the others that were murdered, and a second for those who attempted the coup. I only attended the one for Deanne. My previous relationship with Brad resulted in Sarah's birth, but I didn't want anything to do with him when he was alive, so attending his memorial made no sense.

"I don't think I'll miss him much," Sarah says. "When Brad first showed up, I was so confused. Then happy. He was nice to me and acted like he was sorry for missing out on my life, for the way he treated you.

"But things have been different since Tate was born. I know he was holding out hope there could be some way to use the cord blood to help Victor. After that ended up not being an option, he withdrew from me. Oh, you know, he'd still come over. And I'm sure him telling me not to go to the wedding was an attempt to keep Tate and me safe. But I don't think he really cared for me—or about me. He wasn't a dad to me like Jamie was or like Jake has been. They both genuinely cared for me. Jamie treated me like his real daughter. Jake does too. I guess it's true: biology isn't what defines family."

She lays her head on my shoulder. We sit quietly for many minutes as we watch the fire dance in the woodstove. "When are they going after the geese?" Sarah asks.

"A couple of weeks still. The hunting doesn't usually get good until mid-February. Plus, Evan wants to make sure everything is stabilized and Doris is getting around okay before he leaves." Doris went down hard on her leg, injuring the fragile bones that were in the process of healing. While Belinda doesn't believe she rebroke it, she's being cautious and has Doris only using the wheelchair again.

"I'm surprised he's even willing to go, after what happened last time he was gone."

"Me too. I half think he'll change his mind."

"But Jake will still go?"

"I'm pretty sure he will. The geese were popular last time and gave us a little variety. Harvesting more is a good idea."

"So . . . you never answered me. Do you think it'll always be like this?"

I bite my lip as I think of my response. "I think we need to trust in God but not be foolish. We need to put on the whole armor of God."

She gives me a long look. "Isn't that scripture talking about our spiritual attack?"

"Yes, but when we have the full armor of God, the Holy Spirit guides us and supports us in our actions, helping us to make good decisions. There has always been evil in the world, at least since the fall of Adam and Eve. We each have free will. Some people will exercise their free will for evil. Some may think Dawson was mentally ill, some may think he was evil." As I say these words, I realize locking Dawson up before he did anything would not only have been a violation of the Fourth Amendment, but of his God-given rights, the rights our Constitution and Bill of Rights are supposed to protect as opposed to give.

"And Brad? Was he mentally ill, or was he evil?" she asks.

I shake my head. "I don't have the answer for that. All I know is they're not alone. There will be others who are evil, mentally ill, or even good people who make bad choices."

"I wish we could find someplace safe. Someplace I can raise my children without worry."

"So do I, Sarah. So do I."

Chapter 52

Friday, Day 242

Jake

"I'll be home in a couple of days," I say, as I hug Mollie goodbye. "Make sure you rest like you're supposed to."

She gives me a nod. "I'm doing fine, you know."

"That's what you keep telling me, but I know you." I plop a kiss on her nose. "You're ornery."

"Is that why you're leaving me on Valentine's Day?"

"Ha. Have we ever once celebrated this day? As far as I'm concerned, every day with you is made for romance."

"Aren't you a sweet-talker," she says, as her cheeks color crimson. "I'm glad Evan's going with you."

"I'm pretty sure Doris is forcing him, says the hunt will do him good."

"It'll do you good too," Mollie says, lifting to meet my lips.

"Yeah, if I don't fall off the horse on the way down the mountain."

"That's true. I can't believe Dusty talked you into riding. At least they gave you and Evan a few lessons."

"Yeah, we'll see how it goes. I might not walk right for a week after this. And after the last couple of days of snow, it could get interesting."

"Do you think you'll slide down the hill?" I tease.

"There's a good chance of it. I'm hoping they got a little snow down there too. Might make the hunting better. I've got to go. The sky's starting to lighten. We should be able to see well enough to ride shortly. See you on— " I try to remember what today is. Mollie made a point of saying I was leaving on Valentine's Day, but the day of the week escapes me.

"Monday," she says. "You'll be home on Monday."

I kiss her again, then head to the corral. Like Mollie, I can't believe Dusty talked me into riding either. Bottom line, we're conserving fuel. While it didn't use a ton of fuel last time Evan and I went, we need to be diligent. And when there are other options, we need to use those options, no matter how unappealing it sounds. I'm the last to arrive at the corrals. They already have my horse in. Even though I've saddled him before, Dax talks me through the process of brushing him and getting him ready to go.

There's six of us this time: Evan, Dax, Dusty, my neighbor Pete, Noah Hammer, and me. We take two extra horses, outfitted with pack saddles and panniers, to haul feed down and then to haul the geese home.

While I'm not overly excited about being perched on top of a horse, I do have to admire the sunrise as we make our way off the mountain. My horse, a seventeen-year-old gelding named Domino, takes it nice and slow. He is so slow and calm, he sometimes forgets we're on a mission.

We only stop once to rest and water the horses. My body is screaming when I get off at the break—so much so, getting back on is near torture. The several inches of snow we got on the mountain made it down to Bakerville too. I'm excited thinking about how good the hunting may be. It's crisp and cool, probably around twenty-five degrees. While goose hunting is usually excellent when a storm is coming in, afterwards can still be good. I'm hoping we're in a break between storms and the geese will be moving a lot.

When we're within eyesight of the river people's western guard tower, Dax flaps a bandana to let them know it's us. We continue moving slowly forward, watching for a response.

We're about eight hundred yards away when Evan says, "Everyone stop. Something's not right. They should've responded."

"What do you want to do?" Dusty asks.

"Let me check it out," Evan says, putting his binoculars to his eyes. I grab mine and look also, as the others follow suit.

"Something's definitely not right," Dax says. "There's no one in the guard tower."

"I don't see anyone anywhere," Noah says. "I know we're still a ways out, but shouldn't we see people at the houses? And where's their livestock? They were easily visible last time we were here."

"Let's keep going," Evan says. "Stay alert."

The guard tower is nothing more than a tree stand used for deer hunting, set about five hundred yards from where the group of houses being used by the river people begins. There's a similar tower on the north and south of the community and a hill on the other side of the river used to keep watch over anyone approaching from the east. When we reach the tower, it's empty.

"What's that?" Dusty asks, pointing to a snow-covered lump.

"He fell out of his tree stand?" Noah asks. "Why didn't they come and retrieve his body?"

"Off the horses," Evan hisses, as he clumsily slides down. Holding the reins, he makes himself small.

Once I'm on the ground, the body of a man is obvious.

"Keep watch," Evan says, as he duckwalks to the body and then removes some of the snow on it. "He didn't fall. He was murdered. Probably a couple of days ago."

Dusty looks over and says, "That's Roy McCracken. He arrived with us from Prospect. He was a good man."

"Sorry for the loss of your friend," Pete says.

I give a solemn nod, never sure what to say in these circumstances.

"Shot?" Dax asks.

"Nope," Dusty says. "There's an arrow in him."

I jerk my head in the direction of the body. "An arrow? How'd they get close enough? Did they come down the tree line?"

Evan uses his binoculars to glass the area. Satisfied there isn't an immediate threat, he says, "Noah, I want you up in the tree. They set this up so you should be able to see in most directions. You have your whistle?"

"Yes, sir."

"Okay. Three long, loud blows if you see anything suspicious. Dusty, where can we put the horses? We need to walk the rest of the way."

Dusty looks around a bit and says, "These trees are the best choice. Let's line them up along the creek, back the way we came."

"You and Dax make that happen. Jake, Pete, Noah, stand guard."

A few minutes later, Noah's in the tree. Unlike the previous occupant, he uses the rope to tie himself in place. The rope wouldn't have stopped the arrow but may have kept him in the tree stand where the incident would've been immediately obvious.

The rest of us follow Evan as we cautiously make our way to the first house. All of us are part of the militia, but I can't help but think Evan's wishing for his well-trained security team to be here instead of us. While each of us has done what was needed since the attacks started, we don't have the same level of training and expertise as the security team. And since we've moved up the mountain, most of our militia duty involves only sitting and watching.

There are three snow-covered bodies in the first house; one is obviously a child, an adult arm covering it in a protective pose. I choke back my emotions. A dead body at the lookout. Dead bodies in the yard. Missing livestock. There are more remains in the house and the barn, all still in their beds, some having been knifed and some shot. The next house along the river shows the same results.

Dusty finds more of the McCracken family in a camp trailer parked in the barn at the second house. Evan says he thinks it had been an elaborate assault with many assailants attacking at the same time. The up close and personal nature of the killings leads him to believe it happened during the night, with the attackers sneaking in the homes and other sleeping quarters and taking people out silently until they could no longer do so. He suspects they timed it so they could all strike at once.

By the time we reach Gabe Griffin's place, I have little hope of finding anyone alive. We find Gabe's body in the front yard, his wife by his side. Several other family members are in the house. After we clear the house, Dax says, "Where's their children?"

Evan shakes his head. "Maybe they were at one of the neighbors?"

"I haven't seen them. I— " He takes a breath. "I think I'd recognize them. They kept asking to pet my horse last time we were here. The boy, Chandler, asked if he could ride him when we move back down in the spring."

"Maybe the garage," Evan says.

The garage is really more of a metal barn, with a high-roofed center and a loft above. It's lower on each side with a double garage door in the center and a single door on either side, plus identical doors on the back to allow the vehicles to drive through. Evan opens the man-door and quickly enters. Just like the homes and buildings we've already gone in, there's a creepiness to this space. With the cold and the snow, the odor of death has been minimal. Even so, it's here also.

The cars, which stopped running with the EMP, have all been pushed out of the garage. There are a couple of older snowmobiles and three quads inside, along with several bicycles. There are also three tents set up, allowing another family or two to stay here, in the assumed safety of the group. The woodstove in the corner near the tents is cold. The remains of a man and a woman are still inside one of the tents. We're just about to leave when a slight scratching noise catches my attention.

"Shh," I say, putting my finger to my lips. In the quiet, the sound comes again.

"Mouse?" Dax mouths.

"A mouse making that much noise?" Pete says in a low voice. "It'd have to be a mutant."

The rest of us shrug. I point to the loft space above us, then look around for the stairs. In the far corner is a circular metal staircase.

Evan pulls us close. Barely audible, he says, "I'll go up first. Dax, you're behind me. Dusty, behind Dax. Jake and Pete, you stay down here. Be ready for anything."

With my heart pounding, I set up at the bottom of the stairs with Pete on the other side. Evan is at the top of the stairs when a voice yells out, "Don't come any closer! I have a gun!"

Pete and I share a look. A child?

"No problem," Evan says evenly. "We're just here to make sure you're okay."

"Chandler? You're Chandler, right?" Dax asks. "I'm Dax. My horse is Fritz. Do you remember meeting us?"

"I . . . you're the Bakerville people who moved to the ski resort?" he asks unsteadily.

After a pause, Dax says, "Yep, we are."

"Did you . . . did you see my dad? My mom? They're— " His voice fades away.

Pete shakes his head and mouths, "Poor kid."

"We can take you home with us," Dax says. "You can ride Fritz with me."

"I don't . . . I can't leave."

"Why's that?"

"I have to take care of the others."

"The others?" Evan asks. "Other children?"

"I'm the oldest. I'm in charge."

"Well, that's no problem," Dax says. "They can come too."

"Really?"

"Yep. Where are they?"

There's several seconds of silence before he quietly says, "Hiding in the cupboards."

"Do you want to ask them to come out?" Evan asks.

"Are you sure? Will it be okay for us to go with you? All of us?"

"Of course."

A few minutes later, Evan calls Pete and me upstairs where we meet Chandler, another boy, and three girls. Chandler's gun turns out to be a Red Ryder BB gun. We piece together the information they give us. They were having a sleepover, and their parents let them use the loft.

"There's no heat up here," Chandler says. "But the stovepipe still warms it up. We had our sleeping bags laid out around it." He motions to the stovepipe snaking its way from the downstairs through the loft floor and out the roof. "I woke up when I heard shouting and then shooting. I made the others be quiet when I woke them up, and then I put each one in a cupboard." He motions to the storage cabinets lining the edge of the loft. "Since I had my gun, I stayed on watch. When it was finally daylight, I peeked out the window and saw them taking our cattle. I had to hide when I saw some guys walking to the barn. When I looked again, I thought one of the ladies saw me, but she turned away really quick and then started walking away, so she must not have."

"We had to stay in the cabinets for too long," one of the girls says.

"I could barely walk when Chandler finally said we could get out," the younger boy says.

"When was this?" Evan asks.

The little boy shrugs, and Chandler says, "We've been sleeping here three nights. I mean, three *after* it happened. I think they were the people from Prospect."

"Why do you think that?" Dax asks.

"When they came in the barn, I thought I heard them say it'd take a couple of days to get back to Prospect while driving the cattle. They took all our cows, horses, even our chickens and goats. They took most of our food too."

"We're orphans now, Lottie and me," the youngest boy says, pointing to the tallest of the girls. "Our mom and dad are still in the tent. Chandler told us. They're orphans too. We have to make do on our own."

"Jake? Can I talk to you a minute?" Evan asks, motioning me to the edge near the built-in cupboards the children hid in. I'm surprised they were able to stay quiet and the murderers didn't check for them.

Once we're out of earshot, he says, "We need to finish clearing the houses and check all of the lookouts."

I nod my agreement.

"I'll have Dax stay with the children. They seem to like him. After we're done, let's take everyone to your house, get a fire going and get them cleaned up. I'm fairly sure they haven't been bathrooming properly."

"Yeah, I didn't want to say anything, but yeah."

"After we get the kids back to your house, we need to come back and take care of our people. We can't bury them, of course, but we can put them all together in one of the sheds. And tomorrow morning, we hightail it home. We need to prepare—be ready for them to come after us."

"You think we can wait until morning?" I ask. "They might be headed to our place now."

"I don't think so. We didn't see anything concerning on our way down, which is the way they'd go up the mountain. Plus, they'll want to get their booty home before raiding again, maybe even celebrate their haul first. We've got time, but I still don't want to waste it."

"Understood," I say.

Dax reluctantly agrees to stay with the children while we clear the rest of the buildings. As we move through each one, we look carefully to make sure there aren't any additional survivors in hiding. Chandler said he was sure no one else was around; he hadn't seen anyone outside the few times he went to the house where they have some hidden food and more clothes and blankets.

After we're done with the rest of the homes, buildings, and north guard tower, Evan uses his binoculars to glass the hill on the east side of the river. He locates the lookout and zeros in on it. Several feet away, he finds the body of the guard. We'll check the south lookout on the way back to Noah's perch.

Back at the garage, Dax has managed to get the children dressed and mostly ready to go. Chandler, at nine, is the oldest. Lottie is eight.

The other boy, age four, is the youngest. And the two girls—Chandler's sisters—are between Lottie and the boy in age.

"How about Dad and I go get the horses?" Dax suggests. "That way, they won't have to walk so far."

"I'll help," Pete says. "Do we leave Noah on watch?"

"That's probably best. Bring all the horses except his," Evan says. "We'll signal for him when we're ready to leave. Tell him to keep an eye out. And why don't you guys check those houses and buildings again, just to make sure we didn't overlook anyone. And also check the south tree stand. I suspect there won't be any surprises, but we need to know. I'll keep watch from this window." He points to the same window Chandler said he saw the men from. "Jake will keep watch from the window on the other end. We'll be ready when you guys return."

"Good idea," Dusty says.

A short while later, we're back on the horses. The youngest boy and girl are riding with Dusty, and Dax has Chandler. Plus, they're handling the pack horses. Pete has Lottie, and Noah has the other girl. Since Evan and I are complete novices, it's decided we can only handle ourselves on the horses. I agree with the choice.

As we climb the hill leading to my house, Noah says, "Is that an elk track?" He points to a track in the snow, barely visible due to other snow blowing over it.

"Not unless an elk is wearing horseshoes," Dusty says.

"Everyone off," Evan commands. He hands his reins to Dax. "Jake, you're with me. We're going to make ourselves small while we check out the top of the hill."

"What's going on?" Chandler asks in a loud voice as Evan walks stooped over.

I pass my reins off to Noah and quickly follow.

"Shh. Let him check things out," Dax quietly reprimands.

Evan and I are now on our bellies as we crawl the final feet.

With his binoculars in place, he says, "Better have a look, Jake. There's someone in your house."

Chapter 53

Friday, Day 242

Mollie

As Jake requested, I've been taking it easy today. I even went back to bed after we got the children off to school. We stopped lessons until this week, giving time to get past what happened inside the ski lodge. We didn't even eat in there for several days afterward, choosing instead to make the meals at the firepit and let everyone take home what they wanted. Our lodge kitchen was also used while it was doubling as a hospital. Those were crazy days—days I don't ever want to repeat. I'm reminded of my conversation with Sarah a few days ago. Will we always have troubles? I hate to think so.

Sarah, Angela, Katie, and I are sitting in the great room working on the mending. Sarah's walking well enough that she and Tate are no longer sleeping in the den, so we've closed the room off again. Calley has a radio shift today.

One big change since the judge was assassinated is the news is now posted daily. Radio listeners are no longer sworn to secrecy and the news filtered through the council. As soon as someone finishes their shift, they add the news to a whiteboard in the ski lodge. If something urgent comes across, the runner immediately adds it to the board. So far, there's been nothing urgent.

Funny thing is, while Dawson made it sound like the judge was the one keeping us from learning things, it was him who was the main culprit, insisting it'd be better not to worry people.

The council and bylaws are being dissolved. We've decided to go with a different form of government suggested by Jude Poppe, formerly of Prospect. Jude's girlfriend, Tricia, was one of the people killed. He suggested looking toward certain Indigenous Americans and how they structured their government, allowing everyone a say in the process.

I don't know exactly what this will look like for us in the end, but maybe the idea of more than just a few people providing input and making decisions will work better for our small community. A representative government makes sense for the United States, even for Wyoming. But maybe, if more people had a direct say in what was going on, neither us nor Prospect would've had a coup.

Or maybe it's like Sarah and I were discussing; there is evil in the world, and things will always happen.

"You've got your color back," Katie says to Sarah. "Are you sleeping better?"

"Some." Sarah shrugs. "I still have the dreams."

Katie and Angela each give a nod, knowing what Sarah means. Like Sarah, they've had their own brushes with death, and each had to take a life to save their own. I've been there too. It's not easy to get past, and I still wake up sometimes from a nightmare, reliving the incident.

"Where's Alina?" Angela asks.

"Working on cleaning out the rest of Brad's things," Sarah says. She hasn't called him dad since the day of the shooting, referring to him as Brad or sometimes just *him*. Alina and Victor have officially moved in with us. He's sharing the room with the boys, and Alina is sharing Karen's room.

It's been almost three weeks since Deanne and the others were killed. Deanne's husband and son seem to be doing okay. Her daughter, Sheila, isn't doing well at all. Kelley and Belinda have been so worried about her, they've essentially put her on a psychiatric hold, having her live at the clinic with twenty-four-hour supervision.

Madison and Laurie, who became exceptionally good friends with Sheila early in the attacks when all three were in the pit of despair, spend as much time with her as possible. Even though Calley is back to work, she too is still in deep mourning over Deanne's death.

"Who's going to live in the Tiny House?" Angela asks. "Has it been decided?"

"Not yet," I say. "There's going to be quite a bit of moving around. Roscoe and Moira's children are moving in with Zeb and Ellen. They've become close living right next door."

"I've heard they're turning the family room in the basement into bedrooms," Katie says.

I nod. "Someone will be moving into the guest house, too, but I'm not sure who."

"I think Shelby and Grant should get one of the places," Angela says. "With the baby, it makes sense. I can't imagine living in one of the dorm rooms with an infant.

"Definitely not," Sarah says. "Sometimes I feel bad when Tate cries in the middle of the night here, and this is my family. I can't imagine living with a bunch of strangers—even though we're not really strangers anymore."

"It's hard to believe this is your due date," Katie says. "Or what we thought would be your due date."

"At least it wasn't twins," Angela chimes in. As if on cue, Tate lets out a large sigh from his bassinet box. He'll be outgrowing the box before long. Doris has a playpen for Sarah to use as a crib. One regular crib was found in the houses we salvaged from; Madison's little girl Emma is using it now that they're settled in the cabin with Dot. I have a suspicion Jake is working on something for Tate. He's keeping his plans secret, even from me, but I'm sure he has something up his sleeve.

"Is Dodie going to sew with us?" Sarah asks.

"Didn't Karen tell you?" I ask. "They're both helping at the school today."

"No, I knew Karen was but not Grandma Dodie. I think it's wonderful how she helps so much."

"It's definitely different than how she liked to stay to herself before."

There's a knock at the front door. Another change has been us locking the lodge door except for during designated shower hours. Before, it was to be open from 0600 to 2100 for showering as desired and locked only at bedtime. Now, showering is scheduled from 0530 to 0700 and 0900 to 1000. If lunch prep is happening at our lodge, they also arrive by 1000, and we can lock the door once we're all inside. Showers happen again from 1900 to 2100. It's much nicer not having people in and out continually through the day. I'm not sure why we didn't do something like this in the first place.

Being able to have the door locked while we're inside brings a measure of comfort. We're all a little jumpy after what happened. Unfortunately, we've been unable to find a key to the lodge, so we couldn't lock up when we were gone. Doris solved that issue by producing a hasp and padlock.

Katie answers the door, saying, "Hey, we were just talking about you. Glad you're home."

"You talk about me?" Alina asks in her slightly broken English. "Or— "

"About you, and how happy we are you're living here."

She gives a solemn nod. "It is good to be part of the family. I come in and talk about what I find?"

"Of course," I say from my rocker. "Sit with us. We won't even make you sew."

After shrugging out of her coat and removing her boots, she perches on the edge of the sofa. My eyes land on the briefcase she's carrying, the same one Brad had the first day they showed up in Bakerville.

"Yes," she says, "I have Victor's medical records."

"Is everything okay?" Sarah asks, alarm lacing her voice.

"Medical records don't change. Victor he—as Dr. Sam say last time he look at him—fit as a fiddle. But inside case for papers, I find something. Here, I show you."

She opens it up, displaying the multicolored folders. Each holds different records for Victor. As she moves the folders to the coffee table, she says, "All this time, I think this is all there is. I never know about secret pocket." She slips her hand into one of the sections, and the separating sound of Velcro fills the room. "These are surprise I find." She pulls out newspaper clippings.

"What are they about?" I ask.

"Shooting at Groyver school."

"The shooting in Groyver, Wyoming?" Angela asks. "The one Sam and June were involved in?"

Alina gives a combination nod and shrug. "And he has photographs." She lays several pictures printed from a computer onto slick photo paper on the table.

"Dr. Sam?" Katie says. "And June? Why does he have their pictures?"

"I know not the answer," Alina says.

"Who are the others?" I ask.

She hands me two photos so I can look at them. I flip them over, but there isn't any writing or information on the back. I hand them to Sarah, who also examines them.

Alina is holding a photo and says, "This one I know. He is policeman who died while we were staying in Wyoming. He died days before planes crashed."

"What does this mean?" Sarah asks

I bite my lip. When Brad and I were together, I suspected him of being hired muscle for a guy. I knew he'd done some questionable things. But this, this is like something out of a movie.

"Is he a hitman?" Katie asks softly. "Was he? Do you think?"

"Hitman is person hired to murder?" Alina asks in her usual stoic manner.

I give a slight nod. Katie nods vigorously.

Sarah stares at the pictures and says, "It kind of makes sense, some of the things he told me about traveling for work. He said it was for computers, but he didn't really seem like a computer guy."

"He plays on laptop, but that is all," Alina says. "I don't know what else he does with computers. But true, we travel. All over country we travel. World even. When Victor was not sick, we go."

"So you think he was in Wyoming to . . . what?" Angela asks, shaking her head. "Kill Dr. Sam?"

"Look," Katie says. "This article mentions a gym teacher from Groyver who helped Dr. Sam stop the shooters. He was killed in a car wreck."

"Right," I say. "And the secretary from the school died a few days later. Suicide. Boy, were the conspiracy theories flying. And, of course, Sam and June said both deaths were murders."

"I think they're right," Alina says. "Here's the gym teacher's article. See his picture in it? Look. Isn't this the same guy?" She points to one of the photos we've all examined.

"Looks like him," Angela agrees. Sarah and I share a look.

Katie then pulls out an article about the school secretary and her death. The other photo is undoubtedly her. "Seems pretty clear," Katie says.

"Brad was happy when work brings him to Wyoming. He only find out about Sarah a few days before. He may have been doing this bad stuff, but finding Sarah was important to help our Victor."

"So, that's it then?" Sarah asks. "He was an assassin hired by someone to hunt down and kill Sam and June?"

"Why bother?" Katie asks. "Things had already fallen apart when he shot Sam. Did he think he was going to get paid for it?"

"Brad like to say he always finishes job," Alina says.

"He didn't kill June," Angela says. "It doesn't make any sense. Why wait so long to shoot Sam? You were in Bakerville for a couple of months before Sam was shot."

"We not know Sam," Alina says. "Kelley is our doctor for Victor."

"That's right," I say, remembering the day Brad and Sam met. Something crossed Brad's face, something was in his eyes. Maybe it was recognition. Sam was shot the next day. He didn't die until two months later, but the gunshot is what killed him.

I jump at an urgent knock at the front door. "Mom! Mom!"

"What's happening?" Sarah cries.

Katie rushes to the door, cautiously opening it. Calley falls in, wrapping Katie in a hug.

"It's over! It's over!" she says, jumping up and down, dragging Katie with her.

Katie, looking bewildered, pulls away.

I'm standing by my chair as she comes bouncing toward me. "Mom! Its over!"

"What's over?" I ask, smiling at her excitement.

"We're going to be okay. I heard it on the radio. The president—he's alive and he's sending help to people who need it. He's going to have the lights on soon. Maybe even before my baby is born. Maybe there will even be a real hospital. For both of us—you can get well!"

"Praise God," Sarah says, grabbing onto Alina.

Angela and Katie are hugging each other, crying. Even Alina's eyes aren't dry.

"Thank you, Jesus," I whisper, pulling Calley into an embrace.

Chapter 54

Friday, Day 242

Jake

"How do you know someone is at my house?" I ask, crawling toward Evan.

"Because they're standing in your house, peeking out the window. See? She's checking us out with her own binoculars."

I put my binoculars to my eyes. "I don't believe it."

"You know her?" Evan asks.

"Yep, so do you. Remember when Mollie's boss and his wife visited?"

"Your wife's boss from Oregon?"

"Yeah, you met them last time they were here."

"Well I'll be. I think you're right. That does look like the wife."

"I wonder where her husband and son are? And Bart—her father-in-law. She shouldn't be alone."

"How'd she get here from Oregon?" Noah asks.

"I have no idea," I say. "But I suspect it's an amazing story."

The Bakerville saga continues in My Refuge and Fortress: Havoc in Wyoming, Part 7.

Wondering how Mollie's boss got to Wyoming? Find out in Havoc Peaks: A Havoc in Wyoming Story.

Wondering what Christmas in the apocalypse looks like? Find out in Christmas on the Mountain: A Havoc in Wyoming Novella.

Thank you for spending your time with the people of
Bakerville, Wyoming.

If you have five minutes, you'd make this writer very happy if
you could write a short Amazon review.

I appreciate you!

Join my reader's club!

Receive a complimentary copy of *Wyoming Refuge: A Havoc
in Wyoming Prequel.* As part of my reader's club, you'll be the
first to know about new releases and specials. I also share info on
books I'm reading, preparedness tips, and more.

Please sign up on my website:

MillieCopper.com

Now Available

Havoc in Wyoming

Part 1: Caldwell's Homestead

Jake and Mollie Caldwell started their small farm and homestead to be able to provide for an uncertain future for their family, friends, and community. They have tried to plan for everything, but they never imagined this would happen.

Part 2: Katie's Journey

Katie loves living on her own while finishing up her college degree, working her part-time jobs, and building a relationship with her boyfriend, Leo. When disaster strikes, being away from family isn't quite so nice, and home is over a thousand miles away. Will she make it home before the United States falls apart?

Part 3: Mollie's Quest

Two or three times a year, Mollie Caldwell travels for business. Being away from her Wyoming farmstead is both a fun time and a challenge. They started their farm to be able to provide for an uncertain future for their family, friends, and community. The farm keeps the entire family busy, meaning extra work for her husband while she's away. This time, while on her business trip, terrorists attack. Her weeklong business trip becomes much longer as she tries to make her way home.

Part 4: Shields and Ramparts

The United States, and the community of Bakerville, face a new threat . . . a threat that could change America forever. As the neighbors band together, all worry about friends and family members. Have they found safety from this latest danger?

Part 5: Fowler's Snare

Welcome to Bakerville, the sleepy Wyoming community Mollie and Jake Caldwell have chosen as their family retreat. At the edge of the wilderness, far away from the big city, they were so sure nothing bad could ever happen in such a protected place. They were wrong. Now, with the entire nation in peril, coming together as a community is the only way they can survive. But not everyone in the community has the people of Bakerville's best interest at heart.

Part 6: Pestilence in the Darkness

Surrounded by danger, they band together with the community of Bakerville to move to a new defensible location. But they weren't prepared to have to give up so much for the security they so desperately need. And they quickly learn trust must be earned, not freely given.

Part 7: My Refuge and Fortress

When Jake and a group of hunters return to Bakerville and find their former neighbors slaughtered, they realize there is a new, even more deadly threat. Will their reinforced location be secure enough? And what about the radio announcement from the president? Will his promise of help arrive in time?

Find these titles on Amazon:
www.amazon.com/author/milliecopper

Acknowledgments

Thanks to:

Ameryn Tucker, my editor, beta reader, and daughter wrapped in one. I had a story I wanted to tell, and Ameryn encouraged me and helped me bring it to life.

My youngest daughter, Kes, graphic artist extraordinaire, who pulled out the vision in my head and brought it to life to create the original cover. And to Dauntless Cover Design for the amazing current version.

Sheri at Light Hand Proofreading for not only looking for those pesky typos but also sharing in the creative process.

My husband, who gave me the time and space I needed to complete this dream and was very patient as I'd tell him the same plot ideas over and over and over.

Two more daughters and a young son, who willingly listen to me drone on and on about story lines and ideas while encouraging me to "keep going."

My amazing Beta Readers! Thanks to Ginger, Barbara, Dianna, and Tammy for your help in creating the final story. Your insights and abilities to see the things I miss are very much appreciated!

And to you, my readers, for spending your time with the people of Bakerville, Wyoming. If you have five minutes, you'd make this writer very happy if you could leave a review. I appreciate you!

About the Author

Millie Copper, writer of Cozy Apocalyptic Fiction, was born in Nebraska but never lived there. Her parents fully embraced wanderlust and moved regularly, giving her an advantage of being from nowhere and everywhere.

As an adult, Millie is fully rooted in a solar-powered home in the wilds of Wyoming with her husband and young son, milking ornery goats and tending chickens on their small homestead. In their free time, they escape to the mountains for a hike or laze along the bank of the river to catch their dinner. Four adult daughters, three sons-in-law, and three grandchildren round out the family.

Since 2009, Millie has authored articles on traditional foods, alternative health, homesteading, and preparedness-many times all within the same piece. Millie has penned five nonfiction, traditional food focused books, sharing how, with a little creativity, anyone can transition to a real foods diet without overwhelming their food budget.

The twelve-installment *Havoc in Wyoming* Christian Post-Apocalyptic fiction series uses her homesteading, off-the-grid, and preparedness lifestyle as a guide. The adventure continues with the newly released *Montana Mayhem* series.

Find Millie at www.MillieCopper.com
Facebook: www.facebook.com/MillieCopperAuthor/
Amazon: www.amazon.com/author/milliecopper
BookBub: https://www.bookbub.com/authors/millie-copper
Instagram: https://www.instagram.com/cozyapoc
YouTube: https://www.youtube.com/@MillieCopperWrites